The Write Way for Love

A MOONSHINE ROMANCE NOVEL

BROOKLYN DEAN

WTP

The Write Way For Love

Cover: Melody Jeffries Design

Editor: Sue Copsey

ISBN: 978-0-6456910-2-3 (print)

ISBN: 978-0-6456910-3-0 (ebook)

For anyone with a wonderfully quirky,
cheesy sense of humour

The Write Way for Love

Content Warnings

Dear Reader,

The Write Way for Love was inspired by my love of puns, cheesy rom coms, and my friend Rachel's intense dislike of feet. You will find food puns and foot fetish jokes within.

While this story is intended to be a light-hearted, feel-good romance (usually soft and fluffy by the mere nature of the genre,) it does contain some potentially sensitive topics you might like to be aware of.

Please be advised that *The Write Way For Love* contains: instances of familial violence and bullying (on and off page), crude humour and language (AKA Australian English) and clowns. Also 'open door' scenes, sexualised talk, and the word 'moist'.

Author's Note

This book is best paired with beer and snacks, or a white wine and cheeseboard selection. Unless you're lactose intolerant. In that case, please – for the love of everyone in your immediate vicinity – DO NOT EAT THE CHEESE!

For a holistic reading experience, I have created a Spotify playlist for you to listen to as you read. Scan the QR code to start listening.

Lastly, thank you for being here. You are intelligent, very good looking, and have an excellent sense of humour if you've made it this far. I hope you enjoy Sam and Anita's story.

I'll meet you back in Moonshine soon!

Brooklyn
Dean

Prologue

DEAR DIARY,

Shit. Do people even write that anymore? *Dear Diary*. Bleh. It feels so cliché. Who cares though, right? This is my journal, so I'll do what the damn doctor suggests and just get the words out.

Dear Diary,

Wanna know what's hard to do? Write a novel. An even harder thing? Cook up a sequel. My first book just spewed out of me. Writing 'Heat in the Kitchen' was so organic, and I never looked back to my old job at Beauford's Catering. The Covid lockdown meant I lost that job anyway – not that I enjoyed the hospitality industry. I spent more time daydreaming about the food and nibbling its edges into immature phallic shapes than priding myself on customer service and cleanliness.

Writing was the only job I'd wanted since I was five, so when old

Marty Beauford gave me the flick, I decided to sample the creative lifestyle. Writing that novel (with a healthy side of daytime cooking shows) made me feel something deep. Something I hadn't felt before. Pride or some shit, maybe? Like it was 'my calling' or whatever? Predestination? I don't know. But it was good. Like, drunk on love and whiskey good. Writing 'Heat' was organic.

Flagpole Publishing – a major player in the romance world – signed me. A publicity wizard started a TikTok account under my pseudonym, Sammie Hart. The world was still reeling from the global pandemic, so in-person meetings weren't on the table. That was fine by me. It made hiding my identity easy. I did a few online interviews using a blurry, sexless silhouette figure, composed text responses to predetermined questions, and a filtered voice-over to disguise the fact that I am, in reality, a dude.

Somehow, I went viral. Not in a gross, sexually transmittable way, but in the New Age Internet-Famous sense. Like, people recognised that silhouette and went, "oh, that's Sammie Hart!" How weird is that? It was a blob. Nothing like me. Not at all.

The amazing corner of the internet known as #BookTok rapid-boiled 'Heat' until it skyrocketed into a hit. Like, how did that even happen? People actually ENJOYED my spicy food-pun-riddled word vomit? Shit yeah! My dream manifested into a delicious reality.

For the past year, no one's seen my face, or knows my real identity. Except for my publisher. And my best mate, Reece. Oh, and Grandma Edith, bless her. Keeping a low profile as a penis-packing romance writer has been pretty easy ... until now. Now, they want book #2. And I am FREAKING THE SHIT OUT!

Last time, it was like a jack in the box. It just popped out. The book I mean, not my dick. It was like an ejaculation I couldn't control. Now, I have no jack. There is no box. I have diddly squat happening in my creative brain. I need a muse. I need ... shit, I don't know. Something.

Reece says I need to get a life, have a wank, get a girlfriend. Whatever. I'd prefer to do 'homework' by watching those sappy daytime dramas and MasterChef. They inspired my writing and got me through it last time. Well, that and Sandra. She was there too, obviously. Until she wasn't. Just like everyone else, she left me. Not that I have abandonment issues or whatever, but it hurts a little less when you expect the same old rejection. I can't really blame Sandra. Not entirely. All that build-up, all through high school, then WHAM! Orgasmic sexual awakening. The world tilted on its axis. Sex and watching MasterChef became my life. And when I wasn't engaging in those activities, I wrote about them. Our time together was ... well ... It's like escargot – you never forget your first. But I ended up spending more time at my laptop trying to describe sex than I did actually doing it. Then, one day:

'Bye, Sam, it's been fun, what with the pandemic and all, but now we're allowed out in society again, I'm moving out of your dingy one-bedroom flat and in with this burly, tattooed biker I met last night at the bar while you were preoccupied with fiction.

P.S. You'll never get another girlfriend if you keep wallowing in your underwear, Samuel. Stop torturing yourself by eating cheese and then fart-bombing the flat. Lactose intolerance is not attractive'.

Yeah, I know right? Ouch. She's kind of right, I suppose.

I don't know for sure that he was a burly biker, but in my head, the dude she'd chosen over me was my opposite in every way, so the biker image comes pretty close. Who wants a gangly nerd with 'olive-oil' hair? Not Sandra, who coined that not-so-delicious description. Not anyone else in Moonshine. I'd never had luck fishing this pond.

At least she left before 'Heat in The Kitchen' went from 'manuscript' to 'millions of copies sold'. Before the mysterious silhouette, before those page-flipping quote reels, before the frisky food-and-book-loving cyber world exploded.

Sandra never saw the fruits of my labour. She knew I spent an inordinate amount of time scribbling in notebooks, on napkins, and covering faded receipts with new ink. That was her sum knowledge of my ambition. She hadn't even cared WHAT I was writing, just that the scratch of my pencil – I know, I'm old school – kept her up at night. Cohabitation in small spaces, with a guy who wrote about food rather than eating it, shrunk the apartment.

Thinking back, numerous red flags waved, signalling relationship doom. If my passion irked her, that wasn't an indication of long-lasting love. Whatever. I'm nobody's first choice, I get that. No one sticks around for losers who prefer love stories to real life and overuse food-related puns in everyday dialogue.

I spent lengthy periods inside my head instead of inside her, and it put me on the outer. So, she hopped on that mountain of hairy muscles and roared away on his Harley. Ironically, it was at sunset. I hope they're happy. Really. Maybe.

With Sandra gone, I was in a weird situation. I had no lover, but the love story I'd worked hard at was my life, and it demanded more from me than she ever had. Within what felt like moments, I became the 'hottest debut author of the year'.

They all assumed I was a chick. Probably because I'd penned a sweet pseudonym. And I'll admit it to you, and you alone, Dear Diary. I'm drunk. Really, really drunk. And I hate how I've turned out like my dad, drinking nightly.

But not only that, I have to admit it – I am Sammie Hart. Samuel Harthrup is Sammie Hart, the romance writer of your wet dreams. And I need to vomit.

I need to write a sequel.

I need the cash.

What kind of dude writes romance novels anyway?

Shit.

The Witch

SAM

"IT IS MY PROFESSIONAL opinion, as your doctor and best friend for life, that you need to leave this flat. And shower." Reece's nose crinkled as he clinked beer bottles with Sam, shimmying to the other end of the couch. "Dude, you need to get out of your own head. You've been trying to write this book for, what, a year now? A change of scenery would do you good." Reece took a long swig before retreating to the other brown leather sofa. "Seriously though, shower."

Since Doctor Dickhead had started enforcing the 'we only drink socially' rule, Sam's productivity *had* improved, if not his mood. Huffing the air from his lungs, Sam launched his pencil toward the wall.

"Why isn't this working?" The beer slid cool and heavy down his throat. *Ah, that's the stuff.*

"What? The romance thing? I dunno, maybe because you

haven't had a date since high school?"

Reece was technically right. It had been a *long* time, and the date he referenced hadn't gone so well. Sam had been seventeen and sweating like a mountain goat in that darkened cinema. *Wait, do goats sweat?* The way they clung on to sheer cliffs, hundreds of feet off the ground, they had to, right? If not from a fear of extreme heights, then surely from the exertion of gripping onto inch-long ledges with only hooves and teeth? *If I was a mountain goat, I would have been shitting bricks in that situation.* Sam mentally scribbled out that analogy.

Regardless, Sam had been seventeen and sweating – profusely – when his anxiety-induced vomiting struck Breanna Henderson's new Doc Martens suddenly. The mellifluent splash – and the horrified shriek that followed – drew embarrassing, unwanted attention. It had been chunked with popcorn and alarmingly red from the raspberry Fanta bubbling in his gut from too-fast consumption. The night had ended in tears (his), reflexive gagging (hers) and a mutual agreement that their evening had never happened. Breanna was the bubbly, outgoing sort of girl who spoke to anyone and everyone like they were long-lost best friends, but Sam and Breanna had never spoken again. To this day, Sam insisted he'd never been to the Moonshine City Cinema, or seen *Star Wars*. Which one? Sam had no idea. The whole franchise had been off-limits since The Unfortunate Date. Reece couldn't even convince him to sit through that scrolling, shrinking text intro.

Then there had been Sandra. She had swept him off his feet the week after graduation, admitted to long-time pining, introduced him to alcohol, despite his insistence that he didn't want to drink it, then kept him in bed for weeks. They'd never 'dated', as such, but Sam had been so inspired by the experience that she'd moved in. He winced now, thinking of it. The faster the fall into bed, the harder the fall out of it, it seemed. Sex with Sandra had been a total inspiration though, his writing increasing tenfold. Lockdown happened, and he completed an entire novel.

"Also, maybe the romance genre is just a chick thing, you know," Reece continued. "Last time I checked, you were a dude. Not that I'd judge if you went another way." He threw his hands up in defence as Sam threw the blank notepad at his face. "Just saying, I'd love ya no matter what. BFFs for life."

Sam raised his beer in a toast, mumbling thanks.

Reece resumed. "It's just that women seem more medically pre-disposed to writing romance books. Not being sexist or anything, you can do anything you set your mind to. I think it's just an uphill battle, you know? I mean, you do already have one book. Isn't that enough?"

Ah yes, the one book. The worthless 81,356 words, bound forever in the pages of *Heat in the Kitchen*, Sammie Hart's debut novel. The book inspired by sex. The surprising hit to which, for whatever reason, he'd been unable to add a sex scene. Not because he completely lacked inspiration – Sandra had been very inspirational at the time – but because he'd cringed through all the descriptions and synonyms for body parts, and describing the act was just too ... *icky*. That wasn't a particularly masculine word, but it was how it felt. He'd cringed when writing intimacies, so had shied away, covering the awkwardness with *MasterChef*-inspired sexy food puns and humour.

Readers had gone wild for *Heat*, labelling the 'heat' of the book with fanciful food-related terms like 'slow burn,' 'sizzle' and talk of 'spice,' despite its lack of actual sex scenes. It had been excellent PR, according to Flagpole Publishing. Sam and Reece had laughed for hours at the reviews, preferring the more masculine, cinematic descriptions of 'fade to black' over the rest of the romantic guff. That was then. Now, instead of praise from the publisher, there were only increasingly short emails from the Flagpole Publishing editorial team who passive-aggressively requested updates on his latest manuscript. Just thinking about the long list of unanswered emails in his inbox made Sam sink further into the couch.

"But if you want it, you can do Book Number Two! Specific goals, man," Reece said. Sam watched his best friend wander into the kitchen, the most impressive space in the dingy little flat, ticking off words on his long fingers while searching for snacks. "Specific. Measurable. Achievable. Relevant. Timely–"

"Thanks, Doctor Smartarse, I *do* know what SMART goals are. I went to school, same as you, remember?"

"What I remember is a little dweeb a few grades below me, who desperately wanted to bang my little sister." Reece picked up a life-sized plushie of Thor's mighty hammer, Mjolnir, from the marble benchtop and threw it at his friend's head. Sam ducked, the full force of Reece's homebrew hitting behind his spectacles. The room swum and shifted. He felt the familiar guilt rise in his gut, mingled with the underlying anger that always accompanied a hangover. *I am not my father,* he affirmed, pushing the feelings down and grinning wickedly at Reece, desperate to distract himself.

"Yeah, well, grades and ages don't matter so much when the school's so small that everyone ends up lumped into the same classes. Plus, your sister's *hot*. Everybody wanted to tap that." Sam knew he was pushing a big red 'Do Not Go There' button.

"Dude, she's got three kids now."

"There's an acronym for hot mothers, you know–"

"Don't," Reece warned.

"I think it's spelled ... M –"

Reece left the kitchen, eyes thin as sugar snaps.

"I –" Sam grinned, adding "L" as he retrieved Mjolnir from the floor, tapping it into his open palm a few times, testing it's plushie weight. For a heartbeat, the world froze. Time stopped. "F!"

The room exploded into action. Reece jumped the sofa, his long legs swooping, knocking Sam to the floor. A tan-cotton-clad knee pressed into his chest, pinning him to the crumb-infested carpet. Kneeling over his prey, Reece pulled Thor's mighty hammer from Sam's grasp, pounding him repeatedly until he got an, "I give!"

Reece slid off, just as Sam released the wind that had been gurgling in his stomach. A loud fart echoed through the flat.

"RANK!" Reece's hand flew to his mouth and nose as he jumped backwards across the room, trying not to laugh but failing miserably. "Dude," he cried, chuckling and attempting to hide a rather impressed expression. Sam felt like patting himself on the back. "Lactose intolerance is not a joke! Stop it with the dairy!"

"Pretty funny to me." Sam settled, arms hanging wide across the couch cushions, basking in the stench. Within seconds

Reece was at the door, yanking it open to flood the room with fresh air and light. Sunlight bounced off the grey walls and took a little depth from the stale flat. Sam hissed like a vampire at the sudden brightness. Mjolnir zoomed through the air and struck his temple. Somewhere in the distance a kookaburra laughed, and Sam felt betrayed by nature itself, mocking him.

"Smartarse." Reece fanned one arm wildly, coughing as he forced his way back into the kitchen, sliding the window open to create a cross-breeze. "You stinky, stinky smartarse."

Sam laughed, the sound foreign to his ears. Brushing blond tendrils from his eyes, he slid the remnants of breakfast under the sofa. The small plate of stale crackers with cheese and a half-finished tub of strawberry yoghurt would go better unnoticed. *There's a fine line between pleasure and pain.* Sam smiled to himself. After a few long moments, the air returned to normal and Reece's face unwrinkled.

A warm springtime gust flooded the room. It looked like another glorious Moonshine day. Fresh air wouldn't be so bad. Sam usually made fortnightly trips to the farmers' market, stopping at Friday's Café for caffeination and a chin-wag, but right now, he couldn't remember when he'd last had an excursion into town. *Maybe I should get out more.*

"BFFs for life?" Sam held out his closed fist, by way of reconciliation.

"BFFs for life." Reece bumped it. "But seriously, you need to shower, Sam, and get out of this place. You treat yourself like some princess, trapped in a tower. You're stifling your creativity, being locked away in here alone. Get out! Get some vitamin D and exercise. Doctor's orders."

"Not alone." Sam hiccupped. "I've got Johnny, Jimmy, Jack–"

"Not healthy, man. You shouldn't drink alone. I'm saying this as your doctor and your bestie." Reece paused before adding, "Hey, I know, come out with us tonight!"

"Us?" Sam adjusted his glasses, pushing up off the floor. *Since when was Reece an 'us'?* For as long as Sam had known him, the only *us* the good doctor referenced was their duo. Sam had never been on the outer side of 'us'.

"The Starlight Foundation are taking Donny Wilder out tonight. Cirque de Fortuna. They're only in town for two weeks, but tonight Donny's the ringmaster. Somehow, the town librarian made it happen, organised the whole thing." A weird look crossed Reece's face, though Sam didn't understand why.

"Laura Ahn? She's part of the Starlight Foundation crew?"

"Yeah." Reece's dark eyebrows rose, analysing Sam like a bug under a microscope. "You know her?"

"Reece, Moonshine's a ten-minute drive from one side to the other. Everyone knows everyone in this town." Sam mentally filed through their school acquaintances, settling on a black and white image of Laura, a serious-faced girl, looking studious as she held a chunky textbook and stared into the camera. "I don't know much about her, personally, but I think she's always liked books." Sam added a mental sticky-note to start a dialogue about literature with his old schoolmate. His future as an author, whether he 'came out' or not, could very well include Laura as the local librarian.

"Anyway, Donny's been looking forward to the circus for

ages. You know there's jack to do here in Moonshine, especially for kids. But now his vitals are good and the chemotherapy has been ..."

Reece slid into doctor talk and Sam tuned out, relishing the final gulp of cool beer sliding down his throat. *That explains the face. Poor Donny.* Cancer sucked. It more than sucked. No kid should ever have to go through all that. No parent, either. The diagnosis was too prevalent in Australia and Sam knew how personal that battle was for his friend.

Reece was right, too. In Moonshine there was precisely *jack* to do. Well, except drinking, working, and screwing around – and not always in that order. There was the occasional bout of cow tipping and, once a quarter, an old-fashioned barnyard dance at the Moonshine Community Hall, out on Brindabella Road.

Sam, currently jobless, screwless, and with no dancing bones in his body, had only one option. Sure, small town life was great if you needed a cup of sugar from your neighbour. Or you were into rural markets and quaint harvest festivals, or whole town events based around whatever flower was in bloom. If you enjoyed the entire world knowing your life story – including the most embarrassing chapters, like how you shat your pants in the third grade – the cow-pat laden fresh air of rural life was bliss.

Otherwise, Moonshine was just another pastoral Australian place stuck halfway between two major cities. Civilisation was an hour's drive in either direction, and almost two hours inland from the pure sapphire-and-sand coastline.

At least the town was plonked right on the major highway, so a steady stream of tourists kept the petrol stations and bakeries in business.

"So, five, yeah?"

"What?"

Reece rolled his eyes. "The circus, you dweeb. Five o'clock. You don't have to stay with me, or Donny, or the Foundation volunteers. Just come out! Enjoy the show. Talk to real life people out there in the big bad world. You never know, you might find some inspiration for that romance you're cooking up, chef." He winked, ruffling Sam's hair so it fell into his eyes again. Reece's face screwed up as he rubbed his fingertips together before shaking his hand violently. "Have. A. Shower," he ordered, wiping long lines down his shirt.

Sam popped the lid off another beer, raising the bottle to his friend. "Every thing's gunna *brie* alright," Sam chuckled at his cheesy joke. "See you at five. Love you."

Reece's eyes rolled into his carefully combed hairline. "Love *you*, loser."

Cirque de Fortuna rolled into Moonshine like a breeze. Swift as ants sensing rain, they moved quickly and efficiently to establish their transient tent city. In no time, a colourful base rose from one of Moonshine's community ovals, transforming the static field into a hive of activity and noise.

Numerous vibrant marquees created the long lines of 'sideshow alley'. They ran parallel, leading from the ticketed gate to the Big Top Tent, a huge, red-and-white-striped wonder, dominating the centre of the field. Two circular ticket booths stood at the entrance. Sam couldn't help but wonder if an aerial view of the circus would look like a giant, glowing phallus in the rapidly darkening field. Maybe his mate, walking tall beside him, was right. Getting out of his flat and his head was a necessity. And if Sam was seeing giant dicks and balls everywhere, maybe Reece was right about the *other* thing, too. He needed to get laid. Clear his head and body of any toxins that might be soaking up his creative juices. Toxins he'd accumulated over the last year or two. *God, has it really been that long since Sandra left?*

Head out of the gutter and into the circus, Harthrup! Focus! Ear splitting screams from too-loud children near burst his ears. Horses whinnied loudly, and the carnies complained through gap-toothed smiles. Lost in noise and thought, Sam stumbled past cages, caravans and fenced-off staff areas that blurred together.

"Are you sober?" The good doctor was asking for the millionth time, already knowing the answer.

Sam hiccupped. "Be proud! I found inspiration today, in your home brew. At the bottom of it, exactly. It's pretty good stuff, bestie. Bit too heavy on the hops, though."

Reece rolled his eyes, setting his face into its usual doctorly composition. Serious and scowling, arms crossed, he shook his head at Sam. *Work Reece is here tonight. No fair!*

Reece had always been either too light or too dark, fun and fluffy or serious and solemn. As his closest (and only) friend, Sam learned long ago to take whichever 'self' Reece Hargraves offered. Didn't mean he had to like it.

"Can I have my fun friend Reece back for a bit please? I don't like the Doctor Jekyll thing," Sam begged, tugging on Reece's sleeve. Sure, it was a bit juvenile, but if they couldn't be kids together, they'd have to be adults. And that was just a bit too … scary.

"Hyde was a violent manifestation of Jekyll's evil subconscious urges. The dangerous side to a split personality disorder. You want me to be *that* guy?" Reece didn't give Sam time to think. "There's Donny's family," he said, his pointing finger turning into a paternal waggle in Sam's direction. "Stay out of trouble." He scuffed Sam's hair, offering a small smile. "Glad you found the shampoo and soap. You're almost human now." Reece pressed a large sticker to Sam's chest. "What's that?" He pointed to three white blotches on Sam's otherwise black t-shirt.

"Stain remover." Sam shrugged.

"Well, at least you've done your laundry." Reece sighed. "Finally."

Sam looked down at his t-shirt and jeans, the same simple style he had always worn. Black and denim were the only ingredients he needed. What was the point of an adventurous wardrobe when all he did was actively work on the butt impression on his sofa, and occasionally try to write? Sure, he would move to denim *shorts* come summer, but otherwise Sam maintained a rather generic avatar appearance, only 'levelling up' with his simple, thickly glassed, circular spectacles. The ones he'd been endlessly teased about in school. Sam peered through these now, smirking at his friend.

"Not everyone can get away with the clean-cut and –" hiccup, "– *very adult* dark-blue-and-b –" hiccup, "beige combos you seem to prefer, doctor," Sam retorted, taking a few deep breaths that somewhat settled his spasming diaphragm, but seemed to swirl, tornado style, behind his eyes. Pinching his nose, Sam added, "You seriously have two colours in your entire wardrobe, you know. Who owns tan shorts anyway? And those loafers!" Hiccup. "You look like you've stepped out of the casual section of a Ken Doll magazine."

"Funny." Reece didn't laugh. "Don't lose this." He jammed a finger into Sam's chest, denting the foil sticker that now adorned his t-shirt.

"Whazzit –" hiccup, "– for?" Sam said the words slowly, concentrating on pressing his feet solidly to the grassy earth. The world was inclined, and he felt the steep uphill climb when he looked at anything other than the sticker. It featured a glossy yellow hand with a blazing blue eye in the palm.

"Work perk. Free entry and selected sideshows." Reece smirked, before running off to greet the Starlight Foundation crowd. "Have fun!" He yelled, adding in warning, "Be good."

Sam watched Reece shake hands with the small group of beaming volunteers, high-five Donny and nod stiffly at a Laura Ahn, older than he remembered but just as pretty. Her pencil skirt, glasses and bun made her look like a sexy secretary, but her scowl rivalled Reece's, tension masking her features. Serious as a heart attack, she gripped her metallic clipboard.

After shaking hands with a portly older lady in a too-bright dress, Laura and Reece led the Starlight group past the ticket booth and into Cirque de Fortuna. Sam's clumsy feet carried him in the same direction. He forced another deep inhale, watching Laura's arse sway to the beat in his temples.

Should I go talk to her? Despite years of acquaintance, they had never really conversed. *Maybe I should change that.* He was a writer, after all, and she was a librarian, plus a fellow Moonshine Municipal High School survivor. A love of books and a hatred of school was as much commonality as he'd shared with Sandra. *Yeah, and look how that turned out,* Sam's brain scoffed from behind a muffled wall of alcho-fog. Quickly he changed course.

His gaze staggered skyward as he followed the strung festoon lights through the growing crowd. They were so bright and lovely, little twinkles interspersed with lengths of black cable twisted in a plastic green leaf-filled vine. The spring air was crisp and sweet, full of laughter, excitement, and booming music that shifted tempo from booth to booth. A kookaburra struck up its cackling laugh somewhere nearby, mocking his loneliness. Children giggled, getting high on fluffy pink fairy floss and over-priced, half-melted slushies in odd-shaped, ridiculously giant cups. A heady, herby smoke filled the air.

Following the zig-zag path of the lights, Sam drifted into a flock of garish clowns who sneered and laughed knowingly at his stupor, then past the various stalls offering cheap prizes for trick shots. Another two performers, older men in classic clown make-up, walked a Shetland pony sporting a unicorn horn through the crowd on a brilliantly bedazzled leash. Its heavy hooves thumped slowly as the clowns traded grins and occasional squeezes of their clasped hands. Sam wondered how he noticed such a small, quiet gesture among the overwhelming nature of circus. For all the bright and colourful distractions here, the smallest act of love had somehow found his attention. *Hopeless romantic! That's how you got into this mess in the first place. Go home and write,* commented a nasty voice in his head.

The idea of sitting in his flat attempting to make progress with his sequel was tempting, but he couldn't let Reece down. Sam had said he'd be here, so he was, even though Doctor Duty had ditched him for work ... again. Maybe getting out of the flat would kick-start his creative brain once more. With renewed interest, Sam studied the couple.

One of the clowns, a beer-bellied gentleman in bright red suspenders, knelt by the faux unicorn, whispering gentle praise as he encouraged children to weave flowers through its mane. Sam's feet followed his eyes, hands reaching out to stroke the golden horse. A deep, throaty neigh rumbled from the animal, and a wave of children knocked Sam back as they ran, giggling.

The already lopsided world tilted some more. Sam stumbled on something solid and warm, and the world shifted violently. His flushed cheeks hit water as he sunk face-first into a lucky-dip prize pool. Examining his watery world, Sam's brain scrambled to register what was happening. Looking up, he noticed numbers stuck to the stomachs of the rubber ducks that floated by. The flat-bellied yellow birds bobbed unhappily at his imposition. Abruptly, the water splashed in reverse, and he was air-side again, gasping. Two small, warm hands gripped his shoulders tight, shaking, slapping his back as he spluttered, before holding him steady once more.

"There you go!" Two blue eyes smiled at him from beneath a cloud of dark curls.

The duck-pond vendor, a large lady with cherry red victory rolls, growled deeply, like a bear warning a troublesome cub. Meanwhile, the airy, feminine voice of Blue Eyes apologised, her words swirling rapidly, muffled but insistent through Sam's waterlogged ears. *She could talk under water with a mouth full of marbles.* The phrase sunk into his mind as he blinked stupidly, allowing himself to be guided into a velvet-draped chair.

"Sorry I'm drowning you with chatter! I do that ..."

"I'm all wet," he said dumbly, by way of apology for soaking the seat.

She laughed, the sound infiltrating his drunken fog to hit him squarely in the chest, like butterflies landing within his skin. "You sure are! Gosh, I've never had a man fall for me *that* quickly." She laughed again, pushing his soggy blond tendrils over the crown of his head before sliding his spectacles back onto his face. "There, that's better."

Blue Eyes became clearer as the water drained in tiny rivulets down his glasses. He saw her gaze dip to the sticker on his chest and her fingers reached for it, then at the last second she stopped short. "I was wondering when you'd find me."

Breathe. He'd forgotten to breathe. Sucking in a lungful of air, Sam slid a hand over his face, flicking remaining droplets to the side. Lavender, he thought suddenly. *She smells of lavender and vanilla.*

"Who are you?" If he concentrated on sitting still, the world only swayed rather than spun.

"I'm Anita." Her soft, round face floated in front of him. Untamed curls and huge blue eyes filled his vision. "Can I read you?"

Bile rose in his throat. He was torn between *Shit, I'm gunna vomit – it's Breanna Henderson all over again!* and *Shit, she knows I'm a writer? How could she know I'm Sammie Hart?*

"What I mean is, *may* I read you?" The curvy little Roma princess gestured to his hands, spread-eagled flat on the small circular tabletop between them. Blinking, he lifted them up, examining them. Sweat dropped into his eyes. Or was it just duck water?

"Um ..."

"I'm a reader. A psychic. Medium. Witch. Pick your synonym." She smiled, and a soggy gear slowly shifted in his head. "I'm also a Virgo and I love to dance. I'm smart, truthful, I love vegetarian food – with chicken, of course." She added this conspiratorially, as though a chook might just overhear her confession, "and *wow* – nobody ever lets me get this far into a monologue! I'm just making stuff up now. What else can I even say? I love reading, which is kind of funny, because I'm a palm reader ... Hey, are you okay?" She leaned closer, briefly steadying his swaying frame.

"Uh, yeah?" Sam nodded, which didn't help the whole unstable-world situation. "Yes. I'm okay. My hiccups are gone!" The realisation exploded from him like a corn kernel bursting into popcorn. Head still swimming, he focused on her small hands, now holding his.

The fortune teller had a ring on every delicate finger. Her touch was warm and strong as she held him firmly, anchoring him in place, soft waves of heat radiating from her. His fingertips tingled and he was surprised to feel the unusual sensation of his zipper pressing into him. Blushing, Sam withdrew his hands. Reece had definitely been right. It had been a *long* time since the toxins had left the building.

"Here, let me show you what I can do. I am *very* talented."

I bet you are.

She paused, just a fraction, amidst her fussing, picking up items from the cluttered table then placing them down, moving a candle, re-decking cards, clearing space.

There is a lot of shit on this table. She laughed. *Shit, did I say that out loud?* Biting her lip, she appraised him, working to contain a smirk. Wordlessly, the psychic up-ended a green velvet bag, square lettered tiles spilling across the table. Closing her eyes, the woman – *Anita, was it?* He struggled to recall – breathed deeply before selecting three, lining them up before Sam. One by one, she flipped them over.

W. A. S.

She looked at him, curiously. "What kind of name is Was?"

Clever. Rearranging the letters, he allowed a small, soggy smile, grateful for the excuse to shift his lower half slightly as he carefully leaned forward. S. A. Spinning the W spun to become an M, the psychic exploded into light airy laughter that sent butterflies through his chest. The sound was so beautiful, he wanted to record it to play on repeat or set it as his ringtone.

"SAM. Oh! Well, hi Sam, I'm Anita. But you knew that already." She smiled, brilliant and broad. "And now I know *you*."

"What else d'you know?" Did the words sound as slurred to her as they did to him?

"I bet I can tell what you had for lunch." Anita smirked again, folding her arms. Bad idea. The movement drew his eyes to her chest. Her boobs were small, but they seemed to jump up under the weight of her arms, adding *oomph*. Sam stared for a beat too long. If he was honest, Sam was more of an arse man, but nobody would say no to a nice rack. Plus, he couldn't see her lower half over the lip of the table, so he had to take what he could get.

"Easy. I had my fav-our-ite soup for lunch," Sam retorted, eyes flicking up to her cocky smile as he stumbled through the words.

"What kind of soup?" One dark eyebrow raised, Anita leaned forward, affording a delicious view down her embroidered, scoop-neck top. "Whiskey with croutons?"

"Ouch." He blushed, blinking, caught out. *Smooth, Sammie.* He brought a hand to his mouth, breathing then sniffing a few times. "Not that bad, izzit?"

Pushing her long curls over her shoulder, the bohemian princess squared her gaze at him.

"I might be a mystic but I'm no liar, Was." Anita cleared the tiles back into their bag, re-scattering various gemstones, lavender tips and assorted sweet treats. *Was the table always that cluttered?* Anita smirked again, producing a soft-edged deck of tarot cards, shuffling them like a nimble-fingered casino hustler. She arranged the cards into three piles, before motioning around the table at the assorted mess.

"Confectionary?" She selected a cherry ripe from beside an amethyst, devouring the 'fun size' chocolate in one bite. The tip of her finger slid across her lips as she finished the treat. God, if that wasn't the sexiest thing since Nigella sliced bread.

Sam liked a girl with curves, and from what he could see, Anita had them in all the right places. His eyes swept over her as she chewed delicately, one eyebrow arched as she watched him in return. Long seconds passed as they sized each other up.

Sam didn't bother to hide his fascination. He was useless at the cool side-eye thing most guys had in their flirting arsenal. Even if he could master the skill, his glasses magnified his eyes in a rather extreme way, so anything optical rarely went unnoticed. Right now, he knew this woman would see every light brown fleck of his eyes. Eyes that flicked between her lovely blue pools and lush, rose-pink lips. A tiny bit of chocolate clung to the corner of her smile. It mesmerised Sam for a moment too long, as he fantasised about kissing the cocoa from her skin. All of her skin. The woman was walking milk chocolate, sun-browned and gorgeous.

God, I'm drunk. The beer must've really done a number on him. Sexy thoughts like that were for the spank bank or committed relationships. He was a traditionalist like that, something Reece didn't quite understand, but chalked up to Sam's romantic tendencies. The pesky, long pent-up toxins surged again, and he mentally warned his dick to settle down whilst still, rather embarrassingly, ogling Anita's chest.

"Eyes are up here, Was," she teased, uncrossing her arms and pointing to her grin.

His face flamed, and he dropped his gaze to the table to select a consumable.

"Lollipop. Good choice. You are the second man to choose that tonight. Do you ever wonder how lollipops were named? So confusing. I mean, lollies are usually soft and *candied* lollies are hard. But what about a lollipop? It's hard. Shouldn't they call it a *candy*pop? It doesn't make sense–"

"Wazz the point of this?" Sam asked, shifting in the wet seat again. Anita gracefully unwrapped the sweet for him, sliding the sugary ball between his lips.

"The ramble was just a spot of curiosity, but your choice of treat is important. A person's selection can reveal a lot about their personality, Was. I'm a reader. I like to read people. And confectionary is telling, understand? I don't know *what* you are yet, but I do know you needed to just sit down for a bit. And getting some food into your system probably isn't a bad idea either. Okay, now give me those hands."

Her small hand darted out to take his, startling him and sending tingles through each of his fingertips. Her warmth seeped into him again as she stroked each finger, brushing along the palm of his hand and across his wrist. He sucked harder on the lollipop. Anita leaned in, oblivious to his discomfort, peering at Sam's hands.

"You're a creative soul, Was." She smiled up at him, all blue eyes, black hair and dark lashes. "And, unless I'm mistaken, which I very rarely am, you have a control complex, high expectations of yourself and most likely a lot of energy and anxiety associated with your craft."

Sam blinked. "And just how do my hands reveal that?" *She must really be some kind of psychic.*

In preparing for the circus, he'd washed off the greyed smudge of pencil that clung to the outer edge of his pinkie and the heel of his hand, the usual indicator that he'd been writing. Sam didn't know why, but he had always preferred handwriting in HB pencil over typing. His entire first and current manuscripts lay in carefully written pages, piled up on his dining table. So many tiny, scrawled words, amounting to surprisingly large towers of paper he'd dictated into typed text for his publisher.

Anita's finger hovered just above his skin, but he could still feel her touch. "See your middle finger?" She pointed. "It's bent. The bone itself has been curved over time. You bend bones like that with sustained pressure, like gripping a pencil or pen or paintbrush too tight, for too long. So, you're artistic. Someone who works regularly at their craft, with tight control and anxiety over the product's perfection."

"You really are a witch," he marvelled. "That, or Sherlock Holmes."

Anita laughed.

Such a musical sound. She held up her right hand, silencing her laughter and his trailing thoughts.

"See? Mine's the same. I paint. And I sew. I do the costumes and help make all the sets for the show, among other things. The pressure of creativity in the circus life can be immense." She paused, exhaling softly. "But I've always expected too much from myself."

Suddenly, she looked so sad. At least, he thought she did – but he *was* drunk and probably not the best facial expression analyst right now.

In a blink her face reverted to its smiling configuration. "The physical and emotional pressure has changed the shape of your phalanges, Was, my new friend. So, what about you?"

He blinked away a rogue water droplet. "What about me?"

"What's your craft?"

"I ... write," he choked out. *Shit. Don't say anything else!* "I use pencil, mostly. I like the look of a messy first draft and the way the edge of my hand goes black from the lead." He focused on clamping his lips shut, lest he spill his secret.

I'm Sammie Hart! He wanted to scream it to the heavens and into Anita's cute little face. *Perhaps you've heard of my book? Heat in the Kitchen? Biggest debut in publishing since, like, ever. It's Fifty Shades of culinary sexiness and innuendo, apparently, and it's mine, but now I think it was just a fluke and I'm not talented and I have no inspiration and I'm broke and ... and ...*

Sam didn't say any of that. His lips pressed closer than butter on bread and her astute observation rather stunned him. How had he never noticed such a thing before? She was right. The bones of his right hand – his dominant hand, his writing hand – were *bent*. Sam gulped down the rising bile. If he opened his mouth, he'd either betray his secret to this perfect stranger, or vomit his whiskey and croutons all over her sideshow booth. Worrying thoughts of Breanna Henderson's shoes flooded his brain. *Shit.*

"It's funny." Anita giggled, a strange waft of lavender-scented mist causing her to appear almost spectre-like in the fog. "For a writer, you're a surprisingly closed book. Must be all that *soup* –" she made air-quotes, "– tying up your tongue. They say that alcohol is the best social lubricant but with you, I'm not so sure." She grinned as fire leapt into his cheeks at the thought of lubricant. Shit, did she know how weird she made him feel? *No, it's not Anita and lube. It's the booze.*

"Weird, how the universe brought us together. I'm a reader and you're a writer. It's like we were meant to meet, Was," she continued, her hand gripping his again. His zipper wanted adjusting. Warm duck water dripped down his neck. Heat swept up over his body, followed by a wave of cold rolling down. *This is all a bit much.*

Sam was standing up. Why was he standing?

His feet caught in the draped velvet of Anita's tablecloth.

Sit down, idiot! The words swam in his skull as his stumbling feet tangled in the fabric, his body leaning towards the oval, before the world slipped sideways into darkness.

Dirt Perve

ANITA

DESPITE POKES AND PRODS, the writer refused to wake up – which was perfect. It allowed more time to go through his things. *The Universe always provides,* Anita told herself, remembering how the local doctor had rushed over last night when her client fainted (rather dramatically) in a velvet wrap. Not only did the rather handsome physician know the patient, but he also offered to drive the inert, gurgling writer home. *Small town hospitality, right there.*

Anita opened Sam's fridge. *How unsatisfyingly empty.* The refrigerator was like an old profiterole, she thought glumly. Looked great on the outside but didn't deliver the goods.

The few items stocked inside the polished chrome appliance were largely inedible. Was the guy intentionally creating microcolonies of bacteria?

Perhaps he's a scientist. A struggling, underfunded scientist?

Or maybe he's working with the fine-arse doctor on a cancer cure for the kid who had hammed up his wish to be ringmaster last night?

A few individual grapes survived among the shrivelled mass, in a small open bag, fluffy mould sprouting to one side in what she hoped was an experiment in fermentation. *Maybe he's a wine maker?*

Carefully selecting three solid, round, mould-free fruits, Anita popped them into her mouth, relishing their cold, bursting sweetness. Satisfying, but she wanted more. *Pantry.*

Anita's anticipation was met with a slight explosion of dust. The pantry was another disappointment. More cobwebs than crisps. A jar of vegemite. An opened packet of water crackers. *Who lives like this?* Her eyes flicked to the lanky man stretched out and snoring on the sofa.

The writer had the biggest, most beautiful kitchen she'd ever seen, complete with marble benchtops, an eight-burner cooktop, double oven, and gleaming chrome appliances. The kitchen, unlike the rest of the flat, was clean. It was also, to her surprise, disappointingly bare. *Who has a chef's kitchen and no food?*

Anita slapped her hand, rings clanging together harshly, reprimanding herself. *You're not one to judge.* She was in an almost total stranger's house, hunting for crumbs like a mouse. There were fewer edible offerings back at the circus and far fewer places for her to comfortably hide. *Those who live in glass houses, and all that jazz …*

Digging in the back of the cupboard, Anita struck gold. "Yes!" Her fingers curled protectively around a jar of peanut butter as she relished the discovery. Grabbing a spoon from one of the many soft-close drawers (she opened then closed each one, just to sigh at the wonderfully noiseless impact) Anita sat at the dining table, fingering her unconscious host's stack of unpaid bills.

Samuel Harthrup, she read atop each one, right before the word 'overdue' in bold red. If that font wasn't eye catching enough, many of the red warnings had been circled.

"Holy Hera, there are so many!"

One thing she loved about life on the road was having no fixed address – no postal service and no debt collectors.

Among the scattered piles of Sam's half-opened mail were two much larger piles of paperwork. *Heat in the Kitchen*, her absolute favourite romance novel, weighed down the tallest tower of papers. What a strange book to find in what could only be described as a bachelor pad. Smiling familiarly at the front cover, she gently placed it on the table. A quick flick through the papers underneath it made her gasp. The man had copied out the entire novel – long hand. Weird, but whatever. She'd seen stranger things. Hell, most 'normal' moments of her circus life would seem utterly strange to townies. *You're not here to judge, Anita.*

Sam gurgled a wet-sounding snore.

After last night's pre-circus concussion, Anita had offered to visit first thing in the morning and check in on the patient. In that welcoming, trusting, small town kind of way, the cute doctor had scrawled Sam's address, saying he'd meet her there. Only a few minutes ago, he'd properly introduced himself as Doctor Hargraves, welcoming Anita (and her rather pitiful, handpicked flower bouquet) into the writer's shabby little flat.

"I'll be back, later," the doctor had said, his tall, muscular frame nearly filling the doorway. If this was what house calls looked like in Moonshine, she might just be inspired to stay a while longer ... and break a few bones. "Just keep an eye on him." Doctor Reece's scowl reminded her of her brother. Anita reassessed her desire to flirt. He was so serious. *Too* serious. *Not my type.* Not that she needed a man, anyway.

Waving goodbye, she shut herself into the flat with the patient.

Now here she was, sucking down spoonfuls of peanut butter and examining the writer at close range. Collecting his spectacles from the coffee table, she tried them on, giggling at the blurred world they presented – how Was had seen the world last night. Sliding them back to the table, she blinked rapidly, bringing him into focus.

He has the wrong-sized face on the right-sized head. But he's handsome, in a bookish, dweeby way. His blond hair swirled at strange, looping angles that reminded her of a half-sucked mango, and he was long. Well, tall, she corrected, kinking her head to the side. Yes, he'd been tall last night. Her face had barely met his shoulders. As for long ... *don't even go there, girlfriend.* She was glad his body was blanket covered.

So, who are you, Samuel Harthrup?

For the next few minutes, she played her favourite game – 'Which Romantic Hero Are You?' For as long as she could remember, she had wished upon the stars and allocated everyone she met a character look-alike from romance films. Squinting, she appraised his face closely, as though the answer was written in the creases of his eyes, or the set of his eyebrows. Eventually she settled on a cross between Brad Pitt in *Legends of the Fall* and the uber-sexy Ryan Gosling in *The Notebook*. Sam had the same floppy blond hair, tall thin frame and strong chin as those film stars, but with a more disheveled overall appearance.

The doctor, on the other hand, was possibly the most put together man she'd seen in real life. The town's helpful Doctor Hargraves, she pondered, could be an Austenesque Mr Darcy. The stern-faced Moonshine medical practitioner was just as tall, dark, and handsome. His eyes, a dark grey, seemed suitably intense. Like the infamous Darcy, the doctor had that perma-scowl all super serious guys seemed to wear like a tattoo.

"And I am Thelma. Or is it Louise? Wild and free, only twice the weight and half the height." She giggled to the stale-aired room, bowing theatrically to the immobile Samuel Harthrup.

Sam snored, a trickle of drool sliding from the corner of his mouth. Chuckling, she pilfered a few pages from one of the stacks, loaded up her spoon with peanut butter, and glanced at the clock. The doctor wasn't due back for a while, so there was only a tiny chance of getting busted snooping. *Perfect.*

Settling into a dining chair that creaked beneath her, Anita slid the spoon into her mouth, reading. A few lines down, she smiled. Then, it became a grin. Next, an open mouthed, eyebrow arching guffaw. Turning the paper, she looked for a title to the work. "What in the world is this garbage?"

The lump of man snored wildly, stirring. "Witch," he rasped. *How cute. Is he dreaming of me?*

"Hey, Was. How are you feeling?" The guy looked like

crap reheated. Knowing the question was rhetorical, she kept reading, allowing herself to openly laugh now he was awake.

"Keep it down," Sam murmured, sliding upright, one hand to his head. He looked down over his body, visibly relaxing when his hands found clothing. "Oh, good." Waterlogged eyes eventually fixed on her. His hand blindly sought his spectacles. Once they were on his face, Anita repressed a giggle at his magnified brown eyes. His gaze moved to the papers in her hands, body stiffening. "What are you doing?"

"Let me save you some mental effort, Sam. Yes, you're fully clothed because no, we didn't have sex – you'd remember if we did." She threw in a wink to lighten the mood (and assure him she was joking) as his face flushed redder than a ladybird's backside. *Why did you say that?* "Just in case you were thinking that's why there's a woman in your flat, after a night you obviously can't remember. Your doctor friend brought you home from the circus after you nearly drowned then gave yourself concussion." Sam seemed to relax at the mention of Doctor Hargraves. "And what am I doing? I'm reading. It's what I do. I'm a reader, remember? Fortunes. Palms. Tea leaves and tarot. Anita, the witch –" she waved cheerily, "– from Cirque de Fortuna."

Monologue over (she really had to stop rambling in the presence of even slightly attractive men), Anita held out her hand. Sam took it gently, his own large and cool around hers. She remembered these hands. Life line, love line, the tiny valleys that indicated travel and marriage and babies. They were all so deeply etched, there on his palm. She could've spent days studying every aspect of his large, creative hands. Each long finger, slightly bent, told a story. A slow realisation dawned as she looked between the scrawled pages and his hand, still in hers.

"Was, did *you* write this?"

He wrenched his hand from hers, mouth dropping open. "I. Um ... Shit."

Anita was sorely tempted to slide a ping pong ball into Sam's gaping, clown-like mouth. "It's good!" she encouraged, watching his face turn white. *Please don't barf.* "It's a comedy?"

He gulped visibly, his face now darkening into a deep beetroot shade. "Romance."

Anita saw Sam's wince as she laughed. Heck, they probably saw it on Mars.

"Seriously? This isn't a comedy? Why do you want to write romance?"

Pinching the bridge of his nose, Sam sighed before grabbing the peanut butter from its perch beside her, gesturing for the spoon. Licking it thoroughly, Anita handed it over. *Clearly, he is* not *a germaphobe.* She cast an assessing eye over his blotched shirt and the general toddler-in-a-toy-room state of his apartment. *Definitely not a neat freak*, either. Two heaped spoons of peanut butter allowed for thinking time. Anita waited, chipped nail tapping the table in time with the suddenly too-loud clock.

"I've always wanted to," he admitted finally. "That and go on *MasterChef*."

"You know romance is usually written *by* ladies *for* ladies, right, Was? Like, do you even have a penis?"

His head dropped to his crotch, and he moaned at the sudden motion. *Dear Goddess, why are you bringing up his dick?* She needed to get her tongue under control.

"I was joking, but that was mean. I'm sorry," she said at the same time Sam gritted out "Pretty sure it's still there." Their eyes met and Sam looked away, pink staining his cheeks.

"To be fair," he shoved another laden spoon into between his lips, speaking around the mouthful, "it could've been amputated last night, and I wouldn't have felt it." Clearing his throat, he changed the subject. "Anyway, chicks love Nicholas Sparks." The clean spoon pointed her way. "*Everyone* loves *The Notebook*. And what's wrong with going against the norm?"

"True, everyone loves *The Notebook*." Anita grinned, waving the pages at him. "And there's nothing wrong with male romance writers. It's just that sometimes, they're too focused on what they *see*, you know?" Her eyes widened, dancing back and forth between the writer and his work.

"No, I don't see." Sam's eyes were closed, head dangling over the back of the chair. His cute golden spectacles were making a slow slide up his nose, towards the floor.

"Was, are you being funny?"

"What?" He pushed his hair from his eyes, and a pleasant soapy smell wafted towards her. "I am so confused."

"Okay, look." She stood up. "Describe me. What are the first things you'd write?"

"Um, you have long hair and nice ... tits? But I'm more of an arse man. Can't see it, though, because of the skirt ..."

"Oh, my Goddess, do you actually think you're *thinking* all of that right now? Or did you mean to blurt it out?" She laughed as his face flushed easily once more, the scarlet blush running down his neck and under the collar of his shirt. "And I thought

I had a loose tongue!"

She laughed again as Sam diligently shovelled more peanut butter into the gaping hole in his face. Sam wore his pain and embarrassment while guilt and pity churned in her gut.

See, this is yet another perfect example of why men are never attracted to you. You're not ... her brain searched for an adjective ... *meant for polite company.*

Anita knew her list of faults was long, but the top three included that she was technically homeless (unless 'permanently-in-transit-with-circus' qualified as domesticity), overweight (she preferred 'curvaceous' but her brother insisted that was calling mutton lamb), and sometimes confrontationally critical in her readings, both palm and page (insert current awkward situation with Sam-The-Writer here).

"Okay, backtrack. I'll give you an example from your own work." Her finger wavered at the top of the page. "*Her eyes were dark, like moist soil. And those lips – two pink rashers of bacon.*" Anita's dark eyebrow rose high as she smirked. "Then, you scribbled out *bacon* and wrote peach slices."

Sam cringed. "I know, terrible similes. But you can see I'm still editing ..."

"It's more the *wording*, Was. Moist soil? How is *that* romantic, Mister It's-Not-Comedy-It's-Romance?"

"It's a technique. Assonance, it's where–"

"Repeated vowel sounds, I get it, Sam. But saying your romantic lead 'moves like a jewel in the pool' won't win you any literary awards now, will it?" Anita raised her eyebrows at the barely sober man before her, unable to stop her critique. "The simile isn't effective. The comparison is off. I can deal with the description of big hair and small tits. It's unflattering, yet true. But I wouldn't enjoy my face being compared to wet dirt and bacon."

His cheeks flushed a deeper red. *Goddess, that's adorable.* She'd made men blush before, but not at this frequency. It was like Sam was the sun, frequent solar flares exploding just beneath his skin.

"I suppose I see what you're saying," he grumbled as Anita stole the freshly loaded spoon from his hand. "I have been ... struggling ... with this story."

"I can see that. There are more words scribbled out and doodles in the margins than there are coherent sentences. And here," the many rings adorning her fingers flashes as she pointed to a section on one page. "You described the heroine's feet as long and angular. Then, you spent the next page describing how her skin smelled, *in extreme detail*."

His eyebrows rose. "What's wrong with that? The character smells nice, and descriptive writing is important."

Dude, how are you not getting this? Too hung-over to think?

"Yes," she agreed patiently. "But it implies her feet smell nice. Her FEET! I wouldn't mention feet unless it's a fetish thing. And their smell? Look, all I'm saying is that I can see a few problems in this supposed 'Romance Novel'." *I've always had a run-away mouth, but this is next level.*

Sam groaned, snatching the spoon back before digging deep into the peanut spread.

I'm sorry! Sort of! Anita sent the mental message out as she moved to sit next to him. She knew the poor guy probably felt attacked right now, by a stranger (and in his own home no less!)

but she couldn't stop. She pointed to the papers in her hands. "This bit's supposed to be a sex scene, yeah?"

He nodded, cheeks flushing yet again at the mention of sex. *Strange. A romance writer who blushes about bumping uglies.*

"Well," Anita continued, "one – as previously mentioned, delete the feet unless it's a fetish thing. Two – long and angular? Those words have more masculine overtones. Save those kinds of descriptions for the dong. You want a masculine sounding dong. And third–"

"Really, there's more?" He licked the spoon clean. "And who says *dong*?"

"Man meat, then." She nonchalantly flipped her hand. "Third," she repeated, "what's with you and soap? I mean, looking around this place, you're not exactly Mister Clean ..."

Anita took in the chaos. In one quick sweep, thirtyish novels, six pairs of underwear, two t-shirts, one wet, musty towel, at least three empty alcohol bottles, and a coffee mug for every day of the week, strewn around the dank space. A thin trail of ants investigated a dirty plastic plate that protruded from under the sofa. *You're braver than me, little bugs.* Truth be told, she was itching to tidy the writer's flat. Her world was full of carefully folded tarps and coiled ropes, everything in its place – including her. The mess and chaos of Sam's life was almost too much.

The guy needs help in so *many ways.*

Sam slammed the peanut butter down on the coffee table and stood up, his long legs brushing through Anita's skirts. He swayed, steadied himself, then pinched the bridge of his nose. "Her skin smelled like soap," he said. "That's an okay description, right? Her nice clean soapy smell?"

"Yes, that's totally fine. A brief mention. 'Her skin smelled like rose petal soap with enticing jasmine overtones,' or whatever." She was clearly teasing him, but he rapidly gripped a pencil, scribbling down her suggestion furiously.

"Seriously, Was?" she said, regaining custody of the peanut butter jar.

"How are you so good at this, just off the cuff?" Sam dropped the pencil, looking at her with interested yet wary eyes. They were deep brown, the colour of warm chocolate milk, she decided, holding the peanut butter spoon upside down in her mouth. *Chocolate and nuts.* She allowed the peanut butter to smooth across her tongue. *My favourite treat.*

"I'm not done yet, Was, not by a long shot. Not if that whole stack of paper over there reads similar to this kindling."

"*Kindling?*" he spluttered. "Ouch!"

"I don't mean to be overly critical. I just love to read. In any town Cirque de Fortuna visits, my first stop is the local library. Librarians are the best people in town to ask for recommendations, books and otherwise. They know all the best local haunts and hot spots, and authors too. She's a cutie, the Moonshine Municipal Librarian. Oh, but you probably already know that, living here and being a writer and all ..."

He moaned at her rambling. It was a reaction she was used to: the groan of a man sick of her apparent ability to breathe through her butt and maintain conversation at the same time. *Right, get on with it, girl!*

"Anyway, Laura – the librarian – mentioned a few Moonshine attractions. She said the architecture and stained glass of the church were gorgeous. I love things like that. She also said to have coffee at Friday's, and that the best meals are at The Pope. But she didn't mention that random lighthouse on the hill. What's that about, anyway?" Anita pointed through the window to a Rapunzelesque tower on a hill overlooking the inland town.

"Bet she didn't bring up the pirate ship that's docked on the riverbank, either?" he muttered, picking up his spectacles from atop a novel and sliding them on.

Anita's curls tickled her cheeks as her head shook. "She didn't mention a river."

"Cuts right through town and comes with the Jolly Rodger. My best friend's house backs onto the water, so we're pirate spotting all the time." he shrugged. "This town's only small, but it's full of ... quirks."

As he struggled over the last word, her gaze fell to the novel he'd scooped his spectacles from – *Heat in the Kitchen*. A cog seemed to shift in her head, thoughts spinning in motion. Her mouth dropped as she picked it up, reading the cover.

"Quirks ..." she muttered to herself, eyes shifting from the cover to her hung-over host, then one of the many overdue bills, reading the addressee's name from the top corner. "Samuel Harthrup – Sammie Hart!" Excitement bubbled through her.

Sam buried his head in his hands, sighing as she tapped the cover of *Heat in the Kitchen*.

"*No way*! Was, you sly fox, you're already published! But under a pseudonym, so nobody–"

"Nobody knows!" His hand grasped hers as he pleaded. "Nobody can know. *Please*."

The puppy-dog eyes, magnified by his spectacles, melted her.

He seems so desperate. She stepped back to consider him, running the spoon slowly around the rapidly depleting peanut butter jar. Holding the loaded spoon out to him, she sighed. Hesitating, he took it between his fingers.

"Wow." *Holy shitballs, one of my favourite books was written by a dude!* "Mind. Blown. Well, Sammie Hart, if this –" she waved the papers once more, "– is your sequel, then what you need is *help*, not a whole-page outline of each soapy ingredient that made her strangely square foot attractive in what is *almost* a sex scene." Anita couldn't stop herself from smirking. "If this is what you've been working on, Was, it's no wonder you were trying to find inspiration in oblivion last night. The bottom of the bottle isn't helping though, is it?"

Shaking his head slowly, he'd unearthed a half loaf of bread from the depths of the pantry. After a suspicious sniff, four slices fell into the toaster. Her mouth watered, stomach grumbling. Sam sighed, clearly defeated.

"If I need help, what should I do?" He picked up one of the many lead pencils strewn around the room, pinching the bridge of his nose once more, stress and frustration pooling between his deep brown eyes. *Talk about tells,* she smirked to herself. Maybe this man *was* an open book. Maybe all he needed was a good reader.

Anita laughed, plonking the peanut butter jar onto the table. "Jeeze, isn't this supposed to be a sex book? One whole page outlining soap and then a fade to black where, I assume, he made love with her pointy, angular toes? Help is necessary, my friend. Like insulin for a diabetic, *you need it*."

"Did your crystal ball tell you that?" he retorted. "And it is not –" he lowered his voice, attempting to snatch the pages from her hands, "– a *sex* book."

"Wow, you really struggled to say that, hey? It's just a word, Shakespeare. You can say it. Sex. Go on. *Sex*."

"Stop, please." He blushed. *Goddess, that is the most adorable thing.* "It's not *that*. It's a romance."

Anita blinked. "Are they different?" She could see it all over his face. He was mortified. Genuinely mortified. "Just teasing. Lighten up, Was."

She watched the grumpy writer scrape the last smears of the peanut butter across the hot toast. It melted in, just the way she liked. Lowering her voice, she licked her lips. "Like I told you last night. I'm a reader. A psychic. Medium. Witch. Whatever you want to call it. I believe in signs and tune into the universe. I honestly believe I've been sent here to Moonshine to help you."

He dropped the toast onto a single plate then *hmph*ed down at the table, head in his hands. "You're mean, Witch. Less Samantha from *Bewitched* and more *I'll get you my pretty, and your little dog, too.* Has anyone ever told you that?"

"So frequently, I hear it in my sleep." Sitting opposite him, she leaned across and ruffled his soft, light hair, smiling brilliantly. "But it's not true. You'll see. I'm completely charming, like *Sabrina, The Teenage Witch*. Original version." Sam's head thumped heavily into his hands, and she chuckled, shoving toast beneath his bowed head. "Now, do you want help with this manuscript or what? The circus is only in Moonshine for two weeks and I'm a willing reader, but only if you want help. I'll be honest but constructive. And honestly, you need me, Sam. Otherwise –" she threw her handful of papers into the air as Sam's jaw dropped to the floor, along with his work. " – this trash will never get you a movie deal."

The poor guy looked so forlorn and lost, her heart almost broke. He bent to collect a lost page, chewing slowly. Sam placed the page beside the remaining stacks on the table.

"Okay, fine. But this is a professional interaction. Nothing more."

That will NOT be a problem. Nobody ever wanted her. She was too soft, too round, too curvy, despite all the confident adjectives she used to the contrary. And Sam was cute, in a nerdy kind of way, but he was so introverted and opposite to her, there was no way he could light her fire. No way at all. Especially with his lacklustre personal grooming habits and garbage-dump-themed living quarters. But in spite of how gross the place was, a firework of excitement had exploded inside her. Here it was – her project. Something to preoccupy her when she wasn't working.

Filling two (almost) smudge-less glasses with fresh tap water, Anita handed him one. "Nothing more. There's no time for more, anyway." She grinned wickedly. "Two weeks. To you, Was." The solid clink of their glasses echoed throughout the flat.

"And you, Witch."

His Adam's apple bobbed up and down as he skulled the cool water and her hand somehow made its way to his forearm. Sam froze, two large eyes over the rim of the glass. His spectacles gave his eyes an owlish expression, appearing about three times too big for his face. She smuggled a grin behind the rim of her glass.

"It won't be terrible," she assured him, fingers squeezing reassurance into the cool flesh of his forearm. *Stop touching him!*

Every time their skin connected, he froze, the metaphorical deer in headlights. Clearly, he did not enjoy physical contact.

I wonder if that's why his book is so ... lacking. Still, she let her fingers rest on his skin.

"From what I've read, the bare bones are there," Anita told him, gently rubbing his arm in small, tentative strokes, as one would a pet moody cat in its rare moment of comfort-seeking. "Your descriptive writing is lovely and from my perusing while you slept, your overall story is structured well. Their first kiss? That waterfall scene? Oh!" She clutched her chest, eyes closed and grinning up to the sky. "*Hot.*"

His eyes widened dramatically. "Shit, how much did you read?"

"But ... The rest of the writing fell flat because there was no real *emotion*. No *physicalness*."

"That's not a word."

"*Samuel.*" She assumed the tone of an impatient parent. "You've got to describe *emotions*, not just write about the physical happenings using strange similes and food-related puns. Which, frankly, are deliciously disturbing. Once you fill in a few literary holes ..." she kissed her fingertips and sent it into the air, "you'll be a master chef of romance ... again." She waved *Heat in the Kitchen* before his face, grinning and waggling her eyebrows. Her brother hated that face. He called it 'childish and silly'. But right now, silly and childish might just be what was called for. Samuel Harthrup needed to lighten up. And, if she was honest with herself, this was exactly the time-consuming project she needed right now. It gave her the perfect excuse to escape the daylight hours that would otherwise be spent with

Cirque de Fortuna, and explore this new town with a new friend.

"You really think it's that easy?" With toast and water in his system, the fog of Sam's hangover was beginning to lift. Anita could sense his curiosity and his pride. She'd hurt it, she knew, but the truth hurts sometimes. It was better coming from her now (with kindness as its intention) than later (through scathing book reviews).

"Rainbows are only visible after a downpour," she told him. "I'm not saying it'll be easy. Writing seems like a lot of hard work. *Dull* work, especially compared to circus life. But I know you can make it better and I know I've been sent here to help with that."

Sam dissolved into a quiet, pondering silence once more, before muttering something about spells and magic and literary-style emotional blackmail. "Shit. Alright." He rubbed his hands over his face and through his hair. "What do you suggest, Anita?"

Her breath caught. It was the first time he'd said her name. All gruff and resigned, barely awake and completely hung-over, Sam spoke her name like a mountain-dwelling Bigfoot finally agreeing to leave his cave after years of being invited to come out and play.

Gulping water, she had to think, *fast*, like Superman-saving-Lois-Lane fast. An idea struck with surprising force. "Come to the circus tonight," she said.

"But I saw the show last night."

"No, Was, you didn't. You saw the back of your eyelids before the show even started," she scoffed. "First you tried to drown yourself, then you attempted blunt force trauma to the head. An effective way to avoid the show, by the way. That reminds me, McDreamy said he'd check on you later."

"McDreamy?" His eyes widened behind the glasses and she couldn't help but laugh at his expression.

"The doctor. Anyway, tonight isn't about seeing the show. Not really. Seeing isn't the project." Another cog slipped into place as she figured out exactly how to open Sam up and tailor to his needs. "Yes, that's it! Projects! Assignments!" She snatched a pencil from the table, flipped a page (to his utterances of protest) and began a list. "You're a nerdy guy, you'll like projects. So, number one is tonight."

He leaned forward, reluctantly intrigued. His knee bumped hers under the table. It was warm and hard against her own. Blushing, he moved away. *So cute.*

She continued. "Tonight is about what you *feel*. Listening to your body, focusing on emotions and feelings, not what things *look* like."

He raised an eyebrow at her, swallowing the last of the toast. "I know how to describe feelings."

Anita picked up *Heat in The Kitchen* in one hand and a few pages of Sam's draft manuscript in the other. "Do you mean, *Her slippery tongue danced a magical spell upon my own and I was ready to burst from the ecstasy of her kiss*?" She placed *Heat* onto the table. "Or, *I felt like a pig in mud, consumed by the mess of her hair.*" She groaned, slapping the paper back to the pile, then scrutinising the room. "Sloppy head, sloppy house, sloppy writing. And *again* with the moist dirt. Honestly, what The Almighty Mother is that about?"

"Witch," Sam mumbled.

"Ooh, Was, name calling, I like it. You're getting some spunk back." She smiled up at him once more, batting her eyelashes. "I ask you, what have you got to lose, dirt perve?"

"Two weeks of my life?"

"Two weeks is all I've got to give you, Sammie Hart." She smirked at the name, wondering how many others knew this man's secret identity. "I'll need to be at the showground by four thirty this afternoon, to set up before the show. It'll be around ten before I can escape. So, from ten tonight to four thirty tomorrow afternoon, I'm all yours."

Stop touching him! Her hand had made its way to his again, somehow. Shrugging, she gave a small squeeze before letting go. *Encouragement. That's all it is.*

"That works, late nights are my thing," he said.

"And early mornings are mine." Anita beamed. "Throw in breakfast, and you've got a deal."

Cirque de Feeling

SAM

Dear Diary,

Shit, she knows! Can I trust a circus-dwelling witch? She's got a bit of a mouth on her, little miss Anita Fortuna. She's a nomad for God's sake! She could go spilling my beans all over the country! Wait, does that sound sexual? Like, a sexy baked beans pun? Ah, forget it. Only Nigella Lawson could make baked beans sexy.

But seriously, if the witch even told ONE person at each town the circus visits … But she wouldn't … right? She's cute, but not crazy. Well, maybe a bit crazy and a bit more than cute. Okay, I'll be honest, she's hot – in a curvy, soft, flowers-in-her-hair bohemian kind of way. Anita, that is. But no, this isn't about that. No sexy beans or sexy Nigella or sexy Anita.

The most frustrating thing about the witch is that she's right. I'm stuck with a manuscript that is, in her words, more fizzle than sizzle. My editor is on my back, but that kind of pressure-cooker situation isn't motivating.

What helped last time, with Heat, was someone on my FRONT. Sandra inspired the words my brain required. This time, I'm celibate as ... well, myself, pre-Sandra. I don't want another relationship to ruin me at its inevitable end. So, I have to keep things professional.

People leave me. It's what they do. I get it. It probably sounds dramatic, but facts are facts.

My sequel's deadline is looming. With my romantic life solidly on the backburner, I need a new recipe to whip up this novel. Maybe a totally platonic working relationship with a liquorice-haired fortune-teller is exactly what I need. It can't hurt to try at least. Maybe Anita is exactly the critique partner I need. She's here for two weeks and I'm already so far behind in this project, what's another fortnight?

I need to clear my head, especially if the witch is assigning 'homework'. Shit, I must be a total dweeb, because that sounds fun.

She's certainly no muse, but right now, I'll take whatever help I can get.

From: Suzannah.editor@flagpolepublishing.com
To: Samuelharthrup@hotmail.com;
Sammiehartromance@flagpolewriters.net
CC: editor.in.chief@flagpolepublishing.com

Subject: Heat in the Kitchen Sequel

Hello Sam,

Please update the editorial team regarding your progress with the sequel to your New York Times Best Selling smash hit, *Heat in the Kitchen*.

As you are aware, the contract awarded to you was for a duology, and is dependent on receipt of a second novel which is due to be delivered by November 30th.

As discussed previously, there is demand for more detailed intimacy. This sequel will require more explicit sexual intricacies.

We look forward to hearing from you regarding your progress. If you could please return my phone calls, or respond to this email with an update, it would be greatly appreciated.

Sincerely,

Suzannah Browne

Editorial Director, *Flagpole Publishing*

"Two nights in a row, bud?" said one of the hand-holding Shetland unicorn-walking clowns. "You sure must *love* our popcorn!" He handed the red-and-white-striped box to Sam, who was finding the sideshows less interesting than he had the previous evening. The paracetamol had curbed his headache and a carb-heavy lunch had done wonders, but he wasn't ready to put up with a two-toothed man wearing huge, painted-on red lips. The striped Big Top pointed into the clear, starry Moonshine evening and the crowd swelled as show time drew nearer. Somewhere close by, the extraordinarily loud rumble of a motorcycle filled the air and the ground shook – though the sensation could have been caused by Sam's nerves.

"There you are!" Anita's small, curvy frame popped out from behind a curtain. Had she shrunk? For the first time, they were standing face-to-face. Well, her face to his chest, to be more exact. "I'm so glad you came, Was!"

"Uh, hi, Anita."

Her hand reached out to touch his arm, like it had earlier that day. His skin was left numb and pleasantly tingling when she quickly removed it.

Stepping back, Anita spun in a slow circle, smiling up at him from beneath dark, sparkling eyelashes. "Like my uniform?"

His mouth dried faster than cotton in high summer. Gone were her hippy layers and free, untamed hair. Tonight, she wore a green and black leotard that looked more like a sexy, lace-infused swimsuit than a 'uniform'. Her wild curls had been twisted into a crown atop her head, and a gigantic feathered headdress sprouted in fluffy plumes from the top, affording her an additional three feet in overall height. She appeared so at home here, all sequins, lace, and tail feathers.

"Well? How do I look?" She twirled, grinning.

"I thought tonight wasn't about what I *see*," Sam mumbled, scratching the tingles from his forearm. She laughed, sending butterflies through him. *Goddamn it, get it together, man!*

"Cheeky nerd." She giggled, touching his arm again. "I see you're in your denim-and-black-shirt combination again."

He shoved his hands into his pockets, annoyed to have been ridiculed twice in two days for his fashion sense.

"I love it. Classic," she said. "As for your homework, quick learning will be necessary. Two weeks is *not* long." She launched into a detailed description of her plans for his evening, but the feathers swaying before his eyes were too distracting. No matter where he looked, his entire face was filled with her hairpiece. He tried to look down to her face, but all he saw was ruby red lips and her boobs, packed tightly into the mesh-like fabric of the theatrical bodysuit.

"Like I said earlier –" she hooked her arm in his and led him to the stands, "– I think you need to work on editing that piece of kindling, not rewrite the whole thing."

"Are you always this ..." he searched for the right word. *Rude? Blunt?* "Honest?"

"Yes." She shrugged. "Fatal character flaw, I'm afraid. I'll be labelled as 'brutal' or 'bitchy' until my hair is white, then when I'm a senior citizen my behaviour will nearly be socially acceptable." He considered her words, realising just how true they were. His gran and her elderly friends got away with saying whatever they pleased, no matter how outrageous.

"Societal perceptions suck," Sam said.

"Write on, male romance writer. No stigma." She winked, pointing to an empty seat in the stands. On the other side of the sawdust-smothered ring, a clown ran a comb through his whiskers, watching them with interest.

"So, what about me?" Sam asked.

"What about you?" Her dark eyebrows collided as the crowd began to file in and find their seats. Clowns banging drums swarmed around the arena. A fun, anticipatory atmosphere settled, the hushed eagerness of the theatre before the main event.

"What's your perception of me? Of my character?" he asked. *Is it me, or is she starting to look nervous?*

Anita's feathered head turned left and right, and while her mouth held a smile, her big blue eyes were clearly scanning the room.

What, or who, is she looking for? A saviour to take her away from this conversation? From me?

"You sure you want to know?"

Honestly, he wasn't sure, but his mouth betrayed him. "I really want to know."

Without preamble, she said, "Your face is too small for your head."

"Solid start," he mumbled into his large box of popcorn as his heart belly-flopped into his stomach.

"But you have big, *lovely* eyes." She adjusted his glasses, her sweet smell of vanilla and lavender floating around his face. "Owlishly huge."

Is that even a compliment? "With the depth of expensive chocolate?" Hey, a guy could hope.

She grinned. "They're the colour of moist dirt, if I'm not mistaken." The word 'moist' in her mouth curdled his stomach.

He groaned. "Any other razor-sharp observations?"

"I think your hair is a bit ... uneven or something." Her hand flew to the base of his skull, gently smoothing over the short hairs found there. "I think this bit needs to be longer." Gently, she stroked the back of his head. Heat rushed over him in pleasant waves. How long had it been since anyone had touched him there? So softly? The light hairs on his arms prickled. She pulled her hand away. "Growing it out would suit you better," she said, "and it might make your face look more proportioned. And if you got rid of the glasses ..." Her hands moved to the arms of his spectacles.

"But I need them." Sam swatted her away as an unusually well-endowed male acrobat in a white sequin-trimmed suit called Anita's name. He nodded towards the ring. *That has got to be padding,* Sam hoped, staring directly at the guy's crotch. *Holy shit*! The Cirque De Fortuna leotards left nothing to the imagination.

Anita nodded, almost imperceptibly, to the acrobat. "Well, I'm just saying, the glasses make you look like an owl. A cute owl, but still."

"You think I'm cute?" He smiled his first genuine smile in a very long time. *Shit, am I blushing?* This little bohemian was ripping him – *and* his writing – to shreds and he was *flirting* with her? *Get your head in the game, Harthrup.* He was too out of practice to flirt. *Or write well,* he added mournfully. "A manly, rugged and hyper-masculine kind of 'cute'?" Again, a guy could hope.

"If you invested in contacts, grew a bit of stubble to cover that chiselled jaw, give your face some depth ..." She continued to label his flaws. *Great*. She shrugged. "Hey, you asked."

"I know." He sighed. The woman had no filter.

"You really shouldn't ask questions if you don't want to hear the honest answer," she said, readjusting the deep green sparkling belt that slung low on her wide hips. Unable to stop himself, his eyes roamed her again, though he wasn't sure if it was Anita's words or her spandex-and-sparkle-clad figure that were grinding on his mind. She seemed to be appraising him in a similar way. His gut tightened.

"Why do I feel a makeover montage coming on?"

"Probably because you've seen too many rom-coms." She grinned, looking around the ring once again. The moustached, big-bulged acrobat was back, shooting Anita a pointed look. "Was, I have to go, but remember the assignment, okay? See and *feel*." Louder, she added, circling the crowd, "Enjoy the show, folks!"

Anita strutted into the centre of the ring, commanding the crowd's attention. *My God, that arse.*

The crowd went wild as the clown band struck up and the lights dimmed. Anita executed a cartwheel, landing in the splits rather sensually atop a clown's midsection. He honked his big red nose in mock lust. The crowd went wild, raucous laughter filling the Big Top. Jumping up, Anita pantomimed shock, strutting a few feet away with a pout on her ruby lips. Overhead, the acrobats did final checks of their ropes, watching the clowns pointing and smiling along with the crowd. Mister pants-padding dusted his hands with white powder.

The clown, now walking on comically stiff legs, grabbed at Anita with clumsy arms. He encroached menacingly. The acrobat launched from his platform, swinging low to snatch Anita away at the last second. As she flew through the air, grinning at the crowd and slowly turning her legs as though she was walking in mid air, Sam knew right then that it was going to be a great show.

Throughout the circus acts, Anita found ways to communicate the next steps of his project. At one stage she told the audience, her big blue eyes lingering on his section of the stands, "Close your eyes and feel the vibrations through the stands, the tension in the air ..."

Like a good pupil, he spent the next five minutes with his eyes squeezed shut, focusing on how it *felt* to be surrounded by pure energy. Heart pounding, he felt rather than heard the band set the tone for each act, each note coursing through his veins. The air seemed thicker and felt heavier, laden with anticipation. The thrilled hum of the audience had Sam's heart in his throat, excitement and awe choking him with each act. He enjoyed *feeling* the circus so much that he repeated the task again, repeatedly closing his eyes for long hot beats, the rush of life returning to his veins.

Reece was right, Sam begrudgingly admitted to himself as a huge metal ball was rolled into the centre of the ring. *I have spent too long locked up in my own head.*

During the 'Ball of Moto Moto', an act where multiple motorbikes zoomed around the enclosed metal ball, narrowly avoiding collision and defying gravity, Sam felt adrenaline like he hadn't in years: chest constricted, breathing raspy, his legs twitching with energy. It was incredible.

Sam diligently catalogued his bodily responses and feelings, wondering how they might apply to writing romance. With each new act he became more comfortable closing his eyes and simply feeling the world around him. There were only two acts he couldn't tear his eyes from. One was the white-clad acrobats. The fellow from earlier, who may as well have had three legs, swung in daring loops and arcs with a lithe blonde woman, another muscular, younger man, and a gap-toothed girl who looked tiny and breakable next to the rest of the troupe. Their act was captivating. The combination of the massive men and the tiny girl, all in white, soaring, tumbling and flying through the air, stole his breath. At the finale of their air-ballet, perfectly timed to a dramatic operatic overture, Sam had been surprised to find a tear rolling down his cheek. *Get a grip, Harthrup!* He clapped until his hands hurt.

The other performance he was unable to tear his eyes away from wasn't an 'act' at all. It was meant as a crowd distraction whilst the circus crew changed the set. 'Distraction' was an understatement.

A single beam of blue light pierced the darkened tent, shining down upon the Ringmaster and Anita as they slowly performed to a sombre version of *El Tango de Roxanne*.

Anita's feathered headdress had been abandoned for a curled up-do, and she wore a deep purple burlesque dress, all wire and lace. Long strips of skirt revealed glimpses of her thighs as she moved. Transfixed, Sam found himself leaning forward as the band struck up. He wasn't the only one. It seemed the entire crowd had their elbows on their knees, eyes wide. Slow music and a deep, gravelly voice rippled through the crowd.

Anita slowly circled the Ringmaster, who watched greedily as her bare feet trailed through the fine sawdust. The man was a head taller than Anita, Sam noticed. His black top hat was abandoned to the floor; a white-gloved hand thrust out to stop Anita as she strode by. Her head snapped sideways at the exact moment their bodies connected, music rising. Locking eyes, they began the tango. The light shimmered blue as the music intensified. Mesmerised, Sam watched them. The possessive Ringmaster's hands gripped tight, his dark eyes contrasting the cheery red of his jacket.

Anita attempted escape. The Ringmaster dragged her back into his arms. They swayed, and he thrust her to the floor in a brutal act of choreography, love and dominance. Anita's breath rushed out as sawdust flew skyward. She peered up, eyes wide. The audience leaned in, expectant, collective breath held as the Ringmaster towered over her. His muscular physique exuded dominance; his black-ringed eyes intense and mouth curved into a sneer. It made Sam's blood boil, watching the powerplay as Anita cowered before the man.

She simpered in the sawdust, backing away as his hand rose in warning with the song's crescendo. Lights off, pitch black. *BOOM*. The bang of a drum ended the song.

The audience exploded into applause as the lights illuminated the Big Top once more and several dark horses thundered around the ring in a Greek chariot race.

Shit, what an act. Sam was gasping for breath as he resumed his seat. He hadn't realised he was on his feet.

"Excuse me, sir." The young female acrobat appeared,

tugging at his sleeve. "Are you Anita's Was?" His name whistled through the childhood gaps in her teeth. His heart still behaving like a novice chef facing off against Gordon Ramsey, he nodded, his eyes searching for the witch as the next performance began. Anita was nowhere to be seen.

"Yes, I'm Was. Your act was wonderful!"

"Thank you." The child's face flushed at the praise. "Anita said your project is done? I don't know what that means, but she said you can meet her now. The show is over once the horses leave the ring." The swirl of horses cantering in a circle distracted them both momentarily. "I can show you where her vardo is. Come on." She smiled endearingly, and Sam allowed the girl to lure him from the crowd.

"Vardo?"

"It's a special trailer. It's pretty. Come on, I'll show you."

Anita's vardo was a typical Roma-style wagon. Built on large, spoked wheels with a domed roof, it had been built atop a double-axle trailer with a tow ball fitted, to secure onto a motorised vehicle rather than traditionally hitched to a horse. Ornate patterns swirled around the doorways and windows, and a small 'Do Not Disturb' sign hung from the antique-looking door handle. As they approached, Sam saw a shadow slip behind the window. The night was unusually light. The festoon lights smothered the twinkling, starlit sky, and beams from the Moonshine Whine, the lighthouse, circled overhead, slicing heaven and earth.

Moonshine was a beautiful town, made more lovely by the renewed passion Sam now felt for his work. Anita had been right about this project. If she kept helping him for the two weeks she was in town, he would rapidly improve his *Heat* sequel.

"Thank you." Sam smiled down at his guide, taking a step towards Anita's wagon.

"Wait," the girl said. "She'll have it padlocked inside. You need the secret knock." The little girl rapped her knuckles into his open palm.

"Got it," he said, knocking the beat back onto her pigtailed head. The acrobat giggled, wiggling from his teasing knocks. Her unabashed childhood smile beamed up at him.

"You're funny," she declared in that charming, direct way all kids seem to have. "Will you come back another time?"

Sam laughed, shrugging. "Perhaps. See you around, Robin."

He'd made the Batman reference out of some lame attempt to connect with the small acrobat. Robin was the only name he could think of for an acrobatic joke. But he couldn't help but grin into the night as he heard her whisper reverently, "He knows my name!"

Homework

ANITA

ANITA STRUGGLED INTO HER cardigan as 'Under the Sea' sounded upon her door. She placed her latest treasure, a HB pencil stub smuggled from Sam's flat, against a gemstone on her drawers, blowing out the candle.

"Coming!" she called as the tiny smoke trail danced skyward. Sliding the deadbolt, she peered out into the night.

"Hi, Was. *Feel* like you had a great night?"

"Hey, wow. That was ..." The writer's smile lit up the night. "Wow."

"You, Samuel Harthrup, are clearly a man of many words." She joined him on the small front step, turning to lock the door behind her.

"I only word good on paper." He laughed lightly, energised from his experiences. "So, what do we do now?" he asked, clapping his hands together.

She winced. *Great Goddess, I hope nobody heard that.*

"Now –" she grabbed Sam's arm, dragging him towards the darkened car park, "we run!" Anita took off into the field, her skirt swishing between the cars as she laughed.

"Any of these yours?" she said, breathing heavily, a few moments later. She flapped the open cardigan in wide waves, cooling herself down.

"I walked tonight. Thought I could use the fresh air. Reece thinks I need more oxygen to my brain."

She looped her arm through his as he walked along the path that wound into town.

"Reece?"

"I think you called him Doctor McDreamy."

"Oh, right. The hot doctor." His arm tensed beneath hers. "*Cranky* doctor," she added, looking up at Sam. In the moonlight, his hair was the colour of spider webs, and just as fine. Behind the spectacles, his eyes were two dark pools that reflected the glow of streetlights. Samuel Harthrup by moonlight was eerily beautiful. Like the ghost of a tall, lean, dishevelled Leonardo DiCaprio.

"Reece is a tight-arse about work stuff, that's all."

"He's a close friend?"

"Always has been. Ever since I fancied his sister, and he took pity on me when she obliterated my heart. That, and he was the only one to step in and save my sorry arse when I got into fights at school."

Anita nodded slowly, imagining it. "I've never been in one place long enough to make a steady acquaintance, let alone a *friend*." Jealousy pooled in her gut, and she said three quick affirmations to banish it. She wanted to say more, but instead breathed deeply, feeling Mother Nature alleviate her need to compulsively fill silences.

After a while, Sam hesitantly suggested, "I could be your friend, Witch." He smiled down at her. Gosh he was tall. She could tuck neatly beneath his arm, if she tried.

"That would be lovely, Was. Thank you." A friend. A colleague. Even if just for two weeks. Perfect. "Look! The evening star!" He followed her finger, face turned to the sky. "Make a wish, Was." She ignored his skeptical expression, noting the twinkle of each star as she sent a small, silent dream out into the universe. *Star light, star bright, first star I see tonight. Wish I may, wish I might, keep the wish I make tonight ...*

They walked companionably, the sweet spring air teasing their hair. Arms looped through each other's, Sam chivalrously escorted her towards town, passing colonial farmhouses with wide expanses of land, then the smaller city blocks, before entering Moonshine's Central Business District. Soon, the glowing lights that lined Moonshine's Main Street illuminated their path.

The main drag of town comprised about five civic blocks, lined with double-storey Victorian-style buildings, retail space fitting snugly below residential flats. Each store featured a large window display and its own brightly painted door, reminiscent of bygone times when automatic entrances didn't yet exist.

Huge trees split the main street, arching high above the wrought iron streetlights, offering rare glimpses of the star-filled sky. The wide, paved footpath led to a beautiful, shadow-filled park.

"Main Street Park," Sam sighed, clearly as enthralled with the sight as she was. The size of a city block, the park comprised an abundance of carefully manicured gardens, a vast grassy picnic area, and gnarled rosebushes circling a white rotunda. Gigantic, liquid amber trees waved starry leaves at a bottom-lit fountain, which had pride of place in the centre of the idyllic space.

Anita felt as if she'd stepped back in time. "Moonshine is old, huh?" she said, waving at an old lady on a mobility scooter. She was reversing slowly from a bustling business whose sign read 'The Pope'. Anita laughed, eyeing the building. "The Pope is a pub?" Her gaze travelled across the huge sandstone building. "And people say *I'm* a heathen."

All sorts of delicious smells emanated from the tavern, along with the tell-tale pub stench of stale beer and slight splash of urine.

"The librarian recommended this place."

"No doubt." Sam smiled down at her. "The Pope has the best grub in town. C'mon, let's chat over dinner."

"But it's so late, surely the kitchen's closed?" Anita protested, her voice nearly as loud as her grumbling stomach.

Sam opened the old wooden door for her, and an explosion of garbled conversations and country music burst from the building.

"The kitchen here is never closed," Sam said. In another act of old-world gallantry, he offered his hand. She examined his curved fingers and the deep lines etched across his palm, longing to hold them, read them.

"Why, thank you, sir." She curtsied with a smile before

accepting his gesture. They stepped inside, warmth and noise swallowing them as the door swung shut.

"One reason everyone loves The Pope," Sam shouted, barely audible, "is you can always get a hot meal here, even if Billy's gotta make it for you himself."

Weaving in and out of patrons, Sam gripped Anita's hand lightly, dragging her deeper into the din. Barely able to see over heads, Anita struggled through the mass of bodies, grateful for Sam's height. It allowed a definite advantage in a crowd. Reaching the bar, Sam dropped her hand, waving towards the broad, tattooed bartender, ordering two drinks.

Holy Goddess, now that *is a hunk of man.* Anita watched the mile of chest turn to fill two tall glasses with cola and ice.

"Billy Carmichael, meet Anita."

Billy slid a glass towards her, nodding briefly before turning to Sam. "It's good to see you out and about," he said, his voice rich and rumbling over the din of the bar. "Only kiddie stuff for you tonight." It wasn't a question. It was a demand. Billy had that drill-sergeant manner that allowed no argument. A second tall glass slid next to hers and soon both brimmed with icy cola.

The bush telegraph works fast! Anita marvelled as Sam leaned into converse with Billy about Doctor Reece.

While their voices mingled into the cacophony, Anita eyed the massive man who was The Pope's publican. Billy had one sleeve rolled up to the elbow, revealing a heavily tattooed expanse of arm. The other forearm was missing, his shirt folded and pinned crisply at the elbow. She watched with interest as he spoke to Sam while pouring drinks one-handed.

Billy Carmichael seemed capable and strong, the sort of man

who would never ask for help, either suffering in silence or not at all. He had a large, rough hand (very unlike Sam's two smooth artist's hands) and Anita itched to analyse it in finer detail. What would his one hand reveal? Surely more than most hand pairs might tell her. Curiosity piqued, she forced her arms to cross, holding herself at bay.

The giant publican was also a tornado. Billy turned the whole of his barrel-like chest left and right to reach for bottles of spirits lined up high on shelves behind him. He was as quick and efficient, serving, cleaning, pulling levers on the beer tap – all one handed. Anita's gaze followed the foamy golden liquid he was pouring as it waterfalled over the side of the glass, ensuring patrons got their fill of lager, not a glass of white froth.

Sam paid for the drinks, and she took hers eagerly, grateful her hands were distracted from reaching for the intriguing Billy Carmichael. Gripping their glasses, they found a tall table tucked into a corner. Stepping into the cozy space had the effect of plunging her head into water. Somehow, the music curved around this small section of the pub, muted and slightly muffled.

"This is a nice bubble," she said to Sam. "I can hear myself think, unlike out there." Her head nodded to the bustling bar beyond.

"Yeah, it's a good spot to sit and chat with a good view of the other Pope patrons."

"You come here a lot then?"

Sam didn't reply, watching as she struggled up onto the high barstool, smothering a laugh. Extending his arm, he assisted her up. "I didn't realise you were so short."

"And I didn't realise you wrote kissing books under a penname," she retorted, moving Sam's glass, water condensing on its outside, onto a coaster. There was absolutely no way anyone could have heard her quip over the ruckus of the pub, but Sam *ssshhhhhed*, cheeks flaming. *Who knew men could blush so much?* Those pink cheeks did something strange to her, like when you see a puppy running towards you for a belly scratch. She focused her eyes on Billy, amazed by the way his body moved and worked, quickly, in this fast-paced environment.

"Amputated at the elbow, when he was five," Sam told her, his cola-laced breath tickling her ear. *When had he moved so close?* The hair at the nape of her neck stood on end. "Accident down at the train yard," he added, and a creepy feeling settled low in her spine.

"We saw the train yard as we rolled into town," she said. "Looks like a graveyard for huge metallic condoms." Anita laughed as Sam spluttered, spraying tiny droplets of cola onto his already rather splotched t-shirt. It seemed that all this man owned were stained black tees.

"Maybe," he chuckled, wiping his mouth with the back of one lightly haired wrist. "But it's a dangerous playground for kids."

"Who lets their kids play there?"

"They didn't," Sam said, shaking his head. "His parents are great, unlike some." The words hung heavy, but she didn't get a chance to probe further. Sam's tone lightened as he added, "But four boys have a way of making big fun ... and finding big trouble."

As though sensing their conversation, Billy's bulk sauntered over. The man was huge, solid, with muscles like a lumberjack's. Up close, he was even bigger.

"You two eating?" His voice was deep and rich, pitched just above the buzz of the bar.

"Two of the usual, Billy. Thanks."

"Can you call it 'the usual' if I haven't laid eyes on you in months?"

As they argued the finer points of being a local and a regular, jealousy (a familiar green-eyed monster) clawed its way into Anita's gut. She had never lived anywhere long enough to have a 'usual' order.

Sam turned to her apologetically. "Sorry, did you want to choose your own meal, or–"

"I'll have what he's having." She smiled brilliantly at the publican, already playing her game and trying to place him as a romance Leading Man. "Film heroes are just never that ... broad."

"What?" Sam blinked, pushing his glasses higher onto his nose.

"Billy here." She hooked her thumb towards the towering publican. "He's like some Viking God body builder. I'm having trouble thinking of a romance hero who has *that* body and beard ... and all the tattoos!" She grinned up at him, looking to Sam. "The closest I can get is maybe Luke from *Gilmore Girls,* the later seasons, but more ... lumberjack-like?"

"You have a strange thing for romance heroes," Sam commented, shooting an apologetic glance to his old friend.

"And *you* have a strange thing for strawberry shaped nipples."

Sam's cheeks darkened, eyes widening in horror. With a

raised eyebrow and a smirk hidden within his beard, Billy spun back towards the bar, leaving them to their conversation. "Oh yeah, Was, I read it," Anita continued. "And you know the nipples are just the poky bit, right? The entire coloured circle is the areola, which is what I think you were referencing when–"

"Okay, *thank you*." He coughed loudly, eyes sliding sideways as he changed the subject. "So, that was a quick getaway tonight …"

Anita's heart leapt into her throat, but she was saved from commenting about the circus as Billy returned with two burgers. No, not just burgers – delicious towers with the lot *and then some*. Sam's 'usuals' were magnificent leaning towers of thin beef and crisp lettuce, relish, pickles, avocado, beetroot, carrot, bright red tomato, and a fried egg, all delicately layered between a soft, seeded bun, then skewered with a long wooden stick bearing a flag that read 'The Pope's most religious experience'.

"Oh, my Glorious Goddess, these superb burgers have *everything*." Saliva was already pooling in her mouth.

"No cheese," Billy growled, skewering Sam with a meaningful look. "Doctor's orders."

Anita grinned. "Ah, small town charm. Everyone knows everyone else's business." Sliding a look at Sammie Hart, she amended, *not everyone's business …*

"C'mon, Billy. The cheese is the best part!" Sam complained.

"*No cheese!*" Billy repeated, sliding one plate from his hand and the other from his forearm. Never in a billion years would Anita be able to carry two plates on one arm, at once, but here Billy Carmichael was, making it look easy.

"Thank you!" Anita sung to Billy's retreating mile of back before turning to Sam. "Why no cheese?"

"I'm lactose intolerant."

"Really? You lack toes?" Anita peered down, down, *woah, such a long way down,* to his feet. "It's a sad day to have a foot fetish," she teased. "No wonder you droned on for one long-arse page."

"I do *not* have a foot fetish." Sam rolled his big, chocolate brown eyes, completely red faced. "You're a crack up, Witch."

"Like an egg, or so I'm told." She ducked as a pickle flew her way.

"Sam!" Billy's voice thundered across the music. For a second, everyone froze. "No food fights!"

"Sorry." Sam shrunk into his chair, stuffing the burger into his mouth. The Pope breathed back to life.

"You know that's not a real thing, right? Lactose intolerance." Anita called Billy back to order some cheddar slices. "Your body just needs to get used to it. Build up a tolerance."

"You're wrong. So, *so* wrong," Sam said, his golden hair flopping side to side as he shook his head.

"I'm not."

"You are," Billy's deep voice countered, arriving to slide four perfectly cut slices onto her plate. "And you'll regret it, I assure you."

Defiantly, Anita added two slices to Sam's burger and two to her own. Billy mumbled under his breath about gas masks, retreating once more.

"Carpe diem, Was."

"Cheese the day, Witch! This will be worth the pain."

Sam took a huge bite of the burger, eyes rolling back in his head. Anita followed suit, groaning in delight.

"Wow. *Oh wow.*" She hadn't moaned like that since Cameron Lavinsky, and the rendezvous in that Melbourne food truck. The burger was a religious experience indeed.

"I see my wording good is contagious," Sam said with a grin, his mouth full of burger bits and his glasses fogging up. They lapsed into silence as they ate.

Occasionally she'd look up between bites to discover Sam watching her enjoy her meal, which was weird. She'd never had anyone watch her eat before, but he was doing it in an almost parental way, like she deserved a sticker or to be told she was a 'good girl' (with a slightly condescending pat on the head) at any moment. Licking her lips, she sighed in bliss, sinking into the curve of the chair.

Gulping the last of her meal, she pointed to a long chalkboard above the bar. "What's that?"

Sam swivelled to see what she was referring to. "The tally from the keg book," he said, finishing his own burger and licking his fingers.

"The *what*?"

"The Pope's always kept a keg book. It's a tally of how many drinks have been served in its history."

Anita's eyes bulged at the lengthy chalked number. "Okay, I am impressed! That's a *lot* of beers poured."

Sam laughed. "Moonshine's an old town. So, Anita ..."

Her traitorous hand reached for him. *Stop it!* She ordered, squishing both hands beneath her thighs.

He gave her a strange look before continuing. "How did I do tonight?" She blinked, not understanding. "My homework?"

"Oh! Yes! Well, the project isn't over yet." She yawned, the length of the day suddenly bearing down on her. With the show done and food in her belly, Anita's body decided it was finally time to release its residual tension and simply rest.

"How can you be tired? I'm buzzing with energy. All that *feeling* I did at the circus has me –"

"Feeling like writing?"

"Well, yeah!" He seemed to be running on endorphins and adrenaline, practically bouncing in his seat.

"Good. So tonight, night owl, you write. And Miss Anita will grade your papers in the morning."

"And what about tomorrow?"

"Tomorrow I'll adjust the parameters of the projects moving forward, to help you with whatever it is you actually *need*. Like, if you need to detox from feet, I'll keep mine covered at all times." Sam's pointed elbow nudged into her arm in jest. She winced.

"Shit, sorry. I didn't mean to –"

"It's okay," she said quickly, tugging on her cardigan. "So, does that proposition sound fair?"

"Fair." Shaking hands, they nodded at each other, before Sam assisted her down off the bar stool. She teetered, gripping his gorgeously lined palms tightly.

"Where are we going?" Anita laughed as he hurried her into the darkened streetscape once more. The Pope's doors swung closed behind them, and the quiet of the night sighed into her bones.

"Home." He grinned, dropping her hand and offering her his arm.

Such a gallant gesture. "Why, Was, I thought you'd never ask."

A few minutes later, Sam jingled the keys in the lock, and Anita crossed The Pope off her mental 'Moonshine to-do' list.

"Hey, your door is blue," she noted, through barely open eyes.

"Yeah, so?"

"It's my favourite colour."

"Is that why you picked it for the tango spotlight?"

Her body tensed. *The tango.* She could tango all night, with the right partner.

"No." Anita looked around, suddenly feeling very exposed. Following him quickly through the door, she asked, "You sure it's cool if I sleep here tonight?"

"Totally." Pencil and paper were already in his hands. "One of us should make use of the bed and it won't be me. Not while my head's going a thousand miles an hour. I have to fix this now." He waved his handwritten manuscript towards her before pointing to the closed door of a room she hadn't explored this morning. Head already bent towards the page, pencil flying, he called "Good night!" without looking up.

Pride swelled in her chest. *I did that. I'm making a difference.*

Opening the squeaky door, an almighty stench wafted from behind her. Pinching her nose, Anita swung around accusingly. "Goddess almighty, what is *that*?"

"Ah." Sam's cheeks flamed, his eyes comically wide. "Me. Sorry." He raced to prop open the blue entrance door. "I told you lactose intolerance was a real thing. Sorry ... Maybe it's best if you sleep with the door closed?" Another tiny toot squeaked out from his tensed body and his already red face impossibly intensified in hue.

"Farts are always funny," she told him, laughing as his body released another and his face turned the deepest shade of crimson she could imagine.

"I'll leave you to your work," she chuckled into her hand, allowing him privacy to die in his humiliation. Intensely absorbed in his work, Sam mumbled a response. Anita slipped into the bedroom, closing the door gently.

Sam's bedroom was, like the rest of the flat, untidy. Piles of clothes comprised his *floor*drobe. Books, papers and pencils covered the hard surfaces of drawers. His large bed looked unslept in. Its blankets, pulled flat, were at odds with the rest of the generally wrinkled room.

As she moved beside the bed, her foot snagged something. A big, black box peeked out from beneath the dark wooden frame.

Porn, she scoffed. Ignoring the box and flopping onto the bed, she inhaled Sam's scent wafting from the sheets. Soap, and the slightly woody smell of pencil shavings filled her head as she pulled up the covers and sighed into the soft mattress.

Tired as she was, she couldn't sleep. Somehow, the box had dug its sharp edges into her brain, an itch she needed to scratch. Rolling to the side of the bed, she dragged the container into sight. It was one of many tubs beneath his bed, and, from a quick look, she saw they were chock full of chic flicks. *Sleepless in Seattle, A Walk to Remember, Gentleman Prefer Blondes, You've Got Mail, Sixteen Candles, Titanic, How to Lose a Guy in Ten Days, The Princess Bride, Sweet Home Alabama, The Seven Year Itch.* Sam's collection was vast. Impressive. Odd. He clearly cared for his craft.

Classic and contemporary, Sam had stockpiled every title she'd ever seen on daytime television, or wanted to watch, plus a few she had never heard of, as though there was a love-zombie apocalypse about to hit and he'd curated a doomsday stockpile of essentials. Smiling, she slid the box back into place and snuggled into the warm sheets, a mishmash of romantic scenes playing through her head.

Anita awoke in the near dawn to a persistent banging. *What the fuck?* Bleary eyed, she stumbled to the door.

"YES?" she snapped. *Whoever this is had better have a darn good reason to be assaulting my vardo this early.* She'd been having a most pleasant dream about owls and bacon and burgers (oh my). Brushing dark hair from her eyes, she blinked a few times, eyebrows drawn as the mental fog started lifting. *Oh, right. I'm not in the vardo anymore, Toto.*

"Uh, hey, Anita. Good morning." Her hand rested on a cool forearm. *Sam.* Great Gods, he was handsome in the mornings, all scruffy and sleepy in his crinkled t-shirt. His face was better proportioned without the optical magnification of his glasses. His hair kinked up at strange angles, but who was she to comment? Her own hair fluffed out into an afro overnight. *I must look terrible right now.* Patting it down, she exhaled.

"Hey, Was," her voice croaked, the salty taste of dream-bacon still on her lips. "What are you doing here?"

"It's my room," he reminded her, one eyebrow raised high. "May I come in?"

"Are you a vampire?"

"What? No."

"Then why did you *very formally* request entry?"

"I think that lore only applies to the threshold of a house, not one room." He blinked sleepily at her. "And it isn't your place. It's mine. But to answer your question, I asked because it's good manners. It's consent. You know ..." he shrugged, "because chivalry isn't dead and all that shit. And even though you slept in my bed, I'm not expecting to, uh ..." His voice trailed off, the permanent blush he seemed to wear raced down his neck, attempting to hide under his crinkled t-shirt.

"Yes." She leaned in closer, propping herself up against the door frame, transfixed by the redness of his skin and the rapidly bobbing apple in his throat. "Go on, you can say it ..."

"Well, *you know.*" He blushed.

Heavens help me. Her stomach did somersaults, gurgling loudly. "I think I'll put a spell on you," she teased. "Loosen your tongue."

Sam hesitated. "Seriously?"

"Oh yes. All us circus sideshow mystics are very powerful witches, you know. Actually, I can't back that up. But I do subscribe to some Pagan beliefs." She uncrossed her arms and stepped aside, allowing him entry to his own room.

"Really? Like what?"

"Well, if a God exists, there has to be a Goddess too, right? Feminist? Nah, *equality*ist. And it got me thinking, if there's two, maybe there's more out there? Like the ancient Greeks and Romans and Vikings all believed in multiple divine rulers, so I can too."

"Wow, you're really ..." Sam searched for a word.

"Unique? Wonderful? Beautiful? Honest? Charming?"

"You," he sighed. "And *equality*ist is not a word."

"Of course I'm me." She beamed under his scrutiny, ignoring his quip. "Who else would I be? Except for someone heading out for coffee? I noticed yesterday you didn't have any instant. Not that it's real caffeine, anyway. And as part of our deal, you did promise breakfast." *Goddess, I'm rambling again.* How did this man cause her such immediate verbal diarrhoea?

Sam hesitated, his handful of pages fluttering lightly as he lowered his hands, dejected.

"Okay," he agreed. "One coffee. Then, work. But Anita ..."

Her hands were on him again. Why couldn't she control them?

"Yes, Was?"

"Maybe change out of my t-shirt first ... and," he coughed, eyes unable to focus on one spot. The warmth of his blush pressed into the arm beneath her fingertips. "Put some pants on."

Looking down, Anita grinned. She usually slept in her underwear. She must have stripped off last night, while warm and comfortable and safe in Sam's bed. Winking, she said, "You got it, boss."

Dealing with the Devil

SAM

WHEN HAD SHE CHANGED into one of his shirts? That was weird, right? They'd only met last night. Well, two nights ago technically. *Shit, and she's already slept in my bed!* Sam inwardly groaned, hoping he wasn't giving this intriguing little nomad the wrong impression. Impressions of an off-the-page romance or relationship, involving all the stuff he was too embarrassed to write about in his novels. He should find the balls needed to set this straight with Anita, just in case she was getting any strange ideas. *Speaking of strange ideas...* Sam surveyed his room. Anita had cleaned. Tidied. Organised. Alphabetised.

His clothes, usually scattered around the floor, were now folded in neat denim-and-black towers atop the dresser. His books and paperwork had been stacked high in one corner.

Everything had been rearranged. Neatly.

It sounded like a bad joke – or a raunchy fairy tale. *Man gets rip-roaring drunk, meets girl, wakes up next day, she's semi naked and she's cleaned the house ...*

Sam was grateful Anita hadn't emptied his bins. The last time he'd done so, the clinking of empty bottles had warned of the slippery slope he teetered on. He'd called Reece, trying not to be upset by the recent upturn in his drinking, and had been too ashamed to look at himself in a mirror for a few days. When he did accidentally catch his own eye, he saw his father's reflection, and a lead weight dragged through his core.

Now, he seemed similarly unable to comprehend the truth. Sam was desperately trying not to look down at the semi-naked hippy in his room, but there was just so much to look at. She filled his bed and his senses with her goddamn lavender and vanilla sweetness. Once his eyes made it past the bird's nest that was her dark hair, he tried to ignore how Anita's chest filled his shirt like she'd been made to wear it. Her smooth, tanned flesh curved out from beneath the fabric, rolling away from the tiniest peek of blue panties.

Shit. His dick reacted before his brain did. Turning away, he attempted to breathe through a very unprofessional boner, trying not to replay that image. While his pants suddenly felt too tight, his brain kicked in. Something wasn't right.

He spun to face Anita. "What's this?" He dropped his pages onto the bed before gently turning her arm.

"Just bruises. From the circus." She pulled her cardigan on, covering the purple blotches. "Happens all the time. Dangerous job, somersaulting over clowns and animals, swinging high.

Sometimes you fall." She was laughing, shrugging. Sam gulped, standing back to look down her legs.

"Sam." She called his eyes to her own. It only added a few feet of upward gaze, but still. "I'm okay. I promise. My line of work is different to yours, that's all. Your greatest chance of a workplace injury is a paper cut. We defy death every day at the circus, not that I will jinx it." Anita laughed lightly, hands doing some elaborate jinx-defying symbols before wrapping her skirt around her hips in a flourish of fabric. Sam swallowed hard.

"So, breakfast?" She tucked his t-shirt beneath the waistband, running her fingers through her crazed tresses to no avail.

"Just let me check my emails quickly." He diverted his full attention to his laptop, hoping to wipe that thin strip of blue underwear from his mind.

From: Samuelharthrup@hotmail.com
To: Suzannah.editor@flagpolepublishing.com

Subject: Heat in the Kitchen Sequel

Hi Suzannah,
Sorry I haven't responded until now, I have been kidnapped by inspiration. The sequel is progressing. I don't want to jinx it, but I think you will be pleased. Please see the attached photographs of the draft for consideration. I will send through more pages at the end of the week.
Sincerely,
Sam

Friday's Café was open almost as frequently as The Pope. A crowd had already begun to build as the café sprung to life, the scent of freshly ground coffee thick in the air despite the early hour. Friday's held pride of place directly across from Main Street Park. Wedged between a bank and a charity clothing store, it boasted a bright awning and large arched windows that overlooked the leafy green park. Inside, two domed display cases brimmed with multi-tiered cakes, sandwiches, salads, and quiches, clearly homemade with love and skill. Anita smiled widely at the fresh, colourful delicacies, as Sam ordered, then led her to a table by the window. With a contented sigh, she sunk into a soft armchair, ducking her head to examine the books, board games, cards and toys stashed on built-in shelves beneath each window.

"So, this is Friday's! I didn't realise it was a café," Anita said, beaming. "I get to tick another Moonshine site off my list. According to my source, now there's only the lovely architecture of the church to see, and then the quaint town of Moonshine will officially have nothing of interest left to an outsider like me."

Sam tapped his pencil on the table, distractedly.

"Well, except you, of course."

He didn't hear her.

"Hellooo! Earth to dirt perve. You in there, Was? Blink those moist soil eyes of yours once for 'yes' and five times for 'no'."

"Witch." His lips struggled into a smile. "Sorry, I'm tired.

Long night, you know. Productive one, though." He reached into his satchel and retrieved a stack of papers, shoving them under her nose.

"It took you exactly two seconds longer than I expected to talk books," Anita said, squealing in delight as she received his work from the night before. Sam *shush*ed her again, trying to disappear into his seat, his arms crossed.

Beneath the table, Anita's leg brushed Sam's and his shin warmed with the heat seeping through her skirts. She leaned back against the window, relishing the pages with a grin, oblivious to the pleasant tingle that had settled upon his skin.

"Was, this is good. So much better. I won't call it kindling anymore." She sighed dreamily, smiling at the papers in her hands. "Yep, this is a *draft* alright. But ..."

Sam groaned inwardly, preparing his defences for her onslaught. "Here it comes."

Friday Evans, the barista and café's namesake, deposited two Big Buddha Bowl breakfasts before them, quickly followed by pastel-coloured cups brimming with coffee.

"Thank you *so much*." Anita said, looking up at Friday. "You are the reason I'll be tolerable today."

"Barely," Sam grumbled, fork already laden and raised to his mouth.

Friday laughed, his eyes flicking between them. "You two have a good day, now," he said, winking at Sam as he moved to greet more customers.

"You know what sucks? The lack of New Zealanders in romance films. I can't think of one movie hero I can compare Friday to," Anita told Sam, nodding towards the barista. "You should pitch an idea for a Kiwi-based Hollywood-filmed love story, complete with native tattoos and long hair pulled into a high bun, like Friday."

"Do you assign everyone you meet to a romantic film character?" Sam asked.

"Yes. Everyone." She pointed to a woman by the window whose mop of blonde curls was straight out of the 80s. "She's *so* Meg Ryan in *When Harry Met Sally*. Look at that hair! And that man there is one hundred per cent the sexy Prince Henry from *Ever After*. Best Cinderella story ever, by the way."

"So who am I?" She didn't hesitate to consider, and Sam scoffed when she told him. "*The Notebook* guy? Really?"

Anita simply shrugged. "Have you seen it?"

Sam didn't answer; didn't need to. The witch knew his secret, the ones boxed beneath his bed, and she was baiting him. She prattled on, not waiting for his admission or deflection.

"I thought the novel was good. I love Nicholas Sparks, but the film adaptation?" Anita moaned, the sound muffled as she shovelled food into her mouth, eyes sparkling with mischief. Pointing to the food, her eyes rolling back in her head, moaning again. *Talk about* When Harry Met Sally*! The noises the woman makes when eating are damn near indecent!*

The sun streamed in through the window, heating his skin. Shaking his head, he watched her eat and drink, trying to get comfortable in his seat. All the while she chatted about this and that, then, most importantly, she started to read.

With intense anxiety, he watched her. *Does she like it? Is it shit? The good kind, like bat guano or that coffee made from cat-poop? Or the bad kind, like–*

Anita shot him a look, seizing his thoughts. Grinning knowingly over her cup, she sipped her coffee with delight, and occasionally commented on the bitter-sweetness of the chocolate powder atop the foamy milk coffee. Or the delicate flavours of the Buddha Bowl. Or the gorgeous view of the park beyond the window, as if she was looking at the greenery and roses circling the rotunda. Comments about his work? His hand-written pages in her hands? Never. It was killing him.

For what felt like hours Anita ate like a turtle, picking carefully, chewing slowly and making little pleased noises designed to drive him mad. She finally met his gaze over the top edge of the draft.

"Sam –" her eyes sparkled, "– you're inches from my face." He blinked. "*Back off*, or I'll throw these papers into that coffee roaster over there."

"Okay, okay!" Sam put his hands up, a move Friday mistook as a silent call for more caffeine. Sighing, he removed a deck of cards from beneath the window, laying out a game of solitaire with clammy hands.

A few card placements later, Sam broke the silence, nudging Anita's leg under the table. "Well?" His eyes tracked everyone in the room, hoping that his secret wouldn't be spilled here, in Moonshine's favourite coffee house.

"Stop worrying about what other people think," Anita said, nudging him back with her knee. "Except me. Care about my professional opinion. That is your mission, should you choose to accept it."

"How are you so well versed in pop culture?" Sam wondered, in response to the *Mission: Impossible* tag line. "You grew up in a circus commune, right?"

"Family," she corrected, patting his cheek. "My circus *family*. They really are mine. The circus is, at least. My last name is Fortuna, after all. Did you know that? I'm not sure if you knew that. Plus, caravan parks have free Wi-Fi – did you know that Wi-Fi is an Australian invention? – and usually there's access to a TV, so that's why I'm well versed in pop culture." Her words tumbled into her nearly empty coffee cup, and she raised her hand to order another from the attentive Friday. The barista nodded in acknowledgement, while her mouth ran away with her again. "I love movies," she continued. "Not just romance, but, yeah, okay, *especially* love stories. They always end well. I love a good Happily Ever After. I think that's why I loved *Heat*, and why I'm into reading your story."

Hope and ... pride? ... flared in Sam's chest.

"Here you go." Friday delivered two fresh cups of dark coffee, nodding at Sam. His top knot didn't even wiggle.

Anita sighed. "I wish my hair would stay that still in a bun," she said to the barista. "Mine has a mind of its own." Her small hands waved vaguely in the vicinity of her curls, truly wild things.

"Practice makes perfect." Friday smiled politely before shooting Sam an amused look. "Getting a word in edge-ways, Sam?"

"No. She talks enough for a whole school of kids."

Mouth full of coffee, Anita crinkled her nose at him.

"He's got a nice tattoo, too," Anita commented as Friday ducked into a cake display, one arm holding the glass door open.

"Honestly," he sighed, "do you ever shut up?" She ignored

him.

"Tribal. I think it's just the one, as intricate as it is. Not a collage, like Billy's. It seems to start on his forearm, but I wonder how far it goes ..." Her head tilted sideways as she followed the pattern from his forearm to under his shirt, where it disappeared.

"Anita Fortuna! You have the hide to call *me* a perve," Sam said, shaking his head in mock disgust as he took a long swig from his cup.

"Goddess, protect me from all the hot guys in this town," prayed Anita to whichever of her deities was listening. "Send me a chastity belt." She grinned wickedly, sending a pang through Sam's gut. "Or a fat box of condoms."

A tightness gripped Sam's chest. Any man in Moonshine would be lucky to have this ball of talkative energy in their lives, or in their bed. He was just grateful she was helping him polish his work, contributing to the success of his next novel.

"Friday might be older than me, but he is very attractive. Older! That's it!" He saw the idea form in her brain like lightning hitting sand, forming a solid, crystal-clear epiphany. "Sam, can I borrow your phone?"

He looked skeptically at her, handing it over. "You don't have your own? I hope you're not searching for sexy tattoos and tarnishing my stellar internet search history ..." Lies. All lies. His body might be virus-free from lack of activity, but his phone? That was a different matter.

Anita didn't respond, tapping away at the touchscreen. Sam tried to peer at her internet search. "Is this about the tattoos?"

"Why, Was, you got any?" Her eyes flicked up from the

screen, a grin teasing her lips.

"Wouldn't you like to know?" He tried to appear smug but was pretty sure it came off as a strange grimace. "What about you?"

"Wouldn't *you* like to know?" She mimicked, wiggling her eyebrows until he blushed, looking away. She rose from her seat and stepped outside to make a call. When she returned, she slipped the phone straight into his pants pocket. Sam jumped as it slid onto his thigh. Anita, seemingly oblivious to the fact that she'd literally stepped away from the conversation for five minutes, picked up where they'd left off.

"Anyway, as I was saying, your mission will be a series of assignments. You like to write. You're a word nerd. So, we'll do this like school."

"That is wildly inaccurate, stereotypical and –"

She leaned forward, grabbing his chin between her fingers and squishing his lips into two puffy flaps. "No interruptions. Listen." She released his jaw. "From what I've read –" her eyes flicked over him, head to toe, "– and observed, you need a total of three things to significantly improve your manuscript."

"Oh yeah, and what are these three things?" Sam tapped his pencil loudly on the table. The incessant, repetitive, stress-induced tapping started to turn heads. Friday was too polite to comment, but his head kept popping around the huge, square coffee machine to blink pointedly at Sam, who took no notice.

Anita took the pencil from his hand, writing notes on the back of a paper menu. "One. Sensory descriptions – the touch. Two. Raw emotions – the feel. And three, at least one good

..." she paused, "hot ..." she breathed heavily, gripping the table edges, "*sensual* goddamn sex scene!"

Sam's cheeks flamed and he was torn between mortification and being slightly turned on by her words.

It was like Meg Ryan in *When Harry Met Sally*. Everyone wanted what she was having, and it felt a little ... *weird* ... to hear her wanting it. "The fade to black is so unsatisfying. Your readers want–"

"Keep your voice down!" he interrupted, nudging her leg under the table.

"Naw," Anita cooed, assuming the air of a condescending mother to her poor child. "I'll admit, there are now *four* things. You'll have to get over your prudishness, too. Get comfortable with all the words for the," she winked, "*hard stuff.*"

Desperately hoping he wouldn't regret this deal he'd made with this she-devil, Sam buried his head in his hands.

"Do you trust me?" she asked.

"No. I trust expired yoghurt more than you." He sighed. "But ... Short term pain–"

"For long term gain," she finished. "This is your new approach to both writing and lactose. Now, come on. We've got homework to do, mister romance writer."

"First, sleep?" he asked hopefully.

"First, more coffee." She pushed his cup towards him, signalling Friday once more. "Then, a short drive."

The Knight's Court

ANITA

A<small>NITA REMAINED TIGHT LIPPED</small> about the assignment, using Sam's GPS to navigate them through the town while he drove.

"You know, I re-read the 'About the Author' section in *Heat in the Kitchen* last night," she said, watching him shift gears. Sam had barely spoken once in the car, going into hyper-focus like a teenager learning how to drive – vigilant, and exerting way too much mental energy concentrating on the road. He grunted in response.

"It's all SO obvious now!" Anita cried. "Turn left here." Sam clicked on the indicator early enough for cars three streets over to know they were turning. "Your bio had no picture – first clue to a hidden identity. The second," she quoted the book, "*Sammie is a debut author, enjoys long walks on the beach and massive breed dogs. When Sammie isn't reading, the Moonshine-born writer enjoys watching MasterChef and getting creative in the kitchen*."

"You memorised it? Is it okay? Do I need to re-write it?" Sam bit his lip, pinching the bridge of his nose.

"No, Was. That wasn't my point. Jeeze, you're wound tighter than a necktie in church." She sympathised with his discomfort, the belt buckle digging into her already bruised thigh. One of the horses had knocked her into a bucket last week, and the bruise was only starting to turn purple. "The point is this – zero pronouns. Very clever. But not clever enough. Plus, from what I saw at your apartment, you're a total bachelor. Not even a dog in sight. And urgh, seriously, long walks on the beach? It's cliché and the beach is nowhere near here." Anita felt her nose scrunch as she looked out the window. The entire town of Moonshine was a half hour's leisurely (very leisurely) drive from one side to the other, with nothing for a further hour in any direction beyond that. The circus' drive here had been long and boring, filled with kangaroos bounding through grassy farmland, random stony homesteads among the gumtrees, and road kill. The nearest beach was almost two hours away and over a mountain range, so Sam's GPS had informed her.

"Turn right here," she instructed.

"How can you *not* have a phone?" Sam asked suddenly.

She cackled. "Us witches just hop on our broomsticks and fly off into the night to speak to each other among the stars." Sam's eyes remained fixed on the road, but he did crack a small smile. "Or we use smoke signals from our cauldrons. Turn left here."

Sam indicated, waiting for every other vehicle in the universe to roll past before creeping his old Holden through the intersection.

"This road goes to Saint Jude's, the retirement home." He laughed suddenly, the sound reverberating around the car and straight into her chest cavity. "Why are we here?" His eyes darted sideways, his body suddenly tense and on edge.

"You'll see." Anita unclipped her belt, sliding from the car in a whirl of skirts. Sam followed a few paces behind, hands shoved deep in his pockets. Fidgeting and unfocused, he was clearly, deeply uncomfortable. *Buckle up, buttercup,* she mentally urged, leading the way into the facility.

"Fortuna, Anita," she told the nurse at reception, trying to ignore Sam's chest in her back. It was as though he were trying to shrink his six-foot-plus height behind her five-foot-nothing self. "We're expected."

"Sign the guest register," the portly nurse ordered. Sam shot a small, worried smile at Anita, reading over her shoulder as she scrawled their names in small, loopy handwriting.

"Fortuna," he said. "That can't be your real last name." An old man in an open dressing gown and incontinence pants strolled past, nodding to them.

"You know that scene in *Robin Hood: Men in Tights,* where Latrine tells Rottingham she'd changed her name from Shithouse?"

Sam laughed, nodding. "Of course. *Classic.*"

"Well, it's a bit like that." She grinned.

"Anita Shithouse, I never would've guessed," said Sam, smothering his laugh respectfully as a nurse wheeled an elderly lady in bright pink lipstick past the reception desk.

"What's in a name? A rose by any other name would smell as sweet."

"Urgh, *Romeo and Juliet*. Such a tragedy."

"Not that you can comment, Sammie Har – Oh! Hello!"

A nurse with fairy-floss pink hair and semi-circle spectacles waved them through the door. "Welcome to Saint Jude's. You must be Anita and …" She checked her clipboard. "Was?"

Sam scoffed.

"We sure are," Anita said, chuckling, "and we're ready to meet our Knights."

Sam's brow furrowed. "Knights?"

"You know, Arthur's round table?" *His sleepy confusion is so darn cute.* "Just trust me," Anita whispered, linking her arm through his with a ripple of excitement.

"Shoes off," the nurse ordered, pointing to a neat line of slippers by the door.

"What?" Sam spluttered as Anita slipped her flats into the formation. "Isn't that against workplace health regulations or something?"

Anita grinned at the nurse, whose cool eyes appraised the tall young man like a bug who needed squashing.

"He's just joking. He loves feet. Tell her how much you love feet, Was." He shot Anita a look, and she buried her face in her hair. Mumbling incoherently, Sam brought his knee into the air, wiggling on one foot as he untied the white laces of his sneaker.

"Happiness is a key ingredient to health, especially in the older population," the nurse said sagely, nodding as Sam's bare feet hit the ground and he dropped his mismatched socks onto his shoes. "Plus, in the courtyard, the grass is lovely and soft. Trust me, grounding is good for your soul."

The courtyard where the Knights of St Jude's held 'court'

was an enclosed, highly manicured garden at the centre of the complex. It reminded Anita of a mystical fairy hollow. The tall walls cut off the cooler spring air, locking in the warmth and sweet scent of the season. Two solid, abundantly flowering trees branched overhead, throwing chunky, playful shadows around the seats and picnic table in the centre of the small garden. A number of elderly Moonshine residents had assembled, laughing easily, leaning heavily, and all topped with snowy white crowns.

Anita didn't try to name the senior citizens after happily-ever-after heroes and heroines, sticking with their real names so as not to confuse the poor dears, who probably already struggled with dementia. Cecilia, Shirley, Mary and Ethel all came to greet them, then John, Harry, Lucius and Benjamin ('not Ben', as he'd told them already, numerous times. 'Ben is for young whippersnappers. I'm old. I'm Benjamin. Got it?' Benjamin was a bit of a grump, but nothing Anita couldn't handle).

A couple, who remained seated a few hobbling steps away, waited until last to be introduced. She pointed them out to Sam, encouraging him to approach, watching in amusement as his face turned beet red. The couple dropped hands immediately, like teenagers caught making out in the backseat of their parents' car. Sam approached the pair stiffly. Anita watched the snowy-haired woman speak to the writer, her face the same cherry colour as Sam's. *There really is no age limit on love.*

Anita's first love had been the unnamed Prince from *Beauty and the Beast*. Somewhere, she'd heard him called 'Adam', but it was universally acknowledged that The Beast was better than

The Man. She'd always had a thing for tall, hairy grumps, and living in an enchanted castle with *that* many books wouldn't have been a problem, either.

Her second love had been Pete, a menagerie man five years her elder. He had been wonderful with the animals (and with her, too). He'd smelled of aftershave and hay, and sometimes manure, but she hadn't minded so much. Pete had kissed Anita exactly three times – the same number of months he'd spent with Cirque de Fortuna.

Then there had been Thomas, a sweet boy and mechanic for the carnival rides. His hand had snuck down to her skirts quicker than an oil leak from an old motor. He'd lasted six weeks with the circus.

They never lasted long. She sighed, rubbing a hand over a bruise on her arm. *It's not an easy life.* People romanticised it, alright, a life on the road. New places and faces, glittery costumes and endless popcorn and fairy floss. But underneath all that, the life was tough.

The swarm of encroaching seniors snatched her from the memory. The couple Sam had been speaking to had departed and the nurse called them over, introducing them to the remaining gathering.

"Everyone, this is Anita and Was. They're going to join you today and they're doing some interesting research for a book that I think you'll all enjoy." The nurse winked, a grin transforming her face. The crowd descended in a cloud of talc.

"Anita!" Multiple pairs of warm, soft arms threaded around her and she melted into their squishy, frail bodies. Never having had grandparents of her own, she often relished the easy company and many stories of the elderly community. No matter where Cirque de Fortuna visited, the local wizened-ones always guaranteed her some great local stories.

"What kind of a name is Was?" Benjamin asked, scratching his wizard-like beard.

"It's Sam," he offered, shaking hands. "Uh, Samuel."

"Sam," Benjamin sniffed. "A whippersnapper's name. Samuel is much better."

The women shoved Benjamin (a little too viciously) aside, Sam collecting awkward, stiff hugs from them.

He's not a hugger. Anita smiled at the realisation, watching with fascination as he was pulled into the crushing embrace of the ample-chested, voluptuous Cecelia.

"This," she told him as Sam extricated himself from her bosom, "is going to be fun."

"Come, Knights!" a voice proclaimed. "Assemble. Let's get this show on the road!"

The Knights of Saint Jude's were a lively bunch of geriatrics. Five men and five women, between eighty and a hundred and one years of age. Adorned in their Sunday best, they felt like old friends, if not long-lost relatives. Anita battled the tears in her eyes, sniffling back the simple warm, familial sensation. *I love old people,* she thought as she was released from yet another squishy, maternal cuddle.

Family, to Anita, had always been a motley crew of crazies, creatives and caravans. It had been that way since her grandparents started Cirque de Fortuna. After an illustrious career in one of the world's premier circus troupes, they had decided to avoid the big cities and outrageously expensive shows. Their hearts had always beaten for the country, for small towns such as Moonshine, so they devised a way to connect with the smaller communities and less-fortunate citizens who couldn't afford hundred-dollar tickets. That generous heart had been the backbone of their business. They had lived long enough to ensure an illustrious engagement for their daughter to the wealthy strongman they'd adopted after an Olympic event, but not long enough to meet their grandchildren. As Anita received yet another squishy, talc-scented hug, she grinned at her new, short-term grandparents, seated in a circle around the picnic bench, some in wheelchairs.

"This book you are writing, my dears. What is it about?" the refined Mary asked.

"Sex," Anita proclaimed, at the same time as Sam said "Love". They looked at each other. Sam's blush turned his face into a small sun. She could feel the heat radiating from him. Their elderly companions giggled.

"Well, which is it?" Ethel's eyes shrunk into her round little face.

"They're the same!" Benjamin argued, huffing into his beard.

"They are not," Ethel argued. "Sex and love can be completely different! Why, my poor Arthur and I–"

"Now, Ethel, Ben," Cecelia cautioned, interrupting what could have been a long-winded story. "Let the youngsters speak."

Sam's words seemed awash in his blush, so Anita took the lead. "We're here to talk dirty," she told the geriatrics, who twittered excitedly. "We're working on a romance book, but the words are–"

"Confronting?" Harry suggested.

"Embarrassing?" John offered, chuckling.

"Naughty!" Mary added, her posh exterior slipping into a cheeky grin.

"Icky," Sam finished. All eyes swung to him.

"What kind of grown man says *icky*?" Benjamin huffed into his beard.

The kind of man who isn't affected by toxic masculinity and wants to write a swoon-worthy romance to set women's underwear on fire. Anita was about to speak when Ursula interrupted. "It *can* be a bit icky, but it's perfectly natural, dear."

Cecelia's large bust swung to face Sam, her hand patting his leg familiarly. "I know! Let's start by making some lists. Synonyms for penis and vagina." The congregation nodded while Sam melted into his chair.

"And euphemisms for sexual intercourse," added Lucius helpfully, his shaking hand pointing to Anita and Sam. "That'll help them."

Anita watched the Knights' aged hands flapping around, pointing this way and that. *I'd love to read these people. Know their palms, their stories. It would be so interesting! I could spend days here.*

"Oh my God." Sam slunk further towards the grass, pinching the bridge of his nose beneath foggy glasses.

"Oh, deary." Shirley grinned wickedly. "I think you need a drink, young man." She giggled, slipping him the flask that had already been passed around the group beneath the table. "That'll loosen your tongue." She winked, lifting an eyebrow. Sam downed the remaining booze.

A white-clad nurse slid in on a breeze, adding a record to the vinyl player propped in one corner. Soft, fuzzy jazz settled the oldies into a calmer tone. Anita watched Sam look longingly after the nurse as she slipped from the courtyard. A half hour later, the nurse returned with a huge smile for Sam, delivering a huge tray of cheese sandwiches, and thick, creamy milkshakes. Anita dived in, watching Sam squirm.

Holy Hera, this is going to be an awesome day!

S.O.S.

SAM

THE BATHROOM, A SOLITARY heaven on earth, provided an almost perfect reprieve.

Sam: `SOS! Witch. St Judes. Lactose. Trap. OMG WTF am I doing?`

A heartbeat later, his friend responded: `Are you drunk?`

Sam: `What? No!`

Reece: `High?`

Sam: `Hell no. This would probably be funny if I was. I've been poisoned.`

The sharp pain in his stomach threatened a well-known tale of repercussions. *Damn lactose. Damn cheese sandwiches! How can you say no to grannies?* It had been the best way to avoid this embarrassing situation, to stuff his face, consequences be damned. Avoiding conversation had seemed a solid plan. Now, he was *very* damned and very much feeling the sharp gurgling of those consequences.

Three dots emerged on the screen, indicating Reece was typing. `Lactose isn't poison.` Another popped onto the screen seconds later. `Actually for YOU it totally is. Just eat right man, seriously.`

His doctorly lecture done, Reece sent another text. Must have been a slow day in the medical world.

Reece: `So, St Judes? Seeing Gran? Say hi for me. Tell her thanks for the strawberry jam.`

Sam: `Not Gran. Did see her but she bolted with Eddie. Now we're talking sex. Send help.`

Reece: `What? You're talking about sex? With who? You barely talk sex with your BFF.`

Reece: `You sure you're not intoxicated?`

Sam's thumb hovered above the phone's keypad. As he considered his reply, a knock sounded on the door.

"Sam, you okay?" Anita's voice was laced with worry.

"No," Sam answered honestly, glad he had legitimate reason to hide in the bathroom, away from grannies saying 'vulva' and grandpas arguing 'penile length' versus 'girth'.

She giggled, as she'd been doing all morning, the buoyant bubbles of her mirth filling his chest. *Bloody witch.* Anita had made this day even more extremely uncomfortable for Sam, joining in with the discussions while he sat on his hands. As his cheeks burnt like lava, she added filthy words to the long list being created by the Knights. Milking a cat would have been easier than listening to the Knights hold court for their special-interest project.

Sam had spent the last hour or so willing his ears to seal up forever. It had been mortifying. At some point in his intense perma-blush, he'd wondered if someone had written a dictionary of smut, considering the commercial prospects of that product. Not that he could ever create that book. He'd have to lock himself in the flat and sit in an icy bath while writing. He was pretty sure lunar astronauts would be able to feel the heat in his rushing blood. Just listening to this 'court session' was as open as he'd ever been about ... *IT*.

If there had been a laughter track playing in the background, he could have considered today a sitcom. At least Gran had left, after Sam promised to return the next evening for dinner, *thank God,* but the sexual deviants she'd left behind were making life a living hell.

Who knew the elderly were so open about sex? It was mortifying. Truly, deeply mortifying. It felt dirty. Wrong. *I need a shower.* He yawned widely. *And a deep sleep. Man, it's been one heck of a strange day.*

"Was?"

"Coming." He quickly texted Reece: Love you, loser. Say something nice in my eulogy.

He couldn't hide in the bathroom all afternoon, even if the sharp stabbing pains in his bowel threatened otherwise. Sam flushed the toilet, despite not having used it, then ran the water and wet his flushed face.

Shape up, Harthrup. This is research. This is good. It'll help you get your groove back. Short-term pain for long-term gain. A catalogue of clichés formed in his mind. Cheese the day, Mister *MasterChef*. You need this.

Emerging from the bathroom, a long list of dirty words, in spidery handwriting, was shoved into his hands.

"This will help," one lady said, winking. "Now, onto more interactive adventures." *Oh, shit ...*

One of the elderly men clapped loudly for attention before suggesting they play spin the bottle. Apparently, the flask was empty. It was play time.

"Oh, I think we should get going," Sam said, looking at his watch. "Gotta get this w–" he was going to say 'witch', but considering how the oldies adored his circus-dwelling critique partner, he changed the word mid-phonic, "–ONE here to work." He placed his hands on Anita's shoulders, using her as a human shield.

"Tomorrow then, Was," an elderly lady promised, winking.

"Tomorrow?"

"Oh, yes." The portly nurse had returned with a tray of neatly labelled medicine cups. "Miss Anita booked you in for a three-day crash course with the Knights."

Three Days? "How–"

Anita shrugged. "Every town has a special club for the elderly, who are often the most loose-lipped about the type of stuff *you* need to get comfortable with, Sam." She shrugged again, content with the whole arrangement. "They're always great company and we're lucky that Moonshine's nursing home is very welcoming and accepting of random requests."

Shit!

"Great," Sam managed, weakly, hope fading faster than the collagen in their wrinkled skin.

As soon as the afternoon air hit his lungs, Sam inhaled deeply, the fresh tang of freedom washing over him. Adjusting his glasses, he blinked in the light, exhaling slowly.

"It wasn't that bad, was it?" Anita nudged his arm lightly. "Look at this long list of ideas for your intimate scenes! They were so helpful! And it'll keep your internet browser clean, no nasty viruses for your poor PC."

If only you knew ...

"I don't think I could do that again," he moaned. "*Twice.*" Anita laughed, her skirt swishing merrily as her wide hips swayed towards the car.

"You can and you will, or my name isn't Anita Fortuna."

"Your name *isn't* Anita Fortuna." He raised a brow. "It's Witchy-poo Shithouse."

Anita exploded into laughter. "See, you *can* keep up. Put that energy into fixing your manuscript. Now, my good man, to the Circus!"

As his car pulled onto the oval, Anita became increasingly quiet, her snorts and giggles fading. He glanced at her occasionally, wondering if he should say something. The woman was a talkative bowl of pure energy, and to suddenly lose her excited chatter was like watching your favourite meal rapidly burning on the stove.

Maybe she's just as tired as I am? "Big night tonight?" he said, to break the silence.

"Hopefully." She shot him a small smile.

"I think you left all your energy at the nursing home."

"Possibly. Eight sexy seniors will steal your buzz."

"So ... that wasn't embarrassing for you? Like, at all?"

"No. Why would it be? It's kind of inspiring to see people being so open and honest."

"Brutal honesty is *your* thing," he mumbled, negotiating the roundabout carefully.

"It is my thing." She nodded, looking out the window as the circus came into sight, the festoon lights flickering on. The Ferris wheel started its slow rotation behind a row of well-stocked stalls. She sighed, and he saw her putting on a brave face. His hand reached out for hers. Her warmth curled into his palm, sending jolting tingles up into his wrist. He stared at their hands, so different, but fitting so perfectly together. *This is fine,* he told himself. *This is still within a professional boundary. This is a welfare check. That's all.*

"Anita?" Her hand squeezed his. The tingles leapt into his chest. "Are you sure you're okay?"

"I'm ..." Her ocean-blue eyes rose to his, a heavy tension filling the air. Her gaze flicked beyond him, out the window, and she froze. "I'm fine. I have to go. See you later, okay?" Her small fingers retreated quickly as she exited the car. He watched her walk round the bonnet and towards the ticket booth, where a stern-faced Ringmaster stood, arms crossed. His head jerked inside, and Sam saw her shrink behind the wall of wavy hair.

Anita Fortuna had stamped herself upon his flat. It hadn't smelled this clean, this delicious even, since ... well, before he moved in at least. Her scent clung to the lounge, encasing him as he sat, pondering, tapping his pencil against the notepad.

Opening his laptop, he tried to shake Anita from his head, eyes snagging on the five double-sided pages resting on the table beside him. The Knights had really gone to town in their efforts to help him create that word bank. As mortifying as the day had been, his creative brain had fired up in the most delicious of ways.

Sam scratched at the two-day stubble itching his chin, hoping his fingernails would rip the tiny prickles from his face. Little suckers were stuck in there good. He considered the need to shave and shower, his brain circling back to the list.

A day with geriatrics should *not* be arousing. He wouldn't let it be. *It was wrong. So wrong.* Sam needed to sort out the strange tug-of-war between his brain and his boxers. This 'homework' with Anita wasn't meant to heat him up personally, just professionally. Whipping out his phone, he opened the chat labelled BFF. *I need a distraction, stat.*

Sam: `Beers tonight?`

The response was almost instantaneous.

Reece: `You're on, brother.`

The benefit of Reece co-owning his medical practice was that his work was usually restricted to business hours ... unless there was an emergency, like a tractor accident at a farm, or an intense IBS attack on his best friend. Reece set his own schedule, so they could hang out every other day.

Most Friday evenings the PlayStation ran hot; they watched

films, shot hoops, or stood around a barbeque skolling home brew. For Sam, it was the perfect balance of 'alone time' versus 'peopling'. Being social had never been a Sam Harthrup skill. If it had been, he might have admitted his feelings to Breanna Henderson, spewing feelings instead of ... actual spew. And Sandra would have broken him much sooner. But then, *Heat in the Kitchen* might never have happened.

Absently, Sam opened his laptop, scanning emails. Sighing, he clicked on the little red flag that sorted his editor's correspondence from the Bitcoin, offers of Russian brides, Casino Free Spins and penis enlargement technologies that somehow escaped being filtered as 'spam'.

One day, I'll sort out folders, Sam promised himself for the umpteenth time, opening the new email.

From: Suzannah.editor@flagpolepublishing.com
To: Samuelharthrup@hotmail.com;
Sammiehartromance@flagpolewriters.net
CC: editor.in.chief@flagpolepublishing.com

Subject: Heat in the Kitchen Sequel

Hello Sam,
Thank you for your update. An outline by the end of the week is acceptable, however we would love to see a work sample? ...

He scoffed. That little question mark was fooling nobody. They wanted pages, and they wanted them now.

... **Please update soon with the 'meet cute' at least. We remind you that the manuscript, in its entirety, is due by the end of November. We look forward to reading your opening scenes.**
Sincerely,
Suzannah Browne
Editorial Director, *Flagpole Publishing*

His eyes flicked to the stack of filthy terms from St Jude's Retirement Home; he resisted the urge to scan each page in and send them off with the email. With spite in his mind, and a literal pile of synonyms for private parts before him, Sam picked up his pencil, pushed the lead onto the paper of a familiar notebook, and started writing.

Dear Diary,

Today I discussed (in extremely graphic and surprisingly imaginative vocabulary) the art of lovemaking, with people who have had as many sexual encounters as they have wrinkles ...

As usual, the diary writing led into manuscript work. Fact into fiction. His hand cramped from the pencil, the sign of true productivity. Time flew. A few thousand words later, Sam sat back, head bobbing side to side as he stretched his neck, then rubbed his stinging eyes. *Not bad. Not bad at all!* He wouldn't admit it to Anita, but the Knights had helped. Not with the meet cute, of course. That kind of language didn't belong in the first meeting of the lovers. But the outline he'd promised (and not yet actually completed) had been fleshed out to a healthy length.

Smiling in happy disbelief, Sam glanced at his watch, noting the blurred numbers and hands. A wave of fatigue hit like a sugar crash.

"A quick nap," he told Mjolnir. "Just a little snooze to recharge the batteries."

There was one problem with that plan, though – Anita. The sweet smell of her clung to his sheets, making sleep difficult. As he curled onto the mattress, she seemed to waft up and around him, cocooning him in lavender and vanilla, like she was finding a way to contact him, touching him, even now. The scent pulled Sam down into warmth and comfort, where eventually he lost himself to exhaustion.

A huge, dark hulk moved through the shadows. With the same dreaded skin-crawl of realisation that dinner is burning, Sam felt someone standing over his bed.

"SHIT!"

"Rise and shine, dweeb." Reece threw a hot pizza box onto Sam's stomach. "It's home brew time."

Five minutes and one lacklustre, cheese-free pizza later, Reece was kicking Sam's arse at Donkey Kong.

"So, you're telling me," Reece said, stealing Sam's floating banana stream, "that you spent most of your afternoon at St Jude's talking sexy with the geriatrics?"

"Not exactly ..." Sam rolled, smashing barrels. "But sorta, I guess. Anita says it's research, but it all went pear shaped."

"Anita?" Reece jumped into a tree. "You mean the circus lady you literally fell for? You drunken arse." Without taking his eyes off the screen, he kicked Sam's leg. "Nice."

"It's not like that." Sam rolled across a rickety, vine-covered bridge, missing the jump for bonus bananas. "She's a reader. A sharp critique partner. She read my draft and ..."

The words 'Game Over' danced on the screen. Sam threw his controller to the floor, pinching the bridge of his nose. Reece danced atop the lounge cushions, gyrating and singing "boo yeah!" His classic happy dance. Next, he would do the sprinkler and his latest favourite move, The Floss. Sam both admired and cringed at Reece's Dorky-Dad dancing.

"She's hot, you know," Reece commented, jumping to the floor.

"Dixie Kong?"

"An-i-ta." He separated each syllable. "Did you even notice, egg head?"

Sam stared at his empty beer bottle. He had noticed. Been trying *not* to notice. Actively ignoring the curve of her hips, or the smaller but just as luscious arc of her breasts. Or feel the ripples her touch sent through his body. How her fingers were magnetised, reaching for him. Hell, he hadn't even been able to make eye contact with her while the St Jude's Knights had thrown around words like 'erection' and 'sheathing', 'slick slide' and 'hot ecstasy'. Just the thought of their crinkled lips curving into wicked denture-filled grins, their vivid descriptions and the innuendo-filled language had set Sam's cheeks on fire, sending shivers down his spine.

Helpful? Yes.

Decent? Shit no.

If he didn't have strange, and potentially confusing sexual

nightmares tonight, then Sam was more minced meat than man. And, he supposed, it would be preferable for Anita to star in those dreams, rather than any member of the Knights they'd held 'court' with today.

"Earth to Sam!" Reece knocked on his skull. "The fortune teller?"

Sam shook his head, clearing cobwebs, cheese sandwiches, 'cock' from crinkled lips, and crinkles in general from his mind.

"We only just met," Sam said defensively, trying to control the new wave of rampant, inappropriate ideas racing through his brain. *Her hair. Her filthy, critical mouth. The way her lips formed the word 'moist'*... Sam shook his head again. Violently.

"We have a deal. It's nothing more than professional. I can't afford for it to get personal again. I can't deal with a Sandra 2.0 situation." *Besides, even if I did choose her, nobody chooses me.*

Sam wasn't desired. Not 'quality boyfriend material' Sandra had said. 'Unlovable'. Overlooked and discarded. First by his family, then by Sandra. Now, the literary world was about to drop-kick him out of his kitchen and over the fence, unless he delivered a sexy, food-inspired manuscript.

"God, your head is so far up your own arse sometimes." Reece shoved a fresh beer into his hands and Sam outlined the terms of the arrangement. His friend listened, shaking his head. "So you have a hot chick, who's only in town for two weeks, sneaking into your house each night, spending the night, and you're cooking for her, going on day dates and *not* getting laid? Dude." Reece exhaled slowly. "Raw deal. It's honestly amazing how quickly you've been totally Friend Zoned."

"*Egg*cellent deal," Sam corrected, adjusting his glasses and grinning at Reece. "The Friend Zone is *exactly* what I need to get this sequel off the ground. Departing from being barely friends and short-term colleagues is highly unlikely. She's barely *pudding* up with me," he grinned, ducking an attacking, flying Mjolnir.

"No more food puns." Reece pointed a finger in warning. "Sex, on the other hand ... I could stand to hear about that." He waggled his eyebrows hopefully.

"Too bad it's not happening. *I'm serious!*" Sam said in response to the doctor's rebuking glance. "That would just complicate things." Sam threw Thor's hammer back, the plush toy hitting his mate on the nose. "And I haven't cooked for her. I should, though. She eats trash. Junk food mostly, from the circus. It's *muffin* compared to my food."

"Man, if you cook for her, she'll fall head over heels for your skinny arse."

Mjolnir tore through the air, knocking Sam's glasses to the floor.

"I remember when you cooked for *me*." Reece batted his eyelashes, his hands clasped before his chest, bottom lip protruding comically.

The full force of Thor's mighty hammer struck Reece's face three times as Sam attacked. Unaffected by the plush toy, except for one wayward sweep of spiked hair, the almost statuesque lump of doctor sighed, frozen in position.

"You sure you wanna start, Samuel James Harthrup?" Reece blinked slowly. "Are you *sure* you wanna go there?"

Sam got halfway through his one syllable response before they tumbled off the sofa. A tangle of legs and arms, they grappled for control of Mjolnir, to prove once and for all (for the millionth time) who was the more worthy man.

It was midnight when Sam woke to Reece's snoring and farting shaking the walls. Despite it all, he loved having a brother. Being the only child of disconnected parents had been too isolating. After the embarrassing poetry recital incident with his sister, Reece had taken a liking to Sam. Over the years, they had become closer than bread and butter. Finding Reece had been like Aladdin discovering the cave of wonders.

Shit, did I just reference Disney? Anita's obsession with movie-style Happily Ever Afters must be rubbing off on him.

You need a good rubbing off, a totally more southern brain encouraged, whilst the other, skull-encased kind screamed. *Don't! No innuendo!*

In your end-o.

Stop it!

While Sam's two brains waged war, he had dreamed of peaches. Peaches and vanilla ice-cream, with a hint of lavender. The scents lingered in Sam's mouth, as though the dream itself had been breathed into his lungs.

Gone were his musings on the brotherly bonds of male friendship. If he had to throw Reece through the thin veils of the universe to reach Valhalla, he would. In a totally platonic way, of course.

He dodged the tangle of Reece's legs, splayed across the other sofa. He loved boys nights with his pseudo-bro. Nights where they ate and talked shit and practically fell asleep where they stood, exhausted from each other's ribbing and antics.

His temples pounded as he stumbled towards the sink,

half hung-over, half horny, and a *lot* conflicted about being hung-over and horny. A thin thread of light gleamed from under his bedroom door, snagging his attention. Sighing, he wondered if Anita had snuck in. When? How? He'd half expected it, but the revelation of the light jolted him awake. *I really have to start locking my door.*

Carefully, he tiptoed into the room. A curvy lump of sheets greeted him. Dark hair sprawled across his pillow. Paperwork was strewn across the covers; Anita had fallen asleep reading his manuscript. A smile played across her lips and he wondered what she was dreaming about. He hoped that, maybe, his words were conjuring some kind of literary love spell for the witch.

Shit, he wanted to touch her. To brush her hair back and just watch her smile in her sleep. *No, that was creepy and not what a totally platonic co-worker should do.* It wasn't professional. Then again, how would she ever know? The lavender and vanilla smells swirled around him, the floral delicacy drawing him closer.

Sam bent gently, sweeping a stray curl behind her ear. Anita's face changed and her body stilled. He froze, heart pounding. *Shit*. He shouldn't be here. Shouldn't be standing over her, watching her sleep, like some creep in a horror movie. He waited until her tense body softened back into his sheets before moving to the lamp. Sam cast a final glance at Anita. Her cardigan had slipped. From this angle, he could see a trail of discolorations rolling around her shoulder. Moving closer, he inspected the marks. Four, no, *five* perfect circles. His hand curled, the circular indents disappearing beneath his fingertips. She flinched, the tiny hairs on the back of her neck prickling. A whimper escaped her lips, and not the sexy dream kind he might have enjoyed hearing. Sam whipped his hand back and flicked the lamp off, resolving to ask her about it in the morning. She was honest, brutally so. She would explain. The white pages of his manuscript draft glowed out from the darkness. He could see notes scrawled into the margins. Wanted desperately to read them, but he remained rooted in the open doorway, watching her.

Go back to the lounge, his brain demanded. A snore echoed from Reece. The old brown sofa wasn't an attractive sleeping place. Not nearly as tempting as his bed. But like spaghetti, he just had to suck it up.

The salty tang of bacon filled the air, but it was Anita's laughter that sent a pang of hunger through him. *When did I last laugh like that? So happy and free?* Even Sandra couldn't coax such unbridled happiness from him on their best days. *Wait, who is making her giggle so much?* Sam straightened his neck against the sofa's too-hard arm, one hand searching for his spectacles. His best friend and critique partner were sitting at the kitchen bench sipping coffee from steaming mugs.

"Good morning, Sunshine." Reece threw Thor's hammer with precision, smashing him in the face, just as he slid the glasses onto the bridge of his nose. "How do you feel?"

"Like a bag of dicks," Sam said, sitting up.

"Reece! Sam said dicks! He *actually* said dicks!" Anita set her coffee down, giving him her full attention. "Was, I am so proud of you!"

"He is a bit of a dick and he *has* a dick, so he should be able to say it," Reece told Anita, turning to Sam whose cheeks flushed tomato red.

"Don't discuss my ... manhood ... with my work colleagues please, Doctor Dickhead," Sam implored. His best friend simply laughed, a mischievous glint in his eyes.

"He said it again!" Anita clapped, overjoyed.

"No more home brew?" Reece's eyebrow quirked, and he shot him that doctorly glare.

"No more for me."

"Good. I have succeeded in turning you off alcohol forever more. Healthy choice, Mister Harthrup." They exchanged knowing glances.

Anita patted the stool beside her at the kitchen bench. "Meet my new husband," she said, nodding at Reece. "That is, if you don't mind me stealing him away."

Wait, what? His mouth was suddenly dry.

"The good doctor here is cooking me breakfast. I think I'm in love!"

"*Cooking*." Reece winked at Sam. "The way to a woman's heart."

Sam punched the doctor's arm. Reece didn't move, but Anita flinched like she had taken the hit herself.

"Is violence really necessary?" she asked. Sam's gaze flicked to her cardigan-covered bruises.

"With this one? Completely," Reece said, oblivious to the tension in her look. He grabbed Sam in a bear hug, pinning his arms to his sides then lifted him easily off the ground. A huge rush of air spilled from Sam as Reece squeezed his spine and ribs, and he thrashed, kicking, trying to break free.

"Stop, doc," he laughed, "or I'll puke!"

Something in Anita's face made them stop their scuffle. She smiled as Sam's feet hit the floor. Reece's phone rang, a short, sharp, piercing noise that split Sam's head like a neenish tart.

"You are such a lightweight," Reece laughed, ruffling Sam's hair fondly as he stepped into the bedroom to take the call.

"He's cute." Anita grinned at Sam. "I can see why you like him."

Sam barely had time to respond before Reece flew from the room, collecting his jacket. "Sorry Anita, Sam, I've gotta go. Medical emergency. Get out of this flat today, okay?" He rushed for the door, calling "Love you!" as he exited.

"Love you too, loser!" Sam called. "And we will." The idea of being here all day with Anita, and the image of her in his bed, was a dangerous combination. "We'll get out."

Anita's eyebrow rose; she lifted a crispy strip of bacon to hide the curve tugging on her lips.

After breakfast they visited Saint Jude's again. This time, Sam was more confident in engaging with the conversation. The combination of work, sleep, breakfast, and adjusted expectations of the Knights had placed him in much better humour today.

It was Monday, and the week was shaping up to be productive. The retirees were thankfully less focused on anatomy, and more on how they'd first found love.

"My husband, bless his soul," Ethel said to the group, "used to bring me a flower every single day, then walk me to school.

Not a word for three whole months! Just a flower picked from his garden. Those little wet-the-bed daisies, so nothing terribly special, but they became special to me. We'd smile and stroll. He was a shy boy. Quiet. I fell head over heels for him in half the time he'd spent courting me, but it wasn't until the three-month mark when he actually spoke. And when I heard his voice, I knew I was a gonner." Her bosom heaved as she gulped down her emotions, and the group nodded mournfully.

Harry raised a refilled flask. "To Walter."

"To Walter," they toasted, taking turns to swig.

"My wife pursued *me*," said the bearded Benjamin, his worn hand flexing atop his cane. "Used to write me love letters, even when I went to Vietnam. Always the same. *I miss you. I love you. Come home safe.* I swear, the woman's sheer will and determination to see us married saw me through the war. And God help the Viet Cong if they'd tried to stop her!" They all chuckled, sending another toast up to his departed wife.

"The love of my life had the most amazing hair." John's eyes misted over. "I fell in love with her hair, before I even saw her face. An almost copper, strawberry blonde. Long, and soft as silk it was."

Shirley scoffed. "Your wife's hair was brown, John!"

"Who said I was talkin' about my wife, dammit?"

Raucous laughter echoed around the enclosed garden. Benjamin leaned heavily on a thin tree, shaking loose a shower of tiny pink petals. They fell in slow motion, settling in snowy hair.

Holy shit, their stories are gold! Wiping tears from his eyes, Sam gasped for breath, scribbling notes furiously, as he had been doing for hours, between bouts of mirth and the occasional question.

Unlike the day before, Sam was relaxed and intrigued by the Knights, his curiosity piqued by these oddly inspirational older people. His gran talked about the Saint Jude's residents often, but nothing could have prepared him for the reality of the golden oldies.

"Thank you all so much," Sam said with a wave, offering Anita his arm as they departed that afternoon.

"That was fun." Anita was grinning ear to ear. "But I noticed that you didn't say yours."

"My what?"

"Your first love story."

He inspected his watch, unlocking the car. "No time."

"No time like the present," she quipped, sliding into the passenger seat. "My first love was Prince Adam."

"Prince who?"

"Duh, the Beast, from *Beauty and the Beast*? Oh! That library!" She groaned in pleasure, her small hands grasping at her skirts, gripping her thighs. Sam felt his upper legs tingle, as though her fingertips had brushed his own skin. "For a reader like me, it was a dream come true. Only added to the fantasy of true love conquering all, I suppose. You see ..."

Like yesterday, Sam plotted a course through town to the oval space where Cirque de Fortuna was based, Anita chatting the entire way.

"Do you breathe through your butt?" he asked, parking outside the ticket booth.

She shrugged. "Must do. I know I talk a lot. Sorry. Nervous

habit, I suppose."

"You? Nervous?" Sam laughed. "That is *not* a word I'd use to describe you, Anita."

Her hand came to rest on his forearm; goosebumps raced across his skin.

"How would you describe me, then?" Her voice was nearly a whisper, face buried beneath her hair. Gently, he swept it back, spearing her with a look.

Those eyes, so lovely. Start there, his brain ordered. A blush crept up as he opened his mouth.

"I'd say ... Your eyes have a depth that would rival the wardrobe to Narnia. With the sparkle of Egyptian blue, like an ancient Nile goddess is seeing the world through them."

She blinked those big eyes up at him. "Was, that's ... kind of beautiful." She shook her head with incredulity. "How does *that* sweet image come from the same guy who wrote about feet smell for *one whole page* when one whole sentence would be *MORE* than enough? No, really ..." She reached for his arm again as he scoffed, crossing them. "That was *much* better than your first attempt, when my small tits featured in the description." Anita grinned, her gaze hot and heavy as she scrutinised him, pushing her luck as she leaned closer. "What else?"

If this is a test of my progress, I'm sure as shit going to beat her in this game.

"Your hands," he said, dropping his eyes from hers. He took one hand lightly, turning it palm upward and tracing its lines. "I'm no witch –" he grinned, "I don't know palmistry, but I can tell that you've lived a hard life. Full of ..." he gulped, "love. And loss. But you're strong ... Withstanding. Everlasting," he added quickly, curling her fingers inward, his hands folding over hers. "Every inch of your skin is soft and sweet, I could compare it to gelato ..." Peering up at him, her eyes shone in his description. "But I won't," he coughed lightly. "And I know your lips are not rashers of bacon, and your feet are definitely *not* sexy."

Anita's burst of laughter mingled with the sharp *KNOCK KNOCK KNOCK* of the Ringmaster's knuckles, hard against the car window. He peered down at their clasped hands, his eyes two blue slits smothered by dark eyebrows that clashed in the centre of his forehead.

"You're *late*," he said, arms crossed, glaring at Sam. "Ginny needs help with the horses. Jerry's suit needs mending, and–"

In a flurry of skirts, Anita leapt from the car, mumbling excuses to both men.

Sam watched her disappear, slipping between caravans and tents, before he turned the key in the ignition. He was just about to drive off when there was another loud, angry *KNOCK*.

"Yes?" Sam lowered the window.

"Be careful with her," the Ringmaster advised, nodding towards the circus. "Anita's got her head in the clouds as often as there's a man between her legs. You don't wanna go messing around with the likes of *her*." He spat the word like it was poison in his mouth.

"Don't worry," Sam assured the brawny man. "I won't. It's a professional ..." Avoiding the word 'relationship', he settled for "arrangement."

The Ringmaster grunted, slipping his business card in through the window. Neither man broke their intense eye-lock as the card fluttered to the floor.

"Make sure you leave her money on the nightstand, then, Mister *Professional Arrangement*. And if you need me, *townie*, to come clean up one of her messes, or take her off your hands ..." his eyes darted to the tents, then back. "See that you call." The Ringmaster turned on his heel, red coat blazing, and stormed back towards his circus.

Collecting the card from the floor, Sam shook his head, too shocked and flustered to think beyond the growing rage and disgust that pumped through his blood. *What. A. Jerk. How can anyone think of Anita like that?* With a flick of his wrist, the card fluttered out of the open window.

Family is ...

SAM

MUCH LIKE THE EVENING before, Sam retreated from the world, losing himself in edits and rewrites. When he reached the shocking description of his leading lady's fingertips as 'five scorching fires', he thought of Anita. The little psychic was hell's kitchen in a skin suit, always seeming to burn and glow. She would make some leopard-print-underwear-toting Strong Man very happy one day. An ache rolled through his chest. *I wonder if, one day, someone will choose me?* He could only hope. He wasn't exactly the picture of 'healthy relationship material'. Hell, his relationships – his whole world – only revolved around two people: Grandma Edith and Reece.

Sam's eyes flicked to two small framed photos on a bookshelf. In one, taken when he was a teenager, his grandmother's already grey hair rested lightly on his shoulder. The camera had captured mirror grins, the day crisp in his memory.

It had been winter. Their cheeks, reddened from icy wind, burned as they gulped steaming hot chocolate, sheltering in Main Street Park's rotunda from the gentle fall of snow. He was pubescent and pimpled in the photo, but beaming from winning a small creative writing prize, awarding him one thousand dollars in his pocket and his name in the newspaper. Grandma Edith had taken him out to celebrate. With the last sip of his cocoa, a snowball had slammed into his face like a fist. Sam's spry little granny had ducked, cackling like The Wicked Witch of the West.

"Reece Hargraves, you little wretch! Come here!" Another white ball of pressed powder hurled by.

A vigorous snowball fight had ensued and, at the end, panting and grinning, red, scratched and dripping wet, they'd immortalised the moment in this image. Reece had snapped Edith and Sam, arms wrapped around each other, white all around. That was the last time Moonshine had seen snow.

In the second and only other photo in his flat, Reece and Sam were pictured, heads bent together, having just arrived home from a fishing trip. Both grinned wickedly from within the bright, summery image. What the photo didn't show was the fishtails poking out from down the back of their pants – an elaborate dare taken too far. Gran, the instigator of the bet, having outfished them both, had snapped that particular Kodak moment.

The insistent, high-pitched beep of the oven shattered the productive silence of the flat. *Time for dinner.* Sam quickly filled some microwavable plastic containers, scooped up his car keys, and began the drive back to Saint Jude's.

"You came!" Sam's grandmother, Edith, seemed surprised.

"It is Monday, Gran," he reminded her.

"I know, I know. It's Monday the tenth."

"It is?"

"You creative types have no sense of time." Gran threw her arms around him, and he leant into her stiffly. "You'd fail the Alzheimer's test before I do, young man!"

Gran pulled him inside. As he stepped into her single-bedroom home, his eyes appraised the neat and tidy space for any signs of deterioration.

Grandma Edith lived in the Independent Living Section of Saint Jude's, where the elderly retained their autonomy in small, uniform, cabin-style accommodation. Each unit was fitted with a big red button, to call for assistance from on-site nursing staff, if needed. It was part of Saint Jude's 'Tiered Assistance Programme'. Those making frequent red button calls would be moved into the Assisted Living Studios, on the other side of the property, before eventually moving into the intensive or palliative care wings.

Edith had moved from her home in town to the facility nearly ten years ago, but had so far needed no additional aid. Still, each Monday Sam looked for signs of decline in her physical manner, her mental health, and her lifestyle. Edith, as always, was clean, tidy, and sharp as a butcher's knife.

"I'm reliable. I show up. I'm here," said Sam, kissing her soft, crinkled cheek. Edith's smile warmed him and he added, "I am *not* like my parents."

Edith closed the door. "That's for damn sure." She patted his shoulder. "You're much better company, despite the fact that

your hug was like one from that golden robot from *Star Wars*.
C3PO, is it?"

"Gran, you know I haven't seen *Star Wars* ..."

She winked. He blushed. Aside from Breanna, Gran was
the only one who knew truth of his ill-fated date, and he was
grateful she kept that truth quiet.

Taking sparkling clean cutlery from her orderly drawers,
he rewound the subject. Trying for a casual tone he asked,
"Have you heard from them?" His voice, strangled and squeaky,
betrayed him.

Gran's lips pressed tight as the crash of cutlery on the
polished timber table broke the heavy silence. "Not in years,
darling." Edith shook her head. "I'm afraid that ship sailed
many, many drinks ago." Her whole body sagged as she sighed.

Sam heard her unspoken thought. *How could I have gone so
wrong as a parent?*

"Anyway, we don't dwell, darling. We don't dwell. How
was your day? I was surprised to see you with the Knights."
She leaned closer, eyeing him over the rim of her half-moon
glasses as he slid three of gran's chipped ceramic plates on to
the table. He had tried to buy her new dinnerware, but she
insisted on keeping these, reflecting that they had been a gift
from his parents. One happy moment among many tainted
family memories. Pushing invasive thoughts aside, he focused
on the conversation. "They're deviants, the lot of them. But
excellent for a laugh. Our sides hurt for *days* after we go to court!
Eddie and I firmly believe that laughter prolongs life."

Ah, yes. Edward.

"Happiness is the key to health," said Sam, quoting the nurse.

"Will Eddie be coming to dinner tonight? I've cooked up some culinary puns I thought he'd like to sample." Sam had set three places, expecting the boyfriend-next-door to shuffle over on his walker to join them. Sam had never known his grandfather, but Eddie had been in his life for over a decade now, the only stable figure in his and Gran's lives.

"Not tonight, darling. I gave him the night off from kneading these old bread rolls." She winked, and he rolled his eyes away. "You're so cute when you blush like that." She pinched his hot cheeks the way she always had, a little too hard and with too smug a grin. "You know, you're an adult now, darling. We should be able to talk about—"

He couldn't help but drop his gaze to her chest. "Your bread rolls? More like pancakes." He smirked, ducking her swatting hand. "*Anyway*," he said, removing one setting from the table. "I brought dinner."

"Ooh, I am the luckiest woman in the entire village. What did you cook for me this time, Master Chef?" Edith's hands rubbed together as she licked her lips.

"I was thinking we'd go vegetarian tonight."

"Be still my heart." She clutched her pearl necklace, eyes dancing as Sam unloaded the grocery bag. "A man who is *pea*-sed about eating vegetables!"

Sam laughed, shaking his head. "They say *corn*y humour is inherited."

Gran giggled. "You must be well. You found your humour again! Where was it? Tucked in your top drawer?" They grinned at each other, inhaling deeply as Sam's dinner filled their senses. "The Knights have a habit of unlocking cheer. Good thing too."

She peeked under the lid of one container. "I was starting to wonder if whatever stick Reece has up his toosh is contagious. You've been too serious for too long, Sam."

Edith offered wine, Sam shaking his head lightly as he carefully served their dinner onto the plates, explaining the artistry of their meal. "The trick to making traditional Greek spanakopita is the pastry." Edith listened intently, sipping wine as Sam talked. "It's made with spinach and feta, with a garnish of fresh pimiento, oregano, shallots and pine nuts."

"Is feta lactose free?"

His cheeks heated. "No. But to atone for my future gastrointestinal sins, I also made you some profiteroles for dessert."

Grandma Edith beamed up at him. "Custard filling?"

"Of course."

"And that fancy chocolate sauce you make?"

Sam laughed, serving her a healthy slice of the spanakopita. "You *do* have a reputation to maintain as the luckiest and best grandmother ever." He grinned, his fork loaded with the savoury dish.

"You are *shrimp*ly the best!" Edith smiled around her mouthful.

They ate quickly and in silence, her pink tongue darting out to catch the flaky pastry crumbs cupped in her palm.

"So, tell me about her."

Spinach lodged in Sam's throat. "Who?" he wheezed around the sudden lump in his throat.

"That young lady, with that beautiful swishy skirt. Reminded me of a fancy layered cake! Though all that hair evened out her top half quite a bit." Edith chuckled, helping herself to another slice of spanakopita. "So, who is she?"

"She's ..." Sam gulped down a mouthful of water. "Anita. She's with the circus. A fortune teller. A reader." *She's obnoxiously honest, extremely critical, which thankfully is exactly what I need right now, and she has wandering hands ...*

"A reader, hey? Reading you like a book, dear?" Gran winked again.

"Uh, yeah, kind of. She's a bit unnerving, honestly." He rubbed the back of his neck.

"You like her?"

He shrugged. "Sure."

"Sam, do you *like* her?"

"I don't *like* what you're implying, Gran." He shot her a disapproving look, heat flushing his skin. "And anyway, why would she like me? I'm not really–"

"Not really what?" She set her fork down forcefully, giving him an even look. "Smart? Funny? Creative? A goddamn brilliant cook?" She leaned closer and grabbed his hand across the table. "Samuel Harthrup, you are worthy of being liked. Being *loved* even. If your grandfather were here–"

"But he's not, okay Gran? Neither is Dad, or Mum, or any of them!" Sam's fork clattered on the table. "The only one who ever wanted to put up with me was *you*!"

"Sam–"

"No, Gran." He cleared their dishes, dumping them into the sink, glaring down.

Edith rose shakily to meet him, gripping his arm silently in support. A lengthy silence stretched between them.

"I'm sorry for raising my voice, at you." He lifted her hand, kissing the back of it tenderly. "I didn't mean to be rude. But I don't want to talk about this anymore, okay?"

"I'll forgive you." Edith smiled up at him, her kindness melting his mood. "If you remember that family is who we choose to show up for." Her voice dropped. "I'll always show up for you, Sam."

Swallowing hard, Sam struggled for words.

"I'll shut up with the sappy stuff ... but only if you clean up," she offered, squeezing his arm lightly.

"Deal."

She watched him scrub, splashing suds everywhere, continuing to sip her large glass of wine. The rhythm of washing soothed him, and Gran kept finding more coffee cups and half-finished plates of cheese and crackers for him to clean. He smiled, considering how similar he was to this old woman.

Eventually, his mind turned to Anita. The warmth of the dishwater was too like the heat of her touch, making those thoughts impossible to escape as Sam scrubbed. He hoped she would have a good show tonight, pondering what would make a *bad* night at the circus, other than pre-show concussions of local drunkards like himself, or maybe the faux-unicorn getting stroppy and biting a kid's hand.

"Remember that I know you, Sam. You can't hide the truth from me." He froze at Edith's words, ice seizing his veins. *Shit. How did she know I was thinking of the circus? Of Anita? Was it written in his pink cheeks?* "I know about your literary adventures, remember?" *Breathe. Just breathe.*

"And I just want to say ..." Suddenly she was beside him, her frail arms encircling his waist, pink and frilly from the apron he wore. "I am so, *so* proud of you, my boy."

When Edith's eyelids became too heavy, Sam kissed her forehead and started for the door. Edith shuffled behind him on slipper-clad feet.

"You stay inside, Gran. It's spring, but the night air is still chilly." He bent to wrap her in a clumsy hug, his grandmother's frail shoulders digging into his arms.

"Thank you for dinner, Sammie, darling. Whatever would I do without you?"

"I don't know – live with less pains in your arse? Less food in your tum? Less cheesy puns? A *feta* life? A *gouda* chance to–"

His grandmother laughed lightly, shaking her head. "Sam, you're worth more than you know. One day, someone will choose you and you will make that woman so happy. So happy. Then, you'll be making her laugh and cooking for *her* instead of me."

Yeah, right. Then she'll leave, just like everyone else. No one stuck around. Not for him. Not his parents. Not Breanna. Not Sandra. Not Anita, who would be running away with the circus soon. The thought of it caused his gut to clench. Could he finish his manuscript without her?

Shaking his head clear, Sam smiled at Edith. "I'll always cook for you, Gran," he said, peering down at her fondly. "And in return, don't you go and *leek* my secret, okay?"

"Never! But since you seem to be neck-deep in a boiling pot, my dear, may I offer a word of advice?" Grandma Edith squeezed his forearm, not waiting for his reply. "Watch out for the Knights. They're old as the hills, but they're prone to pranks. And you, my darling, are a cute little snack they'll eat alive, if you don't watch out."

"I used to be the king of pranks, remember?"

"Oh, I remember. You and Reece used to tease me to the very end of my goddamn tether, that's for sure! But, you did learn from the best." Her shoulders rose, a cheeky grin twinkling in the night. She kissed him lightly, the sweetness of custard still clinging to her breath. "See you next week? Eddie would love to see you again."

"Next Monday, same as always. I promise."

Arriving home, Sam found Anita, curled like a comma in his bed. The witch must have used some kind of locator spell to find his spare key, or was an adept lock picker. He didn't mind how she'd found it, either way. It was kind of … *nice* … he decided, coming home to another person.

Titanic played on the television. Rose and Jack and that damn door which, of course, they could both have fitted onto. *Why do I even own this?* Sam pondered, drawn in momentarily by the James Cameron masterpiece. *It's not even a romance. There's no Happily Ever After. It's a tragedy!* Sighing lightly, he clicked the 'off' button, Kate Winslet's shivering, blue face fading to black.

The rough edges of his night smoothed as he watched Anita sleep, arms looped around his pillow, her riot of curls tumbling this way and that, stretching into the darkness. Gently pulling the covers over her, his foot tapped one of the storage tubs beneath the bed.

It had spilled across the floor. *Or has Anita been snooping through my things?* The idea struck like Mjolnir, smacking into his forehead.

He examined his secret stash of romance films. *Holy shit, she's alphabetising them!*

Anita murmured into the pillow, smiling as she hugged it to her body. She looked so soft and comfortable in his bed. And once again, he was watching her sleep, like a total freak. *Get outa there, Harthrup!* Sliding from the room, he closed the door softly before picking up his pencil and journal.

The morning had been unhurried. Familiar. Anita left Sam to sleep on the brown sofa, quietly tidying his flat until the groan of her stomach roused him. Friday's Café welcomed them back for a long brunch where Anita talked, and talked, and talked, then listened intently to the responses he offered to her questions. Time slipped away until their final 'Court' session began.

"We're down two Knights?" Anita cautiously asked, clearly fearing for their wellbeing. Sam's chest tightened at the concern in her tone.

"It happens," the nurse explained. "The elderly become tired and unwell. But don't worry, the other Knights are in *fine form* today." Her tone was laced with warning.

Sam soon realised the two absentees were the quiet moderators of the group, and the others seemed heightened in their cheekiness and vulgarity today. After an unproductive and spine-chilling discussion detailing erogenous zones, during which Sam desperately tried not to imagine anyone naked, lunch was served. Cheese sandwiches. Sam's stomach lurched, anticipating hours of torment. *Why couldn't they just spread on some Vegemite?* He quickly sent up a little prayer to any bowel-related deities, begging for help.

Someone must have been listening – the tray of sandwiches tipped suddenly from shaking hands, triangles scattering across the courtyard, coating themselves in freshly cut lawn clippings.

"Oh, dearie me, look what I've done!" Shirley cried. "The cleaner's cupboard is over there, dears." A craggy finger pointed to an almost invisible doorway.

"I'll get a dustpan," Sam offered, desperate to escape the awkwardness the Knights inflicted.

Anita smiled, motioning at the mess of lunch and white-haired Saint Jude's residents littering the courtyard. "No, I'll go. You stay. This whole shebang is for you, after all."

"I think you should *both* go," Shirley encouraged, watery eyes dropping to the grass. "I made *such* a mess."

In hindsight, they would later agree that alarm bells should have been ringing. In the moment, however, they both hurried toward the cleaning supplies, eager to help their Knights.

Opening the cleaning cupboard door, Sam and Anita peered into the darkness.

"Look to the back!" John cried from his wheelchair.

They stepped further into the storage room. Then, faster than a Knight taking their midday pills from the nurse, daylight was snatched away as the door slammed shut. Giggles sounded from beyond, followed by a wolf whistle and some snorting.

"Seven minutes in heaven, dearies!" Cecelia's voice crackled with mirth.

Sam moaned into the darkness. "We've been pranked by geriatrics." *Shit!* Gran had warned him.

Anita's laugh bounced off the walls of their confinement. "No shit, Sherlock. You refused 'Spin the Flask' three times in as many days, and they want their kicks somehow. Today is their last chance with us."

"This is better than daytime TV!" a voice whispered loudly outside, to a chorus of "Ssshhhh!"

"I think they're listening," Anita whispered into the darkness, her hand somehow finding his back. "Oh, there you are." Her hot palm spun around his midsection, hands coming to rest on his sides. "You know, when I called you dirt perve, I didn't ever imagine it would lead me to a forced proximity situation with a broom shoved into my arse. Let me just ..." He felt her move slightly. An almighty clatter arose as the contents of the cupboard crashed like dominoes around them. She leaned into him, avoiding the attacking shadows, and something heavy hit his ankle. Sam pitched forward, his shoulder colliding with her skull.

"OUCH! WAS!"

"Shit, sorry!"

The Knights giggled. Sam was glad Anita couldn't see his ruby red face. The room had been built for minimal cleaning equipment storage. Maybe a mop and a broom, and the lawnmower for the courtyard, not for one twiggy writer and a curvy goddess such as herself. He reached out hesitantly in the dark, until his hands found the top of her head. Chuckling, he patted the soft curls.

"I forgot you were so tiny."

She scoffed, and he smiled into the darkness, sliding his hands down the waves of her hair until he touched her face.

"*There* you are." Holding her cheeks in his palms, Sam asked, "Your head okay?"

"It's fine." Sam's hands travelled the length of her arms, until he grasped her ring-covered fingers. Something scampered through the shadows, and Anita let out a little squeak, stumbling. Reaching out, Sam steadied her with a grip on her hips. *She's so warm. Soft.* And close. *So close.*

The darkness seemed to grow denser, the air changing.

"Step with me. You go forward, I'll go back. Ready?" he proposed, guiding her gently, allowing more space for her in the tiny closet. She sighed, the heat of her breath tickling the base of his neck.

"Well, this is–" she started.

"Inconvenient. And unproductive."

"C'mon, don't be like that." She squeezed his shoulders, the warmth of her hands seeping through his shirt.

God, she's hot. She radiated enough heat to melt the sun's core. The curve of her moulded to his palms in the darkness. Gently, their bodies swayed.

He felt Anita's cheeks lift as she pressed into his chest. Her slow, contented exhale warmed his cotton t-shirt. *She's smiling? Happy?* His own lips tugged up. "Dancing in the dark." Her soft voice wafted up to his ears. "How romantic, Was. Reece will be jealous, you know. I bet he's the jealous kind. He's so ... *serious.*"

Sam's body stiffened. *What? Why would Reece be jealous?* He tasted betrayal, heavy and sour.

It wouldn't be the first time someone had fallen head over

heels for his best friend. Reece was, in that timeless *Mr Darcy*ish way, tall, dark, classically handsome and generally brooding. Women seemed to like that combination. And Sam? Sam was more like Austen's Bingley. Or *The Notebook*'s Noah, according to Anita. But he wasn't them. He could only *wish* he was them. Sam was just a lanky blond guy with big glasses. A strained writer of romantic food porn that needed more sex scenes, according to his editor.

His chin dropping to the top of Anita's head, Sam sighed, mentally cursing his best friend. Yes, the fortune teller was off limits to *him*, for professional reasons, but the good doctor had never made that bargain with the witch.

Anita's face pressed into his chest.

What the shit is going on? one side of his brain screamed whilst the other cheered: *Just go with it, you over-thinking bastard!*

Anita's hands smoothed the shirt on his back, her skirts swishing around his legs. Soft and warm, her body pressed against his. A tightness gripped his gut, slowly melting into the dark as he breathed in the soft lavender scent of her hair.

This is some kind of witchcraft, he told himself, pressing her closer. Inhaling her sweet scent once more, his chest and stomach pushed into the nooks and crannies that remained between them.

The grannies giggled loudly, pondering their captives' sudden silence.

"What now, Witchy Poo?" Sam whispered into Anita's hair. It was strange, and unnervingly comfortable, how her head fit so tidily under his chin. "Jump on the nearest broomstick and fly us out of here?" He felt her body shake with silent laughter. *Damn it feels good to make her laugh.*

"Oh, definitely. Just let me practise my signature nose twitch." Anita's breath caressed his skin and he bent into her warmth. Noses grazing, hesitating and unsure, he snuck one hand into her hair, holding her close.

Acutely aware of the hum of electricity and heat between them, he closed his eyes, absorbing it through every minute touch of their bodies. *I have enough pent-up sexual energy to power a small city, like Moonshine.* He exhaled shakily. Reece was right – he needed to release this pent-up tension. Clear the toxins from the building. Take matters into his own hands. It was no good for his body, for his head, keeping a tight lid on his needs. And he needed, alright – that much was becoming embarrassingly clear.

"Anita ..."

Her sweet breath curled on his tongue and he leaned closer to the shadow that was his witch, his reader, his ...

"TIME'S UP!" Like a hot knife through butter, blinding light cut though the moment. Wrinkled hands gripped the open door, dentured grins aimed their way.

Sam jolted back – and straight into the mop bucket. It sloshed to the floor, mocking them as it met the ground in a moist kiss before spraying water across his legs. "Shit!"

"You can come out now." The geriatric grinned. "You've exhausted your seven minutes in Heaven."

Pulsing with adrenaline, a dash of shock, and a solid, surprising pinch of lust, Sam wasn't sure 'exhausted' was how he'd write this encounter into his diary.

The Ringmaster

ANITA

ANITA WAS NINETY-NINE PER cent sure that her lifetime of fairy floss, popcorn and Coca-Cola had caught up with her. Heart pounding and light-headed, struggling to control her own body, beyond her control. It was all Sammie Hart's fault, she told herself. It certainly wasn't Samuel Harthrup's. The man was as tense as a teenager on a first date! But *Sammie Hart* ... She sighed, her stomach somersaulting at the thought of the sizzling *Heat in The Kitchen* moments, the sexy food puns that still made her drool.

Goddess, please, I need to stop touching that romance writer, she prayed, hoping her shame wouldn't end in complete and utter embarrassment. She had never been handsy before. Never felt as though her body was betraying her and acting of its own volition. She'd never felt the insane urge to touch or (Goddess help her) *kiss* any of her new friends-slash-daytime-distractions during the circus' fortnight in town. But something about the writer was flipping all her 'nevers' on their heads.

Keeping my emotions locked down would be easier if I could just stop myself from reaching out ... Anita slid her hands under her thighs.

The spot where he'd inadvertently head-butted her throbbed. Another deep throb echoed, closer to her core. Anita kept her eyes fixed firmly on the horizon as Sam silently drove her back to the circus. His hyperfocus when driving enveloped them as he drove carefully, vigilant and aware of every aspect of their trip except, it seemed, for her. Anita filled his silence, talking compulsively (and not really saying anything, *but Goddess I just can't shut up!*) Sam barely acknowledged her chatter. Had she crossed some kind of line? Yes. Yes, she had. And the poor fellow seemed unsure what to do or say about it. And poor Reece!

Damn you. She cursed her hands, squashed between her legs and the seat.

Sam flicked the indicator on, pulling off the road and onto the oval. The striped Big Top loomed, swaying slightly in the breeze.

"Thanks, Was." Her stomach grumbled. They hadn't eaten, after the sandwich fiasco. "See you ... later?"

He cleared his throat. "Dinner?"

Her stomach spoke before her tongue could form a reply.

"Tomorrow night?" he went on. "You need a decent home-cooked meal." His eyes flicked over her, head to toe. A rush of self-consciousness followed his appraising gaze, her skin tingling with delight. Had she manifested a meal, simply by imagining it? Her stomach growled again. Or, maybe he just had functioning ears. *Perhaps he reads minds like I read palms?* No. More likely the deep, frequent noises that erupted from her gut were the cause of his offer.

"I work at dinner time," Anita reminded him. "But I'd be up for a late evening meal?" She closed the door, leaning in through the open window. "Will Reece be there?"

Sam scowled, pushing his spectacles higher onto his nose. "Actually, he's already got a thing ..."

"Oh?"

"Dr Hargraves is working overtime, meeting with the Starlight Foundation again, fundraising and compiling some report on their circus excursion with Donny Wheeler."

Donny Wheeler ... the night I met Samuel Harthrup. She'd known him for less than a week. Heck, she'd known the non-existent writer Sammie Hart for longer. There was no reason to feel this ... unusual.

Keep your cool, Anita warned herself, her peripheral gaze collecting a dark shadow beside the ticket gate. Her heart leaped as the Ringmaster came into view. She dropped her voice lower. "I remember Donny. Best Ringmaster we've ever had." She gave a sad smile. *Poor kid.* The real Ringmaster had taken the night off, allowing the sick child to take his place for one night only. The air had been lighter and the world more vibrant under the rule of a sick child rather than her own brother. The circus had breathed easier in his absence. Every night, the world was his saw-dusted arena, and all the players mere puppets.

"Well, Reece or not, I'm saying yes. *Definitely*, yes. Your kitchen is easily the biggest and most glamorous space in your whole flat. Such a shame when a man's got a big one, and doesn't know how to use it." She winked, and Sam immediately blushed a deep strawberry pink that caused her stomach to growl once more. "And if you cook half as good as how you described the food in *Heat in the Kitchen* ... I mean, you made *salad* sound sexy ... I know my tastebuds will explode."

Salad had never been a turn-on. Not until Sammie Hart's surprisingly delicious debut novel. She backed away from Sam's car with a small wave.

"So ... yes?" He clarified, cheeks blazing.

"Yes. Thanks for the ride, and the ... *interesting* ... day."

Sam nodded, eyes fixed on the wheel, gripped by marshmallow-pale knuckles. "Let's never go to Court again," he grumbled.

"Never," Anita agreed, to ease his discomfort. She would miss the old deviants, but this wasn't about her, or the Knights at Saint Jude's. This was about Sam. *For Sammie.* She had to make this about him. "Those soft cheese sandwiches *really* don't agree with you," she said with a wink, in response to his immediate and profuse apologies. "Bye, Was." She chuckled again, unwilling to enter the circus, praying to whomever was out there in the Universe to give her more time. More freedom. More easy fun with a new friend.

"Hey, Witch?" Sam drew her attention one last time. He was holding out a flower, one of the small pink blooms from the trees in the courtyard. "I really am sorry," he said, pressing it through the open window and into her palm. The cool of his fingertips lingered with the small pink blossom. Nodding, she carefully cupped the treasure.

As she turned her back, she heard Sam exhale, almost feeling his body relax. A familiar noise made her giggle as he rushed the windows up, trapping a foul waft of air inside the vehicle. Sam's face held its familiar tomato hue, eyes glued to the road as he drove away. Loosing the laugh that had bubbled in her chest all day, she waved to Sam's tail lights before sliding back into the circus grounds.

Clutching fingers sprung from nowhere, constricting Anita's bicep as she was pulled into the Ringmaster's private tent. "Who the fuck was that?" Adrian barked. "I've seen that guy drop you off before." He threw his black top hat to the floor.

"He's one of the Starlight Foundation crew from the other night," Anita fibbed, shrinking as Adrian loomed over her. It was easier to hide the truth and hide herself (as much as possible) from his outbursts. "We've just been having coffee."

Her brother barked out a callous laugh. "Guys never want *just coffee*, Anita. You're an idiot if you think that's the case. You're whoring yourself out to him, aren't you?"

"No," she whispered before reinforcing her voice. "No. I–"

"Don't you *dare* talk back!" he boomed. Adrian's eyes, stormy and bloodshot, radiated rage, his height seeming to increase with his temper. His dark hair, a shorter version of her own mess of curls, fell over his face in a shadowy mask. She knew this look, this thickening in the air. Biting back her tongue, she waited, watching his face with caution.

"Just go get ready," Adrian ordered, digging his fingers into her fleshy upper arm as he pulled her to the tent edge. "And the acrobats needed their mended costumes *yesterday*. They'd better be ready, or *so help you*, Anita ..."

He shoved her through the open flap. She stumbled, and pain seared through her ankle as it twisted sideways. The flower hit the ground a few seconds after she landed in a heap of skirts at the too-large feet of Claus, the clown. His big, painted eyes dropped to the dirt. Wordlessly, he helped her up. Soft-stomached yet strong, Claus was surprisingly gruff for a sixty-year-old in make-up. Scooping the small flower into her pocket, Anita shot a thankful look to her old friend.

"See that my *slut* of a sister is ready before the show's due to start," Adrian ordered Claus, scooping his top hat from the ground and shoving it down hard onto his head. "And no food for her again tonight. If she doesn't work during the day, she doesn't earn her way. Everyone earns their keep here. *Plus*," he sneered, a nasty curl on his top lip, "she's already too fat to fit into her corsets. She should be living on lettuce."

Sexy salad. The pitiful thought, half mental retort and half Sammie Hart, struggled into her brain. Claus gave the most imperceptible of nods to Adrian. Holding his arm out as a barrier between Anita and her brother, the clown supported a wincing Anita to the vardo.

The circus folk, pooling money, resources and time, had built the vardo caravan purely for her, in an act of silent defiance of the Ringmaster. Constructed upon an old car trailer bed, it was mobile and sturdy, a safe place Anita could retreat to and lock the door on Adrian's brutality. As she staggered past Robin, the child reached out, depositing a palm-sized biscuit into Anita's hand.

Thank you. My real family. *Thank you.*

Claus helped Anita down onto her bed. "You know he

dislikes it when you's gone durin' the day." He had been with Cirque de Fortuna for decades, practically raising Anita and Adrian. Sneaking her candies whenever her brother played horrible pranks, or helping her tidy up when Adrian left a mess. Claus knew them better than most.

"I know. I just can't stay during the day, Claus. I can't stand being here if there's no show. Has he been–"

"In anyone else's grill? Nah." Claus examined her ankle, *tsk*ing as she sucked in air sharply, teeth gritted.

"Good." She sighed against the mattress.

"Anita Fortuna – ain't nothing *good* 'bout how yer brother treats you. If yer Daddy was 'ere–"

"Well, he's not, Claus. He died. *They* died. And it threw Adrian over the edge. He didn't used to be like this. It's the stress, and he worries about me." *Too much*, in his own way. She was her own woman, smart and fun, vivacious and curvaceous, but somehow, since their parents' passing, Adrian had started to see her through a different lens. Her brother had become protective, aggressive, and unable to control his temper towards her.

"Ain't no excuses for that sort'a misbehavin'." Claus' painted red lips refused to turn down, but the tight line of his mouth said more than his brightly made-up expression. "You gotta get outta the life, Anita. Ain't no place for you 'ere, not with *him*. Meet some nice townie, settle down, pop out some lil clowns of yer own. That's what I'd be doin', if it weren't for Barney."

Barney. A townie turned carnie turned clown, Claus had met his match beside the spinning lights of the Whirl-o-Tron, and no one's lives had been the same since.

"You're lucky to have him." Anita smiled, eyes shifting to Claus. "He's the other pea in your pod."

"Yeah, well, it took me long enough to see it. Kept throwin' his way inter my space like a damn donut ring tryin' ter catch on a peg. Takin' over my stalls, tyin' my tent ropes like I hadn't gone done it a million times afore. Believed he was alpha-male'n me, till I knew better." His true smile was a much gentler version of his painted lips. "Who ever thought a circus clown ter be queer?"

Anita chuckled, shaking her head. "That word is outdated, Claus."

"*I'm* outdated." He nodded over her ankle. "You know Barney's a Moonshine man? Born right 'ere, 'e was, an' right 'ere's where we met all those years ago."

No, she hadn't known that. Barney had left this quaint little place and run away with the circus? Why? It seemed like such a lovely country town. Full of history and interesting people. Hell, their love of liquor extended to naming the pub The Pope! But Moonshine's quirky charm didn't explain the complex emotions she was feeling for this place.

"How could I leave Cirque de Fortuna? Leave you and Barney? Robin and Leo?" She pushed his fleshy chin up, looking him in the eye. Claus' meaty hands ceased strapping her ankle with the crisp bandage he'd pulled from his oversized, wire-hoop-waisted red overalls. Securing the end before struggling to stand on cracking, dodgy knees, the clown mumbled, "Old Leo would miss yer, sure as rain. Who else'd make a new sparklin' horn for me little pony, when the silly thing eats it again? But the rest of us?" His lips twitched and he rose to full height, offering a hand to help her up. "Yeah, we likely wouldn't miss you so much." Huffing a laugh, Anita took his hand, wincing as she rose.

"You'll be goin' easy on that ankle fer a few days, missy."

"Thank you, Doctor Claus."

"I mean it, Anita. I know Adrian'll make yer work tonight, but after that – rest. An' maybe spend tomorrow here, durin' the day. Show yer face around the joint. Show Adrian yer willing to play ball. Earnin' a few brownie points ain't never hurt no one … an' *nobody* should be hurtin', darlin'." He looked at her pointedly, pushing the thick curtain of hair from her face. "No one. Now, where's the leotard fer the first act? I'll help yer get ready."

By the end of the show, one thing was abundantly clear – there was no way Anita could proceed with her plan to hobble to Sam's flat on her swollen, throbbing ankle. It felt as though Leo had sunk his giant equine teeth into her foot, sucked on it for a while then spat it back out again. She fondly patted the old Shetland, more a spoiled pet than work animal. The bedazzling unicorn garb suited the attention-seeking creature well. Leading him back to the enclosure, Anita draped her arm lovingly over his warm coat. "I'm grateful for your support, old pal," she whispered into his big, golden ears, leaning heavily on him.

Duties done, the click of the lock on the colourful vardo door was a welcome sound. Anita sunk to the floor of the caravan, breathing at a deep, measured pace. She slowly slipped off her sequined high-rise show boots, wincing with each tug of the laces.

There's no way Sam would write a foot fetish scene about

that *hunk of bruised flesh.* Her toes were pale purple mini hotdogs, and a large bruise was spreading around her ankle bone. Hopping to her single bed, she eased herself onto the mattress, lying down to dream about the kinds of meals Sammie Hart had described in *Heat in the Kitchen*. The man *could* write a description, especially when it came to food. It was like he'd been born to be a food blogger, but the culinary arts had been deliciously entwined with more romantic notions of tongue usage.

Reaching into the small nook between her mattress and the wall, Anita fished out three novels. Two were borrowed from the impressive Moonshine Municipal Library. Anita had given the stereotypically sexy librarian her list of interests, asking for recommendations. She wasn't disappointed with the results.

One of the librarian's suggestions was a history of the town entitled *Moonshine Madness: A Short History of One Town and Its Long-Running Love of Liquor*. Anita loved history. The alliteration wasn't amiss either. The book had been shelved next to another local history titled *Meet Me in Moonshine*, but that book had appeared more architectural in theme. Interesting, but not her cup of tea. It had remained on the shelf for another lucky reader to enjoy.

The librarian's second suggestion – a graphic novel called *Pride and Prejudice and Zombies* (an Austen adaptation) – was sure to be a hit. Who didn't love zombies infused into their classic literature?

The third book in Anita's vardo was her much-loved copy of *Heat in the Kitchen*. Its paper was soft and edges curled. The cover was so cracked with wear, she often fancied they could be read, like the palm lines of its creator.

As she sunk lazily into *Heat*, Anita's stomach growled deeply. *Damn, he's a good writer, when he gets out of his own way.* Laying the novel on her chest, Anita breathed deeply and stretched, before placing *Heat* back into its nook beside the bed. The growing warmth and noise in her gut was too distracting for her to read Sammie's words clearly. Carefully lowering her throbbing foot to the floor, Anita hopped the short distance to her altar.

Set atop a single set of drawers, the altar was a small workspace where her real world met her spiritual one. She didn't exactly know how to label her belief system, but 'eclectic' seemed suitable. Travelling the countryside and working late into the evenings did not suit early-to-rise, ritualistically Churchgoing people, and the creatives and eccentrics who inhabited the circus and show-time communities had encouraged Anita to explore her own version of faith. Gods, goddesses – if one existed, shouldn't they all? Anyone who could help, or listen, was appreciated.

Lighting an incense stick and the small vanilla candle Robin had gifted for her birthday, Anita's thoughts turned to Sam – the best listener she'd ever encountered.

I wonder how old Was is? Not that it matters. She guessed Sam to be close to her age, but being an inside-dweller, skin kept from the sun, he might wear his age well and be older than she initially guessed.

Pondering, Anita reached into a small wooden bowl, pinching salt then throwing it over her shoulder for luck, mentally banishing any evil spirits – including Adrian –

from this, her sacred space. She took a small sip of cold, metallic-tasting water from a small silver chalice, before searching her pocket for the pink blossom Sam had given her that afternoon. Its petals were crinkled, brown and crushed from Adrian's ... *her* ... fall, but it was still the sweetest little bloom she'd ever beheld.

"Today," she confided to whichever spirits, guides, deities might be lurking in the shadows of her tiny home, "was a good day."

Anita breathed the momentary peace and quiet of the vardo, safe in the knowledge that her few feet of safety had a firmly bolted lock.

It felt strange, joining the Cirque de Fortuna folk at breakfast the next morning. Robin was thrilled; Barney and Claus patted the chair at their table eagerly. It was safe in the open, with the crew, but safer still in her vardo. Filling her plate, Anita ignored their invitations and retreated. Before entering her mobile home, she circled it, dropping a grainy mixture of salt, basil, clove, cumin and pepper, hoping the charm of the protective circle would be enough to see her through the day. Clouds rolled in overhead, and she worried the threatening rain would wash away the enchantment.

Task accomplished, Anita looked back to the assembled crew. Perhaps Claus had been right. She needed to earn brownie points. *Maybe I should eat with the family ...*

A dark shadow slipped between the trailers. Anita froze, feeling the heat of Adrian's eyes on her. As she bolted inside, she heard him hissing about his "fat, shameful, hussy of a sister." Her last shred of strength and dignity worn away, alone in her trailer, she let the tears fall.

Hobbling through her daily chores was easier with the support of her Cirque de Fortuna family. Even a few of the ring-in carnies helped her out, each with a pitying smile. Anita had never said 'thank you' so many times in her life, or winced so much. Pain shot through her ankle like a hot rod lancing beneath her skin. Doctor Reece Hargraves' face danced at the edges of her agony, but she dismissed him. There was nothing Reece would do that Claus hadn't already managed. The majority of her pain wasn't in her ankle, anyway, but in her chest.

What she needed was a balm for her soul, a Band-Aid of a man who would stick to her heart and hold it together. Someone who would *choose* her, love her, not bully her into the ground beneath his boot. "Circus business is circus business," her parents had used to say. Anita took it as a vow of silence. For Adrian, it was a free pass to torment.

Back in her vardo, her tears fell harder. This was not who she was. This was not the real Anita Maria Fortuna. The real Anita was not a blubbering mess. She did not struggle. She refused to think less of herself. She was strong, and worthy of a sappy, romantic-style Happily Ever After.

A new town meant new opportunities – it was one of the joys of living place to place. In each new location, she could reinvigorate and reaffirm all the little parts that made her who she was.

Despite Adrian's harsh words, she liked her Moonshine self. Assisting Sam with his novel, reading and reviewing and helping him to build a book (one of her most beloved physical objects in the world) was a fascinating process.

She had liked who she was in Wagga Wagga – a town so good they named it twice – volunteering at the local animal shelter in her spare time. When your idea of a 'domesticated animal' included monkeys, horses, (and the occasional, proudly mullet-wearing carnival worker), petting dogs, cats and rabbits was easy.

She had liked who she was in Tamworth – the 'Country Music Capital' of Australia – when she had joined a quirky country music band in need of a backup singer. Their usual girl had just had surgery, and Anita had been only too glad to fill in. Her heart, full of song, had made her feel like a Disney princess in the flesh.

Anita loved giving back to each community that helped her escape, interacting with the locals and living her best life during the daylight hours, away from the performance world.

Looking into her small, hand-held mirror, Anita squared her gaze and began her daily phase of affirmations. "You are beautiful," she told herself. "You are a helper, a reader. You use the psychic circus stall to meet those who seek guidance, because you are a giver." She saw pleas for help in their hands and eyes during her readings. "It's not much, but it's something you can offer the world." Her eyes welled. "You are lovely. You are strong. You're worthy, and you're not the woman your brother says you are."

Taking a deep breath, she crushed a stalk of lavender between her hands, inhaling the sweet, relaxing fragrance. Adrian couldn't – wouldn't – douse her spark.

"One day," she told herself, "your prince will come. White knight, white horse. The whole shebang. Because that's the happy ending you deserve. Not that you even need to rely on a man to make your life complete, you know. You're a strong, bad-arse witch with a heart as big as your backside." Smiling to herself, she extinguished the candle and closed her eyes. She'd sleep until dusk, when the circus would call her to awaken once more.

The spring air became crisp and the shadows stretched languidly, connecting the tents and stalls like oddly shaped beads on a dark, tangled string. Eventually, the increased noise around the tents, and children's excited laughter indicated the crowd's arrival for the evening show.

The Ringmaster was displeased that preparations were still underway, thanks to an accident involving the smoke machine and two spooked horses that bolted from the Big Top. Of course, it was all deemed Anita's fault, and Adrian's mood was filthier than the animal enclosures she'd been tasked with mucking out while a more sure-footed dancer took her place in the ring. It was supposed to be a punishment, missing out on the performance, shovelling shit. But Anita didn't mind. She didn't have the energy to put on a show, to wear a happy mask. And nobody would mess with a turd-covered witch. Not even the Ringmaster.

Later, her work done, as the crowds dispersed and circus crew settled in for the night, Anita snuck into the pop-up amenities block, stealing the last of the hot water. She hoped Adrian didn't catch wind of her 'gluttony'. Dressing quickly, she slipped through the darkness to her vardo, bolting the door behind her. With a sigh, she turned to the quiet, empty space, briefly wondering how Sam's novel was progressing. Gingerly, her ankle throbbing, she slid onto her bed, bringing *Heat in the Kitchen* before her eyes, suddenly desperate to re-enter his world, his writing. Her lids became too heavy to blink open; the novel flopped down to the floor and Anita Fortuna fell fast asleep.

"Witch!" A roar of a whisper slipped between the hinges of her doorframe. "Anita! You in there?"

One eye cracked open. Her ankle throbbed. "Was?"

"Anita! Shit, I was so worried. I thought I'd see you for dinner? Let me in!"

Sleep tugged at all her soft edges, dragging her back down to blackness. "Go away, Was. I'm tired."

"Anita, be proud of me!" Sam's voice was insistent. Exalted. Slowly, his enthusiasm soaked in, rousing her. "I had a breakthrough! I've been rewriting and editing and on a massive roll all night. And then I realised the time and you hadn't come over to read, and –"

If the writer believed he was being quiet, he was sorely mistaken. Even the hearing-impaired Knights at Saint Jude's would start waking soon, if Sam kept this up. Anita shushed him through the closed door.

"Shut up and I'll let you in." Sam fell silent.

Shooting pains exploded with each foot fall. Sliding the bolt, Anita peeked to ensure Sam was alone and (more importantly) that no one would see a man entering her vardo. Aside from the gossip that might erupt, Adrian would surely use it against her. With a nod of her head, she admitted the writer into her world.

"Déjà vu," he mumbled. "It's pitch black in here. Are there any cheeky grannies hiding just out of sight?"

Laughing lightly, Anita set about lighting her few candles.

"Seriously, though, where's the light switch?"

"No electricity here, Was. Not that lucky." She pressed her lips, turning her back to him.

"Very ..." he searched for a word, long seconds passing as he surveyed the small, private space that flickered in the low light. "Mystical."

"How was that one adjective so hard to find?" she laughed. "You word good, writer."

"Only on paper, remember?"

Anita could practically hear his grin as she spun to face him, her ankle slipping painfully sideways.

Sam's long arms gripped her, steadying. "Whoa, Witch! You okay?"

Anita looked up into those dark, deliciously chocolate eyes, so full of concern.

"What's wrong, Anita?"

At the sound of her name on his lips, her traitorous hands dashed to his waist and she sunk herself against his abdomen. The hug was awkward at first, her sobs shaking her body against his. Slowly, Sam's frozen stance began to soften and his arms curved around her shoulders. One hand smoothed her hair as she soaked his t-shirt. She knew this shirt. She'd folded it only a day before, unable to stop herself from tidying his bombsite of an apartment. Sam's fresh laundry smell filled her senses, calming, as soft light mellowed the scene.

"Anita, what's wrong? Tell me, please." The pain in his voice echoed the pain in her ankle.

I twisted my ankle.

No. That wasn't accurate. She would not assume responsibility or culpability. And she couldn't lie. Not to Sam. She would deliver what she'd promised – her own brand of brutal honesty.

My brother twisted my ankle ... Go on, say it!

"My ankle ... is twisted," she said finally. *You big chicken.* At least it was true.

"Left or right?"

"Right."

Sam motioned for Anita to sit on the small single bed, and her stomach started its strange flip flop. His hands swept down the length of her, resting on the hem of her skirt. Anita sniffled, wiping her eyes. Unsettling emotions fluttered like butterflies at his care and compassion. She watched him, noting that the ugly wet blotches she'd left on his shirt didn't seem entirely out of place among the bleached stain-remover stains.

"May I?" Sam was on one knee, her right leg resting upon his raised thigh. She nodded. Flicking up her skirt, the swollen, bruised ankle was exposed.

"Not exactly worthy of a three-page description, is it, Mister

Foot Fetish?"

He grinned up at her, eyebrows rising high behind his glasses. "I don't know, I think a decent painter should be able to work on any canvas."

"Are you calling my ankle a work of art, Sammie Hart?"

He laughed quietly, and the lines of worry etched across her face faded. "It should be okay in a day or two, with rice."

"RICE?" Embarrassingly, her stomach rolled, turning noisy somersaults as his cool hands assessed her injury.

"Rest. Ice. Compression. Elevation. RICE." He shrugged, eyes back on her ankle. "Reece is a doctor, remember? He bangs on with medical acronyms all the time."

"Oh." She felt herself blush, glad that the dim, flickering candlelight would hide her discomfort. *Bang on ...* She tried not to picture the variety of meanings those words held, feeling immature and more than a little flushed. Her rapid pulse echoed in her ankle, a painful, heavy throbbing that the writer's attentions were affecting. *Stop it. He's not available. Not to you. Doctor Reece—*

"Lie down."

"Pardon?" *Focus, Anita.*

Sam's dark eyes met hers. "Lie down."

With a deep breath, she did as instructed, feeling Sam's large hands wrapping around her ankle. At first it hurt, the combination of his gentle squeeze and his unusually cold hands sending pulsing waves of pain through her. After a while, however, his cold compression seeped through the hot skin of her injury.

"Your icy hands are heaven, dirt perve." She moaned lightly

to the ceiling as his hands worked their magic. After a few moments, Sam's hands stilled and she caught him peering around her small quarters. "Please, Was," she whispered, snagging his attention, "don't stop."

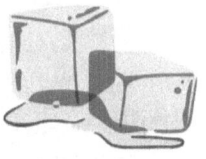

Truth or Dare

SAM

THE INTERIOR OF THE witch's vardo was surprising. Clean. Orderly. Bare, like nobody actually lived here, unlike his cluttered flat. And it was shockingly small, consisting of a single built-in bed, a small desk, and a chest of drawers with an assortment of colourful nick-nacks upon it. A few gemstones, flowers, candles, and one of those fancy Arthurian grail-like chalices brought Anita's personality to less than one square metre of space.

Pity filled him as his eyes continued to explore her trailer.

No wonder she doesn't want to spend time here. I might not have much, but I have more than this. And I have Reece. Who did she have? Sam thought about calling the good doctor, but decided against it. A twisted ankle was nothing Sam couldn't handle himself. And as much as he knew Anita would love to see Reece, Doctor Dickhead was attending another Starlight

Foundation event. Those people weren't letting him off their hook. Finding the right help in a small town was hard, and once they had their claws in you ... Sam felt more sorry for Reece than Anita right now.

Bringing his focus back to the task, he wrapped his hands around her swollen ankle. The heat of it pulsed through his palms. "Please," she breathed. "Don't stop." Sam's eyes snapped back to her face, and shame at being caught snooping rushed through him. As though reading his mind, she sighed. "I know, I know. For all this noise on the outside –" her small, delicate hand motioned to herself: wild dark hair, heavy eyes, flowing skirts, a hodge-podge of colours and textures, "– I really need my *interior* life to be calm."

'Calm' wasn't the adjective he'd choose.

"I like structure. Order. Schedules. Outlines, purposes and goals," she continued, pointing to a thick planner lying open on the small, uncluttered desk. "I like minimalism in my possessions, but not in my personality." Anita bestowed him with a grin.

"You're secretly a highly-strung control freak!" he marvelled. "The perfect critique partner and editor." The sound of her laugh hit him straight in the chest, and his hands convulsed on her skin.

"Ow! Was!" Anita sprang up to sitting, her good foot kicking into his shoulder.

"Sorry, Witch." He nodded towards the chalice. "What's that?"

"My altar." She propped herself up on her elbows and his breath seized. Her tits strained against her shirt, which had slipped to one side, revealing the fleshy curve of one shoulder. With her eyes heavy, lips full, hair a tangled mess, and smothered in the layers of her skirts, she looked decadent and delicious. She glowed under his gaze as his thumbs circled against her hot skin.

One dark eyebrow rose in the hazy, warm light. "That's where I cast my spells on mere mortals." She cackled evilly.

Sam was beginning to wonder if magic *was* at play here. The glow from the candles was certainly casting a charm about the small room. His thumbs continued turning circles, potentially possessed.

"But don't tell anyone, okay? They might drop a house on me!" She said, grinning widely.

Sam had to shake his head, clear his throat. "Tell anyone what?"

The butterflies took flight as she loosed another generous laugh. His hands slid to her calves, kneading lightly.

"That I'm a neat freak witch. Just like I won't tell anyone you're secretly a romance novelist." She winked and fell back onto the bed. A waft of lavender and vanilla floated from her sheets. Above the curve of her waist, he could just see her breasts rising and falling with each deep breath she took. Sam's hands were at her knees.

STOP! he willed them. *This is not appropriate professional contact!*

His body wasn't listening. His fingers dug into the hollows behind her knees and she moaned lightly, causing his body to react in a way he'd forgotten it could. She was doing something to him – some kind of spell. Soft, low light wrapped around them, the world growing hazy while the point of their contact grew sharp and enticing. *Rather like skillful food photography images,* Sam thought absently, her warm flesh moulding to his palms.

Sam's pants were vibrating with pleasant, rippling pulses. This spell was ... pleasant. His leg continued to buzz and tingle.

No, not a spell. The bright, artificial light of his phone screen seared through his pocket, breaking the mystical haze that clouded his mind. Fumbling, he read the illuminated screen.

Reece: `Where you at, dweeb?`

Reece: `Dropped by. Flat empty, except curiously diminishing mess(?) You hired a cleaner? Going through a purge?`

Reece: `Need to talk. TXT me.`

Anita's head popped up once more. "Reece?"

"How did you know?"

"Your face." She sighed, weary and worn. "Give me your palms." Her hands cupped to receive his.

"Why?"

"I want to read something." She slid to the edge of the bed, allowing Sam room to sit beside her. He held out his hands. Her warm touch, sudden and sure, sent tingles through his palms, shooting up into his wrists and beyond. Anita slid her thumb across Sam's palm, opening his curled hand while he watched, frozen and fascinated.

Her fingers traced the lines, barely visible in the low candlelight.

I wonder what she's searching for? He breathed the question into the rare silence between them.

"You have a conic hand," she said, like it meant something.

"With a long slender palm and fingers, a bit bent, as mentioned previously, but full of potential. Your hands are much like the rest of you." Her eyes flicked over his body and he felt the butterflies' wings beating through his abdomen. "You work for the love of it, for the creativity, not for the money."

"Preaching to the very poor choir," he mumbled, his eyes wandering around the caravan once more. He might have very little, struggle to pay his bills and desperately need the Flagpole Publishing advance for the *Heat in the Kitchen* sequel, (*reminder: email Suzannah about Flagpole's expectations of 'more explicit intimacies'*) but he was living in luxury compared to Anita. His eyes swept her skirts once more and he realised that, aside from her two sequinned circus costumes, she had few daytime clothes. She habitually wore the same flowy-style shirt with this multi-layered skirt. She wore it differently, flipping different rows of fabric to the outside to change the overall appearance of the outfit, but every day it was the same skirt. Sympathy curled deeply in his gut. *She deserves better than this poor circus life.*

One finger pushed into his hand, the combination of the pressure and her words bringing his attention back to her ministrations.

"There's loss here." Her finger trailed slowly across his skin. "And emotional hardship. But it's been strengthened by another. See here?" She pointed to a line he couldn't see.

"My gran." The words escaped. "She's the strength in my family." *She's the only one in my family.*

"I've had loss too." She showed him her own palm. "See?" Anita met Sam's eyes. "My parents. They ... died."

Holy shit, is she a mindreading witch?

"Mine too," he heard himself whisper. "Sort of. Might as well have died, anyway. They, uh, left town. Left me with a loaf of bread and half a carton of milk, and just ..." Sam shrugged, "never came back." Swallowing, he went on. "My gran ... she found me after a week or so, took me in." He'd never spoken of it before – this pain – to anyone other than Reece. He was the only one who knew the whole story.

"That's shitty." Anita sighed. "I'm sorry."

"Yeah, well, we all deal with shitty realities sometimes. Like a twisted ankle when you need to perform each night."

She winced, though from pain or the thought of performing, he didn't know.

"I love my job," she said, "but right now I'm not *in love* with the circus. I need a break, but it's hard to get. Especially when your name's on all the flyers. Everyone expects you to ..." she struggled for words for a second, before finishing, "show up. The show must go on, and all that."

A bad idea, *a very bad idea*, suddenly gripped Sam. "Let's run."

"Pardon?"

"Let's run away. Most people run away *to* the circus, yeah? Imagining some wild romanticised adventure on the road? Well, you've lived it, you need a break. Let's run *away* from the circus. Just for the weekend. Just until your ankle is healed and you can return to work."

"Sam, I can't–"

"Sure you can!" He was standing now, pacing. His voice rang loud and clear through the caravan. She shushed him once more and he dropped his voice, realising that when everyone lived in tents and caravans, the walls of privacy were thinner than filo pastry.

"You did just say your name is on the flyers. You're the boss lady! You set the rules, doesn't mean you have to follow them!" He dropped to one knee before her. "Anita Fortuna, your exquisitely swollen, purple-like-blueberries ankle ... which oddly smells of lavender and vanilla, but I won't harp on about it for a whole page ..." he chuckled. "Your ankle demands a break. You *deserve* a break. So, let's go! I'm pumped! I've smashed my writing goals recently and worded *so good*."

She giggled, the sound pure magic to his ears. *How does such a wonderful sound exist?* Sam would do anything to hear it again.

"You're a nerd," she chuckled. Swallowing hard, he struggled with the professional boundary he'd set. This gorgeous, curvaceous woman, was in his hands and in her bed, teasing and calling him names, while he proposed an escape from reality. It was purely selfish, wanting to steal her away, focus her on his words, without the distraction of her work. But in her current state ... Anita needed a break. While she was off her feet, Sam could utilise her mind.

"That's not a no!" He jumped up. "Hop on your broomstick, Witch. We're flying out of here!"

Propped on the edge of the mattress, she considered his proposal. He watched in fascination as her lips pressed together, contemplating deeply. Her sudden silence sent ripples through him. Even though they barely knew each other, he had already grown accustomed to her presence, her easy conversation and jovial condescension of his work, how she filled and replaced the quiet disorganisation of his life. He didn't want that solitude and silence anymore. Like a kid with desserts, he wanted more.

"Have you been drinking?" she asked finally.

"No, Anita. I'm clean and clear and fucking *pumped* about our adventure."

"Sam! You said *fucking*!" Anita smirked, considering. "You must be serious. That or horny."

He was glad the room was so dimly lit, hiding the intensity of his blush.

"Serious as a lion's teeth," he said. "Adequate circus metaphor?"

Anita laughed. It was beautiful. "I prefer your strange and sexy food puns," she admitted. "I *wish* we had a lion! Look, if we're going to do this then I'm the one who'll need alcohol. As a painkiller, at the very least."

Sam helped her hop off the bed, holding her steady as she winced. He slipped an arm around her waist, and Anita leaned on him for support as she slid her shoes on then puffed a few short, sharp breaths to extinguish each candle.

"I'll need to tell Claus ..." She bit her bottom lip, looking up at him, pausing at the door. "He'll cover for me."

"*You* are the boss, Anita." Sam bent his head so he could fix her with his stare. "You make the rules for your own life. Now, c'mon, let's head to the pub for that drink."

The Pope was bustling, as always. Wednesday nights meant karaoke, bringing a lively mix of wannabe pop stars and wanna-perve jocktards into Billy's bar. Sam knew some of them from school. Their antics hadn't changed over the last decade. As they did back then, so they did now, ignoring him as they passed.

Anita, to Sam's amusement, strode in with the confidence of a local. It seemed wherever she went, she made friends easily. Waving to Friday, the café owner he'd introduced her to earlier in the week, a pang of sympathy bolted through Sam. Friday sat with a grey-suited man, a scowl plastered over his usually agreeable features and a stack of paperwork between them. *Perhaps that's the lawyer?*

Reece, who had a finger firmly on the pulse of town gossip, had hinted that Friday's wife had been caught with another man, and divorce was imminent. Big news in a small community. In Moonshine, few things were sacred, but marriage lasted longer than a murder sentence, and religion meant worship with wine at church and beer at the pub. Devotion was Billy Carmichael's Sunday roast at The Pope.

Anita hobbled along beside Sam, raising her foot onto a chair as they miraculously snagged a small table.

"What's your poison, Witch?"

"Anything with eye of newt." She chuckled, the happy noise turning into a hiss as she slid her skirt away from her ankle. "I'll have a something-and-cola, please. Maybe some extra ice for my ankle?"

"Something-and-cola?" Sam laughed, eyeing the bottles lined behind the bar. "Coming right up."

Anita said something else, but her words were swallowed up as a horrible, screeching rendition of Lionel Ritchie and Diana

Ross' 'Endless Love' began.

Karaoke was a legal form of torture, Sam was certain. The couple on stage, clearly in love with each other and their drinks, sung the duet as though no one else was in the room.

The couple fell into each other's arms, giggling hysterically before stumbling back to their seats. The Pope's patrons clapped politely before rowdy male applause accompanied the next singer on stage. A pretty woman with a guitar, Sam hoped she could play.

Moonshine had only just acquired a karaoke machine, and someone who knew how to work it, so The Pope was a hive of excitement. Adding a beautiful air-guitarist to the mix would be too much for one night.

Weaving through the throng of Moonshine locals, Sam made for the bar, wondering if he was still on the Do Not Serve list.

Behind the long wooden counter, Billy was busy serving, pouring drinks, wiping up slops, loading the under-sink dishwasher with hardy glassware, all one handed. Sam almost felt sorry for him. Well, he would have, if Billy actually *let* anyone feel sympathy for him.

Billy Carmichael had that gruff, intimidating presence that terrified the pity right out of you for even *thinking* sympathetically about his perceived infirmity. Despite his grumpy manner, the man was a relatively likeable Hulk who always kept up with his crew, if not overtaking them, despite his disability.

The publican nodded to Sam, voice raised against the noise of the busy bar. "Been a while."

Billy was not, by nature, a talker. Unlike Anita, whose

constant chatter made Sam understand Van Gogh that little bit more sometimes.

Sam shrugged. "Been busy."

"Too busy to grace this honourable establishment each and every damn day?" Billy fixed him with a knowing stare, mouth quirking up behind his thick beard. "Good." Then, as though reading Sam's mind, the publican added, "It was good to see you the other day, off the drink, but you are still banned from ordering anything harder than a fizzy drink. Doctor's orders."

"Then cola it is. Two. Oh, and I need an extra glass of ice."

"Two?" Billy's beard twitched with his smile.

"I'm here with ... a friend. An acquaintance, really. Anita. The woman from the other night?" Sam tried not to blush, he really did, but his body simply wasn't listening. Luckily, Billy let him off the hook.

"Well, you had better get back to miss Anita," the giant publican-shaped tornado, pushed glass after glass towards Sam. "Before someone else tries to snatch her up." His bearded chin indicated over Sam's shoulder. Sam turned towards Anita ... and his stomach fell out his arse.

Shit.

A familiar man was curled into the breathing space of his witch. To her credit, she didn't look uncomfortable. Eyes slits, Sam hastened to her.

"Sprained ankle?" Adam James grinned wolfishly around a lollipop stick protruding from between what Sam had heard described as 'extremely kissable' lips. Closer now, Sam saw the cheeky glint in Adam's eye, the one placed there by whichever gods bestowed manly beauty and charm. Sam noticed the player's large hand, palm up on the table. Anita was reading him, shrewd eyes judging. Despite Adam's proximity, Anita wasn't touching him.

Good choice.

She'd probably catch herpes if Adam scooted any closer.

Sam slid the icy cola in front of the fortune teller, who was examining Adam with one eyebrow cocked. Adam dipped the large fingers of his other hand into a glass of ice cubes Sam placed on the chair beside her ankle. Sliding one out, Adam rolled it slowly over Anita's ankle.

"Looks like you've met Adam," Sam ground out, taking the seat beside Anita, steam billowing from his ears. Pushing up his glasses, Sam added, "He's a childhood ... *acquaintance.*"

Momentarily distracted by the new – thankfully capable – singer, Adam turned his heated gaze to the stage then back to Anita's ankle, rolling the ice cube in lazy circles across her swollen flesh. The heat of her body was melting it, fast. Tiny streams ran down her legs, licking where Adam's hands had just been. It was sensual. It was sickening. Sam wanted to puke. Or punch Adam in the face. Or both. He wasn't quite sure yet, but both urges rose swiftly within him.

"So, truth or dare?" Adam grinned, eyes flicking from Anita to Sam, then back again.

"Go away, Adam," Sam moaned. "That's so immature."

"As immature as hobbling away from the circus?" Anita countered, shooting Sam a look. "Or avoiding certain words ..."

Thankfully her voice trailed off, gobbled up by the perfectly-pitched crescendo on stage.

"So?" Adam pressed, his annoyingly smooth, tanned face

aching to be punched. He was the kind of guy that everyone wanted to be. Even in school, he'd been King Shit. Adam was a bit older than Sam, but not by much. They'd spent their long, long school years in each other's existence, but never in each other's company.

Having been a friendless dweeb for most of his school years, Sam knew about Adam mostly through town gossip, and there was an abundance of that circulating. Had been for years.

"So?" Adam asked again, popping the lollipop from his mouth, dental-ad-perfect teeth flashing. "Truth or dare?"

"Truth," Sam mumbled, at the same time as Anita grinned and said, "Dare!"

Adam ignored Sam, just like he had in school. "Oh, a *daring* girl. The best type," the calendar-perfect jock drawled, leaning over her like a lion drooling over a plump, delicious gazelle.

Adam James broke every rule Sam, as a romance writer, could ever write about love, and he was pretty sure Anita would catch chlamydia if Adam simply *glanced* in her direction for too long. His reputation consisted mainly of fast cars and even faster women, both of which he catalogued online for his mates to leer over. For years now, Adam's personal website, his 'Little Black Book' had been active, showing only a simple black screen and a number, ticking over with each conquest. Sam didn't know *why* he subscribed. Probably for the same reason people watched those epic fail injury videos on YouTube. A morbid fascination with stupidity and the universal need to grimace, perhaps. Almost every day, Adam's LBB sent a notification of an increase in the count. One more on Adam's list. Sam didn't know how the dude did it, aside from the fact that he was uncommonly, inhumanely, unfairly attractive. He'd always had his pick of women. Always seemed to get his way. But Moonshine was only a small town, and Adam James seemed to be working his way through the female population one by one. He was a big, insatiable fish in a small pond. Anita was fresh meat – and like any predator, Adam relished the hunt.

To Sam, Adam was disgusting. The kind of man others lauded as a Legend of the Cock. Sam considered him more as a walking STD. An attractive, sexual predator with the added perk of gonorrhoea. Or perhaps Adam was a thorny rose. Just a pretty thing that would inevitably prick you. Sam scratched his face self-consciously. Or maybe he was simply feeling insecure and prickly himself because he'd taken Anita's critique of his face to heart. There was no harm in trying to fix his 'too small' face with some additional hair, as she'd suggested. But shit, his chin was itchy!

"You're a performer, right?" Adam queried, his lopsided smile leaning much too close to her face. "I'm sure I saw you at the circus. I never forget a pretty face."

Anita smiled a brilliant, Cheshire Cat grin. Her eyes locked with Adam's. "I noticed you, too." Her tone was pure sex. Sam's stomach churned. "You were there with your *mother*, I believe?"

Oh, snap.

Adam smiled winningly, without so much as blinking. The ice continued to roll over her ankle, droplets of cold water running down her hot skin and pooling onto the chair. Sam begrudgingly noticed that the swelling seemed to be going down. How dare Adam hit on Anita *and* steal the doctoring duties from under Sam's very nose!

"Okay, *cirque de lovely*, you chose dare? Since you're here with him anyways –" Adam threw his thumb in Sam's direction, "– I *dare* you to pucker up and kiss this loser." The jock clapped a hand down on Sam's shoulder, in case Anita had misunderstood which 'loser' he'd been referring to.

Sam's mouth became the Sahara.

"Oh no, she doesn't have to. You don't have –" He scratched his face self-consciously, feeling the blush already colouring his cheeks. It was a hell of a night to be alcohol-free.

Anita thrust her hand into Adam's, shaking it in a businesslike manner. "Easy, Adam."

Damn, girl, sly burn! Adam *was* easy. She'd seen through his bullshit looks and charm.

She's gotta be a witch. No mere mortal could refuse Adam James' charms, and while she was playing his stupid, immature game, she was also avoiding his spell. Unlike all the other women in The Pope, whose eyes followed Adam James' every movement.

As Anita turned to face Sam, Adam winked over her shoulder. He pulled the lollipop from his mouth, blowing Sam a silent kiss before sauntering over to the pool table.

"Anita, you don't have to ..."

But her hands were on his shoulders, her lips close to his.

"We won't kiss and tell Reece, okay?" Her cola-laced breath licked his lips.

"I ... We ..."

Words failed him. Feather light, Anita pressed her lips to his. Their sweetness lingered a fraction of a second before they were gone.

"Sorry," she laughed, the sound grabbing his chest and balls simultaneously. "I should have waited ... What were you saying?" A beautiful pink bloomed in her cheeks. Grabbing an ice cube, Anita ran it over her forehead and down the sides of her neck.

Shit, if that isn't the sexiest goddamn path I've ever seen an ice cube take.

Sam opened his mouth, but she was already speaking.

"Do you think Reece will mind?"

"Um ... No?" Sam struggled to get the syllables out.

"Oh, good. I'd hate for there to be tension."

Oh, there's tension alright. Sam shifted slightly in his seat.

Another singer took the stage, and he couldn't handle this any longer. This one could sing, at least – very well, in fact – but the damage was already done. Ears bleeding, chest thumping, Anita's sweet, cola-flavoured kiss on his lips ... This night couldn't get any worse.

"Wanna get out of here?"

"Fuck, yes." She nodded, standing without support, then wincing. "Let's go to your place. There's something I need to do."

And goddamn it if the butterflies beneath his skin didn't take flight, dragging his imagination with them.

Sam tried not to be disappointed when the thing his witch 'needed to do' was some sort of protection spell involving a ziplock bag, salt water, a pen and paper. She hurriedly scrawled a name on a torn corner of his manuscript, much to his horror. Balling the paper with an intensity he hadn't imagined her capable of, she filled the bag with water and salt, shook it up and then threw it into his empty freezer. With a hex mumbled form her lips, she slammed the door. A second later, she opened it again, gawking.

"Sam, you *really* need to buy food. I thought your non-writerly dream was to go on *MasterChef*. Can't do that if you have a useless fridge!"

"I prefer fresh to frozen." He shrugged, settling down on the sofa.

"You know," she said, sliding into the other couch. "That salt water gave me an idea for your book. I have an idea for an excursion, nerd. Tomorrow."

"Speaking of my book ..." he shifted to one side, pulling his curled papers from his back pocket with a grin. "I think you'll be proud of me. No moist-dirt references in there and only one very tasteful allusion to toes."

"No bacon lips?"

The memory of Anita slipping bacon into her mouth grasped him suddenly and he moved a cushion to cover the growing, insistent bulge in his trousers.

No, he told his dick. *She's a colleague. And she wouldn't choose you anyway.* Not when she'd had the hyper-masculine Adam drooling all over her. Hell, if it was a choice between himself and Adam, Sam knew there was no competition. It was like giving a kid the choice between kale or chocolate cake – the winner was obvious. And Anita kept mentioning Reece, like she was interested in him. *Either way, there's a clear choice to the podium there, Sammie, and you wouldn't come out on top, in any case.*

Just thinking the words 'on top' sent his mind into another flurry of innuendo.

What the shit is wrong with me? He shifted uncomfortably as Anita snatched his handwritten pages with glee.

"I do love your sexy food scenes." She licked her lips and his stomach growled, though not from a lack of sustenance. "Wow, that's a big stack." *I've got a big stack right here for you, Witch.*

"I can't wait to sink my teeth into it."

Dear God, is she torturing me on purpose? I wish I could sink my teeth into–

"Sam?"

"What?"

"You've turned white. And now red. Are you okay?"

"Fine," he squeaked removing his glasses and pinching the bridge of his nose. *Thank God I'm not drunk.* Booze dissolved the filter between his brain and his mouth. A filter he very much appreciated right now. "Probably my body detoxing, you know? No more alcohol for me." He tried to laugh it off, taking a few deep breaths before standing (sans cushion) and padding into the kitchen for a tall and surprisingly clean glass of water. He wet a tea towel and wrung the excess water into the sink.

"Sam ..." her voice was barely more than a whisper. "I did my dare. But you owe me a truth." She took a breath and fixed him with a look. "You're not dying of liver damage, are you?"

Not for lack of trying ... Returning to the lounge with the damp cloth, he cleared his throat, wondering how much he could tell her. In the end, it wouldn't matter. She was only in town for another week.

"Truthfully? No. Not yet, at least." She didn't look satisfied. He patted his knee, pointing to her feet. She complied with his unspoken message, resting her still puffy ankle on his knees where he draped the wet towel over them.

"My parents were drunks," he said. She fell silent, an odd state of being for the mouthy Anita Fortuna. Whilst she was a darn good talker, she was also a great listener, he decided. "They … had an accident." He tested the words on his tongue, unused to them – words he kept pushed so far down, scribbled and smudged into dark, unrecognisable shapes. "I'm not good at talking about it, but I know I don't want to be like them." Sam felt his lip curl. "End of story."

For once, the woman had nothing to say. Daylight had started to creep in around the edges of the curtains, striping the floor with light. Anita leaned into him, her hair brushing his chin and nose. Her arms slipped around his waist and she held him tightly, as she had in her vardo.

"That is a heavy truth," she said eventually. "I know about those."

She let silence settle around them, tears rolling down her cheeks. He didn't ask her to stop. Didn't tell her it was okay. They breathed, alone with their thoughts but together in their sadness. Sam reached for her hand, holding it tightly, anchoring himself here and now. The soft patter of early morning rain filled the air with gentle white noise as Sam's thumb circled the back of her hand.

"I think that's why I like writing happy endings," he said, a few heavy heartbeats later. "I get to create all the ways life could've been different, how I could have been happy. Writing it down makes it come into the world, even for a moment, it's almost ... real."

She sniffed. "You write beautiful realities, Sam."

He pulled back, tipping her chin upwards with one crooked finger. Slowly, she lifted her face to his and he cupped her soft cheek.

"I think that's why you like romances." He smiled down at her. "It's not about the magic for you, Witch, or the occasional makeover montage or sudden musical number with singing in the streets. It's the *feeling*. It's about losing yourself in a story that's more hopeful than yours, where a Happily-Ever-After is guaranteed. It's about hope."

Anita pressed her lips together, burying her face in his shirt once more.

"I'm not asking you to tell me your truth, Anita. But ..." he said, his fingers finding the small, curved line of bruises on her arm, thinking his way down to her ankle. "I want you to know that if you want to talk about it, I'll listen. You've helped me so, *so* much, this past week and a half. It's the least I could do to help you in return."

BZZZZZZZ BZZZZZZ. A pleasant vibration in his pants woke Sam a few hours later.

Reece: **Dude, I'm at work but we NEED to talk.**

Reece: **I just saw Adam James. He said you**

were at The Pope with a hot chic?

Reece: Is Anita the hot chic? Is she okay?
Adam mentioned a swollen ankle?

Reece: I'm going to call Billy to
confirm.

Reece: CALL ME, DWEEB!

Sam rolled off the sofa, carefully manoeuvring the lightly snoring hippy who had fallen asleep with her head in his lap. How he had managed to sleep with Anita's warm curves pressed into him, he would never know. Rubbing his eyes, Sam slipped on his glasses, scrolling through the stream of texts Reece had sent in quick succession. He couldn't talk to Reece about this. He'd steal her away, or she would fall on that ankle straight into the doctor's arms and swoon. He'd seen it before. It wasn't Reece's fault. He was a Mr Darcy – tall, dark, handsome and brooding – a woman-slaying combination Sam could only ever dream of. The way Anita kept bringing Reece up in conversation twisted a knife in his gut. In fact, it was a similar pain to his IBS. *Reece, old pal, you mean as much as lactose to me right now.*

Minimising the chat, he noticed the number of unread email notifications. Groaning, he tapped to open the most recent communication.

From: Suzannah.editor@flagpolepublishing.com
To: Samuelharthrup@hotmail.com;
Sammiehartromance@flagpolewriters.net
CC: editor.in.chief@flagpolepublishing.com

Subject: Heat in the Kitchen Sequel

Hello Sam,
The sample you provided filled us with confidence in your progress to date. We realise the meet cute is not the place for the intimacies requested of the sequel, but we remind you that the manuscript, in its entirety, is due by the end of November and there must be (as per reader and editorial expectations, as well as contractual obligations) increased physical intimacies between the pages.
We look forward to reading your next sample soon.
Sincerely,
Suzannah Browne
Editorial Director, *Flagpole Publishing*

With sigh and a sidelong look at Anita, Sam opened his journal.

Dear Diary ... Shit, shit, SHIT!!!

Driving Me Crazy

ANITA

IGNORING THE PANG IN her ankle, Anita slid into Sam's car, tossing *Heat in the Kitchen* into his lap. He flinched, his body curling around the novel. He looked different today, in a crinkled blue shirt and brightly coloured floral board shorts. She wished she could go scour her limited trunk of clothing for something appropriate, but returning to the circus was a dangerous idea. So instead, she had recycled her skirt (as usual) and borrowed one of Sam's shirts. It was a white button-down that was surprisingly flattering, with her skirt flipped and layered shorter, a light blue fabric rippling around the outside. The skirt had several layers of fabric, in various colours and lengths, for a slightly different look each day. Adrian refused to buy her more clothes, saying there was 'nothing in her size' and that she would 'just grow out of it anyway', so the wrap of fabric it was. She tugged at the tie absentmindedly.

"How's your ankle?" Sam queried, eyes glued to the highway as he drove out of town.

Anita flexed her foot. "Good. I think the elevation and your icicle hands really did the trick. Why are your hands so cold, anyway? Circulation problems? Sorry, that's probably a bit personal. What I meant to say was, thanks doc. You were a *major* help." She saluted, leaning forward to set their destination into the GPS.

Today is a good day, she affirmed. *Today will be a* great *day. My name is on the flyers. I am the boss lady.* Her inner voice faltered as her brain circled back to Adrian. Swivelling in her seat to face Sam, Anita started talking, deciding that verbal diarrhoea would help quash the round-robin of her mental dialogue.

"What's with you and old technology?" She slowly flicked through the collection of CDs stuffed into the console and glove box. "First the romcom VHS under the bed, and now compact discs? Even I've heard of streaming music, Was." She rolled the window down and let the sweet spring breeze sprint through her hair. As easily as she'd thrown down the argument, Sam picked it up. Focused on the road, side mirrors, passing vehicles and signage, he continued to argue the merits of each CD, artist, and the dying talent that was cover artistry.

Moonshine was rapidly shrinking behind Sam's car. The greater the distance between Anita and Cirque de Fortuna, the more at ease she felt, to the point where the pain in her ankle nearly vanished. If she believed in such things, she would probably call it a miracle. More likely it was a psychosomatic stress pain in her lower limb. Adrian was probably right – she was weak.

"The trip will take about two hours." Sam nodded to the GPS then to the headset. "No show tunes."

"You have show tunes? I *adore* show tunes. I do work at a show, you realise, so–"

"You won't find any circus sideshow freak soundtracks in there," he interrupted.

"'Circus sideshow freak?' *Excuse me?*" Her voice rose, though a smile tugged at her lips. "I'll have you know, Sammie Hart, you moist-dirt-eyed, foot fetishy nerd–"

They argued for the next hour and thirteen minutes about the merits of a soundtrack to life, what their grand entrance songs might be (if they lived in a film-esque world where everyone had their own theme song), and which lucky CD would be chosen as the backing track for their trip. She pointed out numerous times that his reliance on old-fashioned technology was hindering the enjoyment of their ride. Sam argued that 'old faithful' also meant 'reliable and cheap', and that physical products were more valuable than paying for 'air' (streaming music or TV), especially when one was a 'struggling artist'.

In the end, their trip hadn't required any more soundtrack than their banter, the easy flow of conversation and the breeze whooshing Sam's car as they drove.

"So *that's* why you have a secret stash of films in black tubs under your bed." She grinned at him. "You refuse to stream, so you need the old VHS player!"

He glared at her, colour rising in his cheeks. "You drive me crazy, Witch," he mumbled, white knuckles clenching the steering wheel.

"Ditto, Was. Ditto." Her heart thudded heavier in her chest, and a familiar rolling in her stomach began.

"What's the project today, anyway?" he asked. "How to endure lectures and live through the compulsive talking of a holidaying hippy?"

Holiday. Huh! Anita didn't mind the change in subject. She absorbed herself in the plan and the day, not in what was left behind (or waiting for her return) at the circus.

"Well, I was pondering two things. One, your bio. You said you enjoyed 'long walks on the beach,' but have you ever even taken a long walk on the beach?" She didn't wait for his answer. There was no need. The pallid skin of the man clearly indicated he was more of a domesticated animal. Waiting for him to respond would only allow thoughts of Adrian to slice back through her head. She ploughed on. "Judging by your complete lack of tan, I'm guessing you've never even seen the sun, you vampire." She peered at him closely.

"What?" he said, defensively.

She grinned. "Just checking to see if you sparkle."

"Hey!" Sam protested through a smile, scratching his chin. "Team Jacob, all the way!"

Anita laughed, watching Sam's chest puff in pride. *Of course, he would know I was referencing* Twilight*!*

"Also, while we're on that topic, what makes a long walk on the beach terribly romantic, Mister Romance Writer?"

His mouth opened then closed. It took a few beats for him to concoct a response. "It's ... long?" His shoulders quickly brushed his ears.

Anita's eyes rolled so far back she could practically see the grey matter in her skull. "Oh, my Horned God, you are *such* a man! *Long* –" she mocked his tone. "Not everything has to be a masculine term for what you see. Remember your first project at the circus?" Just saying the word made her stomach curl, so she hurried on. "This needs to be about what you *feel*, too. Can you feel long?"

"This *conversation* feels long," Sam mumbled.

Anita ignored him. "What can you *feel* that will make the act of walking barefoot on microscopic rock shards ... calves hurting because, well, you said a *long* walk on the beach, so that means a buttload of exercise ... while the most raw, elemental weather is beating you up? What makes *that* ... long-winded, I admit ... scenario romantic? Just thinking about it makes my muscles scream from all that resistance exercise."

Eyes on the road, he shrugged off her question about romance. "Do you realise just how many embedded clauses you create when you ramble? I mean, honestly, woman, your long-winded speeches are like fresh pizza dough being kneaded then stretched, back and forth, back and forth ..."

"And the second thing," she continued, completely ignoring his foodish metaphor. He sighed, gripping the wheel tightly once more. "I've been pondering the phrase, 'falling in love'. You've used that phrasing repeatedly in your current draft. Honestly, if I had a dollar for every time ..."

Sam shot her a pitiful look.

"Anyway, just think about those words. Falling. Verb. Who trips and *falls* and finds themselves in love? It's such a weird saying. Like those people who 'tripped and fell' and suddenly they're pregnant?" Her fingers curled with air quotes. "Nuh uh.

Doesn't work that way. It's not like Alice down the rabbit hole. There is no *falling* into Prince Charming, or onto his penis for impregnation ... Though that would certainly spice up the fairy tales ..." She blinked an image of a chainmail condom from her mind, pushing on. "Every little girl needs her knight in shining armour, you know."

"The point is?" Sam prompted, clearly wondering what any of this had to do with him and his book.

"I was reading about how love feels. The dopamine, adrenaline, all that. Do you know that scientists can replicate it? Love isn't any more than a hormonal response to external stimuli, and it can be manufactured. It's a high. A spike in certain chemicals in your body. That's all love is. No 'falling' about it."

He was interested now, considering her with brief side-eye glances. "What does this have to do with today's project?"

"Getting there."

Sam sighed as Anita giggled, aware her mouth had run away with her again.

"As I was saying. That feeling can be manufactured. Even the circus folk manipulate that 'high' to mess with the townies and sneakily get a couple together."

"How so?" He was genuinely intrigued now. His body shifted in the driver's seat; he inclined his head interestedly, one eye always on the road.

I wonder if he's so road conscious because of the accident he mentioned, involving his parents?

"A carefully timed nip from Leo, our favourite unicorn," Anita reminded him, "sends skittish people jumping into their lover's arms. Or a sad, single person joins the Ferris wheel queue only to find themselves suddenly sitting next to another single someone when the ride starts. Then, oh no! The wheel halts at the top! It's stuck!" The backside of Anita's hand flew to her hairline.

"You're so dramatic," he laughed.

Ignoring him, Anita thumped her hand against her chest, mimicking a heartbeat, the heavy thump increasing in tempo as she continued.

"Worry sets in. Breath shortens. Heart pounds. Adrenaline releases." Anita beat her hand hard against her body. "Is this fate? A meet-cute? Love at first sight? No." The loud, crashing beat ceased. "It's manufactured attraction. A sudden injection of panic-laced adrenaline, shared between two individuals. It's science." Anita shrugged. "So today, we're going to examine how all that feels in the body. But instead of falling, we're jumping."

"I don't think I like the sound of this ..." Sam inhaled deeply, his knuckles growing whiter on the steering wheel. "You talk about science and the circus, my manuscript and its failings, but have you ever actually fallen in love?"

Anita's stomach clenched, a heaviness settling in her chest. "I'm not sure 'falling' is the right verb." She considered. "I *thought* I'd been in love," she admitted quietly, a rosy blush warming her high, rounded cheekbones. "But with the benefit of hindsight, and a lack of comparison, maybe I was wrong."

She stopped to consider some more. It was too easy to talk to Sammie, *Samuel* Harthrup. How much could, or should, you tell someone you'd known for only a week or so? Anita had never considered herself a closed book, but just how open should she be with her pages? She let out a shaky breath, turning her attention beyond the window. The beautiful, increasingly lush coastal landscape slid by.

"I've never experienced that spine-numbing, weak-at-the - k n e e s , butterflies-beating-so-fast-in-your-stomach-that-you're -going-to-puke-and-spends-a-whole-page-accidentally-outlining-the-smell-of-their-soapy, square-feet kind of love." She smirked at his silence, unable to bear it for long. "What about you, Was?"

"Honestly, Anita ..."

He'd done it. Said her damn name. And the spell struck. Her hand reached out, connecting them. Her arm draped coolly over the back of the head rests, and her small, pink-nailed fingers lightly pressed into his shoulder. *How does it do that without me even knowing?* Her hand was no longer her own, and she pondered a new phrase now. A phrase involving idle hands being the devil's playground. Maybe Adrian was right. *Maybe I am overweight, idle, unlovable ...*

Sam's grip on the wheel tightened. She needed him to speak. To distract. Fast. Her body might have been betraying her, but it had nothing on the traitorous voice of her brother, creeping into her mind, trying to derail and destroy every affirmation she'd ever said to her reflection.

"Go on," she said, encouraged, squeezing Sam's shoulder.

"Honestly?"

Anita watched him consider how much to reveal in return. "I've fallen more in lust than in love," Sam admitted, shaking his head slightly. Anita noticed his glasses were smudged and fogging slightly. Without a word, she slipped them off his face, clearing the haze in her layers of skirts, before sliding them back with a smile.

"Thanks." His eyes never left the road, and Anita wondered about his desire to claim the trophy as the world's safest driver.

"So, lust?" She dragged him back on track, sitting on her hands to teach them a lesson in restraint.

"It was a relationship of convenience," Sam said. "I was a warm bed and a place to stay when the world came crashing down around us. I was young, naive. I had zero experience and she took advantage of my ..." he gulped, the glasses fogging again. "Loneliness, I suppose it was. My longing for human connection. But when it came down to the wire, our relationship wasn't any more than that. I prioritised my craft over my cock."

Anita couldn't help but gasp, proud of his frankness. "And she had no reason to stick around," Sam continued. "I didn't give her a reason. She said some pretty horrible things. Things my parents used to say. Things that broke me down. Made me feel shit. Worthless. Anita, it was fucking–"

Somehow her hands had escaped. Patting Sam's shoulder with a grin, she encouraged his colourful language.

"*Shit*," he finished lamely. "Then she was gone, TikTok blew up over my book, and Flagpole started demanding a sequel. I freaked out. I started doubting if I knew anything about romance or relationships or how two bodies react to each other. And I hit a deep funk."

"And then you fell duck over water into me." Anita grinned,

squeezing his shoulder.

"Uh, yeah ... Sorry about that, again. The drinking ... I'm working on it."

A neatly painted sign flew past. It read *Welcome to Warner's Bay: Home of The Giant Peach*. Excitement bubbled, curling in her stomach.

"Ooh, we'll have to go there." Anita pushed her hair over her shoulder, imagining the sweet stone fruit filling her mouth. "I love peaches!"

She could have sworn she heard Sam mutter, "I bet."

Sam followed the GPS over a huge white bridge, where children sprung from the sides and into the foamy wash of boats, despite the No Swimming and No Jumping signs. Beautifully clear blue water swelled under them, the hint of a yellow beach on one side, and a large open lake littered with small boats and kayaks on the other.

A winding road led them through a small coastal town that boasted more fish and chip shops than patrons. Anita pointed out an ice-creamery, making Sam promise to stop there for choc chip before they left.

"I doubt they'll have anything lactose free," he grumbled.

"Too bad." Anita grinned. "For you."

"And *you*." He looked pointedly at her, allowing her rare in-car eye contact. Sam was such a careful driver, his attention rarely leaving the road.

We're getting somewhere. She smiled. His walls were slowly coming down.

"Turn left at the next roundabout," the robotic GPS voice instructed. Sam clicked on his indicator.

Warner's Bay township was bordered by the thick bitou bush that invaded all coastlines. The air sharpened and cooled, the thicker tang of salt indicating they were close.

"There." Anita pointed to a gap carved out of the coastal jungle. A small square, barely big enough for one car, probably to discourage camping, Anita assumed, had been cleared beside the tell-tale log-and-wire fencing of the sandy beach access. Sam parked and leapt out, throwing his glasses onto the dash. Anita's heart swelled as he rounded the car to assist her from the vehicle. She felt like a princess waiting for the door of her pumpkin carriage to be opened.

"Really, my ankle is fine." She swatted him away. "Wait, come here for a sec?"

Sam dutifully stepped forward again and Anita leaned on him for support as she slipped her shoes off, tossing them to the sandy grass beside the car wheel. She caught him staring at her bare feet, her toes curling into the cool earth.

"Hey, foot fetish. My eyes are up here." She pointed to her face, grinning as his cheeks reddened. Grabbing their towels, they headed for the sandy trail. The air thickened and warmed among the greenery, opening out to a wide, flat expanse of fine yellow sand.

"Tip! You're it!" she yelled, poking his surprisingly firm stomach.

"What are you, *five*?" she heard him say, already chasing her as she started a hobbled run towards the ocean. Sam's long legs could have easily caught up to her, but he was a gracious gentleman, allowing her to dodge and slip through his grasp as they wove their way closer to the sea.

Suddenly, she stopped dead, her toes inches from the water that reached out.

"Bluebottles!" she cried, too late. Sam crashed into her back, catapulting Anita forwards. With an indelicate splash, she tasted salt.

"Shit, sorry!" Sam plunged his arms into the water, scooping Anita up. Spluttering, she gripped him for stability. As she gasped for air, her fingers dug into his bony shoulders. His cool flesh pressed through her heated fingertips, and a deep, throbbing pulse rippled through her. Anita closed her eyes, breathing deeply, focusing on each fingertip, where their bodies met. Repeated apologies filled her ears as he brushed wet tangled strands of hair from her face.

She smiled. "So," she said, spluttering and gulping, her hands sliding from him. "No more silly business." She coughed again, the sting of the fresh saltwater filling her sinuses. "*Feeling*. Today's homework. Listen to your body and its chemical reactions as we jump."

His voice squeaked. "Jump? Really?"

She crossed her arms, looking up to meet his eyes. "You'll see. Trust me. So, let's establish a base line. What do you feel? Close your eyes and listen to your body and what's around you, like at the circus."

Sam mumbled some more, eventually exhaling slowly and closing his eyes.

Sam looks a lot less owlish without his spectacles ... and when his eyes are closed. She smiled to herself, watching him scratch the growing stubble on his chin. The man sure was open to her feedback.

"I can feel ..." he started, face screwing up in concentration, "the wind on my face," he said finally.

"Good, but what else?"

"The thundering crash of the waves. It's shaking my legs. I feel ... unsteady. Unsure. Wondering if I can trust you to tell me that I'll be knocked off my feet by some giant incoming wave."

"Nice, now you're getting the hang of it." One of his eyes cracked open. He pinched the bridge of his nose, an indication of stress she was now very familiar with.

"How does my body feeling translate into the emotions and the –" he gulped, "'*increasingly intimate scenes*' that Flagpole wants from me, Anita?" He'd spoken the magic word. When he said her name, his lips cast a (thus far) unshakable spell that made her hands seek him. Beneath her palm, his heart beat hard and sure, his breathing deep and steady as she, too, sucked in lungfuls of the salty, fresh air.

"How are feelings and emotions linked?" She laughed in his face, head-butting his chest. "I think I've been giving you *way* too much credit, Sammie Hart."

He opened both eyes and sighed, his eyes dropping to hers, pleading.

"How about this," she suggested, slipping her hand into his. "What do you feel?" He looked down at their clash of tans. "Describe this," she said, raising their clasped hands between them.

"It feels ..." He struggled for the words. "Warm and ... familiar. Like ... two halves coming together?" he suggested, his voice raising high at the end, like a schoolboy about to earn detention for an incorrect answer.

"Wow. That's a huge question mark at the end of that sentence. Maybe leave that bit out of your book," she teased. "But the rest of it was actually kind of sweet. Now, let's go."

"Anita ..."

Her fingers laced through his as she dragged him along the shore.

Lost in thoughts that seemed as deep as the ocean, Sam listened as Anita chatted on about one thing or another.

"How long is a 'long walk'?" Sam grumbled a few moments later.

Anita lifted her shoulders to her ears. "I'm not sure, Was. It was *your* bio."

He was so quiet, strolling along the sandy shore of the gorgeous Warner's Bay. She didn't like it. Quiet led to distraction and overthinking – and not just for Sam. Her own mind began wandering. Has he been here before? Did his family holiday here when he was young? She would've given anything to have had seaside family holidays as a child. A pang struck her heart as she remembered Sam's explanation of his parents. They didn't sound like the kind of people who would play happy families, making sandcastles and applying sunscreen to rosy cheeks with tender care. Then again, her own family wasn't exactly normal. She mentally rapped her knuckles for judging.

I am kind. I am understanding. I am ...

Sam was saying something.

"Pardon, Was?"

He splashed her with a swoop of his foot through the water. "I said, is it over yet? Not that it matters, I'm changing that author bio." They kept walking, bare feet kissing footprints into the transient sediments of the earth. She wasn't sure how long they'd been walking, but eventually their destination jutted into sight. Anita tried to get his attention, but Sam kept on walking, head down, thinking, his hand cool and large, and curled around her own. His lovely, lined palm pressed against hers. Anita skimmed her foot through the foamy shallows, flicking droplets and sand to the giant beside her. They barely splashed Sam's knees. He didn't notice.

He's so often absorbed in his own world, she mused. It must be nice to be in that brain, to have someone want what he had to offer.

Moonshine, Flagpole Publishing and Doctor Reece Hargraves were lucky to have him. And it felt kind of safe, knowing Sam saw her in a strictly professional light. Hell, he'd made that clear enough, several times. *He's completely uninterested and off-limits ... so why can't I stop flirting with him?* Holding hands made keeping a professional distance unusually difficult. Looking down, she saw their fingers entwined, amazed as she squeezed his hand and he squeezed back. Was he unconscious of that reflex?

Sam stared straight ahead, up the beach, his face blank as though he was counting each step carefully. She hoped he was focused on feeling, and maybe cooking up some more deliciously sexy food puns for his *Heat in the Kitchen* sequel.

Slipping her hand from his, Anita bent down in a bow to the ocean, scooping water in her hands before showering his shoulders, shocking him back to reality.

"Hey!" Sam grinned, already bending to splash her back.

"Now I have your attention," she called, squealing away from the water as it flew through the air. "We're here."

"Where?"

Anita pointed up.

"Oh, shit."

They climbed up onto the steep, rocky platform that rose like a wall from the end of the beach. The rocks ran fearlessly into the water at the base, a long lip protruding high like a diver's platform, the perfect drop zone to the deeper water beyond.

"Look!" Anita pointed to the other side of the platform. A small lagoon (with impossibly deep, impossibly blue water) rippled with waves. The wind whipped greedily at their flesh, tossing Anita's dark hair back and forth. Tiny goosebumps had erupted across Sam's arms.

"You ready for this?" Anita grinned at the tall, pale man beside her. He shivered, crossing his arms low on his stomach, as though he were about to barf, mumbling something about popcorn and red soda.

Her stomach flipped. "Pardon?"

"Nothing." Sam sighed, his eyebrows curved in concern beneath his floppy blond hair. He looked away as she untied the knot of her wrap skirt. The layers of fabric fell in a puddle to the rock shelf. She felt, more than saw, his intense blush. The heat of his gaze darted from the cliff to her bare legs.

Anita had always liked her legs. While her face and arms were often darker from days spent labouring outdoors for Cirque de Fortuna, her thighs were a softer tone. Curvy and smooth, the wide expanse of skin was a lovely shade of caramel, reflecting her Eastern European heritage. She was grateful for Sam's shirt, though. Tied in a knot at her waist, it covered her top half, a more motley collage of blacks, blues and the occasional yellowing patch. Tugging the shirt down to cover the triangle of skin between her belly button and the elastic slung around her hips, she scoffed.

"They're just undies, Sam, you prude. And this *is* the beach."

Sam's eyes roamed slowly down her body, before inching back up. She felt like she was suddenly naked on stage, a spotlight revealing every curve and dimple and stretch mark, every freckle, every bruise and scar.

I am beautiful. I am strong. I am brave as fuck. None of this self-conscious bull, Anita. Fuck that. You are a lady boss! And she needed to remind herself of that a lot more often.

Throwing her arms out wide, she tossed her worries into the wind, calling "Kooeee!"

The rocks echoed her greeting before the sea gobbled it up. Turning to Sam, she motioned around them. "This is jump rock! I came here a year or so ago, with some locals, when we were in town. This, Sammie Hart, is where you feel the manufactured biological responses your struggling novel requires."

He nodded grimly, mouth set in a tight line as he shivered, reluctantly sliding his shirt over his head. "Right. Let's get on with it."

Anita paused. *Woah.* She hadn't seen that much male flesh in a long, *long* time. There wasn't a spare ounce of fat on him anywhere, and he was firm, but not excessively muscular. It was the kind of body that came easily to tall young men. He didn't have to work for it, being naturally lean and long lined – a sign of the genetically blessed.

They were both natural and raw, shyly shedding clothing while the other tried not to be caught looking. The wind changed direction and his fresh soapy, laundry-like smell filled her nostrils.

Reece was to thank for that smell. She had seen the doctor's note in Sam's laundry room, stuck to brown paper shopping bags (just as crisp as the doctor himself). 'Use me,' with a winky face emoji and then, 'Doctor's orders'. She had tried not to spy, really she had. But for some reason, everything to do with the strange romance writer intrigued her no end. Finding the new laundry detergent, deodorant and soap, one man's gift to another, had forced a sad little smile. Anita let her eyes travel over Sam, pondering, seeing, appreciating. He was so lucky in his life to have someone who cared.

"What?" Sam demanded, crossing his arms across his lightly haired chest. Goosebumps erupted across his skin and his teeth set in a grim line.

She grinned. "You've been keeping something from me! You have a tattoo!" Anita's feet, like her hands, were traitors. Before she knew it, she had closed the distance between them. Her face inches from his chest, her breasts touched his torso as she scrutinised the little red heart amidst his curly chest hairs.

"That is both adorable and tragic," she told him, giving his ribs a tickle before straightening to take his hand, pulling him closer to the rocky ledge.

"Anita ..." Sam said, his voice shaky, pulling her back. "Anita, stop!" His hand, pressed against hers, felt clammy and like ice, all at once. A cold sweat? Or maybe it was the sea spray? The strangest combination of words spewed from his mouth. "Shit! *Star Wars*. Breanna ... *Shit*!" He tugged her back.

"And you, a writer!" she scoffed. "If this is poetry, it's a bit ... abstract."

"I already told you," Sam gritted out. "I only word good on paper. Verbally, I'm–" Sam's throat bobbed. "Do you think goats s ... sweat?"

What? Where had that come from? Her laugh caught in the wind, whipping around them, swallowing his gasp as they reached the edge. Sam's hands darted out, pulling her back as though to protect her from falling.

White Knight. She smiled. *I'm no damsel needing rescuing.* His eyes locked on her, huge, despite the lack of spectacles. *I am a boss! THE boss!*

"We do this together, okay?" Her toes curled over the stony edge of the cliff. "*Feel*. Fall."

"W ... w ... what?" His teeth chattered, face pale and sea spray slick.

"Hakuna matata, Was! JUMP!" she cried, launching from the cliff. Her grip tightened and the sudden tug of her body was sufficient to tug him down after her.

Sam's scream echoed off the rocks, ceasing only as his feet plunged through water.

"WIIIIIIIITCH!"

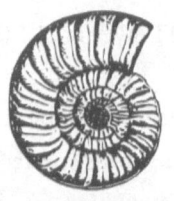

Jump Rock

SAM

SHIT, SHIT, SHIT, SHIT, FUUUUUUUUUUCK!

The witch hit the water first, the rise of her splash meeting Sam's body before the ocean swallowed him. Heart pounding in his ears, he pushed his arms down, propelling towards the water's surface, the anxiety washing away as he broke into the air, gulping. A laugh escaped. *Where did that come from?*

Anita's dark, wet head bobbed just out of arm's reach. She whooped and hollered, clapping her jewellery-covered hands together, a strange kind of siren.

Bloody witch. This would be on Sam's 'Worst Moments of My Life' highlight reel for sure.

His internal monologue circled as he surfaced, small waves rocking his body and pushing him closer to the small sandy strip of the 'Jump Rock' lagoon.

Anita ducked below an incoming wave, surfacing like a

mermaid in slow motion, all smooth curves and fluid motions. Her hair rested in long tendrils over her shoulders, and Sam tried not to follow the lines of the dark tresses to her chest, heaving just beneath the surface. *Damn, she is stunning...* He sucked in a breath, too fast. Too close to the crest of a wave. The salt burned into his lungs. He spluttered, feeling like he'd just French-kissed the world's hottest chilli.

"What?" he asked as she trod water, grinning.

"See? That was easy!" She swam up with broad, powerful strokes.

"Anita, that was –" Her hands slid over his bare shoulders, and he became acutely aware of her feet, kicking in tiny flicks through the water. It sent fluttering waves and tingles through his shins, shooting upward to a more basal pulse beating deep within him. "Exhilarating," he finished. "Scary as shit, but good."

They were breathing hard, grinning at each other as their inhales and exhales aligned in rapid, ragged beats. Her hair, dark and shiny as silk, drew his eyes down. He smoothed a wayward lock back, feeling her shudder through his heated fingertips. She was a blur of hair and boobs before his watery eyes; a smooth, warm wetness in his hands as the waves gently rocked them back and forth in a slow, rhythmic dance.

Suddenly, the warmth shifted, and Anita was in his arms, pressing herself against his bare skin. "Get it off, Was!"

Sam's body stiffened, and he tried to ignore the tug in his shorts, kicking with additional vigour to keep them both afloat.

"What?"

"Get. It. Off!" she squealed, her arms tight around his neck.

"The seaweed, Was, the seaweed!" Her feet were striking at the ocean, at a slimy blob of green sliding past his leg. "It's tangled around me!" Thrashing, Anita nearly dragged him under, climbing him like a tree as the waves rolled around their ears. "Quick! Oh, Neptune below! It's *so gross*. Ew, ew, ew!" Her grip, so warm and tight, welded itself onto him.

Sam laughed, gulping for air and barely scraping the sand as he navigated their way into the shallows at the cliff's base.

Anita pushed off Sam, throwing herself into the water, kicking wildly. Smooth legs flew into the air and a squid-like tangle of seaweed fell on her head with a *splat*.

An explosion of laughter erupted from Sam, a sonic boom that echoed off the rocks and bounced into the surf.

"Get it off. Get it off!" she squealed, sitting chest deep in the water, two fingers picked at the green muck.

Sam laughed. "The way you're carrying on, you'd think it was a spider, not seaweed." He splashed her playfully, watching as she flailed in the surf.

"Seaweed is only good in sushi," Anita protested seriously, a wave catching her off guard to thrust her head under the water. She was a bedraggled, half-drowned mess, *and damn, she looks good that way.*

Steadying himself, Sam dug his feet into the sand, water lapping at his knees. He reached out to help her as the seaweed slipped through her dark hair and down her spine. Sam watched its path, transfixed, as if it were happening in slow motion. Anita's whole body convulsed then sagged in relief as it slapped back into the water. The ocean rumbled, the seaweed reaching for her once more with the shifting water. She leapt up as another strong wave scooped Sam's legs from beneath him, propelling him forward. He crashed on top of her, a tangle of limbs, his skin meeting Anita's soft warmth. Scrambling to right himself in the surf, his hand slipped across her breast. *Shit!* Snatching it back quickly, he spluttered salt water and sincere apologies.

"If you wanted to cop a feel, Was, you could've bought me dinner first." She laughed lightly, the musical noise landing in his chest. "Or asked. Or both!" She laughed again, her hands gripping his biceps. "But I'll never, *ever*, let you near my feet."

A surprising bubble of happiness rose from his gut. They laughed, battling the strong swell as they waded to shore. Sam's eyes rolled up the rocky cliff to the platform he'd just conquered. The platform where he'd nearly shat himself.

Maybe she's right ... The strong pulse of adrenaline still coursed through his veins. Jumping off a cliff might be the inspiration he'd need for his sequel, if he could just ignore the throbbing in his cock.

Water dripped from her nose and lips onto her clinging shirt. His shirt, which rose and fell with each breath. Sam tasted salt on his lips, suddenly mesmerised by Anita's mouth. *Dear God, I want to kiss her.* The realisation hit harder with each wave that pushed and pulled against him.

No, the other side of his brain argued. *NOT professional, man.* He'd been reminding himself of their arrangement all afternoon, trying to remember: professionalism was key.

And he couldn't believe Anita had caught him staring at her toes earlier. How she'd noticed his breath catching suddenly at the sight of her bare feet. He wasn't a fetishist, he wasn't – but they were perfect little toes, manicured and smooth-heeled, the nails painted blue – her favourite colour. Like her hands, they seemed too small for her big personality.

And in that moment, his whole world had shifted. The simple act of seeing her bare feet had seemed ... wrong somehow. Laying eyes on a colleague's toes blurred those personal and professional boundaries. Did this somehow signify a shift in their working dynamic? Maybe Anita was right. Maybe he did have a foot obsession? Or maybe, very possibly, he was overthinking it ... *again*.

Now, Sam moved one slippery hand into Anita's, keeping the spellbinding psychic at arm's length as they tugged each other to shore, waves beating at their backs. A respectable, professional distance grew between them as the ocean ripped their hands apart. Eventually, they sloshed from the foamy white rush and into the gentle, ankle-deep rolls.

"Eee!" Anita squealed again, as a ball of slippery green goop slid by. Jumping towards Sam, she climbed his body like a monkey, to escape it. The feel of her in his arms buckled his knees. The unexpected combination of warmth, weight, and slippery wetness was undoing him. Knees weak, Sam collapsed to the sand. Splayed on top of her, stomach knotted.

"Sorry." Her breath was soft against his cool, damp skin. "Seaweed is just so ..." she winked, borrowing his word to tease once more, "*icky.*" Sand was sprayed across her cheek, and a tendril of hair was tangled in her eyelashes.

"Just let me –" Sam shifted his weight onto one arm, lifting the lock back with his fingers.

She shuddered beneath him, knees curling in and around the

leg that had slid between hers. *Shit, dude. What are you doing? This is NOT a professional relationship, this is ...* He became distracted by her hands on his hips, sliding to his back, exacting the slightest pressure. Pressure that made him want to sink down into her luscious embrace. Savour it. Savour *her.*

It had started in the car, he would decide later. When he'd been too distracted by the seeping warmth that seemed to stretch out from each fingertip to focus on the words tumbling from her lips. She had talked his ear off about the scientific manufacturing of hormones, meddling carnies, falling, jumping and shards of rocks. Not that any of that sounded particularly *romantic* but it had done something to him, somehow, affecting his mind and body in ways he struggled to understand or control. The witch had woven some sort of spell, he was sure. Her constant contact was like being tattooed, her fingers shooting bolts of electricity down into his pants. It had to be some kind of magic. He'd been battling to control himself all day. Hell, the death-grip on the steering wheel was all that had saved him from touching her when they were still in the car!

Now ... Running his bent, white-knuckled fingers through that crazed mess of charcoal hair, he gripped a handful until her head fell back. *She is magnificent.*

Sam drank in her lapis-blue eyes as her lips slowly parted. Lips not at ALL like rashers of bacon, though just as salty ...

Stop it!

His imagination had run away while his body hovered above hers.

No, keep it up (wink wink).

These are not professional thoughts! This is not professional!

War raged within him. *This is not professional.* Touching her was all he'd wanted, and now ...

This is not ...

His hand had moved from her hair to her bottom lip, where a single grain of sand clung. His thighs flattened, pressing her into the sand as she lay still beneath him. The waves licked at the long edges of their bodies, swelling around them in cool bursts as the heat of her skin melted into him.

This is ...

His thumb brushed her bottom lip in a slow, gentle sweep. Her breath rolled into his palm as her lips parted. The deep inhale that followed sent her chest crashing into his. Every inch of his skin rippled, tingling and tight, goosebumps spreading in glorious, electrified waves. Anita was so different. *So warm. So soft.*

His fingers slipped from her lip, through her hair to the base of her skull, gripping lightly and pulling her head higher, out of the growing swell that curled around them. *I'm just stopping her from drowning, that's all.* It was for safety reasons. With the added bonus of inching her closer to his own face.

A little noise escaped her. His cock throbbed, insistent now. Gulping, Sam tried desperately to keep himself under control.

This ...

He couldn't scare her away. He needed her. Oh, how he needed her. His manuscript needed her. His body ... Holy shit, his body wanted her more than it had ever wanted anything.

Sam had been a slave to his brain for years, but never to his penis. He had never been *that* kind of man. He wasn't like

Adam James, led by his dick. No, Sam had a fully functional brain. Yet no craving, no hunger – not even his occasional days of childhood starvation – compared to the way he was yearning for *her*.

This is ... not professional. The warning voice had lost its urgency.

"Anita, can I ..." Another cool wave pressed into the microscopic cavities between their bodies. "Can I kiss you?"

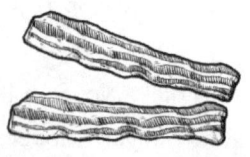

Four Small Words

ANITA

THEY WERE ONLY FOUR small words. Four syllables. *Can. I. Kiss. You.* They shouldn't have been a big deal. But never had someone asked to kiss her before. In the past, her lips had been softly stolen. Others had demanded to conquer them. They had been taken. Never had they been *requested*.

A memory bubbled to the surface. The Pope. Adam James, the man with two first names and a lollipop, daring her to kiss Sam. Anita's lack of control. Sam's shock. She had crossed a boundary. Blurred a line. And she'd felt wrecked about it, if she was going to be honest.

"You want to kiss my bacon lips?" she teased, trying to keep her cool despite the rapid pounding of her heart. As she spoke, she noticed all the places their bodies touched. The long length of his legs, resting on hers, the flat plane of his torso (and something else, too, she noticed with a start) pushing into her stomach. Her chest pressed into his, smothering his tiny, ridiculous heart tattoo. Sam's breath mingling with hers. His cold hand tangled through her hair. The ocean swept up and down, cool water curling around under the back of her head, and time ceased to exist. Moments passed in cold waves and hot breaths, Sam soaking her in as he waited. *He waited!*

Anita tried to breathe through the rapid tingling sensations that swept over her. Every ebb and flow of the ocean slid his cool body in tiny increments along hers. She lost herself to the rhythmic trance of it, locking onto his eyes. Moist eyelashes clung together, and she soaked up the lighter brown spots in his irises. *Chocolate chips in his moist-dirt eyes.*

Her cold, peaked nipples brushed his chest, sending exquisite ripples throughout her body.

He was patient – so damned patient – while his gaze darkened. His eyes devoured her as though she were a wheel of cheese he wanted so badly, but knew he shouldn't. Hungry. Wanting. He waited. She wasn't sure how long. Time was ruled by the crash of the waves that rocked them into a stupor, casting an elemental spell that captured them entirely, each helpless to the will of the swelling sea.

A deep ache throbbed low and hot in her body. She tried to ignore it.

"Anita?"

Her hands splayed on his bare skin, tiny goosebumps rising to meet her touch. Mind sloshing with the waves, backwards and forwards, her thoughts rose up and around. *His body wants me, that's for sure. But his heart ... isn't it already taken?*

"What about Reece?" The words came out as a whisper and

she bit her lip, tasting salt.

Sam's mouth dropped impossibly close to hers.

"What about Reece?" His words caressed her lips. Then, they were gone. "Do …" Sam cleared his throat. She watched the slow bob of his Adam's apple. "Do you like him?"

"Of course I do. He's great."

"Oh. Shit," Sam mumbled, pushing off her. Each hair follicle tingled as his hand retreated. Sam flopped onto his back, breathing hard, an arm over his eyes. Anita tried desperately to keep her eyes fixed on the horizon, the waves, the rocks, the rogue seagulls … anything but the impressive bulge in his boardshorts.

"Do you like him?" Anita asked, feeling stupid. Traitorous.

"Of course I do!"

"So, us kissing would be a bad idea then," she rationalised painfully, feeling like the villainous cartoon character who had stolen the baby's candy. It hurt to say it, but Anita had to stick to her personal brand and be brutally honest. *What do I have, if not my own integrity and values?*

Sam stumbled higher up the beach, his feet sinking into the light, dry sand. Anita sat in the swell, breathing hard, taking her time to calm down, allowing the ocean to soothe her, to take away the adrenaline. She was horny and hungry, and Sam … Had he started that? The weird way food had become an ingredient in her sexual fantasies? When had that started? Was it before or after *Heat in the Kitchen*? Had the delicious thoughts been simmering since discovering Sammie Hart, or since meeting Samuel Harthrup? She waited for her heartbeat to return to normal, allowing Sam time of his own.

He doesn't really want me. Who would? This is exactly as I said. Science. Hormones. Manufactured. Falling. She refused to allow herself to consider that Sam's request to kiss her was all about true feelings. This wasn't real. She had set this up, even explaining the manufactured emotional responses to him. She was helping. Sam needed help.

It's all about the book ...

Her eyes flicked up the sand. Arms looped around his knees, Sam was sitting some way up the beach, his head cocked to one side. The roar of the waves swept away his words, but his lips were moving in a familiar formation. The look in his eyes ... What was he saying? She focused on his mouth. *Anita.* Sam was speaking her name.

Anita's body moved instinctively. His eyes widened as she rose from the water and walked towards him. She could have sworn he said 'holy shit'. Was this a test? Was this some messed up universal spell that tugged her towards him? Ultimately, it didn't matter. Sam wasn't hers to have, even if this whole exercise was confusing that fact.

Before she reached him, Sam stood abruptly. He seemed to have made his mind up about something. His lips straightened in that determined line he'd worn previously, when he'd mumbled incoherently. His eccentricities made her even more curious to figure this man out.

"I think it's a good time to tell you, I *hate* heights." He took her hand, stomping through the soft, warm sand as they started back up the cliff. "But we're doing that again."

She giggled. "Time to conquer your fears?" Relief slid down her body in fine droplets. *I haven't ruined this, after all. We're okay. The project is intact.*

"It's time to take a fucking leap."

Running, jumping, laughing and splashing, they looped from the cliff to the water to the beach, then back again. Time played tricks with the shadows and with every new jump, Sam seemed to forget his request. Unfortunately, Anita's memory wasn't that short.

Can I kiss you? The words burnt in her memory.

Lungs burning, sides aching from laughter, they started the long walk back up the beach. Lengthening shadows were stealing the sun's warmth.

Can I kiss you?

Sam dragged a stick behind him, a long line trailing from the spot where he had scrawled their names in looping stick marks upon the sand. The words, now swallowed by the ocean, had impressed themselves on Anita. It seemed that all of his words affected her, whether written on paper or etched into the earth itself.

Can I kiss you? The words replayed in her skull. Goddess, why had she said no?

Anita had very few moments in her life she might wish to change. The list consisted of the death of her parents and her brother's violence, but they were not things she could change or control. But now, as Sam's words echoed over and over, she pondered regret, hoping maybe (just maybe) she might get a second chance to set this right. Set Sam right. To use her own words and explain why, despite her body's apparent need for him, she had refused his kiss. Could she even explain it? Probably not. Regret sat heavily within her. Hands needing to move, she twisted her rings around and around her fingers. Why the Goddess had she said no?

They reached the car just as the sun slipped behind the bush. Wrapping her skirt around her hips, an instant warmth enveloped her lower half. Sam shivered violently each time the breeze struck him.

"I think in your last life, you were something cold blooded," Anita mused. "A snake. Or an axolotl, maybe, since you seem fond of water."

"No, I was a dog. A wolf." Sam thrashed his head from side to side, canine-style, shaking the lingering water from his hair. Salty droplets splashed Anita.

"Do you *really* want to start that game?" she said, one hand on her hip and the other pointing to her still-dripping tresses. "At this stage, I'll be lucky if this mop dries in two days!"

Sam slipped his spectacles on before throwing his hands up. "Okay, okay! No more water-based shenanigans." He blushed but raced on. "Now, what do you say to dinner?"

"Was, it's like you read my mind."

He laughed. It was such a lovely sound, accompanying a total transformation of his face. *It's nice to see him like this. Lighter. Out of his own headspace.* With unruly, dripping hair and stubble spreading across his jaw, he certainly was handsome. Long, lean and light, it was like the sun shone through Sam (whenever he didn't have his nose in a book).

"Maybe I'm a reader like you, Anita." He beamed as her traitorous hands reached to pat his cool, goose-bumped skin. "Head out? Or cook in?"

She considered. "Let's eat out. And you'll never be like

me, Was. I'm thinking ..." she tapped her jaw, feigning concentration, "a double cheese pizza with cheese-stuffed crust and extra lactose on the side." She cackled evilly, fingertips steepling. "Because. I. Can."

"I can too!" He grinned right back, winking. "And I promise, you'll suffer the consequences more than me!"

Anatoli's

SAM

Sam: Need to talk to you, man. Busy?

Reece: WAZZUUUUUUP?

Sam: Gotta be quick. Anita in bathroom. How do I DATE?

Reece: You're dating Anita in a bathroom? Or some other lucky toilet-loving lady? Either way, dude, your romance skills are RUSTY.

Sam: Gross, man. I THINK this is a date? I mean, maybe it is or maybe I'm overthinking? I kind of think she likes someone ELSE …

Sam: ??

Sam: ???

Reece: LOL calm down, Romeo. I can feel

`your blush from here.`

Reece: `Knowing you, you're overthinking it.`

Reece: `Wait, where are you? PLEASE don't tell me you're locked in a bathroom stall texting me again …`

Anita chose that moment to return to the small, round table of the bistro.

Sam: `G2G`

Slipping his phone back into his pocket, Sam feigned intense interest in the décor of the eatery.

Anatoli's Italian Eatery wasn't a classy white-linen and wall-of-wine-covered-in-vines style Italian restaurant. It was the ruby-hued leather booth kind, with red and white checked tablecloths and bright, tubular florescent lighting that banished all shadows from existence. The kind of place that served the best, most authentic food from a stereotypically Italian man boasting an impressively thick moustache. Usually such restaurants were cubby holes, sandwiched between other businesses with that secretly-the-best-place-in-town vibe, but this place, Anatoli's, was a bustling, seemingly endless space. The black and white chessboard flooring stretched between large windows offering ocean views on one side, and a landscaped garden with immaculate hedges on the other. Life, laughter, music and wine burst through the space. Loud families, teenagers shyly eyeing their dates, comfortable married couples staring at their phones, sunburnt holidaymakers, and a live band filled the restaurant. The air hung heavy with the delicious aroma of fresh tomatoes, basil and garlic.

Sam was glad they had chosen a small table in the garden area. It was quieter out here. Less *peopley*. Tiny fairy lights climbed their way up the trees and speckled throughout the bushes, setting a more mellow scene than inside the well-lit Anatoli's. Sam had been watching the bustling interior, waiting for Anita to re-emerge. Their drinks had been delivered in the meantime and he'd already skulled half his lemonade.

Then, like the stars winking awake in the evening sky – There. She. Was. Sam could have sworn the world slowed down and a cinematic spell settled upon the courtyard. It was the stairs, he decided. So many romances featured stairs – *She's All That, How to Lose a Guy in 10 Days, Titanic.* A pretty woman walking down stairs shouldn't seize time, or change the air around a man. Yet it did. Anita flowed down into the courtyard, a Leading Lady in her bohemian skirt and his borrowed shirt.

"You changed your hair," he blurted. The wild, wet waves had been plaited into a long, thick braid tumbling down Anita's back. It curved at the base of her spine to kiss the top of her arse. She spun to show him. Still wet, it dripped slowly, sticking a large section of his borrowed shirt to her skin.

But her hair wasn't the first thing Sam noticed. His gaze had stuck lower down. The swish of the fabric across her wide, perfect hips made him catch his breath as she moved. He imagined the lovely, olive legs beneath it, remembering the stretch of her thighs, the way her backside curved perfectly like … "Peaches!" he spluttered as Anita sat down beside him.

"Pardon, Was?"

"You like peaches?" *Smooth, Sammie. Smooth.* "Warners Bay is known for them, apparently." He blushed, the word vomit, rather like *actual* vomit, had left a sour tang on his tongue. His palms began to sweat, as he remembered the raging success of his last date with Breanna Henderson.

Anita's laugh filled him with butterflies, stealing away the memories.

"Let's get dinner down before we go dreaming up dessert." She licked her lips unconsciously and his stomach lurched. He had so desperately wanted to kiss Breanna Henderson, but Anita's lips and that tongue tempted him more than he was willing to dwell on. *Popcorn and bloody fizzy soda,* he started mentally chanting, breathing in deep, controlled puffs, trying to keep himself in check.

"Wine?" she asked from behind the large, laminated menu.

"Nah, the doctor will have my guts for garters. Reece only lets me drink under his supervision, to ease me into what he calls The Big Dry."

"Fair enough. Not a bad thing, drying out and sobering up. Henry Lawson had to do it; you should too. The next Great Australian Writer shouldn't be a drunkard, though that would suit a particular stereotype, I suppose. Not that you're much of a stereotype, Sammie Hart." Her merriment bubbled with each word. "You're nothing like I imagined you to be. And avoiding liquor might even improve your writing."

A waiter took their orders, delivering more fizzing drinks promptly as Anita continued her teasing literary insights. She really was widely read, probably even more so than himself. Anita spoke of the great romantics, modern-day classics and lesser-known indie authors. Sam sunk into a relaxed slump as he watched her mouth form words, unhearing.

BZZZZZ. BZZZZZ. BZZZZZ. Sam's phone vibrated through his leg, tingles dancing across his lap and shocking him back to reality. Anita's eyes nodded towards his crotch as she reached for her drink.

"Going to answer that?"

Sam dug in the depths of his pants before examining the caller ID and swiping to end the call. "Nope."

"Reece?"

"Yep."

"*Buona sera,* lovebirds. 'ere you go." The restaurant's owner, Anatoli himself, brought their steaming extra-cheesy margherita pizza to the table, sliding it with pride before their hungry eyes.

"We're not–" Sam started to correct, but Anita's hand curled around his, halting his tongue as though she had captured that part of his anatomy.

"*Grazi*, Anatoli." She smiled up at the moustached man. "*Che bella notte.*"

"At Anatoli's," he beamed, "*sempre*! Always a beautiful night." He smiled, bowing slightly as he left them to their meal.

Sam watched her, slack jawed.

"You speak Italian?"

"A bit." Anita shrugged. "There is always something to learn on the road, from people I meet or the late-night international romances I find on TV." She paused, inhaling deeply. "This smells so good …"

"You're *so* going to regret this," Sam said, motioning to the cheesy, saucy pizza. Tearing off a slice, he held it near his own nose with glee. His eyes rolled heavenward, as much in prayer to culinary heaven as in silent apology to the gastrointestinal gods who would smite him later this evening. He ignored the sudden arrival of Reece's scowling, doctorly face in his mind, lecturing him to avoid lactose, texting him about bathrooms while making sly moves on his little bohemian. Sam dismissed the doctor with a shake of his head.

"Holy *crepe*!" he said around his mouthful. "This is like French-kissing the entire country of Italy."

Anita grinned. "Pancake puns happen when you *yeast* expect them, I suppose. But that's another classically gross Samuel Harthrup description, not a Sammie Hart masterpiece." She licked her lips. "However, I agree. This is the best margherita pizza I have ever, *ever* sunk my teeth into." She gave him a big smile, tomato sauce bleeding through her teeth. An unexpected snort of laughter sucked cheese into his windpipe. Coughing, his spectacles slid from his nose, landing with a moist plop in their dinner. Exploding with laughter, Anita clutched her sides, shaking.

Delicately plucking Sam's spectacles from the pizza, she unceremoniously plonked them back onto his face. Tomato sauce smeared his cheeks, like vampire tears. Anita's laugh exploded again, reverberating through the courtyard. Indignantly, Sam removed his spectacles, attempting to clean both them and his face with wide swipes of a napkin, smudging the red sauce further. After long minutes, Anita's giggles died.

"Pancakes don't have yeast, so zip it, Witch," Sam said, swirling his tongue around stringy mozzarella.

"I *doughnut* take puns lightly, Sam." Anita's deadpan expression made him inhale sauce once more.

"You *butter* believe," he wheezed, spluttering sauce and mirth, "that I'll be writing these down later. Hope I can *sandwich* a few into the manuscript."

"Let's cut to the *cheese*, Sam. You've got to make ends *meat*."

Jaw sore, eyes leaking, he couldn't remember the last time his ribs had ached this way.

"Anita! Stop! You're *bacon* my heart over here with all these *egg*cellent suggestions!"

He'd done it again. He'd said the magic word. Sam watched in awe as her hands flew to his cheeks, her fingers wiping the joyous tears away. He froze as her hand dipped lower.

"You've got sauce ..." Her finger slipped to his lip. The raucous, wine-fuelled noise around them quietened. The warm evening breeze stilled in the darkened courtyard, wrapping them in a cocoon of sudden, flower-scented springtime humidity.

Sam gulped, the heat of her hands on him. Shit, had he misunderstood the strange pull of her spell? The effect of her witchcraft? His breath seemed to seize in his chest, his beating heart amplifying.

Anita looked at her fingertips, stained deliciously red. Her eyes met Sam's and slowly, she slid the stained digit between her lips. Gently, she sucked the margherita sauce until her fingers were clean, eyes focused squarely on Sam.

Every muscle in his body tensed. His groin strained against his clothing. The little bohemian was inches from his face, their legs entwined under the table. When had that happened? Anita had curled herself over him, twisting Sam in a loop of skin and skirts as her magical charm drew their bodies closer. Shaking his head, Sam felt the blush rising.

Anita had been right to lecture Sam about his writing and his ways. He had been so focused on what he could see that he'd ignored what he *felt*, his own words confusing the two. Now, he felt the combination in her warm body against his. He saw her finger in her mouth, tasted the deliciousness that coated his own tongue from their shared dinner ... He needed to get a grip. On himself. On her. On this whole situation. It was all too much. His cock pressed against his fly so hard that the zipper pattern would surely tattoo his skin. Sam's stomach was flipping, and it wasn't from the poisonous lactose that was preparing to wage an internal war with his intestinal system.

Time to be brave, Sammie old boy.

"Anita." He was unsure what else to say, hoping the spell would carry his desperate thoughts into her touch.

Her hands slid up his arms, and he gulped.

"Yes." She breathed the word like an answer to all questions, her big blue eyes locked with his.

"Yes?"

"Yes." She repeated slowly, eyes smiling, as though she had read his mind. "You can. Kiss me, I mean."

Sam didn't need to be told twice. He threw down his pizza slice and buried his hands in her hair, dragging her saucy lips to his.

Their first kiss had been a dare, a stupid dare from a jock who had never grown out of a school-yard mentality. It had been a recipe for disaster soup – the result of a crumbling base of exhaustion, a dash of dropping his guard, three cups of unhealthy masculine jealousy, a pinch of forced proximity and about a gallon of persuasion from some geriatrics.

But this time, *this kiss* ... it was different. This kiss melted him like butter in a hot pan and he let himself dissolve into her. Her heat welcomed home, the warmth seeping into his bones. She tasted like Italy, sweet and tart all at once. *Delicious*. Sam couldn't get enough.

His hands curled into her hair, the warm base of her skull meeting his cool fingertips. A small sigh escaped her lips and he slipped his tongue into her mouth, exploring, tasting. Anita arched into him, wrapping around Sam like a jacket in the depths of winter, comfortable and familiar, pressing herself closer, her lips meeting his with every gentle taste.

"Mmmm *bacon*." He grinned against her lips. Sliding her hands around his neck, her laugh curled briefly in his mouth before she pressed their mouths together once more.

"You're so funny, Was. You know that?"

He responded without words.

Sam wasn't sure when she had slid her legs into his lap, and he didn't care. Anita curled around him in their red-chaired garden booth. One of his hands slipped from her hair, squeezing its way up one leg as she moaned between his lips. Bunching her skirt, he worked it gently aside, tracing a slow line up her ankle.

"This is much better," he told her, fingers circling her ankle as he kissed a path along her jaw. Anita's eyes flew open at his words, as though the spell was broken suddenly, violently.

"Wait, Sam, this isn't what you want." Her head and her hands seemed at war, the words questioning and worrying while her tiny hands pulled him closer. They ran the length of his back, tangling in his hair as she kissed him back. Oh yes, she *was* kissing him back.

"Let me show you what I want," he murmured into her mouth. His erection throbbed, wanting, beneath her legs drawn over his lap. How could she think this wasn't what he wanted? Because of the professional line he had drawn on the page? The line he'd erased and redrawn so many times there was now a hole ripped in the 'stay collegial' plan?

"Sam, stop."

It took a few seconds for the words to register. Breath ragged, he pulled away, one hand still in her hair, the other pausing its inch-by-inch northward exploration beneath her skirts. His body was well and truly beyond his control. Humming and electric, the air between them crackled with energy.

Anita looked away, her hungry gaze gone. "You don't want this," she said quietly. "You don't want *me*. Not really. It's not fair, on either of us." She bit her delicious lip, her hand squeezing his through the fabric of her clothing, acknowledging and officially halting its position, mid-thigh.

Goddamn it. He wanted to lick the worry from her lips. To inch his hand up and ...

He blinked, the words finally filtering through his foggy brain.

"How can you say that? *This* isn't what I want?" he implored, pushing her leg down onto his roused groin. "This isn't a typical day at the office for me. This is ... And you ..." He couldn't help himself. He held the base of her skull, cradling her flushed cheek in his other hand. She arched into his touch. Unwilling to let her curve back too far, lest he sink his lips to the long, caramel strip of her neck, Sam locked eyes with Anita.

"You are perfect, Anita. *Perfect*." He was transfixed, watching her faltering gaze, long dark lashes fluttering downward. "You have no idea what I want." His thumbs resumed drawing lazy circles.

Anita closed her eyes, taking a shaky breath, clearly deciding, then sliding away from his embrace. Away from him. She cleared her throat, looking around Anatoli's courtyard, a rosy blush high on her rounded cheekbones. Sam saw her struggling, grappling for words that wouldn't quite spill from her lips.

Eventually, she took a deep breath. "I know I'm not who men say I am," she started. He went to interrupt, but she held up one finger, silencing him. "I know you want someone to stick around, to help you finish your book. I can't promise that, Sam. Any of that. I never cross boundaries, and this wasn't supposed to–"

"I know, but–"

"What about Reece?"

His gut clenched. "What about Reece?" The words hissed through gritted teeth. *Doctor Dickhead* is *trying to steal my girl!*

"I'm sure he'd have something to say about this. He loves you."

"So?"

"So, I'm not like that."

"Not like what?" *Not liking that you kissed me, because you're actually with him?*

Anita squared her shoulders, a fiery defiance burning in her eyes.

"I am *not* a slut," Anita said, breathy but determined.

"I never–"

"And I'm not *whoring* around each town I go to."

"I know, Anita, I–"

"And I'm not in the business of ruining relationships wherever I go!" She pushed up off the table, their drinks wobbling within their condensing glasses. "I'm *not* stealing someone else's boyfriend, Sam. I won't do that to Reece."

What the shit? Sam balked, trying to squeak a comment in edgeways, but Anita was ranting now, unhearing.

"It ends, now. All *this* ..." Her hand flew between them. "Whatever *this* is! I'm sorry, but prior relationships ... and your book ... they have to come first. That was our arrangement. Professional. And while you are a tall, beautiful distraction ..." She wrapped her arms about her waist, planted her feet firmly into the grassy courtyard. "I think I need to get back to the circus."

Wait ... what? She wanted to leave? To literally run away with the circus *now*? Pinching his nose, Sam exhaled slowly.

"You're telling me that you give me *permission* to kiss you, even though I didn't even get around to asking for a kiss, this time at least. Then, you say you're a slut–"

"*Not* a slut," she corrected.

"Not a slut," he agreed, rounding the table to advance upon her slowly. "Then you insinuate that Reece is my boyfriend? Or is he yours? I'm honestly a bit fuzzy on that ingredient in this mess."

Her eyebrows drew down. "Yours .... right?"

Sam reached out and gently tucked that wayward curl from her face, his entire body quivering as his laughter refused to subside. Their drinks on the table shook, small wells of joy as they captured the vibrations of his laugh.

"Reece ..." He gasped, wiping away tears and gasping for air. "He's just my mate. My BFF."

"But ..." She paused for a split second, before allowing her usual verbal bulldozing style to plough on. "You say 'I love you' to each other all the time. You're always together. He buys you deodorant and laundry products! And what grown man says 'BFF'?"

Sniffing, Sam pulled Anita into a shaking hug. For once, his body didn't stiffen awkwardly at the gesture. He'd never been a hugger, but right now, he pushed Anita to his chest and melted into her, his chuckle rocking through both their bodies. For a moment, she was stiff in his embrace, slowly softening as they clung to each other.

"For the record, Anita –" He wiped another stray tear from beneath his spectacles, taking a few deep breaths to rein in the chuckles, "– I'm straight. In the name of total honesty, I'll admit that I kissed a guy once ... okay *twice* ... but it wasn't Reece and I'm definitely, *totally*, into chicks." Sam pulled back slightly, chin dropping to his chest as he looked down at her, enclosed in his arms. "I'm into *you*," he whispered into her hair. "You are a witch, Anita Fortuna. A goddamn pain in my arse who never shuts up. And God knows why, but you like to clean my flat. You're tidying up my entire life, actually, and despite all your insults–"

"Constructive criticism," she argued, sliding her gaze from his chest to his face.

"Despite your unfortunately relevant yet searing literary critiques, I am firmly under your spell." He saw Anita's eyes darken, a small smile tugging at her plump, perfect lips. "And for the sake of honesty, your personal brand of hell, I want to admit ..." he took a deep breath. "I want you. Shit, I want you so bad, Anita. Can't you read that with those pretty little hands of yours? Because I'm sure it's written on my palms, and my pages, and my face ..." Sam grasped both her hands, bringing them up to press on his chest. He was about to kiss her again, when a loud cough echoed across the courtyard.

"Ah! Lovebirds!" Anatoli's moustache lay heavily over his wide grin. "Get a room," he laughed with a wink, flapping a flour-dusted tea towel in their direction.

"A room?" Sam didn't register the words for a few beats. Not until Anita shot a tiny nod to Sam, and warmth bloomed within him. Hand in hand, they left Anatoli's.

White Picket Fences

SAM

THE WARNER'S BAY BED and Breakfast was a quaint five-cabin resort within a stone's throw of the ocean. A bright neon sign declared *Vacancy* but the thing Anita had *ooh*ed and *aah*ed over was the simple white picket fence that bordered the property. To a woman who lived in a constantly moving caravan and adored all things Happily Ever After, a white picket fence was less a landscaping feature and more a romanticised symbol of domestic bliss.

"It's so homely," she said, sighing.

"I thought a Happily-Ever-After-Castle would be more your style," Sam commented, pulling into a parking space.

"Only if you're on a white steed trotting off into the sunset. But it's already dark, so as long as it's not a candy cane cottage in the woods, it's safe, and it's perfect. For some reason I'm feeling a little bit like Snow White right now, emerging from the woods, finding a cabin–"

"Anita," he laughed, "This place doesn't come with seven little dwarves, you know."

"No? Oh well, I think one giant will do," she said, fingers sliding through his.

They fit together so well, despite their differences. His heart swelled. When had her touch started to make him feel like this? It certainly wasn't the fence, but he agreed that tonight felt like a homecoming, somehow. Sneaking a peak from the corner of his eye, he watched her chin tilt skyward, her mouth moving as she whispered, "Star light, star bright ..."

"You do that every night?"

"Religiously."

"Why?"

"Because, Was, wishing upon stars makes your dreams come true." Her eyes, dark and full of promise, caught his. "And being here, with you?" Her fingers tightened around his. "That's a dream I never would have let myself wish, until today." The words still rolled in his mind as she exited the car, beckoning him into the reception area with a broad smile.

The B&B cabins, beach-facing and connected by neat, flower-hugged paths that led to a grand manor house, boasted high ceilings, spa baths and a late breakfast with an even later checkout.

If Sam hadn't had his eyes glued to the corner of Anita's smile, he would have noticed the small nametag of the grinning receptionist named 'Louisa'. He might have marvelled at the architectural features of the quaint, clean building, the neatly manicured lawns, or the fruit basket on the counter that invited them cheerily to 'enjoy your stay'. He definitely would have noticed his already meagre bank account dwindling further into negative figures. But none of that mattered.

All he noticed, as they entered their hastily rented cabin, was the sharp, modern grey of the door as he pressed Anita's back into it, flattening her against it, rocking her body upwards. Shit, she was so short. His hands reached under her thighs, lifting her higher. She wrapped her legs around him, climbing.

"Bed," she breathed, seconds before they tumbled onto the crisp white linen, panting, laughing and kissing their way up the mattress.

"Sam," Anita breathed between kisses. "I am never like this. I mean ... I'm not very good at *this*." She breathed deeply, pressing herself closer, brushing her body against his. His eyes nearly rolled back.

Shit. Surely, she was joking. He was so hard. His dick strained against the fabric of his pants, like it had been in hibernation for the last few years and was suddenly awake and ravenous.

Anita tugged at the waistband of his pants as he whipped the t-shirt over his head.

"Me either," he admitted, already breathing hard. "It's ... been a while. A *long* while." He kissed a trail from her forehead to her nose, pulling back to quickly whip off his glasses and toss them aside. "But for the record, I think you're good at everything, Anita."

His mouth crushed to hers, or had she closed the distance? All Sam knew for sure was that his bare chest pressed to her clothed one; his hands were lost in her hair. Every time he twined his fingers against Anita's skull, she moaned.

The butterflies in Sam's chest sunk down into his gut. He wanted more. Her hands gripped his backside, pressing closer. Encouraging. Demanding. Ravenous.

Holy shit, she is perfect.

He whispered as much, over and over. She retreated. The warmth of her touch lingered on his bare chest, shoulders and back. He blinked, owlishly. "Did I say something wrong?"

To his dismay, Anita slid off the bed and went to stand, chest heaving, on the opposite side of the room. "No." Her eyes scanned the floor, shaking fingers pressed to her mouth. "No, nothing is wrong."

"What is it?" He moved closer, sliding to the middle of the bed.

Her eyes met his, a shadow of her smart-arse spark flitting across her face. She took a deep breath. "If I was a writer and this was my book, this would be a key scene, yes?"

"Totally." He grinned, wondering where this was going. "You're not making this a teachable moment, are you?"

"You need the practice, Was?" Anita flashed a grin. "Flagpole wants *more*, right? So, how would you write this scene?" She didn't wait for his response, barrelling on, her voice filling the night. "I'd probably describe how you have moist-dirt eyes, and your face is too small for your head, though that stubble is stretching your features more evenly now ..."

Sam crossed his arms, grinning. "Gee, thanks."

How can she be so damn attractive and so brutal at the same time?

"I'd write that you're tall and," Anita looked almost shy now. "You're kind of gorgeous, in a nerdy way that I think is so hot.

Did you know that? *So hot*," she repeated for good measure. "And you're soft–"

Sam scoffed, about to argue that point after feeling a disagreeing twitch in his underwear, but she barrelled on.

"But also strong. Like, you know what you want, and you'll get it, but be gentle and kind about it, too. Does that even make sense?"

"Anita." Sam pinched the bridge of his nose, wondering about her literary lecture. "What does this have to do with anything?"

"Well … I'm strong too." She seemed to make up her mind about something, squaring her shoulders. "Tell me …"

Sam watched the slow path of her hand as it traversed the curves of her body to arrive at the small knot she had tied in her shirt. *His* shirt. Slowly, Anita's hands untied the fabric, the tails of the shirt hanging loose around her thighs.

"How would you write me, Sam? Honestly."

Sam struggled, his tongue wanting to *taste* more than talk. He needed to touch her, to drag her warmth into him. To strip that clothing off, not watch it fall and cover more of her, like some giant's too-long t-shirt. Reaching Anita in two strides, his hands slid to the buttons straining with her every breath.

This is not a good idea … one side of his voice cautioned.

The other side screamed profanities, reminding him that yes, she would eventually leave but he had known that all along. It wouldn't affect his work. He deserved this connection, after so long alone. That side of his brain calculated how long it had been since he'd been with a woman, heck, how long since he'd even paid himself some attention. And it was coming up blank.

No wonder his body was acting like this.

Sam gulped, meeting Anita's lovely blue eyes. For the first time, he noticed the freckles scattered across the bridge of her nose, his gaze settling on the slight dimple at the corner of her mouth.

"Well, since you like my sexy food descriptions so much ..." Sam popped one button, moving upward. Anita shivered slightly, encouraging him to continue with a small nod. "I'd write that you smell of lavender ice cream. The expensive, creamy kind that rolls easily into a big, beautiful ball and melts on your tongue, tasting like heaven itself." He kissed her softly, his hands popping a second button. "Call me crazy, but I can taste it, too." Her tongue darted out, wetting her bottom lip. It drove him fucking nuts.

"I'd write that your skin is the sweetest, most luscious caramel. The kind that demands to be sucked and savoured and ..." Anita shivered as Sam's hands loosened the final few buttons, the shirt now hanging open.

Her eyes shut tight, she held her breath as he ducked his head down to press his mouth to her neck. Her pulse, rapid beneath his lips, urged him on. He trailed a long line down to her collar bone, slowly inching the shirt from her body.

"I'd write ..." Sam drew back to gaze at his prize, ready to concoct more delicious descriptions for the warm woman in his hands, and to bask in Anita's naked form. She froze under his appraisal, her breaths shallow, eyes becoming watery. She nodded for him to continue.

"Don't just look," she whispered. "How does my body make you *feel*?"

Anita had closed her eyes but as he sighed her name, she blindly reached for him, holding steady, a boat adrift needing its anchor. Her head fell to her chest, her warm body shivering under his hot scrutiny. *Holy fucking shit ...*

Drawing back, he held her at arm's length. He looked. And he finally *saw*. His eyes bulged and what he felt, was rage.

His attention flitted between her arms, her ribs, her stomach, from bruise to bruise, scar to still-healing scab. His hands trailed his gaze, gently skimming the top half of her body. He examined her front and her back, gulping as he ran his hands up over the tan-coloured fabric of her bra. It was old, worn, but clean. Nothing flashy or expensive or sexy, like he'd expected, like he'd imagined. Stripped down, his witch was a completely different kind of woman. Only a moment ago, he would have done anything to remove every garment from her shapely body. But he couldn't take that bra off. Not now. Anita was already too naked, too raw and exposed before him. The bruises, the scars ... His eyes kept stock of each injury that tainted her skin.

"Anita ..."

She buried her face in his chest. "I'm so embarrassed," she cried, shaking her head against him. "Who would want me. Want *this*?" She was shivering, her usual warmth drained.

"I do." Sam lifted her chin. "I definitely do." He pulled her into bed, curling her around him as he smoothed her hair, kissing the tears away. "But right now, I don't think we should," he said, hating the taste of the words as they slipped out. Sam wasn't sure if Anita's sigh was of relief or regret, but the shaky sound twisted his stomach more than dairy ever had. "Tell me," he whispered into her hair, his hands gently touching another large, purple and blue bruise on her upper arm. "Talk to me. Please."

Much later, Sam untangled Anita from his embrace and left her sleeping, snoring lightly, in the bed. This day, and this night, hadn't gone to plan.

Sliding the small hotel notepad closer, he picked up the complimentary pen and began scribbling furiously.

Dear fucking Diary ...

I've never wanted to kill someone before, but ...

This wasn't going to be enough paper. His brain was buzzing from an overstimulating day. First, the push and pull of the ocean had lulled him into a horny place, interjected by the rapid rush of adrenaline from jumping off a cliff and confronting his issue with heights. Next, Anatoli's had consumed his sense of taste and his hands on Anita's thighs, under her skirts, had intensified a hunger that had nothing to do with pizza.

But then came Anita's confession. Her heartbreaking story of familial loss and subsequent abuses, both large and small, that her brother inflicted. Adrian controlled her money, her food, and, Sam surmised, a significant portion of her carefully concealed mental state. Her brother was the worst kind of bully. When he found Anita lacking in some small way, he punished her. What had begun as childhood pranks and attention seeking had become malicious, targeted attacks of rage, manhandling and insults. Her confession, halting, infused with tears and sadly whispered into the dark, was seared into his brain.

"When our parents died, Adrian cut off all my hair and said it was a sign of mourning. Then, he called me a boy at every turn, telling me how unattractive I was, how freakish and unlovable. He teased me so much about being a boy, when it was short. It hurt. I didn't want to be a boy. But as I grew and matured, the hair was just a childhood consideration. His insults had turned to other, more prominent parts of my anatomy by then." She shuddered, hands sliding around the curve of her stomach as she spoke. "My hair grew back eventually, and I vowed to keep it long. It was a symbol of defiance, and of my femininity. But he grew up, and the taunts grew with him. Adrian always knew how to attack my body and my self-esteem. To poke at the most tender parts. He'd tell me I was fat. Too curvy, too round, too ..." She had begun to cry in earnest, the words choked. She forced them out. "First, I was too much like a boy. Then, I was too much like a woman. No matter who I was, it was wrong. I couldn't deal. I focused on who I was *inside*, because that's what matters. I decided to be kind and helpful and strong." She sniffed. "It was hard, when he enjoyed knocking me down at every turn. So, I would sneak out, just to be *away*, you know? To meet nice people in different communities, to connect with those who wanted or needed me, even for a small time. To leave my own mark on the world. But then he'd say I'd been out with men. Men who couldn't possibly want me because of my repulsive body. He'd call me a whore and ..." Her words became muffled as he pressed her to him, unwilling to hear more yet unable to stop listening to her sad tale.

On and on she spoke, stories moving between past and present, mixing into a giant ball of rage in Sam's gut. By nature,

Sam was a lover, not a fighter. But everyone had their line in the sand. Seeing Anita quivering, crying, unable to breathe as he held her in his arms? He crossed that boundary. Sam barely knew this woman, yet he believed everything she said to be true. Everything Adrian had said about her was dead wrong.

It hadn't been too far from his experiences with his own parents. The periods of unknowing, waiting for the axe to fall. The drunken outbursts and the shouting. The hidden bruises on his skin and the deeper aches that lived closer to his bones. The want and need to be out of their way whilst being completely under their iron-fisted rule. But Sam couldn't tell her any of that. This was not his story. Not tonight. And Adrian was her brother, not her parents. Sam might not have seen his parents in years, but he had Grandma Edith and Reece to keep him human. Anita only had herself.

Reece was the closest Sam had ever had to a sibling. He couldn't imagine that kind of treatment coming from the hands of one's own blood. *Anita deserves a Reece,* Sam begrudgingly admitted. The kind of man who would buy her laundry detergent, make sure she showered, encourage her to follow her passion for cooking elaborate meals or to wish upon stars. Well, Reece didn't exactly do that last bit, but that was what Anita deserved. Sam wanted to fix it, to help her, like his grandmother had helped him, but how could he? Cirque de Fortuna was rolling out of town at the end of this week. She would leave Moonshine. Leave him. *Shit.* Why did his brain always circle back to that dark place?

Focus. He needed focus.

Sam slipped his shirt back over his head, tugging it deftly

down. His eyes drifted to Anita, the source of his frustration, his pity, and his lust, following the curl of one long, dark tendril of hair as it splayed across the crisp linen. He recalled, in vivid detail, the feel of it, so soft and warm at the base of her neck. His fingers had slid through it like a warm knife through butter. The curve of her hips begged for his hands to glide over them, to shape and squeeze as though gently massaging dough. He wanted so badly to crawl into bed beside her, to pick up where they had left off before their evening had crashed down like an unstable, sticky croquembouche.

New ideas swum behind his eyeballs as his internal body clock came alive. Focusing on the lines of the paper, Sam put pen to paper. It was its own kind of magic, when he became lost in some inky beyond.

At around 2am, Sam snapped a photo of the progress on his phone, ignoring the blinking notification icon that warned of numerous texts and missed calls from Reece. There was also a single missed call from his Grandma Edith. He would reply to them later. Right now, he was on a roll.

Opening the email app, he attached the images to the blank document.

From: Samuelharthrup@hotmail.com
To: Suzannah.editor@flagpolepublishing.com

Subject: Heat in the Kitchen Sequel

Hi Suzannah,
Sorry for the tiny sheets of hotel paper (please see the

attached photographs). Still travelling and unable to type document currently. Inspiration struck and I thought I'd share the good news with you first. I hope this is the kind of sizzle Flagpole is hoping for. I will send through the final pages at the end of the week for your consideration and submit the typed document by the deadline.

Very close now.

Sincerely,

Sam

He didn't want to click 'send'. But, if nothing else, he owed it to himself ... to his fans, to *her* ... to try and meet this deadline. Cracking his knuckles, Sam flexed each finger and rolled his wrists. *Job done, Sammie boy.* Clicking off the little desk light, he heard the sheets rustle.

"Sore hands?" came Anita's sleep-addled voice from the bed. Damn. He'd woken her.

"Yeah. Always. Cramps from gripping my pencil too hard. Probably because I'm a creative control freak." Sam placed his glasses onto the table, fingers flexing before he dug his thumbs into his palms.

"Let me see."

Sliding his feet along the carpet and feeling his way in the darkness, Sam gently perched on the bed's edge. Anita scooped his hands into hers and massaged them.

Sam lay back against the pillows, groaning with pleasure. "Man, that feels so good. If you ever give up reading people's palms, you could become a sexy masseuse to tired old writers and painters and stuff. Knead their knobbly bits." He wiggled his fingers in her grasp.

She laughed. "You really have a way with words, Was."

He chuckled, focusing on every movement of her hands on his. "Wanna know what my favourite word is?"

"Moist?"

"Nope. Though I do enjoy watching the cringe associated with the word *moist*." Sam's lips and tongue slowly formed each letter, mouth curving into a grin as she guessed again.

"Podiatrist?"

"Not even close."

"Tell me, then. I bet it's something totally weird."

He knew he shouldn't, but her hands were already on him, circling the ridges of his hands, turning around his wrists and squeezing the soft pads of his fingertips. Sam wondered at the rules for her spell. Should he tempt fate? Test this strange magic that coursed between them?

"Well? What is your favourite word?" she asked, pressing into his knuckles.

"Anita," he whispered. "Your name ... it's magic on my tongue. It's by far the most amazing word I've ever uttered." He swallowed as her hands froze, squeezed, then resumed their work. "I could never write anything or anyone more perfect than you."

Gathering all his courage, Sam swallowed whatever professional boundary still stood in his way. "I really, *really*, want to kiss you, Anita," he confessed to the shadows. "It doesn't have to be anything more, but ... I want ... I want to ...."

Raising his palm, Anita pressed it to her cheek, her breath

curling against the sensitive inside of his wrist.

Sam's brain lost the rest of the sentence as Anita's teeth grazed the pads of his fingers one by one.

"You want to ... what?" she breathed against his hand. "Paint me like one of your French girls? Or write me as one of your strange fetishes?"

"I can hear your grin, you know." He groaned, his other hand searching for her in the darkness. He wasn't sure, at first, exactly where it landed. Energy rippled beneath his skin, sparking with hers as his hand made contact.

Sliding his fingertip from between her teeth, she murmured, "Kiss me, Sam." He felt her shift closer on the bed. A cloud of sweet lavender filled his nostrils. "Please?"

He pushed himself up, and their noses collided hesitantly in the dark. Sam skated his nose down hers, locating her mouth, allowing the heavy darkness to settle around them. Pressing himself to her warmth, he fought the urge to retreat. Anita was still. Waiting.

The kiss was tentative but magnetic, drawing him deeper. He slipped his arms around her, drawing her softness to him. Every length of skin that touched hers was on fire, tingling and sending shockwaves throughout him.

"You kiss by the book," she said, quoting Shakespeare, arching her neck as he buried his mouth and hands in her hair.

"I'm no Romeo," Sam whispered into her ear, biting the lobe gently. "Dear God, you feel amazing, Anita." Kneeling on the bed, pressed together, her hands slid under his t-shirt, tugging at the fabric, encouraging its removal.

"You sure?" He had to ask.

Her kiss was response enough, all the words he wished she'd say in a gentle stroke of her tongue against his.

Anita slid her warmth over him, straddling his hips, before guiding his hands to the centre of her back, to the clasp of her bra. Sam fumbled with it, hands shaking. Her legs locked at his back. Face to face, stomach to stomach, she didn't seem so short statured curled around him, wrapped in his lap. Sam felt the bra clasp release the fabric sliding from her body. She leaned back slightly, rocking her hips forward.

"God, Anita," Sam groaned as her warmth spread across him in waves. Her hands blazed a trail to the growing bulge in his pants. She gently stroked and rubbed through the fabric of his shorts, kissing him deeper. Sam met her enthusiasm, his hands curling through the wavy lengths of her hair as he rocked his hips upward into her warm, willing hand. They dry humped like teenagers, all adrenaline and breathing and heavy tension as each waited for the other to dictate the next move, enjoying the moment but desperately rising closer to more.

"Wait, slow down." He drew her head back, breathing hard. "I want ... I want to do this good for you, make it good ..."

Anita's laughter hit his face as a wall of warm air.

"Do it good?" She rocked her hips forward, the smooth skin of her stomach and breasts grazing warmly, sensuously, across his bare chest. Her nipples were hard and surprisingly cool, compared to the rest of her body, scorching beneath his touch.

"You know I don't word well," he mumbled, nibbling her ear. Sam breathed hard, Anita's weight on him so delicious.

His hands found her hips and, gripping them tightly, they rolled. Sam lowered himself slowly, pressing Anita into the mattress. She was a beautiful blur of black hair and dark skin on white sheets. Her nipples, just shadows, peeked out from her skirt which had kicked up to cover a portion of her curved stomach. Sliding down the bed, Sam gripped her feet in his hands.

"Are they weird and angular?" Her voice cut through the darkness of the room, adding a jovial air to the heavy, heated atmosphere that swirled around them. "Smell like roses and soap and worthy of a page or two?" Sam kissed the top of her feet, his tongue darting out in tiny licks as he worked up to her ankles, and her calves, his hands gently squeezing a similar path north.

"Delicious," he commented, pausing at her knees. "Salty, like the sea. Definitely worth a solid paragraph, at least."

She swatted at him, but he ducked into her skirts, and she moaned as Sam's lips sucked gently on her inner thigh.

He felt her body tense and quiver beneath him as he continued to lick and suck at the smooth flesh inside her thighs, slowly moving to the edge of her underwear, hands sliding a smooth path after each kiss. Her breath caught, only released when his mouth met the delicate warmth at the apex of her legs. He let his tongue dance and slide, smiling against her thighs as she made a small whimpering noise. He stayed there, savouring the taste, the way she wiggled, the way her breath hitched, and her small groans filled the air.

"Delicious," he repeated, earnestly, raising his head.

"You're stopping?" she said, her expression shocked.

He chuckled, tsking as he rose up, hands moving to the tie of her wrap skirt. "May I?"

Her heavy breath filled the silence for two beats before she whispered, "Yes."

Working the knot, Sam's excitement mounted with each tiny loosening. *Ah, there.* He pulled the fabric slowly, letting it run through his fingers and over her bare chest before sliding it off her body. Curling his hands under her arse, Sam gripped two large handfuls of soft flesh, and a raspy noise escaped his lips.

"You *are* an arse man," Anita giggled. "I'll forever remember that about you."

"I never said that," he protested, massaging.

"Oh yes you did, Was."

He squeezed her behind once more before kissing a cool trail from her belly to her lips, capturing them like a death row inmate might savour his last meal. She responded – equally hungry. His erection pressed into her leg as he ground himself closer, hands in her hair once more.

"I love those little noises you make," he confessed, gripping the warmth at the back of her neck. "I could write an ode to them, if you want?"

"I love–"

He captured her words in his mouth, slowly sliding his hand down her body.

"You deserve the best in this world, Anita." In the darkness, he imagined his hands rubbing away her bruises, his hands stealing the scars and replacing them with more of the soft, warm flesh he'd found at the top of her thighs, where his hand now journeyed. "I'll try my best to make it so. You deserve to be worshipped. An immaculate chocolate torte, layered and decadent." Whatever magic this was, he was firmly under

Anita's spell, and happy to be there. "You're brilliant, truthful, beautiful, and I don't even mind it when you monologue."

Her light laughter hit him straight in the chest; her legs parted in invitation.

"You're quoting me." She ran her hands over his bare shoulders. "The night we met."

"I don't remember *much* ..." he kissed her, pulling the fabric to one side, "but what I do recall ..." he gently slipped his finger through her slick folds, "is that it was magical." She sighed as he sunk his fingers into her warmth. Anita's muscles throbbed around him as he moved slowly. Despite the darkness encompassing them, Sam closed his eyes, focusing on his own breathing, trying to keep his own body under control.

This isn't about you, man. She deserves this. She deserves to know there are good, kind men in the world. Not jerkwads who use their words and fists as weapons. Sam redoubled his efforts, Anita panting breathy little sounds that he tried very hard to ignore. His cock ached, begging for release.

Anita mumbled incoherently, shuddering around him as his thumb brushed the sensitive nub of flesh at the peak of her warm centre.

"Just shut up, Witch. Kiss me." Her lips met Sam's as his fingers slid and explored, plunging deep then stroking light as he moved up and down and inside. "Is this okay?"

"Goddess, yes." Then, "Closer, Was. I need you closer. I need more of you."

His dick strained against its restraints. "I ... I'm not prepared. I mean, I don't have anything ..." He swallowed. "I don't have a condom."

"It's okay," Anita whispered. "I'm on the pill. And I'm so clean, I'm squeaky."

Laughing, he caught her lips. "Say the magic words," he urged, already sliding her now soaked underwear down from her legs.

"Bippity ..." she said, her laugh echoing through his chest cavity, filling his heart with joy before the sensations turned heavier and settled lower, evolving into a deep throb of lust. He threw her last item of clothing across the room, kneeling between her legs.

"Boppity ..." Anita's hands fumbled with the fly of his shorts, slowly popping each tooth of the zipper free while his erection strained against her. She pushed her small hands into his pants and he helped her slide his remaining clothing to the floor. Sam settled back against her warmth, his hands sliding under her waist and shoulders as he positioned himself at the apex of her luscious thighs.

"You sure?" He hated to ask, but it was important. Sam needed to make up for all the wrong in her world, to fix all the broken and bruised bits in her life. He didn't want to just empty himself into her. He wanted to fill her up, like she was a pie dish and the pastry itself, hot and waiting. Anita brought her mouth to his ear and said his new favourite word.

"Boo."

Boo

ANITA

ANITA HAD HAD SEX before, but it had been nothing like *this*. This was the heart-swell of every romantic crescendo, with the sulky womb-throb of all the best romance movies. Sam was attentive and tender yet firm, *oh so firm*. Anita's blood thickened as he inched himself deeper, melting around him, and he sunk completely within her. Breathing, unmoving, Sam froze, his forehead pressed to hers, as they breathed each other in and felt their way in the dark. He muttered something about pastry and she laughed, her muscles contracting around his hard length. He kissed her, then thrust gently, before murmuring "Fuck, Anita," and she laughed again.

"You're so perfect, Witch." He drove into her again and again, his breathing shallow. "So fucking perfect."

She tensed her inner muscles and Sam sucked in air through his teeth, his hair falling to tickle her eyes as his forehead pressed to hers.

"You have a filthy mouth for someone who finds sexy language *icky*," she teased between his kisses, wrapping her legs around his hips, pushing him closer with her heels. Sam groaned, grabbing her arse and rolling once more, so she was on top. She sunk down as gravity settled her firmly to him, marvelling at him, at herself, at how confident she felt. How *right*.

Devoid of self-consciousness, Anita relished the feel of Sam's hands roaming her curves. He touched every square inch of her skin, his cool fingertips exploring her, making her tingle in the most sensual way. Anita loved how, even in the darkness, he gave her pride of position. She felt powerful, possessive, and in control as Sam let her set a steady pace atop him. At every turn he let her win, feel accomplished, and strong. Anita's heart swelled with pride and confidence as her trust in this man became overwhelming. He might not know how to 'word good', but like his writing, he was earnestly working on this, too.

Anita rocked forward and he swore again, gently tugging her hair in that way that drove her wild. Electricity bolted through every twisted, looping follicle until the feeling settled in her skin, vibrating and sensitive. His lips sought hers and he rose up, sitting with his long arms curled protectively around her. Then, his thumb was in her mouth, and she bit down as he thrust his hips up. Each ridge of his fingerprint etched itself onto her tongue and teeth as slowly, she sucked the digit. Sam let out a moan, his breath hot on her neck. He gripped her jaw, pushing something else into her mouth. It melted instantly, heightening her senses.

"Chocolate!" she said, delighted. Sam kissed her, sharing the sweet, smooth treat with his own tongue.

"I knew those little pillow chocolates had to be good for something," he breathed against her, his hands guiding the rhythm of her hips.

Sam filled her heart and soul and now even her stomach. The writer sure knew how to read her, that was for sure.

Rocking against him, Anita savoured their connection and his touch. His lovemaking was sweet. Messy. Hungry. He worked to know her body, and Anita had never felt so desired. She steadied herself, gripping his shoulders, smoothing a hand across his back, moaning as his hands slid between them to cup her breasts, his strong thumbs rubbing her sensitive nipples before returning to her hips once more. Lightning seemed to shoot from her breasts to her clit as the friction increased. She could feel the wiggle and jiggle of her flesh, but joined with Samuel Harthrup, his large, strong hands steadying and anchoring, her usual bodily worries and doubts disappeared. Her softness melted into his harder edges, the flat planes of his chest and stomach meeting perfectly with her curves.

"Anita ..." His thrusts came harder, faster, beneath her. "I'm close. Come with me, babe. Hold on." She met his rhythm thrust for thrust, breathless, and slick with sweat.

"Babe?" The vibrations of her giggle rolled through their connection.

He twisted his fingers in her hair, laughing before crushing her lips to his. "The pig. Babe. Bacon lips. *Joking*, obviously," he panted.

She was losing her mind, like Sam had clearly lost his. Even in the midst of their passion, his brain still came up with the most absurd things to make her giggle. She had never laughed so much in her life than with the romance writer. Was sex supposed to be this funny?

His thrusts increased in tempo, driving harder, faster into her. "Oh, shit, Anita," he moaned.

He could say anything, write anything, and she'd bow at his strangely angular feet. Waves of heat rippled through her, and she felt Sam begin to twitch more erratically.

"Don't wait," she panted. "I'm close." His hand dipped between them and she sucked in her breath as shockwaves rocked through her core. "Oh! Sam!"

"We're in this together," Sam gritted out, almost sounding pained as he rubbed her swollen, throbbing bud. As Anita screamed out, she felt Sam jerk beneath her, losing himself in her pleasure.

"FUCK!" he cried into her hair, pulling her lips to his once more as he twitched and thrust inside her, her own slick walls clenching in perfect ecstasy around him. Her heart threatened to beat from her chest as Sam emptied himself into her, waves of warmth spreading with a pure joy, overwhelming and all-consuming.

His nose skated hers, their foreheads meeting as they sat tangled around each other in the middle of the bed. As Sam's body relaxed, Anita slid her heavy limbs until they lay along Sam's length, clenching her thighs around him. Sam smoothed the hair from her face, tenderly tucking a curl behind her ear. Anita listened to his heartbeat, hard and strong beneath the damp curls of his chest hair. Closing her eyes, she breathed in the smell of Sam. Salty from the beach. Tangy from Anatoli's. The slightly soapy yet musky natural scent of him. She spread her arms around the writer, smiling into his chest.

"You are perfect, Anita," he said. "In every way."

She giggled. "And you're a dirt perve. But I like you a little bit, regardless."

"I can't believe you're leaving town in less than a week," he said quietly, weaving his fingers through her long hair, following the rise and fall of each wave. "It's entirely likely that I won't see you again." He laughed wryly. "You don't even have a phone I could call."

There were times when words were enough, and others when all the words in the world wouldn't adequately fill a silence. This was one of those times.

Anita pressed herself to Sam. His long arms curved around her and they clung to each other in silence. Sliding slowly down the length of his body, Anita held Sam's gaze as she parted her lips and spoke to him in a simple, primal language that didn't require words.

Anita's grumbling stomach signalled lunchtime. Sam pulled out his phone to search for the nearest grocer, frowning as he scrolled through the long list of missed communications.

"Why don't you stay and deal with all that." Anita waved her hand at his phone. "I'll find us something to eat."

"You sure?" Sam's eyebrows drew together as he scrolled.

"No problem at all. I'm well practised at being the new girl in town. I'm used to asking for directions and local hotspots."

"Alright." Sam nodded, pointing at his wallet on the side table before opening an email. A lengthy text filled the screen. Anita whistled, and Sam's cheeks flushed.

He groaned. "My editor."

"I'll leave you to it." Knocking his spectacles askew with a quick ruffle of his hair, she blew a kiss as she headed out the door of their rented cabin.

"Wait!" Sam's cool hand caught hers, spinning her back inside. Without preamble, he pressed his lips to hers, a gentle kiss that assumed nothing more, but spoke volumes. Anita's heart beat against her ribcage, threatening to jump out of her chest entirely. Sincere eyes met hers as a sliver of paper was pushed into her hand.

"I want to cook for you," he said, a fierce, unashamed blush blanketing his features.

Anita raised an eyebrow. "*Heat in the Kitchen* style?"

"Any style you want," Sam laughed, rubbing the back of his neck. "I'll even throw in some cheesy puns, if you add parmesan to the list." His hand squeezed hers, crinkling the note in her palm. "Take my wallet. I don't have much in there, but it's yours. Should be enough to cover that list."

"Thank you. Now, get back to work," she cooed, patting his cheek as she skipped outside and into the sun, leaving him to his lengthy correspondence.

The elderly lady at the reception desk winked as Anita approached, the doorbell still jangling lightly behind her.

"I trust everything is to your liking, dear?"

Anita felt her cheeks warm. "Yes, thank you ..." she looked to the woman's name tag, "Louisa."

"May I help you with something? You or your husband need anything, dear? Clean towels? Or sheets?" Her eyes sparkled as if she were possessed by the cheeky spirit of a Saint Jude's Knight.

Anita's heart raced at the memory of Sam's hands gliding over her, as though he were standing right there, touching, feeling, exploring. "No, thank you. We're fine." With so many rings on her fingers, one of them could have easily been a wedding band. There was no need to correct the grey-haired receptionist about their marital status, or lack thereof. The exact nature of their relationship was complicated, at best. *And won't last much longer, anyway* ... The thought of moving on with Cirque de Fortuna, of leaving Moonshine and Sam left a bad taste in her mouth.

"We need some groceries, though," Anita told Louisa, who nodded seriously, mouth kicked up at one side. "Is there a store nearby?"

Louisa extracted a map from a nearby pile of local brochures and drew a line in thick red marker. It was only a few blocks away and a lovely sunny morning for a walk. Anita thanked Louisa and strolled into the summer day. The sea spray kissed her flushed cheeks as she slid into the shade of a line of beach umbrellas outside a string of businesses. Her ankle twinged suddenly, and she felt the pain in the acute clawing of panic rather than in her joint. *Adrian*. Surely, he would have noticed her absence. What would he do? How would he react? Gulping fresh sea air, Anita tried to calm her mind, shaking off the grip of anxiety that pulled like a knot in her gut, lassoing her lungs and restricting her breath. Through the haze in her head, Sam's words cut through. *You're the Boss Lady*. She damn well knew she wasn't, but the affirmation was enough to loosen the noose. Sam was right, it was HER name on the banners, too. She and Adrian were supposed to be equals and partners. She had to stand up for herself. He had to stop.

The doubt ebbed and flowed for a few minutes, then Anita straightened up, inhaled deeply, and soldiered on to the grocery store, determined to make the most of this weekend – this amazing weekend, with Sammie Hart.

An hour later, Anita rolled down the footpath, leaning heavily on the shopping trolley she'd borrowed to scoot back to the B&B. Kicking her feet in the air, her stomach pressed into the plastic handrail, she clung to the metal sides and propelled herself along, grinning widely. The wind had picked up, whipping her hair, tugging at her skirt, and filling her lungs with fresh, clean, invigorating mirth. *This*, she decided, *is really living*. She stretched her arms out momentarily. Closed her eyes. *Flying*. The laden trolley held her weight perfectly. Sam's wallet was now severely depleted. She felt bad about the money she'd spent, but had purchased only the items on Sam's list, so ...

"Anita?" Her slip-on shoes skidded against the concrete path, slowing her trolley at the familiar voice. "Anita!" Gravel crunched as a car rolled to a stop beside her.

"Zack?" She pinpointed him easily in her mind. *Ashton Kutcher, in any of his romcom roles.* "Hello!" She grinned widely, opening her arms to hug the young man as he rounded the car to meet her.

"It *is* you!" He laughed, his long hair shining in the sun. Zack wrapped Anita in an enthusiastic embrace.

"What are you doing here?"

"Holiday," she said simply, pushing down the pang of anxiety.

"Aw, man, I miss you. I should've run away with the circus!" Zack eyed Anita's transport. "Want a ride?"

She smiled. "No thank you, I'm almost there. How are you? Did you propose to Jenny yet?" When Anita had met Zack, a few months and many towns ago, she'd read his palm and his heart immediately. The poor fellow was lovesick and hurting. She had never seen a more desperately smitten man, full of such heart and wearing it so openly on his sleeve. Zack couldn't make a grand gesture big enough to cement his lover's affections. Anita had two weeks to help.

Zack grinned. "Sure did. Best decision I ever made, listening to you."

"Good for you! I knew you could do it."

"Couldn't have done it without you. You're amazing, Anita, seriously. There's no way my life would be the same without having met you, and the circus, and ..."

A shadow fell over her as Zack gushed, his eyes widening at something beyond her shoulder.

"Anita." The cold voice shot through to her core, every muscle tightening. She spun, almost backing into Zack.

"Adrian," she croaked. "What–"

"Well, isn't this a small world!" Zack beamed. "You're the ringmaster, right? Wait, is Cirque de Fortuna here in Warner's Bay? Jenny and I could come ..."

How did he find me? Why is he here? How did he know? The words crashed like glass to the floor of her brain, thoughts scattering and spilling, flooding the tiny pauses between her questions.

"A small world indeed," Adrian ground out through clenched teeth, his eyes flicking from her to Zack. *Slut. Whore.* The words were flung, unsaid, into her face. Judgement burned in his eyes.

"We were just catching up." Zack smiled, casually looping his arm about her shoulders, oblivious to the furious tension that crackled off Adrian, and to how Anita had shrunk in his shadow.

"I'll bet." Adrian's eyes flicked from the mass of food in the shopping cart to Anita's stomach, to her face. His eyebrow rose. *Fat. Ugly.* "I'll leave you to it." Adrian bowed slightly at Zack, who laughed at the strange gesture, nodding slightly in reply. "See you later, Anita." Adrian's words, an unveiled threat, burned hotter than chilli.

Pressing her feet into the hot cement, she took a deep breath. "Tomorrow." All the hope she'd cautiously built up in her time with Sam rushed out with that one word. *Tomorrow.* She hoped to the Goddess he wouldn't ask her anything more than that. It was all she could give – one day at a time, one hope for a better tomorrow.

"Tomorrow," he acknowledged, his voice flat with implication and warning. He strode to his motorcycle, hidden behind another parked car in the street, and roared away without a backward glance. The deep, monstrous rumble of the black chopper shook the ground, rattling her bones like an earthquake. Without physically touching her, Adrian had managed to shake her body and her confidence. Leaning heavily onto the shopping trolley, she barely heard Zack's exclamation of, "That guy is so cool!" as they watched his thunderous retreat.

"As ice." Anita shivered. *How could he do this to me? How did he find me? Who betrayed me?* Her skin burned with worry as each question settled upon a memory of a bruise.

"If you're staying close by, let me walk you there." Zack took hold of her cart. "And I'll tell you all about how I managed to woo Jenny."

When they reached the cabin, it took all Anita's resolve not to race inside, fling the curtains shut and bolt the door. "Thank you, Zack." She leant in for a hug, the sun-warmed fabric of his shirt comforting against her cheek. "It was lovely to see you. I just know you'll be a great dad in ... seven months, was it? Congrats again, and say hi to Jenny for me."

As Zack's arms looped around her, the door opened. Sam's tall, lanky frame filled the doorway, spectacles lopsided and his hair spiking up at strange angles.

"New project?" Zack's thumb pointed to Sam, eyes flicking up then down the mess of a man.

"Sort of." She tried desperately not to blush. With a cocked eyebrow, Zack nodded to Sam, before smiling warmly at Anita.

"Good luck!" he whispered, waving goodbye as he jogged lightly back to the road.

"Who was that?" Sam asked, as he helped her bring the bagged groceries inside.

"An old friend." She sighed, sliding the door bolt shut, peering out of the window. Was Adrian really gone? *I hope so.* Two men and a hotel ... her brother's imagination would have taken those meagre facts and twisted them into something hurtful. She could feel Sam's eyes on her, but didn't want the focus. This wasn't the tango, and it wasn't the circus. There was no deep blue spotlight on her now. This was about Sam. It was all for him, this trip. She would deal with Adrian, and he would deal with her. Her life would continue on the roundabout it had always been stuck on, a loop of towns and shows and familial pain, but she, Anita Fortuna, could leave her own mark by helping this writer.

Turning from the window, she smiled weakly at Sam. "How's the book going?"

He pinched the bridge of his nose. "Did you get the ingredients I asked for?"

"Of course."

"Then I'll tell you over dinner."

Adrian's surprise appearance had sucked all the fun and heat from the day. She felt like an icy pole with the flavour removed. But watching Sam cook, seeing the way he moved so gracefully around the clean kitchen, laying the ingredients in a neat line on the light blue laminate benchtop before starting, melted her worry.

Anita's mouth watered at the thought of a good meal. She wasn't big on cooking herself, constantly grateful to Claus for his food preparation role in their communal living situation. But Anita did love new foods and flavours, and there was something completely romantic about watching a man moving around a clean kitchen, offering samples from a wooden spoon as delicious scents swirled.

Sam was trying to avoid alcohol, but as they sipped water from champagne flutes she'd found in a cupboard, the same hazy effect took over and she marvelled at the writer.

The way Sam's body relaxed in the kitchen made Anita want to watch him. He clearly loved to cook, becoming oddly chatty as he narrated his culinary ballet. Rinsing, stirring, and searing, he combined pomegranate juice, honey, coriander and cinnamon in a small pot, bringing the delicious sauce to a boil. It was like being in a private audition for *MasterChef*.

As the sauce reduced and became syrupy, a deep ache of jealousy passed through her. Sam was a *whole person*. He was solid and grounded in his life and his craft. He truly knew who he was and what he wanted – even if that meant hiding his secret identity as Sammie Hart.

Anita, by contrast, wasn't the one person, with one path ahead. She could be anyone she wanted, a new variation of herself in each new town. And she relished the unique opportunities she found in each community. She was a transient. A shadow, whose mark on the world would be left in miniscule interactions and helpful tasks. But in this role, with Sam ...

Somehow, he had taken a cheese grater to her soul, slicing away tiny shreds of her life. Sam had peeled her back, exposing the bones of her, plucking at her innermost parts. Never had she felt so raw as she did with him. It was a problem. She couldn't let herself become attached. She never had before. Her plan had always been the same – pay it forward. Do a good deed, and hope that positive karma would eventually come her way. She didn't need to complicate anyone's life – not hers, and certainly not Sam's. And yet ...

Perhaps it was about as complicated as this meal he was

making. The kitchen bench between them was littered with ingredients, chopping boards and utensils. Absently, she started cleaning up the mess.

"Truth or dare?" Anita suddenly asked.

Sam looked up from the scallops he was searing on the stove, spectacles fogged. "Seriously?"

Anita giggled, reaching to slide his spectacles off and clean them on a tissue. "Why not? Need plates?"

Sam nodded and she rifled through cupboards until she found them. "Truth, I suppose," he grumbled, sliding the scallops onto one clean plate, so at ease with this food, this work.

"Tell me about your family."

He froze.

"I didn't mean to hit a nerve. You don't have to," she added quickly. "It's just a silly game, but … you know about Adrian. And you've seen my crazy circus family. I just thought, maybe, I could know a bit about yours?"

Sam focused intently for a moment as he sautéed spinach leaves in a frypan, seasoning them with a flourish of sprinkled salt. Sensing his growing unease, she continued clearing the bench, organising and cleaning, laying more plates out, plopping used knives and spoons into the sink.

"Okay." He nodded slightly, arranging the spinach on two plates and topping the wilted leaves with the seared scallops. Anita's mouth watered as he drizzled the sticky, sweet pomegranate sauce over the meal. A lump formed in her throat as she watched Sam's eyes darting, clearly considering what to reveal to her, what to say.

Placing the loaded plates on the dining table, he slid heavily into a chair. Anita refilled his champagne glass with water, placing it gently in front of him, before taking her own seat beside him.

"This looks delicious," she said, turning to face him more fully, offering a way out of the conversation, an opportunity to backpedal and talk easily of food once more.

He motioned to Anita's plate. "Try it."

She slid a mouthful between her lips, and her eyes rolled upwards as bliss bloomed in her mouth.

Sam began, his eyes on his plate, his fork flicking away a pomegranate seed. "The last memory I have of my parents is ..." He swallowed, starting over. "My parents were arguing ... *again*. It was school pick-up time. They couldn't find me. They were so mad. They had no idea but ... I was pinned on my back by Brent Collins, the school's biggest bully. He was sitting on my chest and his fists were working damn hard to break my face open. But ..." he looked at her, "that's kind of another story." He took a small bite and she let him think, let him tell the tale in his own time. "That's how I met Reece. He pulled Brent off me, smashed him with one solid blow to the chin, hauled my arse out of there."

Anita's hand reached for his and their fingers curled together on the small tabletop. She swallowed lightly, focusing on Sam, lips pressed tight. It was his turn to monologue, for once, and she wouldn't interrupt. There was always time for questions. *Later*. The word was bittersweet, a sudden pain pulsing deep in her bones. Their 'later' was approaching faster than she wanted.

"My parents were furious with me. I wasn't in the pick-up spot. I was late. I was rude. I had disobeyed their authority.

I was the source of their frustration and their drinking and their financial troubles and ... they regretted not terminating the pregnancy. They were never ready for kids. They never wanted me. I heard it all, every day. Dad would whack me around and say these things, and Mum would sip her wine and just let it happen.

"They say family is love, but to me –" Sam's eyes slid to Anita, "that was never my experience. They used to tell me all the time that I was worthless, that I'd ruined their lives, that there was no way I'd ever have a sibling because I was already too much to deal with. They were jerks. I was small and quiet and scared, and ..." Sam's body deflated. "Anyway, they started driving around looking for me, fighting with each other, half concerned and half drunk and a whole lot of pissed off. They ..." he swallowed, "the car hit a girl."

Anita's fingers flexed, digging into his flesh. She turned more fully in her seat, facing him, eyes wide.

"She was in hospital for a month. A few surgeries. And they couldn't deal." He shrugged, his eyes meeting hers. "A small town like Moonshine can be great, Anita. Cups of sugar from your neighbour, first name basis with everyone. But if they turn on you, then there's nothing like the prejudice of a small community." He shrugged again. "My parents weren't strong enough to deal with everything. They left Moonshine. Left me with my Grandma Edith, so I could finish school, they said. But really, they just wanted out. Out of town and away from me, the kid who made their lives suck. They hadn't cared that school had been hell for me. They didn't care that despite all their flaws, I wanted to go *with* them to wherever it was they were going. They were my family, you know?" He blinked hard, trying to hold back tears. "I was staying in Moonshine. I had no say. Neither did Gran, but she took it in her stride, a lot better than me. But from that day on, with Reece by my side, school – *life* – improved, little by little. I had three square meals a day, for once. I was encouraged to pursue my passion for cooking. I had a house without holes in the walls, my own room, and even a cat for a few years." The smallest of smiles played at the edges of his lips. "I lived with Gran until graduation, then I moved into my flat, and I've been there trying to stand on my own two feet ever since. Trying to be better than *them*."

"It's difficult," Anita said, voice low and raw, "to stand on your own feet. Be an adult. Adulting is hard."

"Adulting isn't a word, Anita," Sam scoffed, squeezing her hand. Sitting beside him wasn't close enough. Leaning into him, she slid her hands over his chest, fingers tapping out the steady rhythm of the heartbeat they found there.

"Samuel Harthrup, you have the *biggest* heart," Anita whispered, leaning closer. His breath, sweet and laced with cinnamon, said her name once more. She pressed her lips to his, drinking him in. All his pain, his sorrow; she wanted to somehow suck it from him, to release the tension in those heavy shoulders that bore the sad, resentful memories. She wished desperately to heal him, the way Sam had started to heal her, with soft kisses and caresses and kindness in the dark.

But it wasn't dark. And she wasn't gentle. Anita was hungry with want and need. It pooled in her gut, mixing with the sweet tastes of him, the meal he'd made still dancing on her tongue. She wanted to devour this man, this writer, this chef, knowing that in only a few days, the nomadic life would again swallow her whole.

Sam responded to her like a moth to a flame, matching every kiss and lick and desperate grip with gusto. Their plates clattered to the floor, the pomegranate sauce splashing pink, wilted spinach sliding off in a shrivelled green stream as Sam gripped Anita by the backside, guiding her onto the table.

"This is not professional," he told her, nearly tearing off her clothes.

"You're right," she agreed as his hot lips sunk down, settling low. One hand gripped her thigh, the other splayed low on her abdomen as he tasted the depths of her. Reaching out, Anita found the last chunk of her scallop, popping it into her mouth as her body rippled with delight. It was good. It was all so, *so* good. And Sam revelled in her praise of his skills.

After licking every last flavour from each other's skin (and the plates) they settled on the couch together. Sam was writing intently, so focused on his work that he didn't even notice the world had shifted around him. Anita had shifted. Her whole world was simultaneously falling apart and falling into a place, with Sam. He offered a perfect recipe for happiness, short lived as it might be.

Deciding to let the writer finish his masterpiece, which was really starting to sizzle, Anita pushed the little red button on the remote. The television sprung to life and she scrolled through the apps. Squealing, she clicked on Disney Plus.

As the pre-show credits of a classic Disney masterpiece filled the screen, Anita said, "Did you know that Aurora has the least dialogue of any Disney Princess? She's the protagonist with the fewest words in her own story. Isn't that sad?"

"Mmmm. Dialogue. Gotcha."

Rolling her eyes, Anita tucked into his side, cooling her flushed skin. *This is right.* Sammie was writing and she was ... *safe.* Yes, that's what that feeling was.

Safe. Anita's body relaxed. *I wish this would never end.*

Best Laid Plans

SAM

THE DRIVE BACK TO Moonshine was strangely silent. No rambling. No monologues. Just the almost-comfortable silence between two people who'd had amazing sex. Repeatedly. Sam wasn't sure how Anita was feeling after their weekend away, but he wanted more. The past two days had been a revelation. An awakening. A new dawn in his personal and writing lives. Well, almost. Every time he looked at Anita, or felt the warm graze of her hand, he was only reminded that by the end of this week, she would be gone.

"What are your plans tonight?" she asked, leaning over to place a hand on his thigh.

Sam kept his eyes on the road. "It's Monday. That means dinner with Gran. And I'd better check in with Reece. Maybe not in that order, I'm not sure." There was a pause. "You?"

Anita's hand withdrew. From the corner of his eye, he saw her hands clench tightly together. "Go back, I suppose."

Swerving to the shoulder of the road and stopping, he yanked on the handbrake, blinded by white hot rage.

"Sam! Why did you swerve like that? What's wrong?"

"You can't."

"I can't *what*, Was?"

"Go back. To the circus. To your brother. That life isn't good enough for you, Anita. It's not *safe*." His hands reached for hers. "You can't." *I care about you too much …*

Anita snatched her hands from his. "I have to. There's no alternative, Sam."

"Listen, Anita." Sam growled the words. "You don't have to put up with that. With him! *No one* should suffer domestic violence."

She barked a laugh, loud and dry. "How can it be domestic if I'm technically homeless?"

"*Familial* violence, then," he hissed through gritted teeth. "Label it however you want, Anita. It's wrong. It's fucking wrong and shit and you deserve better than–"

Her warm hand silenced him, her finger pressed to his lips before smoothing against his cheek. "I know. I can handle it. I've *been* handling it." She said the words, though neither believed them. "It's okay, Sam."

"It's *not*," he spat. "And I thought you didn't lie? Don't let that change, Anita. Your honest observations are one of the best things about you." He scrutinised her, jaw aching from his clenched teeth. "He can't do this, Anita." She ran her thumbs across his cheekbones. He was surprised and frustrated they left his face smudged in saltwater.

"Not all men are like that," Sam said softly. "My dad was, and your brother ..." Anita shivered. "But not me." He couldn't unsee the marks that hid beneath her clothing, but he would work damn hard to heal her while he could – even if it was only removing bruises to her confidence. "And from now on, only one man is allowed to touch you."

"And who is that?" she spat, laughing at his absurdity. "You? My scrawny dirt perve nerd? Am I just going to swap one form of masculine controlling influence for a cuddlier variety? You don't get to dictate to me, Sam. You're a beautiful distraction from a pretty shitty existence." She saw him wince, try to backtrack and explain, but she pushed forward, gathering strength to say words she needed to get out. "You're a project and you're *wonderful*, but I'm as transient to your life as Moonshine is to mine."

Hurt coursed through him, but it was too late now. You couldn't un-toss a salad.

"Project?" Sam's grip tightened. Anita's eyes widened, trying to shake his manacle hands from her own. A low whimper escaped.

Throwing his hands into the air, Sam backed as far away from Anita as he could. "Shit, I'm sorry. Anita, I didn't mean ..." Concern, fear, and anger at his own brutish self twisted into a ball in his gut. How could he fix this? Get her to stay? *You can't. They always leave. Everyone does.* Sam set his mouth into a tight line, the hurt and slight tinge of fear in her eyes like a punch to his gut.

"Did I hurt you?"

She shook her head, looking suddenly sad and tired. "I'm

okay, really. But I need to get back to the circus." Her words were a corkscrew to his heart.

"You can't."

"I have to." She smiled weakly. "*Fortuna*. My name on the banners, remember?"

"Shithouse." He hadn't meant it as a joke, but somehow, their previous joke about name changes broke through the tension. Mouths twitched into reluctant smiles.

After a few moments Sam let down the hand brake, clicked the indicator, and with a final check over his shoulder, pulled back onto the road.

"Reece is right. I'm a dweeb. An idiot. I'm sorry." He tried focusing on the road, a side-long glance catching Anita wiping at her eyes. Shit. He'd been stupid. Selfish. And now, he'd ruined it. Them. Her.

"It's not you," she said, blinking back her tears.

"It's me?" He sighed the classic letdown line. "God, Anita, that's so cliché. But whatever. I live in a world of romantic clichés, so I suppose it's fitting."

"Please don't be angry."

"I'm not angry!" Sam snapped. *I'm disappointed* ... And for once, Anita didn't seem to have a response.

The silence stretched until Sam begrudgingly parked outside the showground. The big, hard knot that was his stomach ached worse than IBS ever had. Sharp pangs in his chest made him think of coronary issues, and he was glad to be seeing the doctor tonight. He needed a check-up. A check-up and a cold fricking hops-filled home brew lager.

The colourful tents, flags and banners, the lively music and the occasional lonely whinny of Leo the fabulous unicorned Shetland, painted a brighter picture than the look of trepidation on Anita's face.

She opened the door, then turned. Their eyes met.

"Thanks, Sam," she said, lips tugged up heroically.

His mouth pressed to hers, sudden and desperate. His whole body sought hers, trying to drag her closer. Her hands to his chest, she pushed him back gently.

"Tonight?" she asked. The hope in her voice made him think of spaghetti – a wobbly and tenuous string between them.

"Maybe not tonight ..." Sam couldn't believe the words, even as he said them. He felt deflated, but why delay their separation? She was leaving. There wasn't much point to their charade anymore. Surely, that's all this had been.

"Are you sure? I was looking forward to harassing you about the ending to your book."

He nodded, once, and she bit her lip before nodding in return. Slipping from the car, she closed the door.

"I understand." Her voice was extra-mild curry, devoid of any heat.

"Anita – wait!" he called. She turned back, briefly. He didn't want to ask, but he did. "Is that all I am to you? A book and a safe bed?"

A look flashed in her eyes, but she shook it off, her long, crazy waves curling around her face. "You think that's true? Sam, do you *want* me to stay away?" The look in her eyes was beyond hope. It was hunger, a challenge, a wish.

Sam sighed. "I want you with me. But I need to know. What am I to you? What do you see when you look at me?"

Her mouth quirked up as he played her own game. "It's not all about what you *see*, Was, you big dumb man." Her face melted into a faint, tired smile. Resting her forearms on the window ledge she leaned in and put her hand to his cheek. "You've misjudged the assignment. Again." She sighed quietly. "You're so many things, Sam. But right now, I'm afraid that I can't be what you need. Not for much longer, anyway. I'm here until the weekend and then ..." Her eyes travelled to the circus before them. Three massive banners reading *Cirque de Fortuna* swayed in the breeze. Anita looked back at him, shrugging. "I need to go."

Sam's hand darted out, gripping her wrist lightly. "Anita, you can't."

"You can't stop me, Sam. You have your life and I have mine. Our paths crossed for a reason, and as much as I want to stay ..." Her voice trailed off.

"But—"

"No, Sam." Anita's voice held a raw crispness he'd never heard before. It was the furthest thing from her chest-fluttering laughter, hitting his heart all the same. "I don't think we should do whatever *this* is." She motioned between them. "It was amazing. Truly. But it's not what you need anymore." She wrenched her wrist free; his hand felt ice cold without her heat. "Goodbye, Sam. I can't wait to read your *Heat* sequel. You know the library is always ... my first stop in ... a new town." Voice breaking, she turned away.

Bile rose in his throat as Anita walked off towards the circus. Sam watched her, utterly speechless, brain boiling over with millions of tiny bubbles of doubt, worry, longing, hurt.

"Anita!" he called. But the spell was broken. She didn't linger. The charm had worn off. "Witch!"

She kept moving, disappearing beyond a cotton candy stand. Sam's head hit the steering wheel, spectacles slipping to his lap.

"Shit."

"So, how is the manuscript coming along?" Grandma Edith nudged her grandson as Eddie handed her three clean plates. Well accustomed to each other's rhythms and movements, the elderly couple moved in complete sync, as though in a slow dance around the kitchen. It was a dance of familiarity and love, of tiny touches, small smiles and brushed elbows as they circled each other in their dinner preparations, with a surprising amount of grace for their age.

This is the relationship I want. Sam watched the aged lovers tenderly before the wayward thought sunk in to hit bone. Relationship he wanted? He'd never really thought about relationships and their longevity in a kitchen before. The weekend with Anita had muddled his head. Relationships were for *stayers*. No one wanted to stay with him. Everyone left, eventually. Even Grandma Edith would one day be gone. The realisation hung heavy in his chest as he looked at her. *Maybe*, he consented to the idea, *maybe I do have abandonment issues.*

"So?"

"Sorry, Gran, I wasn't really listening. What did you say?"

"Listening and hearing are different, you know." She flicked his earlobe lovingly. Sam wondered if the women in his life had always been so pedantic about semantics. *Listening, hearing. Seeing, feeling. Writing, creating on-page sizzle, then real-life fizzle.*

"How's the new book coming, Sammie?" Gran repeated, raising an eyebrow and her voice. "Managed to write that erotic scene –"

"SSSHHH!" Sam blushed, his eyes swinging to Eddie.

"Oh, don't worry about him." Edith swatted a hand towards her partner. "He's as deaf as a bat."

"Ay?" Eddie turned to her voice. "What did you say?"

Raising her voice, she touched his arm gently. "Nothing, dear, just talking to Sam about his sex book!"

"Oh, righto!" Eddie turned back to washing potatoes in the sink, humming softly to himself.

Edith winked. "See?"

Sam – practically a puddle on the floor by this stage – didn't want to mention that while Eddie did have large, pointed yet unhearing ears, bats had sensitive hearing that relied on ultrasonic echolocation, so that metaphor didn't stick. He remembered this vividly. It had been his year three science project and the reason his father had forcefully, repeatedly, clapped his hands to Sam's ears every time the word 'bat' had been spoken. Headaches for days and throbbing eardrums hadn't stopped Sam from winning a first-place ribbon, which had been carefully smuggled into his pillowcase for several months.

"Tell me all about it, Sammie Hart. Is this new book as fantastic as the last one?" Gran's hand rested gently on his arm.

Sammie Hart. Every time he heard that name a secretive swell of pride filled his chest. "Much better than it was a week ago," he admitted, adjusting his spectacles. "I knew it wasn't my best work, but I didn't know how off it really was until Anita started ripping it to shreds."

"Ah, she has a name!" Gran beamed at his blush. "This Anita, your muse ... she's been helpful, then?"

Sam didn't appreciate the grin that teased the crinkles of his grandmother's face.

"Actually, yes. Her opinions cut deeper than Japanese steel through a salmon steak, but she makes annoyingly valid criticisms."

"She must be *whipping* you into shape." His grandmother winked. "You're back describing the world through a lens of food."

"I am?"

She nodded, grinning. "Aside from in your writing, you haven't been in that mindset for a while now, dear. Your *MasterChef* mind fell flatter than my flans." Her dentures gleamed as she motioned to her sagging breasts.

Nothing is sacred to the elderly. The Knights assembled in his mind as Gran continued.

"You lost that spark, dear. But I'm glad you're reigniting the furnace, so to speak."

The blush consumed him quickly, his spectacles nearly fogging.

"You know, Sam, I support you in everything you do. But I worry." Edith perched delicately beside him. "I worry about your heart, Sammie. You open up on paper but close yourself off in the real world."

"Yeah, well, fiction is easy." Sam shrugged. "In reality, it's hard to find someone who wants to stick around like a romantic protagonist would."

"I understand. A good character will live in your heart forever, like Mr Fitzwilliam Darcy for me. Tall, dark, handsome and in the social elite. He was every girl's dream. But the reality of a warm bedfellow is so much more than that."

Sam's thoughts shifted again to Anita. *A warm bedfellow indeed.* So hot she was scorching, the witch was the most tantalising spice he could have added to his life.

"Time is all relative," Edith continued, cloudy eyes flicking to Eddie, happily slicing vegetables at the bench. "There's not a day goes by that I don't thank God for giving me a second chance, and more time for love. I truly believed I was done, then I met Eddie ..."

Tears clouded her eyes, and she cleared her throat harshly. Eddie looked to her, a small nod of acknowledgement directed her way. He might not be able to hear their conversation, but he seemed acutely aware of each emotion beneath her weathered skin. The way Gran lit up when she nodded back at Eddie clenched Sam's heart.

Yes, this *is what I want ...*

"Make the most of your time together," Gran advised. "And if you want more time with the circus woman – make it happen! If you want a book, then only you can write it. You have to decide how to invest in the dream, dear."

"It's not that easy, Gran." Sam sighed, pinching the bridge of his nose. Since when had Monday night dinner become a lecture on love and literature?

"Bullshit." Her sudden expletive shocked him. "It's as easy or as difficult as you decide to make it, Samuel James Harthrup."

Eddie interrupted her impending tirade with two ridiculously full glasses of shiraz.

"Oh, thank you dear." Edith's eyes brimmed once more as she sipped the red wine. Eddie collected his own extremely full glass before shuffling carefully to the sofa, just a few feet from the kitchen. Open plan living had its benefits, especially when those included a wrinkled, shiraz-providing interruption that was usually only a few feet away.

"So, Sam," Eddie said, slumping into the couch with a sigh. "Managed to write that sex scene yet?" *So much for being deaf!*

Time dragged on uncomfortably as Sam outlined his novel to Edith and Eddie, garnering feedback from his grandmother and her long-time boyfriend. He let them read sections of the manuscript, nibbling his thumbnail.

"Son, this is wonderful," Eddie encouraged, handwritten papers in one hand and the other gripping Sam's shoulder, shaking it gently. "Really good."

"You mean it?" It was a relief, really. People knowing about him – Sammie Hart – and his work.

Edith chuckled, another chunk of paperwork in her hands. "It's funny! Poignant and *deliciously* described." Her milky eyes met his. "You need to thank that fortune teller. She's certainly worked some kind of spell over you." She shook the paper. "This story is nothing like the, uh–"

"Kindling?" Sam suggested, borrowing Anita's word.

"Well, I wouldn't quite say *that*. But this is more sizzle, for sure!"

"Keep this muse around, son," Eddie advised, his voice loud as he emptied a second bottle of wine between their three glasses. "To Miss Fortuna." Eddie raised his glass.

"To the witch," Sam begrudgingly agreed.

His phone buzzed in his pocket.

Reece: I'm here.

Sam rose, opening Gran's door. The tall doctor beamed from the front step, a huge bunch of flowers before him.

"NANNA EDITH!" Reece Hargraves grinned, swooping in to scoop Sam's grandma into his arms.

"Why, Doctor Reece Hargraves, I never! It's nearly midnight! Way too late for house calls!"

"It is?" Eddie yawned, checking his absent watch, tapping his bare wrist lightly.

"It's never too late to call on you," Reece said flirtatiously.

Gran's cheeks reddened and she swatted his arm lightly before accepting the bouquet. Heading into the kitchen, she replaced Reece's flowers from a fortnight ago. The vase – a chunky, handmade clay monstrosity Sam's seven-year-old self had lovingly crafted for Mother's Day – almost brought a smile to Sam's lips. Almost.

"I just got off work," Reece apologised, checking the time on his phone. "Had to do a few hours at the hospital, covering another doctor. I knew Eddie was cooking tonight, so that meant wine." He slung his arm around Sam's neck, ruffling his hair and dislodging his glasses. "That usually means this dweeb is too sloshed to drive. So here I am, the sexiest taxi service in Moonshine."

"Oh, *you*!" Gran tittered.

"You know, you ALL should be limiting your liquor ..." A cool draught blew in through the open door as Reece assumed his stern doctor's tone. Sam shot a pleading look at his friend. *Please don't ...*

Edith hadn't known the depth of Sam's depression, and the extent of his drinking issues. Reece's appraising gaze took Sam in, his strong jaw dipping in an almost imperceptible nod. Sam's stiff body relaxed a little, knowing he wasn't about to receive another lecture tonight. He began collecting his papers, preparing to leave. "And it's bedtime for the old ducks."

"Who fucks?" Eddie asked the room.

"*Ducks*, Mister Hogan," Reece said, his voice loud and clear.

"Oh bother. Here I was thinking I'd get lucky tonight," Eddie mumbled loudly into his wine glass, his eyelids drooping.

"Oh my God," Sam grumbled, patting the old man on the shoulder, startling him from his shockingly quick slip into sleep. "Good night, Eddie. Thanks for the steak."

Eddie raised his glass, eyes already drooping once more.

Sam brought an arm around his grandmother. "Night, Gran."

"It *was* a good night." She leant into Sam's awkward hug. "See you next Monday. I look forward to the next instalment of your story."

"Bye, Nanna! Pops!" Reece called from the doorway, blowing kisses that Edith readily caught. Eddie snored lightly, glass dipping in his slackened grip.

As soon as the door closed behind them, Reece turned on his heel to face Sam. "Drink?"

"Shit yeah, if the Doctor's buying."

Reece rolled his eyes. "As always. But only if we go out."
Clicking the button on his BMW, they watched the lights
illuminate the retirement village. "I need to get out of my
house and my head. And I'm only letting you drink in social
situations."

"No complaints here." Sam slid onto the pristine leather
seats, tucking his manuscript safely into the pouch behind the
passenger's seat.

"And I think we need to talk about your little impromptu
beach getaway ..." Reece waggled his eyebrows, and it was Sam's
turn to roll his eyes, cheeks already burning.

"Pretty sure I've done enough talking tonight." Sam poked a
thumb over his shoulder, to Gran's front door. "How about I
listen to you rattle on about coronaries, infections, and snotty
kids with hot mums instead?"

The car rumbled to life as Reece laughed. "To The Pope?"

"Let's go to church, my friend!"

"You spiked my drink!" Sam slurred, sunlight streaming in
the suddenly wide-flung curtain.

"No, I asked for your permission. Every time, in fact. And at
each request you donned your horned helmet, raised the mighty
Mjolnir and declared 'indeed!' to the whole bar. Ask anyone!
They'll vouch for me," Reece countered, cracking an egg into
the frying pan with a loud sizzle.

"Where's the helmet?"

Reece shrugged. "I think Adam James stole it. Last I saw, he was chugging beer from it while a bunch of women chanted his name."

Moaning, Sam attempted to sit up.

"I'm glad your breakups are so few and far between, or else I'd worry about your liver even more than usual." Reece thrust a tall glass of water at Sam while the bacon and eggs sizzled merrily away, filling the flat with a stomach-flipping scent. "Scratch that; the doctor in me definitely does worry about your liver, but the BFF side totally loved seeing you let your hair down, bro. And *in public*! Will wonders never cease?"

"Where's Mjolnir?" Sam's eyes scanned the flat. His *clean* flat. Anita was everywhere. In his head and in his neatly stacked piles of laundry. "I really want to hit something."

Reece squinted an eye as he, too, examined the flat. "You left Mjolnir at the pub, with your pride."

Sam groaned, burying his face in the sofa seat. A terrible idea. The couch smelled like fart.

"My tummy hurts, doc."

"Good. You ingested *so* much lactose last night." Reece pointed tongs at him accusingly. A glob of fat dripped to the floor. "You deserve whatever you get after torturing yourself so creatively."

"Does the doc have a sore head of his own today?" *I'd wager, yes.* Sam's BFF gingerly joined him at the table, dark hair spiking between his fingers.

"I'm only sore from your singing at karaoke, man. Pitched like a cat in heat, you are."

Vomit. He should go vomit. Or simply die. *Can you die from pure mortification?*

"I did not do karaoke." Sam's voice lacking the authority needed.

"Did too. Billy Carmichael did *not* appreciate your rendition of Taylor Swift's *Shake It Off*."

"I *sang* at The Pope?"

"*On* the bar." Reece grinned as Sam's mouth fell. "Pretty sure you're banned for life now. Billy was not a happy man." Shuffling towards the stove, Reece flipped bacon then pushed the pre-loaded toaster sleeves down. "You –" a spatula pointed towards Sam, "– shower. Breakfast in five."

The thought of a cold shower, to temper the heat of his embarrassment, was enticing. But a small knock turned him from the idea, his heart leaping into his chest. *Anita*. He raced to the door, flinging it open.

"Ani–"

Sam had expected his constant daydream. His beautiful bohemian. The witch. For an instant, he imagined her five-foot-nothing curves, crazy curls and flowing skirts filling the doorframe.

A gruff voice lamented, "Not quite."

Sam hadn't expected this – a solid mass of cross-armed clown, make-up cracked and smeared, a serious expression on his face and something dark clutched in his hand.

"I'm Claus. We haven't met, not official like. You the townie project?"

Sam gulped, nodding, despite the sloshing wave of pain it sent through his skull.

"But she's not here," Sam said, the words catching in his throat. "She ... left." *Me. She left me.*

The clown's hard, air-chopping finger cut him off. "Mate, I ain't here te bust yer balls about what yer been doin' or not doin' with Miss Anita. She needs yer." The clown held out his hand. A soft wave of lavender scent rose up. "There ain't no excuses for this sorta misbehavin'. There's a line in the sand, townie, an' he's crossed it."

Sam took the offering, drawing it closer, brows furrowed. *What the …?* He knew this softness, had curled his fingers through it before. This darkness, and its lavender-and-vanilla scent – Anita's hair! Horror washed over him, cold as ice down his spine, and realisation struck. Revulsion sent bile soaring into his throat. Throwing the severed ponytail to the ground, Sam stared down, his hands shaking.

"He cut it," Sam heard Claus say, fury riding high in his voice. "He cut it off, took 'er dignity, like he did when they was just kids. Made 'er sit there an' got the scissors round 'er pony-tail–"

"Shit! Shit, shit! That FUCKING BASTARD!"

White hot rage blinded Sam. Swaying on his feet, he lost all sense of self. Imagination running wild, he blinked back tears of pity, sorrow, and hatred. The diamond-painted eyes of the circus clown came closer, the man holding Sam steady.

"Who are you?" Reece appeared protectively beside Sam, eyes flashing between the men, cutting to the dark mass both men glared at, lying beside their feet. "And why is there a chunk of hair on the stoop?"

"We need to do something!" Sam spun to Reece. "Grab your keys. We're going." He moved to push past Claus.

"Hold up, townie." Claus thrust a weathered hand to Sam's chest, pushing him back. "We agree, completely. Somethin' needs doin'. But we'll need a plan fer Adrian, or there'll be trouble fer sure."

"Who is *we*? What the hell is going on?" Reece demanded.

Sam ran a hand through his hair. "Is she safe? Please tell me she's safe, at least."

"We got 'er stashed 'way." Claus nodded briskly. "Keepin' 'er out of 'is way as best we can do." The clown's painted face contorted. "Circus is a family." He barked a laugh. "But sometimes blood's too thick fer its own good."

Reece's eyebrows shot up at the mention of blood. Sam could see his medical instincts kicking in, formulating a plan despite little context.

"We'll need ter be smart 'bout this, townie. An' I think yer her best hope at a normal life."

Under normal circumstances, Sam would have been flattered. But nothing about this said 'normal'.

"Come in." He didn't offer the clown a right of refusal, grabbing the strap of his braces and pulling him into his apartment. "This ends. Now. We're going to fix this." Sam's voice weakened. "If we can."

"We'll need a plan," Claus said again. "An' knowing her, she'll need ter think it's popped outa her brain, not ours. An' she'll need a grand gesture, townie. The whole shebang. It'll be a lot of groundwork, but she's a smart girl, an' she wants more than Cirque can offer. She *deserves* more ..."

"Fix what?" Reece sulked, hating to be left out, as the three men strode into the bacon-scented apartment.

Wishes

ANITA

ADRIAN WAS RIGHT. HOW could anyone ever love her? Sammie Hart was a fantasy. A paperback hero who didn't exist. And Samuel Harthrup? He was no Prince Charming. He was the furthest thing from a shining-armoured romantic protagonist she could've chosen, and despite the beautiful, food-filled fantasy he had offered, he hadn't loved her. Not really. She'd tricked his hormones at the beach, ultimately tricking herself in the process. *What an idiot.*

It had been radio silence from Sam. Cold, hard silence that surrounded her at every moment, like she were living in the freezer section of a supermarket. Rubbing her hands together, she tried to ease the cold permeating through to her fingertips. *Damn hands. This is all because of you. Traitorous things.*

Anita glared down at her palms. If each line told a story or showed a glimpse into the future, then what were her hands telling her? Palmistry had always been for the Cirque customers, but she'd read her own more times than she could count, desperately searching for ... *something*. Hope? Destiny? A clue buried somewhere in the tiny valleys of her skin? She considered them now, heart aching, staring at the lines that indicated matters of the heart, only seeing a W, an A, then an S. Anita's eyes blurred. *WAS ... Sam ... How could I have been so fucking stupid?*

She'd wished upon a star. Several million, in fact. And she'd asked for many things, throughout her life. But love ... movie-worthy, unable-to-stop-swooning *love* had been a constant request. And as quickly as it had presented, Anita had turned away. *Why?*

"Anita!" Adrian snarled. "The show starts in ten minutes! Hurry up! Fix that hair!"

Ah yes, the hair. The long locks he'd destroyed in a fit of rage and possessive jealousy. An act of domination. An owning. He'd done it before, when they were children – cut her hair off and taunted her often, calling her a boy. This occasion was the same punishment for disobedience.

Like he needs to be obeyed, she scoffed, even in her own mind. *Fuck you, Adrian.* She would have said the words out loud, if not for the young company she kept. She was feeling very sweary these days, all other words trailing behind. *Fucking fuck you, you fucking fuckhead of a bastardly mother-fucker.* Sam would die hearing such profanity, she was sure. What he didn't realise was how few words she said while here, at the circus. With Sam, her mouth ran away with her so often, because she'd finally felt as though she had someone to talk to. Communicate and connect with. A heavy ache settled with the cold in her bones. *Sam ...*

Robin's small, slender figure silently appeared beside her in the vardo, her raised hand offering a hair tie. The flimsy plastic band wouldn't be able to tie back the short curls that tumbled into her watering eyes, but Anita accepted the gesture, a smile barely registering.

"Robin, you're not only the best acrobat, but the best friend anyone could ever ask for." Anita squeezed Robin's tiny, muscular shoulder. "Sorry I've been a bit absent lately."

"It's okay," the ten-year-old said, eyes on her shoes. "I understand why you go."

Barney poked his head into the caravan. "You ready, miss? Claus is stalkin' around, impatient. A kid kicked his shin, earlier. Gunna be a rough night."

"I'm ready." Anita stretched her neck left then right. "Let's get this done."

Claus had worn a track in the dirt just beyond the door, a steadily looping trail of frustration as his large red shoes skidded through the thin grass and increasing mud. After only a week, the ground beneath their tents was turning to mush from the constant foot traffic. The earthy scent made her think of Sam. *Moist dirt.* Eyes welling again as she left the vardo, Anita squashed the thought.

Claus pounced. "Ain't nothin' to worry about, Miss Anita. You know what's put into the universe comes back times three. His comeuppance will come, an' when it does, there ain't gunna be no one sorry for his mangy arse." He smiled wryly.

"We shouldn't wish ill on those we love." *But we do reserve our mental cuss words for them.* Anita sighed, allowing Claus to adjust the straps of her blue and black body suit.

"Ye really love him? Yer devil brother?" Claus scoffed. "I know love is blind, Anita, but love ain't stupid."

"You calling me stupid, you old clown?" Despite herself, Anita grinned at her friend, flicking the braces that circled his rounded stomach. His eyes softened, though his voice retained its pointed edge.

"Ain't much else to call it."

"I love *my* family too," Robin added softly, picking at her acrobatic leotard. "But they catch me. They don't make me fall."

Tears caught in Anita's lashes as she scooped the girl into her arms. The child had always been wise beyond her years.

"You guys are my family. My true family." Anita met Barney's and Claus' eyes as Robin's strong arms tightened around her neck, nuzzling in under the curls that had been unevenly slashed above her shoulders. "I don't know what the–" she caught the cuss before it spilled from her mouth and into the young girl's hair, "*fork* I'm doing here sometimes. And I hope comeuppance will come ... But for now, we do our jobs. Let's get this show up and running, so we all get paid."

Robin slipped to the ground, nodding, before running off to find her parents in the Big Top. Anita busied herself with the huge feather headdress. Claus turned to say more.

"Claus," she said, cutting him off with a gently laid hand on his arm. "We leave Moonshine soon. Let's just get through tonight. I'm strong. I'm fine." She hoped the words were true. They *had* to be true.

"Yer not fine," the old clown argued, arms crossing over his bulky chest. "Yer a half-shorn sheep an' ya deserve better than this flock!"

"Claus, I am tired." Anita sighed. "I'm hungry. And I'm pretty fucking sure I'm heart sick. But you know what my hands say?" She held her palm to his face. "I'm strong. I'm determined. I'm a survivor. And I'm meant for … for love." The words choked around the lump in her throat, and she ignored those three letters she'd seen so clearly earlier. "Someday, my prince will come."

"He will." Claus nodded confidently. *How can he be so certain?*

"You're a great friend, Claus. Thank you."

"ANITA!" Adrian barked.

"The show must go on," Anita said, fixing her performance-perfect smile in place as, inside the Big Top, the band struck up the opening number.

After the show, Anita slid through the shadows to her vardo. It had been a tough gig tonight. No matter which town they were in, the local troublemakers would turn up after a while, their protective, small-town, testosterone-fuelled attitude landing squarely on the 'outsiders'. Two weeks in town was enough to entertain the families but escape the troublemakers, who'd start with loosened ropes, progressing to a poke at the horses in the dead of night, and once, the theft of three sets of bright red clown shoes.

It was like the body rejecting a splinter. The Cirque de

Fortuna embedded itself but was then slowly squeezed out. It was another refusal, and she'd sensed the pressure growing all evening. There would be trouble if they stayed in Moonshine much longer.

Anita had spent most of the show with her eyes fixed to the shavings on the floor. She felt every pair of eyes on her. They judged her uneven, wild hair, her tight costume, the meekness in her manner, waiting for her to react.

The shifting gravity hit Anita hardest during the tango. A group of young men had whooped and wolf-whistled at her, carrying on like drunken footballers at a strip club. As the music for 'Roxanne' struck up, one threw a tub of popcorn into the ring, the shower of fluffed kernels littering her hair as she swirled past, falling like pieces of her spirit to the floor. Adrian trampled each speck into the sawdust and later, had tasked Anita with binning each individual kernel.

I fucking hate this. Anita leaned heavily on the side of her safe place. *Is this what I was meant to do with my life?*

Since the weekend away, her world had become more unhinged than ever before. What was her place? Her role? Not just within the circus, but in life itself? Was she doing enough to leave a mark? Had she helped Sam? Or gone too far? Been too selfish? Her brain was a murky soup of worries, doubts and fears. Her getaway with Sam had made Anita question many things, waking a want for *more*. More than this. She felt like it was her first time on the trapeze – the nervous teetering, the feeling of dangling above nothingness ... Knowing you have to take a leap, but desperately worried about the plunge.

Would she? Could she?

Where did she belong, if anywhere? Where was she supposed to invest herself? In the circus? In Sammie Hart's delicious romances? Sam's arms? Anita had always known who she was, but her place in the world? That had never really been a question before. The answer had always been 'the next place on the road'. But now? She sighed, too tired to continue humouring the thoughts swirling through her skull. At least now it was time to rest.

Bolting the vardo door behind her, Anita moved through the darkness to the small side table, lighting a candle. The emptiness of her life sprung into the gentle flame illuminating the caravan in a hazy light.

Here, in her tiny home, life had seemed neatly contained. So clean and safe. Now, it felt small and claustrophobic. She seemed too big; she was outgrowing this place. Its emptiness echoed her heart and suddenly, Anita wanted to fill both the vardo and her life with domestic *stuff*. Piles of laundry. Cups on the sink. A pencil on every surface, like in Sam's flat, where the written word, paper and chaos reigned.

She wanted the cluttered comfort Sam thrived in. The kind of environment that had its own character – safety, multiple spaces and stuff. She wanted the shirts on the floor, the socks in the pantry, and the stain remover that bleached unwanted splotches but left their own kind of mark on her world. She wanted the disorganisation. The food-filled fun. The – dare she say it – love.

Wait ... Love? When had she started to think of Sam and love in the same sentence? Maybe her nighttime ritual of wishing upon the stars had finally produced results. How many times had she wished for love? For a man to somehow sneak into her life and take her away from the circus? Infinity. Her stomach groaned once more. Wanting ... Hunger ... They were dangerous feelings. Feelings that led to disappointment as she watched opportunities shrink in the rear-view mirror. Gently, she collected the now curling, semi-dried flower from Saint Jude's from her alter. The tiny gift of nature Sam had offered.

"I think I love you," she whispered into its petals. "How messy is that?"

Team Romeo

SAM

TORTURE. LIKE EATING COLD, burnt toast with a dry mouth in the middle of a desert. That was the most accurate description Sam could concoct to explain how he was feeling right now. Not that Reece had asked how he was feeling. Reece hadn't asked much since Sam had shown up at the good doctor's door.

But Sam had caught Anita's propensity to fill a silence with unsolicited opinions and observations. He'd been having a one-sided conversation with his bestie all afternoon, not that it'd helped. He was still nervous as hell. At least his friend raised an occasional eyebrow, acknowledging Sam's chatter. Reece's eyes never left Sammie Hart's latest manuscript, though. And as exhilarating as that was, it was laced with terror and a simmering anxiety. His friend's eyes danced from left to right on loop, one side of his mouth permanently quirked up.

Thinking, worrying, *wanting* Anita had been driving Sam

crazy. And he'd deliberately funnelled that huge amount of (often intoxicated) energy into fixing one thing on his list – the sexy sequel.

Sam went to speak once more. This time, his BFF's upheld finger silenced him. Reece was a slow, methodical reader, his attention to detail making him an excellent and attentive doctor, and reliable with preliminary editorial services. Reece left no full stop misplaced or preposition dangling, but watching him read, waiting for feedback, was torture. Like waiting for potatoes to boil. *Bloody frustrating!* He went to speak, wringing his hands.

"Nope," Reece told him, eyes flicking briefly above the pages. "Rack off, mate, or I'll stop reading altogether." He shook the paper threateningly.

Sam busied himself in the kitchen, his favourite room in Reece's two-storey home. It was sterile and clean, unlike Sam's classic bachelor pad. Why the good doctor needed a three-bedroom home and a mortgage for it was beyond Sam. Reece had never expressed interest in families or kids or roommates or any other thing to occupy those empty rooms and, despite years of begging, even Sam hadn't been allowed to move in. The house had a massive backyard they barbequed in. The grassed area was large enough to play footy on the weekends, and the undercover patio was always filled with a huge inflatable pool in the summer. Reece's house was an adult home to fit his adult job, but not his single man's life. Sam's flat was a dingy single man's hollow. He wondered if he'd outgrown that place. If he was ready for something different and something more. Something like this. His eyes roamed the fresh white paint, white tiles, gleaming stainless-steel fixings. Maybe not yet, but hopefully someday soon.

Sam plucked a purple-red vegetable from the fridge, mumbling about how he 'felt beet'. Not even a snigger, Reece was so absorbed. That was good ... right?

Occasions such as these required snacks. Nibbling would improve the heavy literary silence Reece's slow-arse reading had placed them in. *Thank God I went shopping.* He removed a stash of delicacies from the fridge. Reece would have settled for a small handful of plain biscuits, a protein shake or a small bunch of grapes, but Sam's taste ran to more luxurious food, and he was in the mood for a slice of self-flagellation. He slid a wheel of home-grown Australian brie to the growing charcuterie board.

Reece let out a long breath, securing the bulldog clip back onto the stack of Sam's rather large manuscript.

"Well?"

"Well ..." Reece's hand brushed through the short dark spikes atop his head. "I just want to know one thing, I suppose ..."

"Is it about the sushi?" Panic and bile rose in Sam's windpipe. "I wasn't sure about seafood-covered nipples ... and the whole connotation of fish, to be honest. And the scene with the vegemite. I mean, have you ever tried to lick that stuff off–"

Reece casually reached for his own plush version of Mjolnir. Sam's lips pressed shut, his whole body bracing for impact. The twin toys always made him smile with the memory of their school excursion to Luna Park, the place they'd vowed to end their virgin status. The manly competition had brought out the best in both young men, though Sam hadn't hit 'consummation' status until well after school. As per their initial deal, Reece was allowed bragging rights and the first Mjolnir bashing session. Sam eyed it now, warily.

"If you'd let me finish, dweeb," the doctor said, grinning. "Why are you here?"

Sam blinked. "That's a bit existential–"

Mjolnir kissed his face. Hard.

"With *me*." Reece shook his head. "You should be with *her*, man." He held up Sam's manuscript. "This is the bees knees, Sam. Seriously good, strangely sexy stuff. You know I don't read romance, but this shit gives me a partial boner. That's why it was so weird to have you hovering. I reckon chicks will go wild for it and Flagpole will flip. But this –" he shook the papers once more, "isn't about them. This is about you and Anita."

"I can't talk about ... her. Not now. Okay?"

Sam had been too scared to say Anita's name, for fear of conjuring her. Her name on his lips was a spell, he was sure of it. And summoning the witch wasn't the plan. And as hard as it was, he needed to stick to the plan. But her name tumbling so easily from Reece's lips made Sam watchful, peering around suspiciously, expectantly. The doctor pierced him with that all-knowing, medically disarming glare and Sam shoved a large chunk of cheese into his mouth. Chewing. Avoiding. Annoyed that Reece's use of her name didn't manage to conjure her.

Sam swallowed. "You got any beer?" Reece raised an eyebrow in warning. "Hey, we're being social!"

Reece just shook his head. "I'm trying to have a serious conversation here, Sam."

"Well maybe I don't want a serious conversation, Reece. Maybe I just wanna get tipsy with my best mate, play some

Super Mario Kart and forget about my feelings for a while, alright?"

Between them, the doctor's phone buzzed. Jumping, Reece snatched up the device, quickly cancelling the call

Sam grinned. "Who's 'Bookworm'?"

"Nobody."

"Bullshit!" Sam grabbed the phone, holding it at arm's length as it began ringing again. Reece mounted his back like a turtle shell, struggling to pull Sam's arm – and his mobile phone – closer. "You want to lecture me about Anita when you're hiding another bookworm from me? For shame, sir! For shame!"

Reece sighed dramatically, feigning cool. "Fine." He shrugged. "I'll get the beer."

"So, we gunna talk about this mysterious bookworm?"

"You want to talk about Anita?"

"Nope."

"Then *nope* back."

"Mario Kart?"

"Shit, yes." Reece's serious, doctorly scowl had Sam wondering what, or who, had so quickly drawn down his face. "I love you, you know. In a terribly manly, blokey kind of way." Reece donned an unusually sheepish smile. "But I think we should see other people."

"You like this bookworm?"

Reece's silence spoke volumes.

Numerous beers later, one slurred to the other, "You should write a love letter, man. Chicks like that shit."

"Heck yes," the other replied, head lolling. "I will if you will."

The two friends shook hands roughly, grinning.

"To Luna Park and other romantic ideals!"

"Let's go, Team Romeo!"

A grain of hope planted itself in Sam. It was the size of quinoa, but it was there. Claus had returned to Cirque de Fortuna to speak sense to Anita. To protect her as much as possible, until the time came. To create an escape strategy. To rally support from the other circus folk.

And Sam? He'd sulked into Reece's homebrew and had written a letter. It wasn't kindling, he was sure. But, in his intoxication, he had written it into his diary – his most intimate thoughts. There. Laid bare for her to read. The diary was so full of shit, every fear and sexual rumination he'd ever had, all bound in brown leather. And he'd left it for Anita to find and – oh, God – read. Would she be ready – hell, *willing* – to leave the circus when the time came?

"Oh, shit."

"Man, I just hope it works."

"Don't stress." Reece cracked his knuckles, chuckling. "We've got a man on the inside, and if Anita really is a witch, her magical powers, whatever they are, will be on our side."

Long days and nights passed with no word from Anita. Sam's gut was twisted and in more pain than his nemesis, lactose, had ever inflicted. *Is she okay? Was Claus able to convince her to abandon her family? Her meagre home? Is she leaving town with*

the circus, or has she been persuaded to stay? No news was good news ... right?

Claus had barred Sam from the circus, fearing that Adrian's frustration would be taken out on Anita if the writer was seen skulking around, trying to communicate with the circus psychic. He had no way of getting his diary to Claus or Anita, or anyone else who might help him woo her with his on-paper grand gesture.

So after much contemplation, Sam had entrusted his journal, and the love letter it contained, to someone he knew – he *hoped* – Anita would visit before leaving Moonshine. It was a risky move, but it was all he had, short of antagonising the ringmaster and praying to whichever gods would listen. *If there was ever a time to be like the witch, and wish upon a star, it sure as shit is now.* If she didn't connect with the diary holder, if she didn't show up, his words would be in vain. All of his writing would be for naught.

Reece coughed as he flung back the charcoal curtains in Sam's flat. The door had been propped open with a laden laundry basket. Light, fresh air and a flurry of tiny springtime petals flew in to freshen the space. The doctor stood over his friend, prying Sam's eyelid open with medical precision.

"This isn't healthy, bro. What's up with you? I thought the manuscript was going well? I mean, it was all good a few days ago. What's happened since then?"

Sam groaned in response, rolling himself into a beer-sodden blanket burrito. The movement wafted the smell of lavender from the sheets, cocooning him in Anita's scent. Groaning again, he flung the blanket off the bed. Allowing her to sleep in his bed had been a mistake. *Was it all a mistake?* His gut coiled.

Three days. It had been three days of self-inflicted torture. Three nights without a visit from the witch. Sam had spent the time typing, mentally punishing himself, eating his body weight in cheese and crackers, washed down with Reece's too-heavy-on-the-hops beer. He had 'the impeccable diet of the rare male romance author', or so Reece warned.

The doctor, now propped against the doorframe, rolled his eyes. "You are so dramatic," he scoffed. "Seriously, dweeb, what's going on?"

I miss her. The circus is leaving Moonshine today. I ate too much cheese and desperately need to fart but for some reason I'm trying not to be rude, so I'm holding it in ... Sam had a list of reasons why life sucked balls right now. Instead of choosing one, he pointed to the lengthy email that dominated the laptop screen. The doctor scooped up the device, holding it in front of his chest as he read.

"*Dear Sam, Flagpole Publishing is extremely impressed with the sample work as provided to us, by you, ahead of your deadline* ... How is this a problem? This is great!"

"Halfway down," Sam mumbled from beneath his arm, shielding his stinging eyes from the light. "*As per our negotiations.*"

Reece scrolled down, and his words filled the room once more. "*As per our negotiations, we would like to extend your contract for another three novels ...* THREE NOVELS!" Reece's heavy frame shook Sam's bed as he sunk down. "That's amazing, dude! They obviously love you and your weird sexy food thing, as they should! As I do!"

Sam groaned.

"What's the problem?"

"Inspiration," Sam sighed, sitting up slowly. "Or the lack thereof."

"What, not enough cheesy puns in the world? Can't *brie* bothered to write anymore. Think you're no *gouda* at romance?"

"Is that really what I sound like when I food pun?"

"Totally, bro. *Eat* them up, while you can." He chuckled. "Just *camembert* it. This kind of inspiration won't last forever."

"Urgh, you're in a good mood. And camembert sounds nothing like 'grin and bear it'."

Reece's eyes rolled. "I'm *always* in a good mood. And yes, it does, Mister Food Fetish."

Sam's head throbbed. "Whatever."

"I'm a culinary, literary, freaking inspiration over here!" Sam could practically hear Reece's grin, making him groan once more.

Clearly Reece's letter had worked. There was no other explanation for his annoyingly chipper mood.

"That's the problem, Reece. Inspiration. She's gone. I have no inspiration left."

"Who's gone? Anita? Man, I told you – you need her! You *lurve* her ..." The doctor made wet, kissy sounds that threw Sam right back to their high school days. Reece laughed, shaking Sam's leg. "Go get her, man! Cirque de Fortuna is still there, I passed the tents today, but they're coming down quickly."

Sam slid off the bed. "She's a witch, Reece. Honest to God. It's like I'm under some kind of spell! I wrote that damn letter, handed over my whole brain, heart and soul in that damn diary. She hasn't responded, so I don't know if she has it. I don't even know if Claus has managed to convince her to leave the circus, or get the other Cirque folk to rally against Adrian, and I'm in limbo over here because they won't let me on site, despite trying my damned hardest to sneak in, and ... what?"

Reece was giving him that crooked, cocky grin that had driven the girls wild in high school. "You didn't deny it."

"Deny what?" Sam pushed his glasses up his nose.

"You're in love!" The doctor shook his head, as if explaining something to a child. "I should have realised it was this serious! Should have read the signs." He thrust a hand to Sam's forehead, then counted heartbeats on the writer's wrist.

"Stop that!" Sam swatted his friend away. "No playing doctor, unless it's the sexy kind. Even then, don't do it with *me*." Shaking a finger, he added, "That's the best way to ruin a friendship, you know."

"Dude. Don't change the subject. You love Anita! Like, you actually *love* her."

"Love?" The word caught in his throat, breathy and weak. "No. I'm–"

"You are." Mjolnir hovered threateningly once more. "Don't make me beat you. But if I have to knock sense into your head, I will! Sammie Hart, I know you. And I saw how you were with Sandra, before she left. She didn't ... how do I say this ..." Reece stroked his chin. "Sandra saw your wounds and turned away without even offering a bandage. She tugged at the edges of the hole until it festered and grew. You learned the hard way how to cover the wound and deal with it. Anita?" Reece shook his head, a smile on his lips. "She seemed to stitch you up. She healed you. She saw the dark, moody parts and the shitty first draft and worked *with* you to mend it."

Sam shifted uncomfortably. The last time Reece had spoken this intimately was when Sam finally broke down in school and opened up about his parents' abandonment. Gran had taken him in by then. Sam had cried, and Reece let him. No judgement, just support. Unlike now, where the good doctor was prescribing a whole lot of solutions in the form of unsolicited advice.

"You a Love Doctor now?"

Reece ignored the comment. "Honestly, the best thing that ever happened to you was Sandra high-tailing it with that scary biker. Tattoos and trouble for days, that bloke. He even squared up to Billy. I know! Nobody messes with a Carmichael!" Reece chuckled as Sam balked. "He backed down saying it wouldn't be a fair fight. Billy, that is. Didn't want to flog the poor fellow in front of the whole pub. It was classic. And you know I'm not a betting man, but I reckon our one-armed bartender would've given Sandra's fling a run for his money."

Sam crossed his long arms over his tall, thin body, unsure what Reece's point was.

"Sandra was never right for you, Sam. But Anita?" Reece whistled. "She's the yin to your yang, dude. She's different."

"She's a bloody witch."

Reece ignored him. "Anita brings out the real you, the best version of my best friend. The guy who laughs and says punny things and then writes this beautiful prose ..."

Sam slipped his glasses on, blinking slowly, mouth dry.

"Beautiful prose?"

"I mean ... yeah, okay ... I've read *Heat* a few times. And your draft for book two. I'm halfway through the initial edits for you, by the way. So many embedded clauses. But it's good, man. SO good. And that's all on you. You're the head, Sam. But Anita? She's the neck. She's helped turn you around, lead you in a better direction." He grinned, winking. "A *loving* place. Yeah, in this metaphor, she's also the heart." The doctor shrugged.

The burrito of sheets suddenly became suffocating. Wriggling violently from their clutches, Sam threw the sheets in a bundle to the floor. "She doesn't want me."

Woah, standing was not a good idea. Sam propped himself against the wall, breathing deeply.

"Bullshit, man. I saw the way she looked at you. I know you're a dweeb, but not a loser. Do not *lose her.*"

"She's leaving."

"The *circus* is leaving," Reece said evenly. "That doesn't have to mean the same thing." What, if anything, had Claus prepared her for? Was she going to sneak out? Was she able to come to him? Or was she moving on?

Reece's phone buzzed and Sam took the opportunity to change the subject.

"Bookworm?"

Reece rolled his eyes as he quickly read the text. "Minor accident requiring stitches. Not worth going to the hospital, so the patient will wait at my office. Some of us don't get to pick our own hours of work, you know." Reece typed a quick response to his receptionist before slipping his phone back into his pocket. "Look, I've gotta go, but I mean it, Sam. Anita is an awesome chick. She's done wonders for your writing. Don't let her slip away. At least go and tell her how you bloody feel, Romeo!" Reece ruffled Sam's hair, hugging his friend before heading for the door. "But first, shower," he demanded, sending a backwards glance over his shoulder as he ran for his car. "And for God's sake, let's both vow to stop drinking for good. Social or otherwise. I can't keep letting you do this to yourself, man."

As the BMW's engine rumbled to life, the window rolled down. "Love you!"

Sam dug a thumb into the palm of his hand, working out a cramp in his muscles. Eyes glued to his palm, he said, "I love you, loser."

Where the Heart is

ANITA

"THANK YOU FOR THESE –" Anita's eyes flicked to the name badge, "– Laura Ahn." She smiled at the pretty yet fierce-looking Moonshine librarian, sliding the borrowed books across the desk. Anita immediately pinpointed the librarian's romantic fiction counterpart: Lara Jean from *To All The Boys I've Loved Before*.

"Did you make it to our local attractions?" Laura asked, already scanning the novels back into circulation.

Sneaking out of the circus this one last time had been difficult. It felt like every pair of eyes was on her, all the time. Claus had been incessantly present, stuck to her side like glue and mumbling often about retirement, when he wasn't throwing his stink-eye in Adrian's direction. He'd said Sam would come, when the time was right. Her eyes slid to the clock.

"Yes, I did see the attractions you recommended. Thank

you."

"Did you go see the Moonshine Whine?"

Anita laughed. "The Whine? No! What's that? It sounds familiar."

"You know that little hill, with the ridiculous lighthouse on top?"

"I was wondering about that! Why does an inland town with no airport have a lighthouse?" Laura's tiny, violent shrug made Anita snort with laughter.

"Who knows. The old drunks who founded this town were notoriously unreliable when it came to common sense and town planning. Now, those quirks make for interesting historical tours and architectural studies, but to be fair to them, the name makes sense."

"A country town lighthouse named 'The Whine' is the epitome of logic?"

Now it was Laura's turn to laugh. It was a light, breathy thing, like she was out of practice, her body too stiff to release her joy. It sounded *almost* happy, but made Anita sad. Laura scanned the next book, tapping the computer keyboard with manicured nails. Anita considered her own, broken and chipped, lined with the hard work and dirty labour that came with circus life.

"It's called 'The Whine' because the first Moonshine Mayor complained so much about hiking up there to officially open the site. So, you didn't visit it? I didn't mention The Whine, but thought it rather obvious, thus unworthy of comment."

"Honestly? I saw the light circling each night but got ... *distracted* ... and didn't end up exploring it."

"You should go, Anita." Laura smiled, then nodded a little

too severely at a child who plonked numerous *Thomas the Tank Engine* books onto her desk. She directed her gaze back to Anita. "I know you leave soon, but I doubt you'd leave disappointed." Laura hesitated, before briefly touching Anita's hand. "And for what it's worth," she added, her tight, dark bun nodding closer, "you'll always be welcome here. Moonshine is a strange little town, but it's also full of rituals and history and heart. Like you, I imagine." The librarian's head notched ever so slightly to the side, considering her.

Taking a deep breath, Anita willed back the tears. *Seen.* She felt seen. *Rituals and history and heart. I like that.*

"Thank you, Laura Ahn." Anita briefly squeezed the librarian's hand. "It was truly lovely to meet you."

This time, Laura released her tight, breathy laugh with a little more force. "You only think that because you don't live here. Most people are scared of the little Asian lady at the library." She air-quoted 'little Asian lady' with a dramatic eye roll.

Unable to stop herself, Anita laughed, the noise filling the vast, empty quiet of the library. A horde of unknown people "shushed" in reverential tones, but Laura Ahn grinned, laughter lines crinkling otherwise smooth skin. The little boy tapped the desk impatiently, his tiny fingers dancing towards the glossy counter bell. Laura cast a sideways glance at him, and he froze like ice under her cold glare.

"Don't you *dare*, Thomas Smith," she warned, blank-faced and calm. "I'll be with you momentarily."

Thomas backed away from the desk, flustered, his dinosaur toy suddenly clutched tighter.

Oh yeah, I wonder why they fear you. Anita grinned at the

woman.

"I wanted to ask –" the librarian's eyes met Anita's once more, "what my future might hold? I usually do not believe in such hokum, but ..."

Anita drew the woman's palm into her cupped hand, examining the lines, dips, curls and whorls.

"Will I ..." Laura's voice dipped to a practised library whisper, "find love?"

Anita looked up from Laura's palm, a sly smile on her lips. "I think you've met someone already. A special someone who most certainly has potential." Laura's cheeks flushed a beautiful cherry blossom pink. "But I think you know that already ..." She curled Laura's fingers closed.

The librarian took her hand back, like Anita had gifted a priceless gem inside her curled fingers, bowing her dark bun.

"Let me give you some advice," Anita whispered. "Don't let him get away. Make the most of your time together, always." With that she nodded, retreating from the librarian who, blushing beautifully, began intently scanning the mountain of *Thomas the Tank* books.

"Anita, wait!" Laura called across the library. Heads swung her way, though nobody dared to ssshhhh her. "This one isn't ours."

Anita retraced her steps, and the librarian shoved Anita's personal copy of *Heat in the Kitchen* into her hands.

"I love this book," Laura Ahn confided. "It's a *delicious* read." She winked and, assuming the tone Anita had used with her only moments before, said, "But I think you know that already."

There was an hour until Adrian's deadline to leave Moonshine. One hour of freedom. The winding road to the Moonshine Whine didn't look that steep, or that long.

Wrong. She was so wrong.

The Whine was the epitome of the phrase 'looks can be deceiving'. Twice she'd had to roll her skirt into a shorter version of itself, pushing through the pain of sweaty, chafing thighs. Wiping her brow, Anita forced herself up the winding bush path while the kookaburras laughed. "Fucking kookaburras," she called to the cheeky birds, determinedly trudging on to see this monument, before being ripped away from Moonshine. She considered hurling *Heat in the Kitchen* at the chortling birdlife, but knew she'd regret losing her favourite book to the Australian bushland.

For a small mound of dirt, covered in spiky grass and scraggly eucalyptus trees, the hill of The Whine sure as shit felt like Everest right now. Anita trudged past the stratosphere and into the mesosphere, breathing hard. As she rounded the last bend in the road, cursing the fact that she hadn't considered booking a taxi for this trip, her breath caught.

The Whine was a huge, Rapunzel-like tower, jutting from the rocky hilltop into the blue spring sky. The stonework alone told of its age. The stairs leading to the door were worn from foot traffic, weathered by people and time. The weird inland lighthouse was a true testament to the original settlers Laura Ahn had called 'old drunks' - the same people who called their beloved pub The Pope. But none of that caught her gaze for long. The thing that did lock her eyes was the tall, thin figure of a man at the top of the lighthouse. *Claus said Sam would come. That there was a plan ...* Was she some damsel in distress, who needing saving? The shadow in the lighthouse moved, and all other thoughts evaporated.

"Sam?" she whispered, surging forward. "Sam!"

Anita pushed off the balls of her feet, barely touching the ground as she raced up the wrought-iron staircase that rose within the tower.

"WAS!" she called, bursting into the open circular room at the top.

The silhouette turned, startled, backing into the giant light bulb in the centre of the room. Surrounded by mirrored panels, the light spun in a lazy circle, its light extinguished during daylight hours but its soul still soldiering on.

"Anita?"

Her heart knew it before her eyes registered the face – it wasn't him.

"Anita Fortuna?" The voice was cracked. Old.

"Oh, sorry, sir, I ..." Words, slippery as fish, escaped.

"Are you Anita?" the man asked, hobbling closer. He leaned heavily on a cane and, despite his height, was rather stooped. Was he a St Jude's resident? He didn't allow her time to allocate a romantic film persona to his aged face. The hike up the Moonshine equivalent of Everest had frazzled her brain, anyway. A trickle of sweat slid down her neck. Running a hand through her short, frazzled hair, she nodded, her heart pounding.

"Yes, that's me."

"I'm Tom. The lighthouse keeper. Usually only up here to check the bulb, takes forever for these old knees to make it up all those steps." He chuckled, knobbly hands gripping his cane. "But today I'm up here with a special assignment. Have to give you this ..." His shaky hand offered a brown leather journal inscribed with the initials *S.H.* "He said you liked books?" He smiled. "Happy reading, Miss Fortuna." Then, as though to himself, "Yes, happy reading." Gripping the wrought-iron railing, he moved slowly, preparing to descend the stairs.

"Tom, wait!"

He stopped, leaning against the wall.

"Why do you have this? And how did you know I'd be here?"

The lighthouse keeper smiled warmly, and gave a bony shouldered shrug. "I'm a bit of a busybody, I suppose. And a hopeless romantic. It's all my wife's fault, of course. Delilah, her name is. Love of my life ..." His eyes glazed over and she sensed the classic pose of the storyteller. Tom was about to prattle on and lose his train of thought.

Reaching out, Anita gripped his hand. The haze lifted with a few long blinks.

"Oh." He blinked once more, dreamily. "I tend to get myself involved in matters of the heart, I suppose. It wouldn't be the first time I'd helped lovers connect, no sir-ee. This place," his broad smile wandered over the ancient stone, "she's an underrated place of connection. The First People of this area used to connect and have corroboree–"

"I don't mean to be rude," Anita interjected, sensing a tangent as his gaze clouded over once more. "Me being here?

How did you know? How did *he* know?" She waved the hand now holding both Sammie Hart's novel and Samuel Harthrup's journal.

Tom shrugged again. "The young fella said it was the only place on your list you hadn't visited yet. Said you'd likely come up here, before the circus left town. I didn't much understand that part myself, but now seeing you ..." He took in her eclectic attire and what must have been crazed hair. "You're a showman for sure. Show*woman*," he corrected, hand on his heart, bowing slightly.

Fuck. He knew I'd visit The Whine? Maybe he was better at reading her than she'd given him credit for.

"Tom, what time is it?"

Fumbling to lift his sleeve, Tom tapped the face of his watch. "Near three o'clock, miss." *Time to run away with the circus.*

"Fuck," she whispered to herself, unconcerned that the craggy man who seemed old as the very stone around them, heard her cuss. Her fingers clenched around the books. "Thank you, Tom. Do you think you could call me a cab? There's somewhere I need to be."

"Can't call a cab. Terrible phone reception up here. But how about I give you a lift?" The old man smiled warmly. "I was just about to lock up anyways."

A few minutes later, she was bundled in the lighthouse keeper's old white Ute, rattling down the rocky driveway, The Whine shrinking in the rear-view mirror.

"I'll get you home safe," Tom said, following the arrowed signs that indicated 'Cirque de Fortuna this way!' Soon, that sign would be gone.

Home... She pondered the word, rolling it like chocolate over her tongue. Eyes dropping to the books in her lap, she flipped open the brown leather journal, smiling at Sam's familiar pencilled scrawl. *Isn't that supposed to be where the heart is?*

Fast Cars, Fast Women

SAM

"Doctor Dickhead, I need the keys to the BMW."

"Seriously? No. Take your own shitbox car."

"Yours goes faster."

"You don't do fast cars, remember? You do ANCAP safety ratings and statistically crash-less cars. Not flashy BMWs."

"Dude, I'm trying to make one last romantic gesture here."

"You don't need *my* car to romance me, bro." Reece yawned, scratching his balls. "Just a six-pack and a G-string and I'm all set."

"Dude. *Anita*. I've gotta try. One more time. Claus said today would be the last chance to convince her to stay in town, and that if she wasn't here by now, I should ... what? What's that look for?"

Reece grinned widely. "That makes more sense. Thought you'd lost all hope and turned. Not that I'd blame you. I am a stud." He belched, grabbing the keys from a tasteful glass sculpture by the front door.

"Maybe as a last resort," Sam said, swiping the keys that now dangled from his friend's fingers. "Get that smug look off your face."

"All I'm saying is, *about time*, dweeb! The circus leaves today, so there's literally no more time to lose." Reece was hot on Sam's heels, running to the car. "And obviously, I will be present in this moment of triumph," the doctor said, clicking the seatbelt with a smile.

"Obviously. BFFs for life, bro."

They fist-bumped and Sam turned the key before revving the engine. It felt unnatural, but now was not the time for slow and steady.

"Think Claus convinced her to leave the circus? Think she wants to?"

Sam didn't want to answer. Didn't want to jinx it. A hot minute later, Sam cursed. The showground was empty. Stray birds pecked at the dead grass, mistaking the brown rot for worms. The oval was empty, back to open grass and a brilliant blue sky.

"We're too late!" Reece's voice fell flatter than a pancake.

"No shit, Sherlock," Sam mumbled, knocking the gearstick into second. "But it's not over till a buxom lady sings."

Indicator blinking in sync with every second heartbeat, Sam slipped onto the exit that headed out of town.

"C'mon, c'mon!" Sam watched the thin red line of the speedometer creep up as he hit the highway, hoping to God he was speeding in the right direction. Cirque de Fortuna found the small country and coastal towns, not the cities. Armed with that knowledge, he was pretty sure the circus would be heading towards the township of Brighton. A small green sign flew past: *Brighton, 20km*.

"Shit." He pushed the car further, faster, ignoring the clammy feel of his hands on the wheel and the pounding in his chest and ears. "I'm not my parents," he said on repeat. "I'm not my dad. I'm not drunk driving. I won't crash. I know that the heavy road trains carrying the circus stuff will be heavier and slower than me." Sam rationalised accelerating over the legal limit, Reece ignoring his friend's pep talk. Their eyes scanned the horizon for the gaudy branding of the trucks they hoped to find, the branded and bannered cars that would be towing a brightly coloured, scarcely decorated vardo trailer.

"There!" Reece said suddenly, pointing ahead. "I can see the carousel!"

"Shit yes!" Sam swerved around a yellow-plated license holder limited to a slower legal pace. Reece gripped the back of Sam's seat, his other hand clutching the door.

"Punch it, Sam. Go get her!"

Sam planted his foot, ignoring the speedometer. *I am not my father. That car accident wasn't my fault.* Passing numerous Cirque de Fortuna vehicles, including Anita's colourful vardo trailer, Sam sped to the front of the queue. *HOONNNKKK!* The horn blasted as he pulled parallel to the lead truck. The driver, the ringmaster himself, peered down from the lofty seat of the vehicle.

Sam rolled down the window; the BMW swerved close to the truck. "PULL OVER!" he yelled up to Adrian. The ringmaster's eyes remained fixed ahead. *BEEEEEEPPPPPPP.* Sam honked the horn loudly, repeatedly, ending in one long note until the ringmaster eyeballed him. "PULL ..." Sam pointed to the side of the road, "OVER!"

Sam saw Adrian's angry sigh. He nodded once and Sam eased off the accelerator. Indicating left, they slowly left the road, kicking up dust in one of the many long-vehicle parking areas that pock-marked the state's highways. The remaining vehicles slowly pulled into the rest stop after them. While the dust settled, Adrian climbed from the truck, stalking towards Reece's BMW.

"Oh, shit," Reece mumbled, unclicking his seatbelt. "You ready for this?" He turned to Sam, whose door already hung open.

"What do you mean, forcing my truck off the road?" Adrian roared, slamming his door closed and stomping across the gravel. "You lunatic!"

Circus folk started leaving their vehicles, closing in on the spectacle. Sam didn't even give the ringmaster a chance. Storming towards him, Sam smashed one clenched fist into Adrian's jaw.

"FUCK!" Sam screamed, shaking his aching hand. He'd never punched anyone before. It hurt. Felt good. "Fuck YOU!" Sam spat, eyeing him like he was nothing more than mould on bread.

A few carnies shuffled forward, Barney and Claus stepping to the front, growling "Stay back" at everyone.

With what could only be described as an animalistic growl, Adrian threw a fist towards Sam. Swinging too wide, he spun full circle. Gripping the ringmaster's shoulders, Sam drove a knee into his gut. A quick uppercut landed as the ringmaster rocked forward, clutching his stomach.

"I've had enough of bullies like *you*," Sam told the curled, dusty man at his feet. "You think you can take what you want, but you can't! People have free will and choice. And I CHOOSE to make you pay for how you've treated Anita."

Sam could have sworn he heard the cheer of young Robin, followed quickly by hushes and a gruff "huh" from Claus, who nodded at him in acknowledgement. Sam caught the clown's eye, trying to convey all his queries in one pleading expression. *Is she okay? Is she ready? Is she staying with you, or coming with me?*

"Choice?" Adrian barked out a laugh. "She won't choose you." The ringmaster staggered to standing, pointing to Anita's small, colourful vardo, the smallest trailer in the long Cirque line. "My troublemaking sister's in there. Locked her in myself, when she came trudging back from her last *whoring* through town, sweaty and disgusting." Adrian flinched as Sam approached once more.

"You locked her in there?"

Throwing his hands up, Adrian's eyes fired with challenge. "You want her? Go. See if she'll have you." The ringmaster forced his voice louder. "Mister Fast Car here deserves a fast woman."

If Adrian had expected a laugh, he was sorely disappointed.

"They ain't puttin' up with yer rot, Adrian Fortuna." Claus barked, eyes thin. The men on either side of him stood taller, crossing their arms as they stared down their boss. "Not no more."

Adrian fixed his dark blue eyes on Sam, huffing through flared nostrils. "If she comes out, you're welcome to her. I'm done." He dusted his hands onto even dustier pants.

"Go," Reece encouraged, fists balled at his sides. "I'll watch him."

"As will we," Barney added, gripping Claus' hand tightly.

"No more," Claus barked again, as Adrian made to move. Even little Robin and her parents came to stand with Claus, a human wall forming to separate him from Anita's vardo. The dark eyed Ringmaster's jaw ticked, but he stayed put.

"Go get her," Robin encouraged, the crowd behind her parting to let him through. "She deserves happiness."

The world quietened as Sam strode with purpose to the vardo. He barely felt the pats on his back and mumbled words of praise and thanks as he passed through the circus folk. His vision narrowed on the vardo door – firmly locked with a heavy bolt. The circus crowd hushed as he knocked. "Anita?"

No reply. Sam slid the bolt aside, knowing there was a similar lock on the inside. Adrian could lock her in, but she could also keep him out. If she wanted to emerge, she would, but Sam couldn't force her.

"Anita, It's Sam ... Was. I'm –" *Sorry? An idiot? Ashamed of myself?* "Here."

Silence.

"HA!" Adrian scoffed, his dark eyes flashing mean and

victorious. "You see? She's a big fat heartbreaker, that one."

Sam turned on his heel, advancing on the ringmaster again. Anita's Cirque family stood at his back. "Fuck off. Leave," he ordered coolly, body trembling with emotion.

"Oh, don't worry, we're going. And we're never coming back." Murmurs rose through the crowd. "Little towns like yours rely on tourism, so as a parting gift, *I promise you* we'll never bring business back here –" he stepped forward, fists clenched, "*ever* again."

Blinking hard behind his fogging spectacles, Sam stood strong. Worry, fear, hurt and anger mixed like the ingredients in a witch's potion deep within him. A feast of cheese, milkshakes and yoghurt wouldn't hurt this much.

Huffing a triumphant noise, Adrian turned away, barking at his troupe to return to their vehicles.

Robin darted forward to hug the writer, whispering goodbyes.

Claus clapped a hand on Sam's shoulder. "Don't fear," the old clown said. "Good things and comeuppance to them that wait." His face contorted – was that a wink? – then he was gone.

Cirque de Fortuna rolled back onto the highway, a thick cloud of dust smothering his grand intentions for a romantic declaration.

She'd rejected him. She'd left. *It was inevitable,* he reminded himself. It was done. The old clown hadn't convinced her to leave the circus, or stay with Sam. It had all been for nothing.

"Anita!" Sam tried once more as the vardo rolled past, tugged and towed onto the busy motorway. Only the sounds of rumbling traffic found his ears. Reece slid an arm around his friend's shoulders.

"C'mon, dweeb. Let me drive you home."

"See you next week?" Reece asked hopefully as Sam opened the door to his darkened flat. Sam grunted in response, head hung. "You tried," Reece said gently. "No one can say you didn't. Who has the balls to chase down the circus? You do!" Reece was trying to build him up, but how could you repair a pavlova when the meringue was completely crumbled? If a foundation was cracked, the whole building would fall.

"Next week." Sam tried to sound authoritative, but it came out like a kid begging for more cake.

"Dixie Kong will be waiting," said Reece, "and I might even have some home brew ready for sampling."

Sam screwed up his nose. "No more drinking," he said earnestly. "None. I need to get my head straight, and your lager won't help me do it."

"You're officially quitting alcohol? You do realise that Moonshine was literally built on the stuff, right?"

"I'm quitting. Officially, forever more. I am not, *nor will I ever be,* like my parents."

"That's for damn sure, mate," Reece agreed. "Solid, healthy choice. Your friend is a bit sad but your doctor wholly approves." Reece winked before his concerned gaze swept over Sam once more. "Sure you'll be okay?"

"Yeah. I'll be *feta* after a good sleep."

"Ah! There's my boy!" Reece started reversing out of the driveway. "Cheesy till the end!"

"*Swiss* off!" Sam flipped up his middle finger. "And thanks ... for today."

"Love you, dweeb!" Reece offered one last pitying smile before his car crunched out of the gravel driveway.

"I *also* love you," he heard from within the darkness of his loungeroom. Flicking the switch, Anita hissed theatrically at the sudden light, startling Sam. She was surrounded by neat piles of fresh laundry, his personal cleaning Goddess.

"Wait, what? I ... what?"

"I see you still word good." She grinned, holding up his brown leather journal. "*Very* good, I might add." She tapped one polished nail on a page while Sam stood frozen in the doorway.

"What ..." he swallowed. "What are you doing?"

From her seat on the sofa, Anita looked around Sam's flat, motioning to the clean dishes drying by the sink, the folded laundry. Every surface gleamed.

"You don't recognise a Grand Gesture when you see one?" Scoffing, she hid a smile by ducking her head, opening his journal. "*Dear Diary,*" she read. "Who even writes that anyway?" Clearing her throat, she started again. "*Dear Diary, I've fucked up. Like, royally fucked up.* Kudos on the cussing, by the way."

His head suddenly realised that they still controlled his feet. With effort, Sam willed them to move. Was she really here? Or had he finally cracked his nut and this gorgeous, curvy apparition was just here to tease him?

"*Wanna know what's hard to do? Write a novel. An even harder thing? Coming up with a sequel. An even HARDER thing? Ignoring your feelings and bottling up emotions instead of expressing them like a goddamn adult. If my parents taught me anything, it's that the lifespan of love and the ideal 'happy family' doesn't last forever, so you've got to make every moment count ... Family is who you want it to be. To me, it's been Gran and Reece. I kept my circle small to limit the impact of the potential future hurt. What I didn't factor in was that people you meet every day, or have short-term interactions with, also affect you in deep and meaningful ways.*"

Anita's eyes watched him take a few tentative steps towards her.

"*Then, I met a witch.*" Her voice cracked, despite the huge smile. Sam knelt before her, and she shifted on the sofa. "*And without even realising it, she snuck into my heart. It happened so quickly, unexpectedly. I was sure her spell had worn off, but ...*"

"Anita."

The diary fell to the floor with a soft thud. Her eyes met his, fingers tentatively reaching towards him.

"*I thought love was a pain in the gut, like IBS ... only a pain you actually wanted.*"

He laughed, sighing as her warm hands met his cheeks. "You rote-learned my diary? That's so weird."

"*But it's not.*" she continued. "*Love is her.*" She chuckled lightly, blinking back tears. "*Anita Shithouse-Fortuna.*"

"Anita ..." His thumbs drew small circles against her wrists. "Why are you here?"

"I couldn't leave ..." she breathed. "I couldn't leave you.

Nobody has ever written about me before," she whispered, tears sliding down her cheeks. "Do you mean it, Was? Or was it an elaborate rouse? The lighthouse keeper, this letter, this diary –"

"Anita," he interrupted, watching in amazement as her hot fingertips stroked his skin. "You are my opposite in every way. You're short and curvy, and you say what you *feel*. I'm not that person, Anita. I'm a dweeb. I'm lanky. I'm never the one who gets chosen. I'm the one people leave because they can't imagine being stuck with me. I'm quiet and I write horrible, terrible sex scenes that include food and feet, and you say you love me for it, which is so weird and now *I'm* the one monologuing ..." Sam took a deep breath, continuing when she nodded. "I know it's insane, and probably happening too fast, but I love you. I have so many questions, but right now all I really want to know is ... can I keep you? Here? With me?" He whispered the request, searching her eyes. So warm, she was so goddamn warm in his hands. He wanted to touch her all over, to hold her, to slide off her clothing and shed her old life along with it. To see them in a puddle on the floor, scoop them up and throw them in the trash, where all remnants of her brother belonged. "Please, Anita. Stay. I gave Tom the diary, knowing, *hoping*, you'd visit The Whine. Please, *please* stay."

"Why?"

He smiled, sliding his hands to her elbows, holding her tight. "I really, *really* want to kiss you."

"Two blushing pilgrims," she whispered back.

"What?"

"That's how Shakespeare described lips and kissing in *Romeo and Juliet*."

Tension grew between his eyebrows and he desperately tried not to rub it away, needing to keep her in his touch. "The point is?"

Anita leaned close, her hot breath fogging his glasses. "You aren't the only writer struggling with romantic descriptions. You. The Great Bard himself ..."

"Is that a yes?"

Swallowing hard, she barely got out the 'Y' before their lips met forcefully. Sam wound his fingers through her curly dark hair, before pulling back suddenly. It was short, but just as lovely. Thinking how the trim had occurred, Sam kissed her harder, trying to take away every pain, every hurt she'd ever had.

Anita pressed closer, pulling him to the sofa. Sam covered her, protectively, lovingly. Wrapping her legs around his long body, she tugged him closer with strong, thick muscles. Closer wasn't close enough. Would never be close enough.

"Witch," he rasped, the word tantalising and filthy all at once. The world disappeared as they lost themselves in the kiss.

"Sam?" Anita breathed into the space between his lips.

He struggled to push himself back, panting, his zipper struggling against her skirts. "Anita?"

"You're kissing me like it's Ragnarök or something," she said, her musical laugh hit him straight in the chest. "Slow down. We have all the time in the world. I'm not going anywhere. Not without you."

"But Anita, it *is* the end of the world as we know it. Don't you see?" He explored the depths of her eyes as he spoke, heart in his throat. "Nothing on this planet will ever be the same again. No word on the page will be the same. There will be no more strangely angular feet, three-page descriptions of how skin smells –" He grinned as she dug her fingers into his arse, bringing him closer as she pushed against him.

"Close those moist dirt eyes, Mister Foot Fetish," she giggled, her laugh gripping his heart. "And kiss me with those ridiculous bacon lips until we're no longer hungry."

"Yes, Ma'am." Sam grinned. "I'll never tire of the taste of you, Witch."

"Good," she said, squirming, sliding her hands beneath the waistband of his pants. "Because I'm never going to let you go."

Epilogue

SAM HAD ONE GOAL, and one goal only right now –
worship her.

"You are the words on the tip of my tongue." He lavished
Anita with kisses. "Words I can't find without you."

"Suzannah and the entire Flagpole Publishing team will be *so*
pleased to hear that. But you know we could be totally still, and
your words will take me wherever I want to go."

"Shit, I love you."

"You're such a poet, Sam." Anita laughed, eyes flicking to her
oversized handbag, brimming with shiny new novels bearing
golden *Signed by the author stickers*. "Did you really have to
bring them here? Today?"

"I promised too many people they could have first editions
of this latest instalment," Sam admitted, cheeks darkening. "It's
hard being 'out' now, with a bunch of books to my name. It's
your fault you know." He swooped in for a long, deep, kiss. "My
muse," he said against her mouth. "My beautiful witch who

grows even more lovely every day." Sam's hand rounded the curve of her belly and breasts, lovingly.

"And you once declared yourself to be an arse man?" Anita teased.

"I'm a *you* man," he told her, bunching her slinky dress in his fist. Sliding one hand beneath the fabric and up the magnificent curve of her thigh, he dragged her closer, wrapping her around his body. "I'm *muffin* without you, Anita Shithouse Fortuna." Sam's cola-laden breath mingled with hers.

Her head tipped back as Sam licked a line up her throat, his free hand swirling in her long, dark curls.

"I'm so glad you grew it out," he sighed into the shiny waves, nibbling her earlobe as his hand slid slowly towards her underwear. "Not that I disliked it short. I'd love you no matter what you looked like."

"You too." She pushed his long golden locks off his face, before rasping her knuckles over the stubble of his cheek. "But I hated your hair short. You know that. I like this long always-seems-to-fall-in-a-different-way kind of hair. It's so interesting." Her fingers weaved through the long blond strands. "Now, you look like a hot surfer dude, or a dapper literary genius when it's pushed back like this ... definitely not some stained-up dweeb whose hair was cut by a blender."

"Ouch," Sam said, laughing lightly. "Well *you* are more beautiful than ever." His words fell lightly on her plump lips.

"I'm fatter than ever."

"It's not fat, Anita," he said sternly before smiling at the strength of her spell, the small blessing of her touch. She cupped his face, dragging him closer as he added, "It's baby weight, my love."

Sam's mouth found hers and he slowly, passionately drank her into him. For a long moment they revelled in tender touches of their lips, long and slow and sweet. "I can't wait to tell everyone."

"Not just yet," Anita reminded him. "It's only been a few weeks since we found out."

Sam's hand splayed across her thigh, dragging her closer as his eyebrow rose. "I. Can't. Wait." Hands full of her arse, Sam pressed Anita into his growing arousal. Laughing, she gripped the lapels of his suit jacket, her thumb rubbing at a slight stain she found there. Their worlds had turned upside down and inside out, but some things, the small stains, the goofy moments, the sexy and often confusing food puns – those things never changed.

Pressing her closer, she groaned into his mouth. Adjusting the angle of her face, Anita allowed him deeper access, pulling him into her mouth as he tasted her all over again. Sam's fingertips clawed her exposed skin.

"Say cheese!" Reece burst in, camera raised. "Oh, shit, sorry!"

Sam dropped Anita's leg, blushing like a schoolboy as she laughed, rearranging her dress. Coughing, Reece examined the floor, giving them a moment to right themselves.

"You ready?" he grinned a moment later.

"Nope," Sam admitted. "You?"

"Never. Who ever thought–"

"I know! It's just too weird–"

"Can you two stop with the bromantic reading-each-other's-minds and finishing-each-other's-sentences thing and tell us what you're talking about?" Reece's better half slid into the room, a vision in sparkling silver, her hair cascading down her back. She looked so different. Sam and Anita found themselves staring. "There is a wedding to get on with, you know, gentlemen."

"Oh, we know."

"Well, let's go!" Anita linked arms with Reece's dazzling wedding date, and they exited the tent together.

"You're one lucky brother, doc." Sam dug an elbow into his friend's ribs.

"Oh yeah, I know. She'll never let me forget it, either."

Peeking through the white flaps of the tent, they looked towards the altar.

"You were such a dedicated bachelor, Reece. When did that all change?"

"Honestly? I'm not really sure how or when ..." Reece's brow furrowed. A brilliant diagnostician, able to see any loophole or misplaced comma, this puzzle was sure to eat him up.

"You're such a loser." Sam laughed, pushing his spectacles higher.

"Says you! So, you think this marriage will last?"

Sam scoffed. "I'd bet my life on it. Hey, check out Adam James." Sam's chin lifted, Reece following his line of sight.

"He's here? Where? Why? Is he going to *truth or dare* the bride and groom into adolescent fun?"

Sam laughed dryly. "Probably. Must be nice, avoiding growing up."

Both men sighed, watching as Adam handed the beautiful

musician a tall glass of cool water from the refreshments table. He was leaning in close and laying it on thick. He exuded the kind of raw animal magnetism Sam could only dream of.

"Leopards and spots," Reece commented, watching their old classmate.

"Now, boys," Edith said, appearing suddenly to lovingly smack Sam and Reece on their backsides.

"Shit! Edith!" Reece clutched his chest. "The Heart Research Institute says that heart attacks are the leading cause of hospitalisation and death in Australia."

Edith looked to Sam. "You brought *The Doctor*?" she scoffed. "I thought *The Friend* was going to be here today." She raised a knowing eyebrow at Reece.

"I am both," he said defensively, adjusting his tie.

Sam pinched the bridge of his nose. "You're a total Doctor Jekyll, Mister Hyde situation, dude."

"Okay, I'll take a chill pill!" Reece shot a look at Edith. "Kidding, Gran. Kidding! Us doctors can have a joke, you know." He hooked a thumb at Sam's grandmother, turning to his best friend. "Jeez, who does she think I am? Some pill-popper?"

"Actually," Edith wrung her hands nervously, "I was rather hoping you'd have something to calm my nerves. Weddings always make me jittery. And the whole town seems to be out there! Even that young fellow you joke about being a walking sexually transmitted disease—"

"Yes, Gran, keep it down!" Sam's face, hot and flushed, peeked nervously back towards Adam James. "The whole town will show up when the wedding is in Main Street Park, you know. It's literally the centre of attention. Check on any map. This park is the heart of Moonshine."

"Do you know, he asked me if I'd play spin the bottle later? Me! Spin the bottle! At my age!" Edith clutched her pearls.

"Who, Eddie?"

"No, that James fellow. The dick on legs."

Reece guffawed. Sam sighed, massaging his sinuses. "Gran, don't say dick."

"It's true!" Edith said, deftly adjusting her flower crown through her grey fluff of hair. "I mean, I'm a looker for my age, I'll grant you that. But the nerve of that young man! Mind you, if I was *younger* ..."

Both men whined. "Gran! No!"

"He's certainly the centre of a lot of town gossip," Edith continued. "I heard he was secretly married, some time ago. Also that he might have killed someone, which is entirely possible with all those muscles. If I chose how I could go ..."

"Edith, stop drooling over our classmate," Reece chided. "You'll ruin your lipstick."

She didn't hear him. "He's a bit mysterious. I wonder what he's like, under all that *gorgeous*ness."

"Gran, *please* don't talk like that. And don't start rumours about Adam. It'll kill his playboy reputation, and possibly land him in gaol, if you go around talking about muscle murdering. And without that bravado, Adam might just shrivel up and die, like his virginity did."

"Solid burn," Reece chuckled, fist-bumping his bestie.

"I swear I'm not making it up!" Edith insisted. "I've been hearing quite a few whispers about that one, and you know

Saint Jude's is a hotbed of gossip and scandal."

"Oh, I know alright."

Edith winked, falling silent. She cast a knowing look Sam's way, sighing.

"You'll be fine, Gran." Sam said, giving her shoulders a light squeeze. "We're here."

Fiddling with her hair, she nodded, then gave a thumbs up to Anita, whose voice rang out, "It's time!"

Edith took a deep breath, nodding for Reece and Sam to part the curtains, exiting the tent. Stepping lightly into the garden that held pride of place in Moonshine's Main Street, she met a round of polite but enthusiastic applause. Sunlight sparkled through her veil as Eddie turned, grinning ear to ear. Sam and Reece each locked arms with Edith, one on each side, proudly walking her down the rose-petal-covered aisle and towards the rotunda.

The wedding singer, sitting tall at the front of the congregation in a stunning strapless dress, struck up a slow Elvis classic. Nervous at first, her voice warbled before strengthening. Closing her eyes, her tone melted perfectly into the rhythm of the moment. As the song went on, Edith slowly shuffling closer, the musician relaxed into her performance, opening her eyes. Voice smooth as her honey-coloured hair, she winked to Edith as she strummed, causing the congregation to swing their heads.

Gran had been right. Everyone in Moonshine had come out of the woodwork. Even the pillars of hospitality must have shut up shop for a while, Sam's friends Friday Adams and Billy Carmichael among them. Still sporting their workwear, the men nodded as he escorted his grandmother to the altar.

Edith giggled under her breath.

"What's so funny?" Sam whispered out the side of his mouth, holding his sliding glasses as he nodded on repeat, silently thanking nearly everyone he'd ever known for being here today. *Such is small-town life,* he mused, cheeks already sore from smiling.

"That boy," Edith smiled generously to Adam James, sitting near the guitar-strumming singer. "He's *besotted* if ever I saw it. He's got the same look on his face as my dear Eddie right now."

"Adam? Besotted? *Never.*" Reece whispered his two cents.

"You're no rose among the thorns yourself, Doctor Reece Hargraves!"

Reece's lips pressed into their usual tight line.

Altar reached, Eddie relieved them of their duties, taking Edith's hand.

Moonshine had put on a glorious day for the wedding, made even more glittery by Gran's only dress code requirement of 'sequins up to the wazzoo'. The crowd glimmered, each person's sparkle shared and reflected by those around them. Pride swelled in Sam's chest as he noted how many were present.

Anita beamed up at Sam from the first row of lawn chairs, her small hands planted lovingly on the belly that hid their growing baby.

At the end of the aisle, the 'besotted' Adam James perched on the edge of a white garden chair. Moonshine's biggest player. The man who had slid ice over Anita's ankle and dared her into their first kiss at The Pope that night. The man who'd offered to play spin the bottle with his grandmother on her wedding day. Adam *bloody* James.

Adam sat still and characteristically chill, a dopey grin plastered on his face. He caught Sam's eye and winked, before blowing a kiss towards Edith. Sam couldn't tell if Gran had noticed the exchange or not, but he blushed enough for the both of them.

Gran had to be wrong about Adam James. She *had* to be. *Besotted?* Unlikely. Still, Sam couldn't discount Adam's doe-eyed expression as he'd looked at the musician Gran had employed for the wedding. The guitar-toting woman looked eerily familiar, but Sam couldn't place her. Whoever she was, she was serving up the cold shoulder to Adam. *What is worrying,* he thought warily, watching Adam trail after the cool musician, *is that Adam James loves the winter.* He lived for the chase.

Turning his body slightly, Sam slipped his phone from his pocket, opening an old app he hadn't accessed in many, many years – Adam's Little Black Book of sexual conquests. Sam's eyes read the number displayed there, a full three seconds before it truly sunk into his brain. It was a disgustingly large tally. If Adam's LBB count was honestly that high, he had earned his title as the town's most fun, and most frequent, hook up. Gagging, he slid his phone back into his pocket as he coughed and spluttered. Reece whacked him on the back. Everyone stared.

Hands still clasped with Eddie's, Gran turned. "You okay, Sam?"

Through watering eyes, Sam managed, "I'm fine, Gran. Carry on."

Locking eyes with Anita, he basked in her smile, eyes misting all over again. Who needed a tonne when you had The Right

One? *I love you, Anita.* As though she'd heard him, he watched her mouth form the words, "I love you, Sam."

After the ceremony, he sought her out, groaning slightly as he saw the company she was keeping. *Shit.* Taking a deep breath, he joined the energetic bunch. After a few moments, Anita caught his eye, a familiar smirk lighting her face.

"Oh, I know *that* look. Some kind of inspiration is hitting. Tell me, who inspired this next Sammie Hart love story? What do their feet look like?"

Sam exploded into laugher, draping his arm around her shoulders and bringing her face to his chest. "You sure have a way with words," he chuckled into her hair. "But it's The Knights, you see. They're, uh, full of ... *ideas.*"

"Oh, so many ideas."

"You need to write about a king and a servant! Historical, you know. I love those," Cecelia was saying to Sam, ignoring the youngster's side-chat. Benjamin started to mumble something, but Ethel's retort was louder.

"No!" she cried, gripping Sam's arm tightly. "I think you should write one of those monster romances. You know, where some horribly sensual fantasy creature with tentacles–"

Coughing loudly, Sam tried desperately to cover the rest of that sentence, and unhear what they were saying. Benjamin continued mumbling, and Lucious had his hand cupped around his ear, clearly straining to follow the conversation. The women argued on.

Help. Sam tried to convey the wish in his eyes as he looked down on his witch. *Anita, please.* Her touch warmed his forearm. "Sorry, Knights, but I have to steal this one away."

"Must you really leave so soon?" the refined Mary asked.

"Is it time for the reception?" Ethel's eyes widened in her round face. "I want to draw out this shindig!"

"Last wedding I went to was decades ago!" Benjamin huffed into his beard. "I'm not ready to go back to Saint Jude's."

"We're not going back," Ethel scoffed. "Not yet! The night is still young!"

"Ethel. Benjamin." Cecelia shook her head at the constantly bickering pair. "Let the youngsters go. Clearly, they have *other business* to attend to." No one missed her innuendo, or her wicked wink. Used to their antics by now, Sam barely even blushed.

"That's right," Anita said, winking right back. "But we'll see you soon."

"At the reception?" Ethel clarified. "I'm so looking forward to the reception."

"Yes, Ethel," John offered, chuckling.

"You cheeky youngsters!" said Lucious. "Off with you!"

"Don't need to tell me twice," Sam laughed, looking around for Anita.

"You coming, Was?" she called, already halfway across the park, heading to his car.

God, I love this woman.

He reached her in four long strides, running a hand through his hair. "So, you wanna get out of here? Blow this popsicle stand?"

"Blow popsicles, hey?" Anita's dark brows rose suggestively and Sam's skin heated.

"Not what I *meant* ... but I'm not saying no! I, uh, have

something to show you."

Her burst of laughter drew so much attention, a sneaky get-away was impossible. "I think I've seen it, Was. But I don't think we should leave Gran ..."

"I have strawberries and chocolates in the car." He purred the words against her earlobe.

Curling into his attentions, she admitted, "That does sound delicious."

"Don't worry about the newlyweds. We'll see them for dinner. Just wave at Edith and come with me now."

"Now?"

"I took a page from your grimoire and worked a bit of a spell on Gran, and she's happy for us to go."

"Seriously?" Anita sought the newly wed bride through the crowd. Clutching Eddie's arm, her beaming dentures were aimed straight at them, and she winked. With a flick of her hand, she encouraged them to leave. Her mouth formed an exaggerated *GO*.

"See? C'mon, *lettuce* get out of here!"

"How do you make salad sound so sexy?" Anita chuckled, calling through the crowd, "See you later, Edith and Eddie!" Sam unlocked the car and they slid in.

"So, can I know where you're taking me?"

"Does it matter?" *Anywhere with you is Heaven ...*

"Not in the slightest." She leant across to kiss his cheek before clicking her seatbelt on. "You could take me to moon and back, Sammie Hart."

"Aaaaand another right here? Samuel Harthrup, I think we've circled Moonshine four times already! Where. Are. We. Going?" Laughing, Anita shook her head. "The old colonial planners really must've enjoyed the bootleg liquor this town is named after. There are no other reasons for the dog-leg corners and five-way intersections that seem to end in a series of cul-de-sacs. Was, I'm new to this whole living-in-one-place-and-getting-to-know-each-street-thing, but even I know you're just cruising randomly." Biting her lip, she looked out the windscreen. "Are we there yet?"

"Actually, yes. We're here." Sam pulled the car to the side of the road, killing the engine. "This is it. Wentworth Avenue." *One of the most expensive streets in Moonshine.* Sam surveyed the vast, neat lawns and heritage homes that lined the street. Nearly every property was bordered by thick, tidy hedges and the white picket fences Anita adored, all shadowed in a shifting, dappled light from huge trees that arched the width of the road.

"I agree about the town planners by the way," he mused, his eyes following thick trunks into their casings of tar. The roads had been built wide and around the towering trees, unlike newer cities where trees were cut and the earth paved over.

"WOW! Was, isn't it beautiful?" she sighed, hands unconsciously sliding to rest on her stomach. He looked to her, so bright and full of life.

"Sure is." Sam's eyes were glued on Anita, to the growing

baby beneath her loving touch. "Simply amazing."

Gone were her worn bohemian rags, replaced with the formal dress that hugged every curve and flowed to her feet in long waves. While she had always been beautiful, now Anita positively glowed. She had changed his whole world, in the simple act of choosing him, choosing them. Something he'd never dreamed possible. But the little witch wasn't done altering his world – not yet. She was in the process of transforming herself, too. He watched her kick off her heels and bury her toes into the soft grass by the footpath, moaning with pleasure.

"You know, if I didn't know any better," he mumbled down into her hair, bending slightly to wrap his arms around her waist, "I'd think that life in Moonshine suited you." The fullness of her felt like heaven as she moulded her body to his.

"It does," she said, arching her neck to catch his lips once.

Sam pointed one crooked finger. "Number Three. C'mon."

Taking her hand, Sam led Anita up the footpath to the letterbox that proudly poked through the white wooden fence palings, the number 3 painted in a dark, luxurious font. As they turned to face the property face-on, he pointed out a meticulously hand-painted clown waving below the mail slot.

"That reminds me of Barney," Anita said, gently stroking the figure. "He's got great talent, you know. He designs and paints all the sets and props for Cirque de Fortuna." Her voice became far-away as she leant into Sam's side. "Did I tell you Barney was originally a Moonshine man? He ran away with the circus. Joined the family decades ago, after meeting Claus by the Ferris wheel." She sighed, surveying the property.

"You didn't tell me that, no. But Claus mentioned that they

always planned to retire here."

"Really? He told you that?" With a sigh, she added, "I'd love to see them here."

"For the last twenty years, they've kept this house for that one purpose," Sam said, nodding towards Number Three. "But they're not ready to retire yet, apparently. They're not done with Adrian, they said."

Her face soured. "Well, I am."

Resting his chin on the top of her head, he inhaled the sweet lavender scent of her. "It's an amazing house, hey? The kind of place I can see two old clowns with twin rocking chairs on the porch."

"True. But ..." she sighed, hands on her belly once more. "Plans change, Was." Turning to him, she lifted her chin, eyes lighting up as she added, "Wanna snoop?"

"You? Snoop?" She grinned up at him as he laughed, "I thought you'd never ask."

Hands clasped tight, they strode across the manicured yard, stopping at the small front porch.

"Use that spell," Sam whispered. "The one where you find people's spare keys and let yourself into their place, like you did with my flat."

"Why are you whispering?" she whispered back with a low chuckle, starting to circle her arms over an imaginary cauldron. "Hocus pocus, eye of newt ... Gods Sam's sexy in a suit. We need a place to go make out ... So pocus hocus, Gods help me out!"

Sam fought a smile, fighting the blush creeping up his neck. "That's it?"

"Well, what did you expect me to say?" Her laughter warmed

his soul. "But look! A key!" Bending to kick the mat aside, she slid a silver key into his palm.

"It worked? Shit, maybe you are a witch!"

"Or, hear me out … maybe I just know the usual places people leave their spare keys?" She shot Sam a knowing look. "Under the door mat or in a pot plant really isn't the safest hiding place, you know."

"You do this a lot?"

She offered a shrug, nodding to the cherry red door. "Go on, open it."

"On one condition."

"And what's that? I already have my shoes off …" Her grin near cut her face in half and all he could do was reflect it back at her.

"No, you infuriating woman. This isn't about feet, though yours are particularly attractive. I want to carry you over the threshold."

"Really? Sam, no."

"I mean, I know it's *corny* –"

She rolled her eyes. "Here we go …"

"*Cheesy* even –"

"Dear Gods." She pinched the bridge of her nose, mimicking him. "The food puns …"

"C'mon, Anita, I want to. Will you let me?"

"*Can* you? I mean, I'm–"

"Gorgeous." He cut off any other adjective she might have used. "Exceptional."

Her blue eyes rolled. "Alright. But if you drop me …"

"Doctor Dickhead will be here in one minute flat."

"Oh, *that's* comforting."

The key slid in, releasing the lock with a soft *click*. "Ready?" Bending his knees, he caught Anita as she jumped lightly into his arms, curling against his chest and around his neck. "Mmmm," she murmured into his neck. "You smell so good. Clean and fresh." He squirmed as she nuzzled into him.

"Stop wiggling!" he huffed into her hair, gripping her tightly. "There's a good little witch."

"I'm hardly little, Was."

Carefully, he manoeuvred her feet around the door frame, swinging her gently into the room before placing her down on the hard wood floor with a kiss.

"Babe, you're like, half my height. You're *tiny* to a giant like me."

"Giant, huh?" She let her eyes flick to his crotch and his blush hit in full force. As she moved further into the house, her hand grazed over his trousers, circling as she took in their surroundings. "This house ... it takes my breath away."

"Go on," Sam encouraged, loosening the tie from his crimson neck. "Explore."

She didn't need to be told twice. Giggling, she took off, commenting the entire time about the grand home, the ornate cornices and wide windows, the sparkling wooden bannisters and the modern kitchen Sam was sure to drool over.

"Was?" her voice drifted through the hallways. "Where are you?"

"In here!"

"Where?"

"Follow my voice!"

Anita hadn't realised they made houses this big, without calling them 'villas', 'chateaux' or 'castles'. But her friend's home was worthy of such a title, especially after so many years in her tiny vardo trailer. The sheer size and scale of the ceilings, the windows, the spaces ... "Breathtaking."

"Don't get distracted!" Sam's chuckle echoed off the clean, crisp walls. "Follow my voice!"

"Sam?"

She found him in the kitchen, of course. Fiddling with a copy of his latest novel, *Chef's Kiss*, he adjusted his spectacles, Adam's apple bobbing as he swallowed.

"Was? What's wrong."

"Nothing." He drew her close. "Absolutely nothing, Anita." Placing her hands on his chest, she looked up at him, marvelling at this man who put so much faith into her. Into *them*.

"This is ..." he shook his head, starting again. "You are ..."

"You word *so* good, Sammie." Knowing he'd find the words, she held him, enjoying the feel of him against her.

"You are the best thing that's ever happened to me, Anita," Sam said, threading his arms around her. "I *donut* know what I would do without you in my lie. You've given me so much already ... a career that is only getting stronger, someone to smooch daily, a family I can be proud of ..." His hand dipped to the curve of her stomach. "The only way you could make me happier right now is if you held a boombox above your head or stood at the door with a series of hand-written signs declaring your undying love."

"You've been watching too many romantic movies, my darling," she said, chuckling. She tapped her temple. "I love it.

I'll file that away for next time, Romeo."

"Actually, I do have one kind of odd request ... Something that would make me happy ..."

She marvelled constantly at the deep blush that overtook him. Watching his face darken now, Anita shook her head in wonder. "But we did it this morning ..."

"No, not *that*, you sex fiend. Jeeze, it's like every time we hang out with the Knights–"

"Sam." She cut him off with a chuckle. "What are you trying to say?"

"Anita Shithouse Fortuna," Sam fell to one knee, *Chef's Kiss* in his hands. "I love you. I adore you to pieces, in fact. And I ..." he thrust the book toward her. "I want you to have this."

"I already have it." Her eyebrows scrunched. "And the drafts."

"This copy is special. Open it ... carefully."

Her blue eyes sparkled as she took the novel, carefully peeking inside the cover. Nothing. A few page flicks and she was wondering if she should be reading the words she'd helped write, edited and proofread a million times before now.

"Sam, I'm not sure what ..." With another page turn, her breath caught. A hole had been cut through the centre of the book – just big enough to fit a small, navy-blue box. "Sam?"

Removing the book from her shaking hands, she watched him work the box from the core of his novel.

"Hand out," he instructed, gently tracing the lines of her hand before resting the box in her palm. Sam started a slow removal of the rings on her other hand.

"You know," he said, eyes wide and sincere, "I don't have

much." He slid the ring from her thumb. "But what I do have, I want to share with you, always and forever." Sam twisted a set of three stacked rings from her pointer finger. "I couldn't be Samuel, let alone Sammie Hart, without you." Another three rings were removed from her middle finger. "I need you, Anita. I want to live with you. Here."

"Here?" She cast a look around the mansion of a house Barney and Claus owned.

"Sshh. I'm doing a thing." He winked up at her from his bent knee.

"Sorry," she whispered around the lump growing in her throat. "Go on. I'll be quiet."

The look he shot her screamed 'Yeah right!' but he drew her attention back to his careful ministrations with a kiss to her hand, sliding the remaining rings from her fingers and pocketing them. "So many," he muttered, plucking the box from her open palm. "Anita."

"Was?"

"Will you do me the honour of living in domestic bliss with this dweeb of a writer?" He clicked the box open, revealing a single blue key on a keyring. *My favourite colour* ... Her heart swelled, fit to burst from her chest. Sam removed the key from the box, sliding the ring up one bare finger. "Live with me, here, till the clowns come to kick us out. They're okay with this plan, by the way. Let's cook in this kitchen and fill the rooms with laughter. Let's raise our kids here. Let's–"

"You're giving me a ... house?"

"Let's make a *home*, Anita. You. Me. The baby. A black cat, if you insist."

"Oh, Sam!" she breathed, crushing her lips to his. "Say the magic words!"

Chuckling against her mouth he spoke through kisses. "Bippity. Boppity. *Boo*."

Acknowledgements

This book is my tribute to food puns and feet. I never thought I'd write that sentence, but there you go.

As I wrote *The Write Way to Love*, I found endless joy in a little group called 'Feet Fridays', established with the sole purpose of freaking out my friend Rachel. To say Rach has an intense dislike of feet is probably an understatement, but the jokes led to inspiration and a whole lot of giggles as I wrote this novel. So thank you to the Feet Friday Crew – Ben, Beth, Caitlin, Cassie, Daniel, Jacob, James, Melissa and Rachel. Without you, Sam might have been a completely different dude.

In keeping with Sam's quirky, foody character, let me dish up some thanks:

A full cup of Special Thanks to my wonderful husband and kids, who *try* to respect my writing time. Your enthusiasm and encouragement to follow my dreams makes me feel valued and loved. Thanks for putting up with all the late-night keyboard tapping and frequent staring-off-into-the-middle-distance as I ponder. Your cheesy humour (and ability to put up with mine) makes life fun. I love you guys.

A Nanna's-sherry-in-trifle-sized dash of Thank Yous to my wonderful 'Bookie' team, for their honest critiques, for steering me in the right direction and keeping me accountable. I am truly honoured to have such wonderful cheerleaders who see the light at the end of the tunnel, and who helped me whip this story into shape.

Speaking of Nanna's trifle, thank you to my grandparents. Shirley, Neville, John and Ann, you each (in some way) inspired the Knights. Your conversations were sometimes disturbing, but always memorable! I miss you.

I want to also sprinkle Many Thanks on two special women who weave magic into my bookish life:

Shelley Breen – savvy businesswoman and fellow gin lover. I don't know what I would do without your wisdom and ability to fix my technological stuff-ups. I'm sorry I forgot to acknowledge you in *Meet Me in Moonshine*. There had to be someone I forgot – apologies!

Sue Copsey – editorial wizard and insight-giver. I am indebted to your willingness to work with me, your wisdom, and critiquing kindness. Thank you for some hearty chuckles and for helping settle the words into their final form.

And last (but not certainly least) let me serve up some thanks to YOU, dear reader, to whom I am eternally grateful.

I look forward to meeting you back in Moonshine sometime soon.

Want a sneak peak

at the next

Moonshine Romance?

Read on

THE INSUFFERABLE ADAM JAMES

THE ADVANTAGE OF SYDNEY'S small, shitty studio life was that there wasn't room to accumulate excess stuff – except when it came to her overflowing wardrobe. Clarissa Wilson's closet was like Narnia. Upon opening the door, you fell into a mystical Other Realm, one full of fabrics and furs, sparkles and sequins. You never knew when or how you might escape, or how old you'd be on emerging. Now, those items were suffocating in vacuum-sealed packages stacked neatly into matching pink suitcases, their zippers straining heroically as she dragged them from the bus stop.

Inhaling deeply, Clarissa took in her rural hometown with its wide streets, huge trees, and tidy, paved footpaths. Moonshine. It was halfway between Here and There, completely in the middle of Nowhere, but right now it was exactly where she needed to be.

Checking her watch, Clarissa smiled. Three o'clock on the dot, and most shops were flipping their 'closed' signs. In the country, a schedule was as solid as the thick wooden signs they were painted on. Work after 3pm was almost unheard of.

The familiarity of the place settled into her bones as she dragged her mountain of bags on their unsteady plastic wheels. Walking along the old, unchanged streets, she adjusted the guitar strap on her shoulder, heading towards the pub.

Despite the new navy carpet, Moonshine's favourite tavern, The Pope, had that reliable pub smell of a place where too many beers had been spilled. The strangely comforting aroma welcomed her home.

It was already buzzing with locals, but Clarissa knew they were unlikely to recognise her. Hell, she'd ensured it. Just another city slicker in for a short stay, they'd assume, taking brief, dismissive glances before returning to the last of their late counter lunches or billiard games.

Clarissa took another deep breath, trying to ease the rapid beat in her chest. You got this, she reminded herself, heaving suitcases over the threshold with one almighty tug, her eyes already searching for Meredith. *It's fine. Nobody will recognise you.*

Clarissa had left town over a decade ago, moving to Sydney for sheer self-preservation and a lot of therapy. Her entire world had been different then. She'd been red haired, freckled, and clinging fiercely to her baby fat. Now she was a completely different person. A woman in her thirties who morphed almost daily with a careful selection of cosmetics, clothing, and enough accessories to fill all the backstage rooms of Milan's Fashion Week.

Catching a glance in a wall tile polished to reflective perfection, Clarissa tucked her long blonde hair behind one ear, eyeing herself critically. The woman watching back was busty and confident, with a country singer style that little farm girls idolised. No, she wasn't that same confused, chunky, spotty, red-headed kid anymore. The little girl she had been may as well have existed on another planet. And even though she was back in town, after years of growth and change … well, it didn't mean she was ready to Velcro those two versions of herself together just yet, either.

Comparing 'then' and 'now' photos, Clarissa barely recognised herself. Beauty school had taught her to do wonders. Makeup wasn't just pigments and powders, it was hours of artwork to become someone new. Cosmetics, coloured contacts, and an affirmation, and Clarissa recreated herself each day.

Clothing, too, she considered as armour. A woman's wardrobe could completely transform her life, and Clarissa knew how to dress for her lean body, her rounded hips and bust. She wasn't vain – she was careful. Every minute spent on her appearance distanced her from the little girl who had once lived here in Moonshine, where 'fashion' was just a word in outdated magazines lying around the doctor's office. As a kid, her 'style' had included mis-matched tracksuits, one pair of 'good jeans' for church, and old denim overalls for renovation work with her father. Those items sufficed, and they all fit into one small backpack.

Clarissa smirked at her huge, pink, pile of baggage. The last time she'd packed these bags was for her sister's wedding, a small, family-only event that had made her heart soar. Being here now was the opposite of that high.

Her boots clinked against the metal leg of a stool as Clarissa surveyed the bar. Meredith. She had to find Meredith. Her best friend always knew how to take Clarissa's mind off the past and drag her – kicking, screaming, and laughing – into the present.

You're not that little girl anymore, the angel on her shoulder soothed.

The devil on her other shoulder teased, *No, you're much more wicked now.*

Though she'd made the occasional day trip back for small family events, sixteen years had passed since Clarissa had been home to roost. Half her lifetime ago. And while some things had changed, others – like the grainy, solid wood of the bar – endured. *Welcome home, Clarissa Wilson … Are you ready for this?*

Her return was long overdue, but if anyone could have convinced her to return home, it was Meredith.

"LISSY!" her best friend's squeal shot through The Pope. "Girl, you're here! Finally!" Launching herself over the bar, Meredith squeezed Clarissa's shoulders with the strength of a boa constrictor. Clarissa squished into her best friend, inhaling the familiar scent of her strawberry shampoo.

Meredith had glorious hair. The kind that fell in mesmerising waves and always looked fashionable without her even trying. Her friend effortlessly exuded an air of Hollywood glamour, like she was runway ready – a look Clarissa worked much harder to achieve.

"Hey, Billy!" Meredith loosened her vice-like grip, turning to her boss. "Lissy has just arrived in town. Can we store her bags upstairs somewhere? One of the rooms?"

A grumble resounded from The Pope's publican, Billy Carmichael. Tall, broad, and easily over six foot, there was no doubt he was the tallest, broadest man Clarissa had ever seen. His piercing blue eyes were as she remembered, but the rest ... *Holy smokes*. The boy she'd known, all those years ago, had somehow grown into a mountain. A literal, hairy, towering, tattooed mountain of a man in a smart button-down shirt. Leaning over the bar, Billy eyed her bright-pink belongings, his hand passing over his thickly bearded chin.

"Here with family?" He searched the tavern, obviously looking for the husband and five children who warranted so much luggage.

"Just me. That's all my emotional baggage." The joke fell flat. Beneath the layers of cosmetics, Clarissa felt herself flush as his familiar light blue eyes flicked over her. *Please don't recognise me ... please ...* In a small town, a little bit of anonymity went a long way, especially when she was desperate to make a new start, on her own terms.

"Staying here?" His gruff voice contrasted with the quiet warmth of the boy she'd once known. He gave her tower of bags the side-eye once more, adding, "Forever?"

"She's bunking with me!" Meredith squealed, clapping her hands together. "So, the leaning tower of luggage will come home with us, after my shift. They just need somewhere out of the way for now. C'mon, boss man, pleeeeeease?"

Billy grunted, his piercing blue eyes narrowing, like he could sense trouble brewing.

He's not wrong ... Clarissa mentally waved the she-devil from her shoulder, banishing the wicked, adventurous ideas

Meredith seemed to coax from her. If 'Walk on The Wild Side' had been a club, Meredith would have been president, with Clarissa half a step behind.

Billy eyed a broad, long-legged man whose black shirt read SECURITY. "Upstairs," Billy said, his head motioning to the luggage.

"No problems, boss." The security guard easily collected her bags, winking dazzling eyes the same colour as Billy's at Clarissa. *So, he was a Carmichael, too. Which twin is he? Connor? Liam? Surely this isn't the eldest son, Graham?*

Clarissa tried not to stare. The genetic makeup of the Carmichael family had always been distinctive. All four Carmichael boys – men, now, she amended – shared those same exquisite blue eyes, and it seemed, a similarly imposing masculine frame. Even as kids they'd been solidly built, their baby blues popping from tanned faces, contrasting starkly with their dark, rich hair. Their features branded the Carmichaels, as did the coppery hair and freckles that ran in the Henderson family. Lifelong neighbours, the Carmichaels and Hendersons were practically the same tribe. Glancing around, Clarissa knew Breanna Henderson would be close by.

Memories of childhood started to push their way in. Obtrusive. Unwanted. Her mental shields were failing. Opening the floodgates was not an option, so she took another deep breath, focusing on rebuilding the buffer in her mind. Visualisation had been Clarissa's favourite part of therapy, and now the bricks had been re-set, she imagined a solid metal wall sliding down as though from Heaven itself, slamming shut. Separating her conscious mind from the darkness beyond.

Forcing herself back to the present, Clarissa watched the Carmichael – whichever one he was – haul her luggage towards the curving, carpeted stairs that led to the accommodation floor of The Pope, amazed by the contrasting sight of her feminine luggage in his manly grasp.

"Wait! Not that one!" She hadn't even noticed him sling her guitar case over one shoulder. The Carmichael carefully placed two of Clarissa's bags on the floor and allowed her to lift the hard case and strap over his head.

"Thank you." She couldn't help but stare into those blue eyes, so cool and familiar.

"Not a problem. Anything for a mate of Meredith's." Those eyes darted back to the bar, searching for her best friend.

"So, Lissy, you any good?" The towering lumberjack of a publican brought her attention back with his own set of baby blues, his bearded chin motioned to her guitar.

Clearing her throat, Clarissa pushed her shoulders back. "I'm very good, actually." Did he recognise her? Would he? It had been so long, and she was so different …

"Hell yeah she's good!" Meredith beamed, jumping into the conversation and snapping Clarissa from her ruminations. "She's been playing all across the city for a few years now, and I even heard a few of her songs on The Cat and The Fiddle. Stupid name for a radio station, but that's not the point. You'd better snap up her talented arse soon, boy, before someone else does!"

"I am no *boy*," Billy growled.

"Boy. Man. Dude. Whatever." Meredith shrugged, her wavy tresses kissing her shoulders.

Clarissa jumped in before her friend dug a deeper hole. "This is Maton." Unclipping the case, she enjoyed the opportunity to show off her acoustic. The guitar, practically an extension of her soul and a gift from her stepsister many years ago, had been lovingly dragged everywhere.

"Nice." Billy's eyes roamed the wood and strings, before resting back on her face. She waited for it – the flash of recognition. That little hint of familiarity. There was none.

Clarissa breathed a little easier, an excited shiver skittering up her spine. Perhaps she had grown and changed so dramatically that nobody would ever identify her as poor little Clarissa Wilson. That unfortunate girl. The one they'd all gossiped about. The one they'd all pitied, such a long time ago. A lifetime ago.

Clarissa eyed Billy's left arm, his one and only. He knew a little something about losing yourself to the past and forging a new future. One you'd never expected. Billy, of all people, knew how life could be cruel; how it could redefine you in an instant.

He didn't waste air with words. "Audition?"

"I'd love to! Anytime. You name it."

He sized her up, appraising. Still no shred of recognition. "Three-song set. Wow me and you can count on a regular gig. Fair?"

"Brilliant!" She shook his hand vigorously. "Thank you, Billy." The name slipped from her tongue, and she flinched at the sound of it, hoping something in her voice didn't give her away. The publican didn't raise an eyebrow. The tension in her shoulders released. Perhaps a clean slate was possible in this town.

Meredith grinned. "Trust me, boy, you won't regret it. She's got the voice of an angel and a peach for an arse. Look at that thing! It's glorious!" She slapped Clarissa's rump playfully. Billy resolutely kept his eyes on the bar. "Plus, she really knows how to handle her instrument, if you know what I mean." Meredith winked at Clarissa before turning back to her boss, sassy as ever. "They'll *love* her."

"To be determined ..." Billy's blue eyes cast around the tavern.

"If you're looking for Bre, I haven't seen her. Not yet, anyway," Meredith told her boss. Mumbling into his beard, Billy shoved a wet beer glass into one of Meredith's hands, then followed it with a crisp, white tea towel. *Your job then*, his expression told her, before he walked off, greeting a patron further down the bar.

Clarissa watched as Meredith spent an entire second diligently cleaning the glass before her head perked up like a kid hearing the siren song of an ice-cream truck in high summer.

"What is it?" The words had barely left Clarissa's mouth before masculine laughter flooded the tavern, and Meredith's head nearly swivelled off her neck as a group of men pushed through the doors. All hope for clean glassware was destroyed. Meredith sunk her elbows to the bar with a blissful sigh.

"Girl, would you look at those *fine* specimens ..." she purred, tracking the men's entry.

The spectacle of Meredith drooling like a Looney Toon spying chocolate cake was familiar, so Clarissa didn't bother turning to look. At least, she wouldn't look right away. Apparently, Meredith's boss was also familiar with her inclination for distraction. Shaking his head, Billy turned on his heel and strode further down the long bar, mumbling about finding more bar staff.

Allowing Meredith a moment to salivate, Clarissa observed her old classmate work the bar. Watching Billy Carmichael was akin to seeing a bear perform ballet – it was mesmerising. The publican was a human tornado, spinning and whirling as he functioned one-handed, completely unstoppable despite his amputated right forearm. The hulking publican was much more interesting than the alpha-bros who'd stolen Meredith's focus.

In the city clubs, obvious ogling was practically a sport. The sweat and aftershave that hung in the humid air, the bass pumping up through your feet – it was all part of the experience. All those heavy eyes and long looks that communicated more than words could in the humid, sweat and aftershave-filled air of in the too-loud clubs. But in a small, quiet town like Moonshine, if Meredith wasn't careful, gossip would label her a sexual pariah. Small town opinions were often formed hard and fast, and a reputation could stick – whether it was warranted or not.

Shoving her towelled fist into the glass, Meredith blew a low whistle of appreciation. Her eyes were glazed. Wide. Typical.

"Is the view *really* that good, Meredith?"

Her best friend only purred in response, arching her back like a cat. *Well then ... What's good for the goose is good for the gander.* And gander she would. However, unlike Meredith, she knew how to play it cool. Chuckling, Clarissa locked Maton back into the case, propped him against the underside of the bar, then watched the men in the gaps between the neatly lined-up bottles in the bar's mirrored splashback.

They were typical night-out-on-the-town dudes, commanding the room, laughing loudly, high-fiving, and slapping backs as they exchanged neanderthal grunts and greetings. She knew their type – Alpha holes. Great tippers. Flirty but relatively hands-off, if managed properly. Some were older versions of the dirty-kneed boys she'd gone to school with, in her former life. She recognised them, pulling their names from the deepest, most forgotten parts of her memory, shuddering. Jesse Miller, Brenton Collins, Jacob Wheeler, Bryce Dodson, and ...

A prickling sensation spread across her skin. Clarissa's immediate flinch was born of pure muscle memory. *No! It can't be! Not on my first night in town ...* The universe sure had a warped sense of humour.

"Oh, *baby*." Meredith sighed further onto the bar, chin resting in her hands. "There. He. Is."

Him. "Adam freaking James." The name slipped out from between clenched teeth.

Meredith purred. "And looking *fine* as ever."

He should have gotten fat. Gone bald. Had a wiry-haired wart or a pimple, or a wedding band on his finger, or something. But no, he was the typically – tragically – tall, dark, handsome, single man her stepsister warned he'd be. Despite the years that had passed, the boy she'd known had grown into a man she instantly recognised. Trimmed, dark hair. That wide, too-white, dentist-perfect smile. Sharp angles, hard ridges, and strong lines. Sensuous lips curving around a pink candy ball he was French kissing into oblivion, the stick of the lollypop caught up in his smirk.

"What I wouldn't give to be that Chupa Chup." Meredith's voice echoed Clarissa's very deep, very private, sentiments exactly. "Girl, you described him, and *of course* I stalked his social media, and I've seen a lot of him since moving to town, but ..." she sighed, "Adam James is a million times more potent when he's in the same room, don't you think?"

Potent was an apt word. *Gravitational* was another. Everyone seemed to lean in as he worked the room like a red-carpet celebrity. Heads turned. Bodies followed. Women stroked his arm. Men offered handshakes or back slaps. A shiver snaked down Clarissa's spine. Physical contact was *not* her love language. But looking and touching were very different things. And look she did.

Dear Lord, his body ... There was no escaping the muscles upon muscles that stretched beneath his clothing. Did he have that shirt painted on? It was obscene. He was ... A myriad of foul names raced unsaid over Clarissa's tongue.

Devastating, she mused. What a perfect descriptor. Devastation was the man's middle name, their history proof of its validity. Eyes burning with hatred, she watched him strut through The Pope. Meredith's eyes shot fire, too, though hers was probably sourced from her flaming ovaries.

"Meredith, stop drooling."

"Neverrrrrr." That purr was back.

"It's a good thing I'm here. Clearly you need me," Clarissa hissed to dead ears. "And an intervention! Stop it!"

As though his ears burned, Adam turned towards the mirror.

She saw his gaze roam the length of her blonde hair, settle for a beat on her arse, then flick up to the splashback. Their eyes met briefly. Those eyes ... She'd nearly forgotten them. Forced herself to forget. They weren't the cool, bright blue of the Carmichael clan. No, Adam's eyes were a stormy sea, flecked with mischief. Clarissa didn't want to recall those details. Not his eyes, or the feel of his fingertips digging into her hips. None of that.

The trance broke as he blinked and turned away. Clarissa exhaled a shaky breath, unclenching her fists and rubbing at the crescent moon dents across her palm.

"Damn, girl, I didn't realise it was *this* bad."

Clarissa stretched out her fingers. "What's bad?"

"The *hate*," Meredith said. "Girl, if looks could kill, that sexy man would be in itty bitty squishy pieces, all blown up over my bar right now."

"*My* bar," Billy mumbled from a few feet away, but Meredith ignored him.

"My eyes make people explode? That's a useful superpower." She shot another glare at the back of Adam's head. Meredith snorted.

Another chill crawled up Clarissa's spine, and she checked the mirror once more. Yep, he was looking at her. Staring. Smiling. *Jerk*. She scowled at his reflection, imagining rapid and spontaneous combustion. Flexing his biceps – did he mean to do that, or did every muscle jump when he moved? – he sent a wink to her still-turned back. Great. Bile burned in Clarissa's throat. Adam James. With any luck she wouldn't have to deal with him. And with even greater luck, he wouldn't recognise her, either ... or things could get very complicated, *very* quickly.

**One immature dare.
Two childhood enemies.
Three kisses to bring
him to his knees.**

Clarissa Wilson *hates* Adam James - his dentist-white smile, his ridiculous body built of muscles-upon-muscles, and that movie-star swagger that carries him into every room. So, back in their hometown of Moonshine — sixteen years later — with a revenge body and a new name, it's a guilty thrill when Adam wants her... and has no idea she's the chubby girl he teased throughout school.

As 'Lissy,' she's determined to live by her own rules and hide her old scars — meaning she needs a plan to deal with Adam, their past, and the present. Luckily, his cheeky dare offers Lissy the perfect opportunity for payback: she has three kisses, and three chances to seduce the man who ruined her life... then leave him in the dust.

But Adam is playing with her heartstrings and rewriting their history, revealing things aren't what they seem. Now, Lissy must decide who she really is and what her heart desires, because three kisses can't undo a lifetime of hate...right?

ISBN: 978-0-6456910-4-7 (PRINT)
ISBN: 978-0-6456910-5-4 (EBOOK)

See where it started

- Small town romantic adventure
- Mysterious notes of love and longing
- Skinny dipping
- Greasy pig chase

About The Author

BROOKLYN DEAN is a perpetual daydreamer from rural Australia. She grew up in Gundungurra country, but now calls Darkinjung land home.

When she's not writing, Brooklyn is often training to become the world hugging champion, drinking coffee, throwing her head back in laughter, or stealing time to nap in the sun.

The Write Way For Love is her debut novel – the first standalone novel in the interconnected Moonshine series of romances.

Connect with Brooklyn on social media, or subscribe via her website for first access to news, giveaways and more:

Please consider leaving a review of this book.

Whether on Goodreads, Amazon, on social media,
an email, a recommendation to a friend ...
reviews are a great way to support an author.

Like water to a flower, reviews help authors grow!

Thank you.

Wattle Tree Press is a small, independent publisher, located on the picturesque Central Coast of Australia. WTP believes that everyone has a story (or two) within them and aims to bring Aussie storytelling to the wider world.

Their growing catalogue can be found at:

www.wattletreepress.com